HIGHLAND BEAR

CELESTE BARCLAY

0 9 8 7 6 5 4 3 2 1

Published by Oliver Heber Books

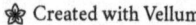 Created with Vellum

SUBSCRIBE TO CELESTE'S NEWSLETTER

Subscribe to Celeste's bimonthly newsletter to receive exclusive insider perks.

Have you read *The Highland Ladies Guide*? This FREE first in series is available to all new subscribers to Celeste's monthly newsletter. Subscribe on her website. Subscribe Now

SINCLAIR FAMILY

Liam Sinclair m. Kyla Sutherland
    b. ***Callum Sinclair*** *m. Siùsan Mackenzie* (SH-IY-oo-san)

        b. Thormud Seamus Magnus Sinclair (TOR-mood
                SHAY-mus)
        b. Rose Kyla Sinclair
        b. Shona Mary Sinclair

    b. ***Alexander Sinclair*** *m. Brighde Kerr* (BREE-ju
KAIR)

        b. Saoirse Sinead Sinclair (SEER-sha shi-NAYD)
        b. Nessa Elise Sinclair
        b. Mirren Louise Sinclair

    b. ***Tavish Sinclair*** *m. Ceit Eithne Comyn* (KAIT-ch
En-ya CUM-in)

        b. Ailish Elizabeth Sinclair (A-lish)
        b. Tate Henry Sinclair
        b. William "Wiley" Matthew Sinclair

    b. ***Magnus Sinclair*** *m. Deirdre Fraser* (DEER-dreh
FRA-zer)

        b. Blake Magnus Sinclair m. Cerys Kerr (CARE-is
                KAIR)
        b. Torquil Lachlan Sinclair
        b. Maisie Blair Sinclair

    b. ***Mairghread Sinclair*** (Mah-GAID) *m.* *Tristan* *Mackay*

        b. "Wee" Liam Brodie Mackay m. Elene Isbister
                b. Alec Daniel Sinclair
                b. Hamish Kincaid Sinclair
                b. Ainsley Maude Sinclair

PREFACE

Welcome to *The Clan Sinclair Legacy*, a spinoff from my *The Clan Sinclair* series. As you join the second generation of this remarkable family, you may recognize heroes and heroines from the first series. For some of you, it may be a chance to become reacquainted with old friends. For those who haven't read *The Clan Sinclair*, take heart: all of my books can be read as standalones, so you don't have to read the earlier series to enjoy this one. Many readers of the original books wondered what would become of the couples from my *The Highland Ladies* series. Fear not. The children of several of those couples will have their chance to find love with the younger Sinclairs and their Sutherland relatives over the course of my next twenty books.

The Clan Sinclair Legacy takes place roughly twenty years after *The Clan Sinclair* ends and about ten years after the final installment of *The Highland Ladies*. In my first series, I never explicitly stated who ruled Scotland at the time; however, King Robert the Bruce and Queen Elizabeth de Burgh appear throughout *The Highland Ladies*. In *The Clan Sinclair Legacy*, David II is the King of Scotland, having succeeded after the death of his father, Robert the Bruce.

King David's reign was complicated during the Second War of Scottish Independence. He spent much of his life either in exile or as a captive. At age four, he married seven-year-old Joan of England, often referred to as Joan of the Tower. Her grandfather was King Edward I, known as both Longshanks and the Hammer of the Scots. Her father was King Edward II, and she was the youngest sister of King Edward III. This means her grandfather, father, and brother tried to oust members of the Bruce family from the Scottish throne. Her mother was Isabella of France, cousin to the French King Philip VI. Robert the Bruce consented to this marriage as part of the terms to the Treaty of Northampton, which ended the First War of Scottish Independence.

King David ascended to the Scottish throne in 1329, when he was five years old. When David was nine, he was forced into exile when Edward Balliol (son of John Balliol, who fought to take the throne from Robert the Bruce) defeated the Scots at the Battle of Halidon Hill in 1333. David, Joan, and the rump of their royal court absconded to France, where King Philip VI granted them Château Gaillard in the northeast region. In 1346, when he was twenty-four years old, David invaded England in support of the French during the Hundred Years' War. It was not a prudent choice. His army was defeated, and he was captured, then held prisoner by the English for eleven years. He was eventually ransomed, but at a cost so high he eventually couldn't afford it. He tried to cancel the debt by bequeathing the succession to Edward III or his successor, but the Scottish Parliament was not amenable. David died childless after Joan died and his second wife, Margaret Drummond, failed to provide an heir, and the succession passed to his nephew by his half-sister Marjorie Bruce, Robert II.

We meet our characters in *Highland Bear* in 1337, when King David II is thirteen and Queen Joan is sixteen. His court had already been in exile for four years. The majority of this story is the product of my imagination. Clan Hannay, mentioned in *A Devil at the Highland Court*, had distant familial ties to the Balliols and remained opposed to the Bruces' dynasty. There is no evidence of disloyalty on the parts of either Clan Cunningham and Clan Home toward Robert the Bruce or David II; their geographical placement lent itself to this storyline. Clan Kerr was ever loyal to the Scottish cause. Our heroine's grandfather would have fought alongside William Wallace, and Clan Kerr continued to support the Bruces throughout the First and Second Wars of Scottish Independence.

Sir Andrew Murray, Guardian of Scotland, plays a lesser role in this story but was, in fact, an important historical figure. He not only held the lofty position William Wallace and Robert the Bruce once filled, he was married to Robert the Bruce's sister, Christina (or Christian). You will find him in the history annals as Andrew Murrey, Andrew de Moray, and Andrew Moray. They are one and the same, but not to be mistaken for his father, who was also Andrew Moray and who was joint commander with William Wallace. The last name can be rather confusing since there was an Earldom of Moray, but it was held by the Randolph family at this time. For the purposes of this story, to prevent confusion about his father or the earldom, I've chosen Andrew Murray as the military leader's moniker.

Our heroine, Cerys Kerr, was the niece of my heroine, Brighde Kerr, from *His Highland Prize*. I want to take a moment to explain the rather tall and many-limbed family tree I've created that links the Sinclairs and Kerrs. For those who haven't read *The Clan Sinclair*,

I shall list the couples. For a more detailed family tree, please see the image after this preface.

Liam Sinclair married Kyla Sutherland in *Their Highland Beginning* and were the parents of the heroes and heroine of that series. Mairghread, the only daughter and youngest sibling, married Laird Tristan Mackay in *His Highland Lass*. Callum, the oldest son and Sinclair heir, married Siùsan Mackenzie in *His Bonnie Highland Temptation*. Alexander married Brighde Kerr (Cerys's paternal aunt) in *His Highland Prize*. Magnus married Deirdre Fraser in *His Highland Pledge*, while Tavish married Ceit Comyn in *His Highland Surprise*. Each of these couples went on to have at least three children, so the illustration on the next page should clarify which child belonged to which pair. I hope you take a moment to look at the family tree and to refer back to it if you need it as you read.

Cerys's father's family has a storied past with the Sinclairs beginning in *His Highland Prize*. Cerys's father, Muir, was one of her grandfather's illegitimate children from his long-time mistress. He was born only a month or so apart from Brighde, Laird Kerr's only legitimate child at the time. When Brighde's mother died, he married his mistress and declared all his children by her legitimate. Mary, Brighde's half-sister and Cerys's aunt, had an affair with the man who was supposed to marry Deirdre Fraser in *His Highland Pledge*. Archibald Hay was killed for his treachery, and so was Mary Kerr. If you've read much of *The Highland Ladies*, you may recognize the name of Archibald Hay's clan. Margaret and Sarah Anne Hay, Archibald's nieces, appear in many of the books as the heroine's nemeses. Wilma Hay, who we meet in this story, is Archibald's great-niece. During this story, the Sinclairs encounter Kerrs and Hays, clans with whom they are not reconciled.

I hope this preface places you in good stead for the

story you're about to read. It's been wonderful to re-visit the characters from the series that launched my career. I'm thoroughly enjoying introducing readers to the next generation of Highlanders. And for those who had a special place in their hearts for *His Highland Prize*, Alexander and Brighde's daughter will have her story told next, in *His Highland Jewel*.

Happy reading,
Celeste

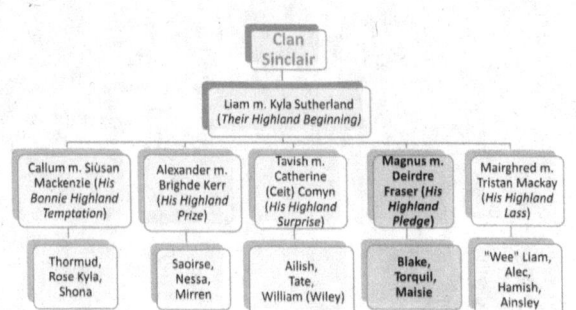

Clan Sinclair

Liam m. Kyla Sutherland
(*Their Highland Beginning*)

Callum m. Siùsan Mackenzie (*His Bonnie Highland Temptation*)
— Thormud, Rose Kyla, Shona

Alexander m. Brighde Kerr (*His Highland Prize*)
— Saoirse, Nessa, Mirren

Tavish m. Catherine (Ceit) Comyn (*His Highland Surprise*)
— Ailish, Tate, William (Wiley)

Magnus m. Deirdre Fraser (*His Highland Pledge*)
— Blake, Torquil, Maisie

Mairghred m. Tristan Mackay (*His Highland Lass*)
— "Wee" Liam, Alec, Hamish, Ainsley

CHAPTER 1

"*A*ll I want is an ale and a willing wench." Blake Sinclair wiped the sweat from his neck as he led his horse into the Stirling Castle stables. He and his family rode hard from Aberdeenshire after spending weeks chasing supporters of the unscrupulous Edward Balliol, pretender to the Scottish throne. His father, Magnus Sinclair, scowled at him while his younger brother, Torquil, chuckled.

"Ye take after yer uncles, Blake, and those habits were nearly their downfall."

"Da, nae everyone can meet their love when they're barely more than a lad. Nae all of us are ye and Mama."

"Ye should listen to yer da, lad." Callum Sinclair, the Clan Sinclair's heir and tánaiste, spoke up. "I nearly lost ma Siùsan because of ma randy past. Looking back, it wasna worth a moment of fun for what it nearly cost me."

"Ma Ceity suffered for ma past, and I regret it every time I'm at this blasted court. I should have been more like yer da. I should have used more restraint." Tavish Sinclair, the third Sinclair son, shook his head as he looked at his nephew.

Blake inherited all the shared attributes that the

1

four older generation Sinclair brothers possessed. His hair was a deep chestnut, and his eyes were a warm whisky brown. He was a strikingly handsome young man, and he knew it. And therein laid the problem. He was a mirror image of his father, Magnus, standing broader than any of the other men. The Sinclairs already towered over most and carried the strength and musculature of Highland warriors. But where Magnus had always been brooding and intimidating when he visited the royal court, Blake was jovial and charming. Few women approached Magnus before he married his wife, Deirdre Fraser, but women flocked to Blake.

"I wouldnae mind that one." Blake and his family emerged from the stables as a petite woman with deep brown hair strode past. She heard his comment and looked his way. The bluest eyes he'd ever seen stared at him. The contrast to her richly deep bronze-brown hair was remarkable, but they pierced him in place. He'd been rude enough to point, and she caught him. He felt his cheeks heat with a blush, something that never happened when women looked at him. Chagrin flavored his smile as he winked at her. He wondered what manner of woman she was when she didn't react in the least. She continued along her way as though he hadn't tried to flirt.

"I think she would mind ye, Brother." Torquil clapped Blake on the shoulder hard enough to make most men wince. Standing just a hair's breadth shorter than Blake and with an ever so slightly narrower build, Torquil made a matched pair with Blake. People frequently confused them for their father and uncles.

"Yer mouth shall be yer ruin, Son." Magnus clapped Blake on the other shoulder, and he suspected both men intended to hold him back from chasing after the woman. He enjoyed the chase as much as he enjoyed the capture. While in truth he had less experience than what he postured, he wouldn't mind exchanging some heated kisses with the bonnie lass.

"Mayhap he isnae ready to remain here alone to represent us."

"Ahem, Uncle Callum." Torquil leaned forward to be in Callum's line of sight. "He willna be alone. I'm staying with him."

"And I dinna need a nursemaid." Blake crossed his arms and spread his feet hip-width apart. This merely made his father and uncles laugh. He'd learned it from the older men. People called it the Sinclair Stance. His mother used to call it the Odin Stance before she became familiar with her brothers-by-marriage. They'd learned it from their own father, Laird Liam Sinclair, the Earl of Caithness. It was infamous among the Highlands, and even the English had learned to fear it over three generations of battles.

"Ye may nae need a nursemaid, but I think a talk with yer mama might serve ye well since ye dinna want to listen to any of us." Magnus cocked an eyebrow at his son. His wife, Deirdre, was much like her four sisters-by-marriage. They all appeared easygoing and jovial, but Hell hath no fury like an angered mama. Blake's eyes widened as he vigorously shook his head.

"I'll behave, Da. I swear." He loved his parents equally, but despite being a foot shorter than her husband and sons, Deirdre Sinclair scared her son witless when she was upset with her children. He would rather spend the day in the lists taking a pounding from his father than face his mother. She had a way of making her children confess without saying a word. He had no idea how she did it, but it always happened. She'd offer absolution with a hug and a kiss that still warmed him as much as it did when he was a wean.

"Let's go inside. I'm starving and still a growing lad." Torquil's stomach growled on cue. At eight-and-ten, two years Blake's junior, the young man hadn't reached his final size.

"Keep yer eyes to yerself. Ye dinna need aught else growing. Nae beneath yer plaid now or beneath a lass's kirtle in a few moons." Callum's voice rang with authority, not only as their uncle but as the future leader of their clan. Blake and Torquil nodded their heads as the group reached the Great Hall. It was virtually empty, which had been rare when Callum, Tavish, and Magnus were Blake's and Torquil's ages.

"It feels unnatural for there to be so few people here." Tavish signaled a serving woman, who brought over a tray of ales. "I canna believe the king has been in France for four years."

"The Battle of Haldon Hill wasna our shining moment. Bluidy Archibald Douglas. If he'd waited a few more days, we could have had the reinforcements we needed. Instead, those of us who lived walked away with our tails between our legs. And the king and queen scarpered off to France." The disgust and anger were still present in Magnus's voice. It was the first battle Blake rode into alongside his father and uncles. He'd been six-and-ten, and it had been a decisive defeat by the English. It only strengthened Edward Balliol's claim as the Scottish king.

"And that's why we're still fighting." Tavish ran a tired hand over his face. They'd traveled alongside Sir Andrew Murray. War broke out for a second time against England as the Scottish continued to struggle to maintain their independence. It had already been five years, and there was no resolution in sight. Not as long as the rightful king, King David II, was in exile. The three-and-ten-year-old monarch was like a cousin to Blake. King Robert the Bruce had been godfather to his father, uncles, and aunt. In turn his grandfather, Laird Liam Sinclair, was the absent king's godfather. They

4

were practically family. It meant the Sinclairs held a personal connection to bringing back the one true king.

While the older Sinclairs continued to talk, Blake looked around the Great Hall. It took only an instant for his gaze to land on the curious woman from outside. Her clothing was modest and unadorned, contrary to what most noblewomen wore at court. She carried herself with grace and poise, but she didn't appear to be a lady-in-waiting like his mother and Aunt Ceit described from their days of serving at court.

He watched as she crossed the gathering hall and stood beside four men, none of whom seemed to notice her presence. The mystery woman appeared to listen, since she said nothing. He noticed one man glanced at her and gave a jerky nod, but none of the four spoke to her before they drifted apart. Seeming to sense him, she looked over her shoulder. Their gazes once more met. Blake felt that same rush of heat to his cheeks as he had when he first spied her. But when she turned away from him with no acknowledgement, his pride stung.

"Do ye think she truly isnae interested, or is she playing the same game ye do?" Torquil's whispered voice made Blake shrug. He hadn't a clue, but he intended to find out. He observed her moving toward the door leading to the connecting antechamber. Blake knew he had the perfect excuse to follow her. He stood from the table and stepped over the bench.

"Garderobe." With one word, he had a plausible reason for heading toward the royal meeting room, which had an indoor latrine beside it. Convenient for both a king and Blake. His long stride carried him to the door, and he hoped it was fast enough to catch the slower-moving enigma. When he passed through the doors, he looked around. There was no one in sight.

How the devil did she disappear? I was only moments behind her.

A soft sound carried to him from the antechamber. He eased along the wall until he could see into the chamber, since the door was ajar. Inside was the woman he pursued. She looked toward a crucifix hanging on the wall. Her shoulders were rounded, and she appeared defeated. He watched her take several deep breaths before she straightened. She pushed her shoulders back and lifted her chin. Gone was the moment of sorrow and returned was the confident woman who intrigued him. She wiped her fingertips across her cheeks, and Blake realized she'd been crying.

"Lass?" Blake didn't know what possessed him to intrude on her quiet moment, but something drew him to offer comfort. When she whirled around, the first sign of emotion entered her eyes. It wasn't what Blake had hoped to see. It was anger.

Cerys Kerr merely wanted a moment to herself. For a royal court that was practically vacant, it felt like she rarely had time to herself. She'd spied the mountain range of Highlanders as they rode into the bailey when she stood with another fellow lady-in-waiting. It had forced her to walk past them on her way back from the kirk as they emerged from the stables. They were an impressive sight, each as handsome as the other, but one man stood out to her. His jovial expression struck her and sent a wave of heat throughout her body.

Then she'd heard him speak. It took all her etiquette and poise training not to react when she realized what the man implied. While part of her wasn't averse to the idea of sharing a kiss or two with the handsome stranger, it embarrassed her to be singled out and in front of four other men. Hearing the new arrival talk as though he were picking her among tavern whores made her temper bristle.

When she noticed him in the Great Hall, it was because she had an overwhelming sense that someone observed her. She knew who it would be before she looked, but she couldn't help herself. She'd seen the group, who were clearly family since they were five peas in a pod, when she entered the Great Hall. She'd cast a glance in their direction as she walked to join her father and uncles. Her family barely noticed her. Only her Uncle Mitcham acknowledged her.

Now she stood alone in the antechamber, where she presumed no one would intrude. She needed a moment to compose herself. This day never grew easier. The pain and loss were still a gaping hole. But each year she questioned herself more and more about why that was. The emotions had shifted from grief to guilt over the past three years. As tears dripped from her eyes, she wondered if it would ever get easier. The feelings were just as intense as the day it happened, but many of the details had faded. Feeling more herself again, Cerys prepared to return to the inevitability of having to be cordial and graceful. A rumbling baritone had her spinning toward the door.

"What do you want?" The words tumbled from Cerys's mouth unbidden. She snapped her lips shut as her eyes widened. The man's shocked expression matched her horror. "I beg your forgiveness. That was unconscionably rude."

"I startled ye, ma lady. It is I who owe ye an apology. I merely meant to check on ye."

The Highland burr wrapped around her like a fur cloak on a winter's day. The raspiness and harsh syllables that mingled with the barely-there letters seemed to fit the rugged man and sent a pulse to her core. She forced her mind to work again as she struggled for a response.

"Thank you. That was kind. I merely needed a moment to myself."

"Did those men upset ye?"

"No." Cerys shook her head and offered nothing more. The man waited, seeming to assume she would say more.

"Do ye need aught? Now that I've intruded, is there aught or anyone I can fetch for ye?"

"That's kind…" She didn't know how to address him. He'd assumed, rightly, that she was a noblewoman. But she didn't know if there was a title she was supposed to use. She doubted he was a laird since there were men older than him who so closely resembled him. One of them was more likely a clan leader.

"Blake Sinclair, ma lady."

Cerys leaned away as she shifted uncomfortably.

Sinclair. Bluidy buggering hell. My bluidy luck.

"I'm Lady Cerys Kerr." She waited for that to sink in. When he leaned away too, she knew he was aware of who she was. His response confirmed it.

"Yer ma aunt's niece." It was almost an accusation.

"I am. Those men are your aunt's brothers-by-marriage."

The scowl that transformed Blake's face from concern to disgust didn't make him any less handsome. It only made him more intimidating. But for reasons beyond her fathoming, he didn't scare her.

"Such a coincidence." Blake's tone made it clear it was anything but a happy one.

She couldn't blame him. She knew the story behind why there was such animosity between their clans. Brighde Sinclair was once a Kerr; she was Cerys' father's half-sister and her grandfather's legitimate daughter. Cerys's father and uncles, however, were born on the wrong side of the blanket. Her grand-mother had been the former laird's mistress for more than a decade when her aunt and father were born only weeks apart. When her grandfather's first wife died, he married his mistress and proclaimed legitimate all his sons and daughters by her. He'd also arranged a marriage for Brighde to a repugnant and violent man. Her grandfather and Randolph de Soules concocted a plan to make money while removing Brighde from the scene. She'd fled and met Blake's uncle, Alexander. She'd married the Highlander, but both her father and supposed fiancé died in a battle against the Sinclairs.

"I may be my father's daughter, but I am not him nor my grandparents. Are you your aunt?" Cerys watched as Blake bristled, and she realized what she implied.

"I would be proud to be like ma aunt. She wasna the one in the wrong. She wasna the attempted murderer."

"I didn't mean to insinuate that, and I realized it didn't sound right once I said it. I just meant we are our own people. We aren't anyone else." She considered how different their accents were. Her Lowland speech sounded boring to her ear, while Blake's Highland brogue intrigued her. They were from the same country, but it felt, at that moment, that they were worlds apart.

"Vera well. Are ye certain ye dinna need aught?"

Cerys offered a soft smile. The annoyance was gone from Blake's voice and back was the softness, the concern.

"I'm well. I merely had a moment, and it's passed. Thank you, though."

"Think naught of it, lass."

"It was still kind. Most men wouldn't have bothered."

Blake raised his chin as his gaze bound her in a

spell. "Nae all men are Highlanders, and vera few are Sinclairs."

Cerys swallowed and felt that same wave of heat course through her again. It wasn't a threat. It was more like temptation wrapped up in a promise. But then she recalled what she heard as she first walked past him.

"I shouldn't keep you from your revelries. I bid you adieu."

"Ma revelries? Is there a feast I didna ken aboot?"

"No. I believe you had plans for your evening. I don't wish to keep you from them. I know you already had your ale. I believe there was something else you wished for."

She'd meant to extract herself from the conversation. Instead, her comment made Blake step closer until she was within his long arm's reach. She tilted her head back as she kept their gazes locked. She didn't want to be the first to look away, yet she felt like she was baiting him. But to what end?

"And did ye hear what I said after that?"

"I did." Her voice was strong but quiet. "If that's what you want for this eve, I am not the right woman."

"Mayhap I've changed ma mind." Blake took another step closer, almost as if to test how she would react. She was rooted in place. But her mind wasn't as slow to move as her body. It suddenly snapped to attention.

"I think you enjoy pursuing ladies as much as you enjoy sitting in a chair with a tavern wench draped across you for a few coins. The difference between those women and me is that I don't need aught from you."

"That doesnae mean ye dinna want aught from me."

"And you didn't deny that you enjoy the pursuit. I

am not a fox for you to take to ground. Though I get the sense you're a hound."

Blake grinned, and his even, white teeth appeared to shine against his suntanned golden skin. "I am persistent and loyal. I dinna even mind a scratch behind the ears from time to time."

"And I wouldn't mind putting you outside for the eve."

"I'll only come back. *Semper fidelis*, ma lady."

Cerys's brow creased, unprepared for Blake to claim he was ever faithful. Was he carrying on their banter? Or was he hinting at more? When he continued, she understood.

"A dog may wag his tail at many people, but there is always but one owner to whom he's most loyal." Blake bowed to her and turned on his heel, but when he reached the door, he paused and looked at Cerys. "Until the morn, Lady Cerys. I'm certain we shall see each other often while I'm here."

The man was a puzzle with several of the pieces already in place. But she wondered if she wanted to put it all together. The thought of encountering him again appealed, but she had more important things—life-altering, history-influencing things—with which to contend. They would need to come first. If only her racing heart would remember.

CHAPTER 2

$\mathcal{B}$lake sat amongst a group of courtiers who either weren't ordered to or couldn't afford to follow the court to France. He, Torquil, and half of their guards shared a few drams at the local tavern, The Wolf and Sheep. It was more reputable than the Picked Over Plum and was likely to land them in less trouble than the Merry Widow. None were the official names of the establishments, but that's how everyone in Stirling knew them.

The Picked Over Plum employed whores who were far past their prime. The women and whisky were cheap, but Blake feared getting more than just sotted. The Merry Widow was the most popular tavern in Stirling, since it was where many married women from court met their lovers for what were supposed to be secret assignations abovestairs. The Wolf and Sheep suited Blake since he wasn't looking for overly attentive wenches, and there were next to no women at court to come to the Merry Widow. But he would have to mind his coin purse, since the tavern was known for its light-fingered wenches and owner.

"The bluidy English scurried back toward the border like bairns pishing their raggies." Blake threw back another dram as he laughed alongside the men. "Murray showed why he's the Guardian of Scotland. He wasna just the Bruce's brother-by-marriage. He's a right terror on the battlefield. Ye should have seen how the Sassenachs ran when they spotted Andrew Murray and a hoard of Highlanders breathing down their necks."

"It's not like the English are entirely unprepared. That bastard, Edward III, is as bad his grandfather, the Hammer of the Scots. There must be something aboot the name. All three of them have had their sights set on Scotland for generations." A young Lowlander courtier, Domnall Cunningham, curled his lip in disgust. He wouldn't have anyone discredit or ignore the role Lowlanders played in protecting the border or the cattle reivers stole from the English.

"We've been fighting to keep them from our doors for nearly two score years. Your grandfather was fighting for the Bruce even before your father and uncles joined in. Mayhap you'll finally accomplish what they couldn't." Another Lowlander, Stanley Home, concurred with his brethren.

Blake fixed him with a gimlet eye. What his family accomplished had helped Robert the Bruce secure his rightful place as the king of Scotland, and they had fought valiantly to keep him where he belonged. Blake's grandfather, father, and uncles were celebrated war heroes. They'd accomplished more than this kowtowing, soft-handed, pretentious prick ever had. He exchanged a glance with Torquil, both in silent agreement not to acknowledge the slight.

"Murray is certainly a mon nae to be underestimated. After being prisoner to the English more than once, he doesnae have any love lost for them." Torquil rested his hand on the wench's hip, who took a seat on his lap. Blake shot him a warning look. They might flirt, but they would both heed their father's and uncles' warnings.

"That prig, Strathbogie, really thought he could lay siege to Kildrummy Castle, and Murray would turn a blind eye. The mon's wife held the castle. As the Bruce's sister and as his wife, Murray wasna going to ignore Lady Christina."

David Strathbogie was a personal enemy of sorts to the Sinclairs. His mother, Joan, was the eldest daughter of John "the Red" Comyn of Badenoch, and cousin to Tavish's wife, Ceit. The Red forced Ceit to spy for him during her time as a lady-in-waiting. It caught her between her uncle and the Bruce, who forced her to be a double agent. The English gave Strathbogie a castle in Ireland because of familial ties. He would have done well to stay there.

Andrew Murray responded by marching eleven hundred men to his wife's defense and routed Strathbogie and the English. It was this battle from which the Sinclairs arrived at court. It was their survival that Blake and Torquil now celebrated. Their father and uncles were likely fast asleep in the family's suite in the castle. Away from their wives and children for weeks, none of the older men, who'd survived countless battles before, were interested in merriment. They loathed being away from their wives of more than two decades, and while Castle Dunbeath was one of the most impenetrable in the country, none felt at ease not being there to defend their children themselves. Blake and Torquil were among the oldest, so their brood of cousins were still young.

"Where do you think the English will pop up next?" Domnall appeared curious, but neither Blake nor Torquil would share anything about future plans with someone they neither knew nor trusted. It was one thing to regale people with their feats of strength and bravery. It was another to divulge battle strategies. There was something about the young man that set Blake's nerves on edge when the Lowlander asked. It felt almost too curious.

"Wherever they want. The only thing predictable aboot them is that they will return." Blake hedged as his eyes swept the tavern. Unlike Torquil, he had found no one who took his fancy. None had bronze hair and blue eyes. At least none until he spotted a woman with brown hair in the kitchen. He hadn't seen her before, so he wondered if she was a cook. If she were, she was probably the tavern owner's wife or daughter. A wife would be out of the question, but a daughter might be willing.

He spied the woman's profile when she shifted to let a servant pass. Blake was on his feet and edging around the table before his brother and guards knew what was happening. He waved them away as he stormed toward the kitchen.

What is she doing in a tavern? It's the bluidy middle of the night. The gates are already locked. She canna get back in. If she thinks she's spending the night in a tavern...

Blake slammed the door open, hitting the wall with it. Everyone in the kitchen jumped except for Cerys. He sensed she already knew he was there, and she'd guessed who possessed the seething rage that filled the small work area. His hands went around her waist from behind as he steered her toward the back door and outside. Once free of the stifling heat in the kitchen, he grasped her arm and dragged her into the shadows.

"The truth." Just two words, but the command was clear in Blake's hushed tone.

"I owe you naught. You met me once."

"Women of yer station dinna gallivant at night in taverns."

15

She had the audacity to snort. Blake inhaled so deeply that his chest nearly bumped into hers. She pressed her lips together, and Blake couldn't tell if it was to keep from laughing or to keep from licking her lips. She looked at him as if he were a flank of beef she wished to devour. He couldn't deny he was looking at her as though she were a fine cherry tart. He noticed her hands fisted her skirts as though it would keep her from reaching out.

"You know as well as I do that women of my station leave the keep at night. There's a tavern named for them."

"Are ye a merry widow, then? Are ye looking for a tumble?"

"Not this eve. I haven't spotted anyone I fancy."

Blake could see her eyes sparkle in the moonlight, and there was defiance radiating from them. "That's because ye hadnae spotted me, lass."

"But I had. I checked the main room when I arrived. And as I said, there was naught there that I fancied."

"I wouldnae have guessed ye were a liar when I met ye."

"I don't—"

"But ye do. We both ken we fancy one another, but ye dinna want to act on it."

"And you do?"

"Aye, but I willna." Blake watched the surprise, then hurt, flash across Cerys's beautiful visage. "Because ye arenae a woman to be found in a tavern. And I willna take what isnae offered to me."

"Then you should go back inside and leave me to my business."

"I canna do that. It's nae safe out here."

"Too true. Some lumbering mountain mon might accost me."

"Lumbering?" Blake chuckled. "One of these days I

16

shall show ye just how agile and flexible I am. And I amnae from the mountains, Cerys. I'm from the sea where the sky looks like it'll meet the water, and they both match yer eyes."

Where the hell did that come from? Blake never considered himself a bard, but that was likely the most flowery thing he'd ever uttered. He went from a randy comment to complimenting her like a lovelorn suitor.

"I don't go to the lists, so I'll never have a chance to see any of your movement." Cerys paused, her eyes searching for something within his. "But thank you for the compliment."

"Ye're welcome. They come easily when I speak the truth." Blake's face hardened as he recalled what had brought him outside. "And that brings us back around to what ye're doing here. Dinna lie, Cerys."

"The truth. Is that why you paid me the compliment? Was it to put me in my place and guilt me into talking?"

"What? Nay. Never. I meant the compliment as just that. I dinna lie. It merely reminded me of what ye havenae told me."

"I'm not a liar either, Blake." At his dubious expression, she grew defensive. "Just because I don't want to admit whether I'm attracted to you doesn't make me a liar. Mayhap I wish to keep my feelings to myself. And as to why I'm here, that's none of your business, Blake. Go back to your men."

"Ye dinna strike me as a fool, Cerys. Ye ken the gates are locked, and ye dinna have a way back in until morn. Ye also ken it isnae safe for any woman, let alone a noble one, to be out and aboot this late at night. That means ye ken there's somewhere ye can spend the night, and I want to ken where that is."

"And I suppose you want to know with whom that will be. That's also none of your business." *Though I*

17

wouldn't mind if it was. Cerys scolded herself for her wayward thoughts. "You can't get back into the keep either. I can imagine where you'll be spending the night. Go seek her bed, and I shall seek one for myself."

Blake pressed Cerys back against the wall near which they spoke. He loomed over her, but he didn't scare her. Any other man, even one of the other Sinclairs, would have terrified her. She would have been clawing and fighting to break free once Blake rested his forearms against the wall, boxing her in.

"Ye said yerself that ye saw me in the main room. Ye saw I didna have a woman near me."

"That doesn't mean you won't."

"Until I spied ye, I didna plan to seek any woman tonight."

"I don't believe that for a moment."

"Ye should. I told ye, I dinna lie."

"Fine. Mayhap you would merely change your mind. You have to sleep somewhere. Why not with a woman as your pillow?"

"I would have slept on a bench while the others did as they please. And in case ye havenae notice, I'm a rather large mon. I would crush a woman if I used her as a pillow. I'd prefer the woman I want to use me as a pillow. Do ye ken who that is?"

Blake watched Cerys swallow. She made no other reaction. She neither denied nor admitted about whom he spoke. He was certain she knew. He dropped one hand to rest at her waist.

"Do ye ken, Cerys?" He repeated his question, leaning to whisper in her ear. His warm breath brushed against her ear.

"It can't be me, Blake. It won't be. I'm no wanton. Find a woman who can service you as you wish."

"I never said, never even imagined, ye're wanton. And I dinna wish to be serviced. I wish to get to ken

18

ye better. I wish ye to let me kiss ye this eve, but I willna ask for more, and I wouldnae dare try to take more."

"A kiss? I doubt you wish to stop there, or you could have drunk in your chamber."

"Ye said I might change ma mind. I did already. I dinna want anyone but this chestnut-haired lass I met today who is equal parts frustrating and intriguing. Unless it's her, I amnae interested."

"Just a kiss?"

"Aye, *leannan*. Just a kiss."

"I don't speak Gaelic."

"I ken. Mayhap a kiss would convince me to tell ye."

"And if I say no?"

"Then ye will have to seek me out and talk to me again." Blake leaned back, giving Cerys room to move if she wished.

"And if I say yes?"

"Then I will endeavor to make it the best one ye'll ever have."

"You presume I've never been kissed before."

"Mayhap ye have been. But the court is virtually empty these days. There isnae as much trouble for a young lady-in-waiting to get up to."

"There are still plenty of men with lips."

Blake chuckled again. "I should hope they have lips. What a strange sight that would be if they didna. What say ye, *leannan*?"

"Are you going to demand I tell you why I'm here?"

"Nay. Clearly, demanding doesnae work. I dinna think ye will tell me even if I ask sweetly. But I will ensure ye're somewhere safe for the eve."

"I will be. I know what I'm doing, Blake. This isn't the first time I've been out this late." Cerys's confession was barely more than a murmur. Blake felt his temper spike once more. He didn't even care why she was away from the castle. It was knowing she put herself in danger that angered him.

"Show me yer dirk." Blake didn't expect her response.

"Which one? The one in my pocket? The ones in my boots? Or mayhap one of these?" Cerys lifted her arms and turned them palm up. He spied bracers with *sgian dubhs* fastened to her wrists.

"What are ye up to, Cerys, that ye need to carry so many weapons, and ye're out in the middle of the night? Ye have nearly as many knives as me." Blake watched as her speculative gaze ran over his body. He felt his rod twitch as he hoped she liked what she saw. "If ye're nice to me, mayhap one of these days I'll show ye where I keep some of them."

"You don't need to. I already saw the ones at your wrists, and I'm certain you have ones in your boots. I don't need to know where the rest are to know there are bound to be more."

"Mayhap I want ye to. Mayhap I want to ken that ye ken how to use them. Do ye, lass?"

"Yes."

To Blake's ear, the admission sounded miserable, as if she wished it weren't the truth. He lifted her chin and brushed his thumb over her cheek.

"Did something happen to make ye ken that?"

"Yes." Cerys swallowed the lump in her throat. "No one tried to—no one—"

"I understand, *leannan*." And he did. She didn't want to, or couldn't, say aloud that no one had molested her. But something traumatic had happened. "Let me walk ye to wherever ye planned to spend the night. I will stand guard wherever it is. I willna be able to leave ye in good conscience. I just canna."

"Why? Why do you care?"

"Because I'm a Sinclair."

"You say that as if it explains everything."

"It does, lass. It always will. The way that I am, the things I do, the way I think. It's all because I'm a Sinclair. Duty and honor are everything. I canna let a woman half ma size roam around at night when I ken what could happen, and I'm big enough and trained enough to keep aught from befalling her. What kind of mon would I be to walk away kenning that?"

"I—" Cerys couldn't bring herself to turn him away. She'd never felt so safe as she did now, even though they were standing outside in the middle of the night, and Blake was a virtual stranger. She'd sensed everything he just said when they met in the antechamber. She still thought he might chase her just for entertainment, but she didn't doubt he would respect her if she said no. And it wasn't just because he was a colossus. There was an air of controlled danger about the man, a sense that anyone foolish enough to take him on was signing their death warrant. But there was also an air of trustworthiness that set her at ease. "I'd like that kiss, please."

The hand that held her chin slid to cup her cheek. The hand resting at her waist slid around her back. He leaned down and brushed his lips against hers as their eyes drifted closed. He straightened and gazed down at her confused expression.

"As starved as I am, I'm nae going to devour ye, *leannan*. If ye wish for more, then ye can ask. But ye didna want to kiss me only a few minutes ago. Though I didna like that, I will respect it."

Cerys rested her hands on his biceps as the one cupping her cheek fell away. She felt bereft of his touch. His hands were warm despite the crisp night air.

"May I kiss you, Blake?" She watched as it was his turn to swallow before he nodded. She went onto her toes, but he still had to lean nearly in half. She pressed her lips to his, allowing a little more pressure than his mere brushing. But it wasn't by much. When they pulled apart, Blake shocked her by pulling her against his chest and holding her. She wrapped her arms around his waist and stood there, utterly unsure of what to do but feeling blissful and protected. This wasn't lust. It was affection, and she didn't know why. "I have a way back into the castle."

CHAPTER 3

$\mathcal{B}$lake didn't expect that pronouncement. Even though they'd spoken in whispers since they walked outside, her admission that she could get back into Stirling Castle when it was sealed and locked for the night shocked him. He was also unprepared to let Cerys out of his embrace. Nothing had felt righter. He wished to keep her in his arms until the sun set on the last day of his life. And it was the most disconcerting feeling he'd ever had.

"How?"

"There are tunnels and hidden passageways."

Blake froze. Very few people knew that secret. It was meant to be that way for a reason. If people knew, it would no longer be a secure way for the royal family to escape if needed. It also weakened the castle's defenses if people knew how to enter without passing through the main or postern gates. He only knew because David showed him and his cousins when they were very young. The Bruce showed his son in case the English attacked. It had been too much of a novelty not to share with friends who were practically family.

Once they'd explored, the Sinclair cousins ran to tell their parents about their discovery. It was the first time all the Sinclair siblings, including his aunt Mairghread, who was there with her Mackay family, gathered their children for a family meeting. Callum, Alex, Tavish, Magnus, and Mairghread had the same conversation with their parents, Liam and Kyla, when they were children. The older Sinclairs knew from having done what Blake and his cousins did. Deirdre and Ceit knew from their time at court. Deirdre's cousin, Elizabeth Fraser, lived at court half her life and used them until she married the Bruce's adopted brother, Edward, and left.

The parents explained the dire importance that they never even whisper about the tunnels amongst themselves, let alone tell anyone. They also emphasized that they were not a place for children to play. There were miles of hidden corridors in which an unsuspecting child could get lost. They'd all taken it to heart, so it shocked Blake to learn Cerys knew about it.

"I've never told anyone that. But I suspect you already knew since I know how close the Sinclairs are to the Bruces. And—I trust you."

"Ye can always trust me, *leannan*. But that's dangerous information to have."

"Or not. If Balliol and Edward attempt to take Stirling, then it may be what keeps me alive. There're not nearly enough warriors here to defend a deserted castle. I'm surprised they haven't come back for it since it's in a strategic location."

Blake kept his face studiously neutral. Just like he would reveal nothing to the courtiers inside, he wouldn't do it with Cerys. The men inside were untrustworthy. Cerys could be in danger.

"How do ye ken aboot them?"

"I can't tell you." Regret filled Cerys's eyes, so Blake opted not to press further. He already knew it would get him nowhere.

"Let me take ye back."

Cerys shook her head. "You wouldn't leave without telling your men. That means they'll know where you're going and will come along."

"If I just said it's dangerous kenning such, why would I let ma men ken? Besides, as ye said, the Sinclairs ken. Torquil kens. Come back into the kitchen, lass, and I'll speak to Torquil. I'll be back in two shakes of a lamb's tail."

Blake gave her no choice, taking her hand and guiding her back inside. They exchanged a surprised glance when they realized what he'd done and how much they disliked letting go. He returned faster than Cerys expected. He drew her cloak's hood over her head and guided her back outside. They walked in silence to the castle wall. Blake knew where to go and led them around the side and away, toward a copse of trees. He held open the hidden door, and Cerys stooped to pick up a torch. Using his flint from his sporran, Blake lit it. Sound carried in the passageways once they were within the keep, so they trod softly. Cerys led him through the warren of tunnels until she stopped and pointed to a door.

Blake eased it open into a music chamber that no one had touched in at least a decade. He pushed aside the tapestry, letting Cerys pass. Once it settled back into place, they crossed the chamber. At the door, she stopped.

"The ladies-in-waiting chambers are down the passageway. I can make it from here. Thank you."

"Go ahead of me, but I'm following until I hear the lock click to yer door."

"I managed to survive here before you arrived. I'll be here after you leave."

"That may well be true, *leannan*, but if ye can share the burden with someone, why nae take the help?"

25

Cerys nodded. She'd been dumped at court two years ago, and she'd fended for herself ever since. She knew she faced less danger since there were so few men around. But it also meant there were far fewer people to hear her scream if she ever did. She'd had more than one threatening encounter. It's how she'd discovered the tunnels and why she knew how to wield her knives. She'd asked her Kerr guards to teach her. Once again, she felt safe with Blake.

"You never told me what that means."

"I ken." Blake crossed his arms and grinned. He leaned forward and whispered. "Sweetheart. And if I have ma way, it'll be *mo leannan*." My sweetheart.

Cerys could guess what the word before sweetheart meant, and she realized she wasn't as opposed to it as she knew she should be. Something about the enormous Highlander appealed to her in a way no man ever should have. But guilt nipped at her for even fantasizing for a moment about what could never exist between them. She never should have kissed the warrior. As she observed him, noting the seriousness, yet softness, of his tone, she couldn't help longing for more of his attention. She'd never imagined she could feel such a draw to a man. It unnerved her.

"We can't stand around here for forever. Someone is bound to pass by at some point."

"Cerys, how many other ladies-in-waiting are there? I saw none this eve and just the one ye talked to when I arrived."

"There are ten of us. Without the queen, we have no real duties. We attend morning Mass together and most meals, but otherwise, we spend our days as we please."

"How do ye spend yers?"

Cerys wished she could divulge how she spent much of her days, but she wasn't at liberty to share. Not even to a man who tempted her in ways unlike anyone other than him. She offered a sweet smile, but that made Blake narrow his eyes at her. He sensed she was hiding something. "I spend time walking in the gardens, sewing, weaving, and reading. Naught different from any lady-in-waiting. I merely have no queen to follow around."

"Why are ye here?"

"My family believes the French court is too depraved. They insisted I remain. The queen is little more than a child, so she has no need of me. She needs tutors more than the dozen women who accompany her."

Blake snorted. "Depraved? Have they never been here when court is full? Nay royal court is exactly a bastion of innocence."

"With it nearly empty, they believe it is. I arrived after the court absconded to France. I serve in title only. My father believes it makes me marriageable."

And yet here I still am. That's what he claims at least. I wished I had stayed home. I was more likely to marry there than find a suitable husband among the unwanted and impoverished who were relegated to remaining here. Then again, being unmarriageable at home is why my father dumped me here.

Blake watched her, knowing there were thoughts running through her head that she didn't share. He'd learned just as much about Cerys from what she left unsaid as he did from what she said.

"Do ye have guards here?"

"Yes. Why?"

"How many, lass?"

She wasn't much fond of returning to being called lass. It felt like a demotion after being called sweetheart. "Two."

"Would ye go riding with me in the morn? After Mass and ye break yer fast."

"Don't you have commitments or training?"

27

"I can take a day away from the lists, and Murray gave everyone leave to rest on the morrow. What say ye?"

Cerys hesitated. Two guards weren't many, but they were enough to serve as chaperones. But her father and uncles were at court. While they would never notice her absence, her guards were sure to report it to them.

"If ye dinna wish to—"

"No!" Cerys swept her gaze up and down the passageway, embarrassed that someone might hear her. "It's not that. I do wish to. But my father and uncles are here. My guards are sure to tell them if I go riding with a mon, especially a Sinclair. It might give them an apoplexy."

Which I wouldn't entirely mind. Cerys! That's wretched to think.

"I suppose it wouldnae be wise to do that." Disappointment filled Blake's voice as he tried to conceive of an alternative. "May I accompany ye on a walk through the gardens?"

"Blake, I can't. I won't have guards with me for that. But someone will surely see us. My family will still find out. My father will seek you out, and it will be ugly."

"Cerys, I do nae fear yer father, but I respect ye and how that would make yer life difficult. I dinna want to do that. But I also dinna want to give up."

"You enjoy the chase, Blake. What will you do if I let you catch me? You'll be here—what—a fortnight, at best? Then what? I'm not losing my reputation and the one thing of value to a future husband."

Blake's warm brown eyes darkened nearly to black, and Cerys wished she could swallow back what she said.

"I may enjoy flirting with a lass now and again, but I dinna ravish virgins and leave them in ma wake. I also think there is far more to yer value than yer maiden-

28

head. But if ye think that's who I am, then ye havenae learned aught aboot me. Ye havenae listened to me at all. I willna keep ye. Go to yer chamber, and I will watch until ye're inside. Goodnight, Lady Cerys."

"I—"

"Goodnight, Lady Cerys." Blake wasn't interested in excuses or prevarications. Her comment cut deep. It went beyond bruising his pride. Rejection he could accept. But her doubt about his integrity wounded him. It felt as if she knew him not at all, that he hadn't proved his character to her when that's all he'd tried to do since he spied her in the kitchen.

Cerys didn't know what to do, so all she did was nod. She gave him a wistful glance before turning toward her chamber. True to his word, Blake followed behind on silent feet. When she reached her chamber, she spotted him lingering near the stairwell. He'd given her space, even been discreet, but he was close enough to rescue her from danger. She noticed him creeping closer when she opened the door, but he stopped where he could hear the door lock. He drew no closer, and Cerys nearly waved when she turned to shut the door. But that seemed childish and petty.

As they both prepared to retire in their separate chambers, both concocted one plan after another to run into each other. By the time they were each in bed, a plot brewed in each of their heads.

29

CHAPTER 4

$\mathcal{C}$erys crossed the bailey with Wilma Hay beside her. She observed the Sinclairs making their way to the lists, Blake amid his kinsmen. Cerys tried to hurry Wilma, but the woman was in no rush. She perused the Sinclairs with clear appreciation. A kind Cerys was certain the men would not return. Wilma's family had as sordid a past with the Sinclairs as her own. Wilma's great uncle, Archibald Hay, was the man Blake's mother was supposed to marry after her parents kept her away from Magnus for seven years. He tried to assault her and even kidnapped her, but Magnus's unrelenting love saved her. It was Cerys's aunt Mary, Brighde's half-sister, who had an affair with Archibald and tried to kill Deirdre. To save their lives, Magnus killed Archibald, and Deirdre killed Mary.

"Let's not dawdle. I wish to pick the flowers and arrange them for the altar before the midday meal."

"I'm taking in the scenery."

"I know, and you're a fool to be so obvious. I don't doubt they know who we are." Wilma was the spitting image of her father, who was Archibald's nephew. The two men had resembled one another strongly enough that people questioned Wilma's father's paternity.

Cerys doubted the Sinclairs wouldn't recognize Wilma, and she didn't want to face Blake yet. It wasn't part of her plan.

But it was too late. Cerys knew the moment Magnus and Tavish spotted them. Their glower could have turned her to dust. She tried to yank Wilma in the garden's direction, but the women held firm.

"Gracious, they are fierce."

"And that's why I don't want to find myself at the sharp end of their sword."

"The Sinclairs don't hurt women. Everyone knows that. It's fact."

"And neither are they the forgetful type, Wilma. My aunt and your great-uncle caused a great deal of trouble for Magnus, and from what I've heard, Tavish was there to support his brother."

Cerys turned her gaze back to the Sinclairs and found all five of them glaring. She focused on Blake, who watched Wilma. At least they didn't direct their entire animosity toward her. But when his gaze switched to hers, she read the disappointment in his gaze. It was bad enough she was a Kerr, but to be seen in the company of a Hay only made it worse. But she had little choice. She and Wilma became friends out of necessity. They arrived at the same time and knew no one. Their personalities were nothing alike, but loneliness made for strange bedfellows.

"Good morning."

"Are you daft?" Cerys was aghast that Wilma called out to the men. She was prepared to acknowledge them with a nod and move on. Now it would force them to return Wilma's greeting, and none looked pleased. They had no choice but to cross the women's path to make it to the lists.

"Lady Cerys." Blake nodded before he looked at Wilma. Cerys's nervousness made her shift her weight as though she wished to take off at a sprint. She wondered if Blake would chase her. That nearly made her lips twitch since she'd accused him of that.

"Blake." Cerys offered the warmest smile she could muster that wouldn't look phony. She offered it to each man, not wanting to single out Blake.

"You're the Sinclairs. Our families know each other."

Cerys wanted to melt into the ground at Wilma's observation. She glanced at the garden and wondered if she could get lost among the hedges.

"We ken." Magnus's stare bore into Wilma, but Cerys couldn't help but feel it in her marrow. It was intense and unrelenting.

"Good morning, we were just on our way to pick flowers for the kirk. We don't want to detain you." Cerys tried to nudge Wilma, but the latter riveted her attention on Torquil, who smirked at her. It only made him more handsome, but unapproachable. Cerys knew Wilma saw it as a challenge. How she didn't understand what a fool she was making of herself was beyond Cerys.

When Wilma refused to take the hint, Cerys debated whether she could just walk away. She glanced at Blake, hoping he might have a solution to this horrifying encounter. But he watched her, cocking an eyebrow when their gazes met.

"I told you I wasn't my family. I am my own person. She isn't her uncle any more than I am my aunt or grandfather." Cerys kept her voice low, imploring Blake to intervene. But it was clear Magnus heard her because he turned to look at her.

"Ye speak the truth, Lady Cerys. But it isnae wise to put a rabbit in front of a wolf and expect it to fight the instinct to pounce." Magnus's cool tones sent a shiver down Cerys's back. She glanced at Blake, but he awaited her response.

"Too true. A wise rabbit would run the other way and find its warren. Unfortunately, not all rabbits heed that wisdom. Isn't that right, Lady Wilma? We'd do well to learn from the rabbits."

"Rabbits? What're you talking aboot? There aren't any rabbits or wolves."

Cerys cringed at Wilma's misunderstanding. Her father hadn't bothered with a tutor for his daughter, and it often showed in her lack of worldliness and reasoning.

"We really should go, Lady Wilma. I'm certain the Sinclairs are eager to train with their men. We shouldn't keep them." Cerys tried again, and this time, Wilma nodded. But not before she flashed Torquil a coy smile. Cerys's stomach flipped at the predatory look in Torquil's gaze. She knew he was likely their age, but he suddenly struck Cerys as much older and experienced. He would be the wolf that swallowed her friend whole.

"Enjoy yer day, Lady Cerys, Lady Wilma." Blake's gaze nearly set Cerys ablaze. She abandoned her original plan and hoped this impromptu idea worked.

"Thank you. It is rather lovely. The kind that makes you pick flowers in the morn and go for a long ride in the afternoon." Cerys saw the flash of surprise, then understanding, in Blake's eyes. He dipped his chin, the slightest acknowledgement. She turned away and practically dragged Wilma into the gardens.

"What was that?" Magnus demanded as he turned to his sons. "Ye looked like ye intended to strip the lass right where she stood, Torquil. I ken that was just taunting. But ye, Blake, ye looked like a lovesick pup. Naught

33

good will come of either of ye dallying with those lasses."

"I have nay intention of dallying with Lady Cerys." Blake tried to keep the defensiveness from his voice, but he nearly plowed his fist into his brother's stomach when he spoke.

"He's likely to return to Dunbeath with a wife and a bairn soon on the way."

"I would never be so careless or dishonorable as to trap a bride, Brother."

Torquil's eyes flashed wide as he realized how Blake interpreted his meaning. "Forgive me. That wasna what I meant. After ye're wed. Only after ye're wed."

The men entered the lists, and Magnus maneuvered himself to his older son's side. "Ye wouldnae be the first to marry a lass from a clan we dinna get along with. We would accept her just as we did yer aunts and yer mama. But dinna think her father would let her go willingly. He's never forgiven Uncle Alex, and he still begrudges Aunt Brighde being the only true legitimate child."

"I ken. But none of us kenned who she was when we arrived. It's nae like she wears a pennant announcing her clan."

"Ye ken now, though. I dinna wish to see ye heart-sore, son. It's a misery I wouldnae wish upon ye." Magnus spoke from experience. He and Deirdre fell in love over several years as adolescents. They handfasted, but it enraged Deirdre's father. He whisked her away from a Highland Gathering before they could tell Magnus's father. Her father kept her hidden at court for seven years. It was by coincidence that they reunited.

Magnus had come to court to resolve the issues with the Kerrs and Hays, but he found his long-lost bride. They'd remained faithful to one another the entire time they were apart. They'd both lived in agony during those years. Even nearly a score of years later, they both loathed being apart for more than a day. The pain had faded, but it returned with ferocity when weeks and months separated them because Magnus was still a warrior.

"I ken, Da. But was it easy to walk away from Mama once ye met?"

"Nay, it wasna. And that's why I offer ye this advice. If she's worth the fight, then dinna capitulate. Ken that it may be a fight to the death in truth, but also remember, we never fight alone. Keep yer brother at yer back, and ye'll both come home alive with yer bonnie lass."

"Do ye really have to leave in the morning, Da?"

"We do. I wish it werenae the case, but we still have obligations to the clan. We've been away long enough. It isnae fair to the guards to continue taking our watches or bearing the responsibility of our leadership. Grandda is expecting us."

"I wish ye could stay. What do I do when I need yer advice?"

"Even if I were here to give it to ye, ye're yer own mon. Ye must make the choices for yerself."

"I'm scared I willna ken which choices to make."

"Then talk to yer brother. He may be younger, but he'll nae steer ye wrong. *Familia prima.*"

"*Semper familia.*"

Family first and always family. It was the laird's family creed and what they lived by. It meant Blake knew he could rely on Torquil no matter what, and his family would welcome his bride, whoever she might be, because she would become family.

"Da?"

"Aye."

"If ye were me, what would ye do aboot her father? Assuming we suit and wish to wed?"

"I dinna have the right answer to that without some

35

serious thought. But a mon like him will put himself first. Yer grandda is now the Earl of Caithness, governing as both the Earl of Sinclair and the Earl of Orkney. It would tie the Kerrs to us twice over and give him a connection that will elevate his status among the pretentious pricks he surrounds himself with. Play to the mon's vulnerability. His pride."

"Thank ye, Da. I'll miss ye, but I ken Mama and Maisie miss ye."

"They miss ye and yer brother, too. Even if Maisie was happy to see the hind end of yer horse when we rode out." Magnus chuckled, and Blake joined him. His younger sister had inherited the Sinclairs' competitiveness almost to a fault. She'd bested him at archery three days before they rode out, and he knew she wasn't in a hurry to defend her win. But he also knew she missed Torquil and him as much as they missed her. While the Sinclair siblings and their cousins squabbled from time to time, never did they forget their family creed. It's what made them happy and kept them as one of the most powerful families in Scotland. Only their Sutherland and Mackay relatives rivaled them in devotion and influence, and they were an unbreakable alliance.

"Kiss them both for me."

"I will. Then I'll have ma own kisses with yer mama."

"Ugh." Blake pretended to gag. "I dinna need any more brothers or sisters."

"And yer mama and I dinna need any raggies to change, either. Fear nae, lad." Magnus and his siblings were still as in love and in lust with their soulmates as they were the day they each wed. Unusual among the nobility, the couples openly showed their affection for their mates and their children. None pretended to be anything but enamored. It embarrassed Blake's generation, but he knew his siblings and cousins aspired to such happiness.

"I will take what ye said to heart, Da."

"I ken. But while ye're off courting this lass, try to remember that wasna the reason for ye staying."

"I ken. I willna forget. I will be in the Privy Council chamber before Murray arrives. Torquil and I will see ye all off, then go there. We're ready to represent the clan."

"I ken ye are. That's why Grandda suggested it. Wee Liam had his mission to Orkney, and this is yers."

"We willna disappoint the clan." Blake felt rising trepidation now that his father's and uncles' departure drew near. He'd been confident when he was with his older family members, and he'd been sure he could bear the weight of this duty. But now that it was merely hours away, he doubted himself. He wanted to prove himself the man his family raised him to be. However, that didn't extinguish the fear that he might fail and disgrace his kin and clan. He reminded himself that he would watch and listen more than he spoke.

"I never thought ye would. I'm proud of ye and yer brother. Ye're fine men who will support Thormud when it's his turn to lead." Thormud, Callum's son, was barely two years older than him. He was as close to Thormud as he was Torquil. But the older generation of Sinclair brothers cast long shadows in which Blake felt he stood.

Blake and Magnus joined the other men. Blake sparred with his brother, while their father and uncles took turns sparring with one another. But everyone not in the match stopped to watch when Callum, Tavish, and Magnus teamed together during the mock battle. They moved with such synchronicity that it could only be nature, not nurture. Years of practice honed their skills, but intuition made them move together like a three-headed beast with one body. The only thing missing was Alex, the last key to them being ever victorious.

"One day that will be ye, me, and Thormud." Torquil crossed his arms and stood with his feet hip-width apart. It matched Blake's stance.

"Aye. And just like Uncle Alex makes them even more invincible, Tate makes us unstoppable." Tavish's oldest son inherited his father and grandfather's barrel-chested build. The four cousins together had been holy terrors since they could walk, but as young men, they were formidable.

"Ye better hope ye're unstoppable when it comes to the lass. She's watching ye."

Cerys didn't have to try hard to spot the Sinclairs in the lists as she walked back to the keep. It was far emptier than the royal lists should have been, but there were very few people in residence and even fewer visiting. She recognized the guards wearing the royal standard, and she spied her guards. But the Sinclairs simply stood out. Everything about them. Their size. Their strength. Their skills. She couldn't stop thinking about how they were like no other men she'd ever met. How Blake was like no other man she knew.

She'd distracted Wilma long enough to gather several large bouquets of flowers that she took to the kirk. She arranged them to celebrate the early June feast of St. Columba. It blessedly took longer than she expected, so it was time for the midday meal when she passed the lists. She wrapped her arm around Wilma's, taking a direct route to the keep, avoiding the Sinclairs as they prepared to leave the training field. She would seek her guards at the meal and tell them she wished to go riding. She hoped Blake would happen upon them, but even if he ignored her hint, she was eager to get away from the castle. She didn't know how an enormous building that stood mostly empty could feel so stifling.

By the time the meal ended, she was in a nervous twitch, conflicted between whether or not she wanted Blake to find her. She hemmed and hawed until a servant removed her trencher, and there was nothing left for her to do but get up. She needed to go to her chamber to change into a more appropriate gown in which to ride. She didn't wear elaborate gowns, since she felt there was no one to impress. At least, before Blake arrived, there hadn't been. But she still didn't want to ruin the one she wore. It would be muddy, and she needed her boots, anyway. When she turned toward the door, her eyes caught Blake's. He offered the same brief dip of his chin as he did when they encountered one another outside. It was discreet, and it made Cerys feel better.

Unlike most previous ladies-in-waiting, Cerys and the others present didn't have to share chambers. There were plenty available, so when Wilma sought some of the other young women to sew and gossip, Cerys slipped away and spoke to her guards. It wasn't strange for her to go riding in the afternoon with her chaperones, so she knew no one would question her. She hurried and was in the stables in fifteen minutes.

When she entered, she heard no one but a stable boy, who mucked out a stall. She looked around, but she was virtually alone. A chill ran over her that had never happened there before. Something felt unsettling. There should have been more than one worker, and there should have been more noise for the middle of the day.

"Lad."

That was a voice Cerys knew, and it wasn't Blake's or her guards'. She ducked down the line of stalls until she came to her horse's. With the air so still, the voices carried, even though they were lowered. She feared she would pish herself when they drew closer.

"Get our mounts fed and watered once we're done."

Cerys listened to hoofbeats and chided herself for where she hid. She should have picked a stall away from where her family always kept their horses when at Stirling. She shifted around her horse's right flank and moved toward its rump. She ran a soothing hand over the animal's hindquarter, ensuring it would remain calm despite her being beyond its sight. She crouched and remained silent. She had years of experience remaining out of sight.

"The sooner they leave, the better for all of us. They swan around as though they still hold sway in this court and in this country."

Cerys cringed as she listened to her father bemoaning the Sinclairs. They did still held sway. A considerable amount, in fact. The bitterness in the man's voice soured her stomach and made it churn the meager meal she'd eaten. She'd heard the complaints before, but it never held significance before meeting Blake.

Merciful Father and all angels. Don't let Blake arrive while they're here. Even if he brings a guard or two, there will be trouble. My father won't let the opportunity go. He's even more bitter than my uncles. Uncle Mitcham is laird, and he doesn't care aboot Brighde or who she married. Neither do Uncle Michael or Uncle Marcas. From what I've heard, Aunt Mary was disliked by everyone, including her brothers. Why does it still matter?

"At least the bluidy turd, Alexander, had the sense not to show up." Mitcham, her father's eldest brother, chimed in. "The others we can ignore. Him? I would plunge my blade into his heart."

Apparently, he did still care.

"Only Alexander? It was Magnus's bitch who killed our sister." Cerys's uncle Marcas joined the conversation. He was the uncle she liked least. There was something predatory about the way he watched Cerys. When he tried to touch her chest when she was eight summers, she decided she would never be alone with the man again. She'd hidden in alcoves, behind furniture, and run down passageways to avoid him.

"No one's forgotten anyone." Her uncle Michael, the second eldest, was the voice of reason. Their clan would have benefited if he'd been the eldest and became laird. But she wasn't opposed to Mitcham, since he was the only one who acknowledged her each time he saw her. Michael was unpredictable, and Marcas leered. Her father ignored her.

"Muir, back to the point. We need to return home. Does Cerys remain here or come back with us?" Mitcham sounded frustrated, as though they'd already discussed her. She needed to hear this conversation, so she remained frozen despite how her knees ached.

"She stays. No one needs a reminder of her and what happened." Her father's disgust no longer stung like it once did. She accepted it, but it didn't mean it hurt any less to be kept away from her home and her family. While her father and uncles were frequently repugnant, her aunt Matilda was a gentle woman, and kind to Cerys after her mother died. She missed her aunt tremendously because she couldn't remember her own mother. The only maternal figure she knew was Matilda. Her grandmother, when she was alive, was a horrid woman, prone to throwing things at children who got in her way.

"You'll leave her here with the Sinclairs sniffing around? Is that wise?" Mitcham wondered.

"They'll be gone soon enough."

"The two young ones are remaining with Murray," Mitcham countered.

Cerys couldn't tell who laughed at the triumphant warrior's name, but it lacked humor. It was derisive.

"They are the sons of a fourth son. They hardly merit mentioning. They are naught more than foot soldiers who run to wipe Murray's arse." Muir's bitterness clouded what everyone else knew. It mattered not where a Sinclair fell on the family tree; they all mattered. She was certain her father knew nothing about her encounters with Blake. All his anger and resentment stemmed from Brighde mostly and Deirdre slightly. It wasn't the first time she noted that every one of the Kerr siblings had a name that began with M, except for Brighde. That alone made her stand apart, and their disregard for her as a half-sibling ensured there would never be a truce. Matilda explained the situation before Cerys came to court. It was more a warning than anything else, but it tore away much of Cerys's naivety and prepared her for courtly politics.

As her relatives' voices faded away, Cerys rose. She moved around her horse's head and reached for the bridle. But she once again heard voices, and none were her men's or Blake's.

Bluidy hell. Why is this the most popular place in the keep right now? I don't know if Blake is going to come, and I can't get out without someone seeing me. And Shaw Hannay is the last person I want to see.

"He must be back across the border right now. It wouldn't surprise me if he's returned to the Cliffords in Cumbria." An elbow to his throat nearly crushed Shaw's windpipe and resulted in a distinct, rasping voice.

"Do you think Murray will chase him? Neither Sinclair would say aught last night." Stanley Home stood just beyond the stall in which she hid. She prayed he didn't take another step to his left, or he would surely spot her. "Cunningham and I tried, but neither took the bait."

"They probably knew what you were up to. You both have the cunning of a toad."

"Hannay, insult us, and you lose our help. You and yours need more clans to back you and Balliol. I have no qualms aboot walking away." Domnall Cunningham's warning rang in the air. Cerys didn't believe for a moment that he would walk away. She'd followed Domnall and Stanley to The Wolf and Sheep the previous night and knew they were fishing for information. She hadn't gone there intending to eavesdrop. Once she realized they were there, she made the best of it. She couldn't go into the main room, but the tavern wenches kept feeding her information.

There was a smug conviction in the threat Hannay issued next.

"Settle yourself. No one is going anywhere unless it's to ride alongside Balliol. I sent a messenger to my father the moment the castle guards spotted those Sinclairs. He'll reach home in two more days' time. While we wait for a response, make friends with the Sinclairs. Wipe Murray's arse with your tongue. I don't give a shite what you do. But you need to learn more, and we know I can't go anywhere near them without it being suspicious. Balliol will make his return and hiding behind France's skirts won't keep the little bastard safe. A fortnight, and it shall all begin."

HIGHLAND BEAST

CHAPTER 5

*B*lake watched Shaw Hannay, Domnall Cunningham, and Stanley Home walk into the stables. He and his men veered away and waited, since he didn't want to get cornered into talking with any of them, let alone all three. He'd watched them in the lists that morning, and it was clear none were the spoiled courtiers they wished to appear. While their skills didn't match the Highlanders, it was clear these border Scots could fight.

Blake's brow furrowed when the men walked out only minutes later, and none with a horse. It made him question why they needed the privacy of the stables. When they were out of sight, he and his men entered the stables. He wondered if Cerys and her guards had already left. He was glad she hadn't been in the stables when the three men were. He didn't trust them around her, even if she had guards.

"Which way will we ride, Blake?"

"Out across the meadow to the river. We can ford it and ride along the ridge, or we can head into the forest."

Blake had told no one why he wished to go riding. He'd merely suggested it and asked which of his men would want to accompany him. He turned toward his horse's stall and nearly jumped out of his skin when Cerys appeared, brushing hay from her skirts.

"Cerys?" Blake blurted as he walked toward her. Without thinking, he shook her skirts, knocking some of the hay from it. He looked over his shoulder, but not to his men. Instead, he strained as though he might see and hear where the three men were once they left the stables. When he looked around, he realized no one else was there. "Where are yer guards?"

"They aren't here yet." Cerys peered around Blake's shoulder at his men before she met his gaze. She lowered her voice so much that Blake could barely hear her. "I heard something. I need to tell you once we're away from the keep. I don't know what to do."

"Are ye hale, *leannan*?"

She nodded and exhaled. She hadn't realized how eager she was to hear the endearment again until he said it. She wanted to wrap her arms around her waist and bounce on her toes like a wean awaiting a gift on her saint's day. She opened her mouth to respond, but her two guards appeared through the doorway.

"Lady Cerys?" Tyree, the senior of the two, glared at Blake and the Sinclair warriors while making his way to Cerys.

"Yes. The Sinclairs just walked in. It seems great minds think alike." Cerys turned to Blake. "I assume you're going for a ride, too."

The look in her eyes told Blake to play along, as if she hadn't overheard him suggest a route. "Aye. It's a fine day to be out and aboot."

"I would have thought you spent enough time on your horse." Lyle, her other guard, crossed his arms. He was not at all convinced of the coincidence. Cerys wondered why.

"We're Highlanders. We ride before we walk." Blake

shrugged as if that explained everything. As far as he was concerned, it did. "Do ye have other guards, Lady Cerys?"

"No. I do well with my two."

Blake nodded but frowned. He already knew she had only a couple of warriors, but he assumed they would ask men from another clan to accompany them if they were riding away from the keep. He considered what he'd heard during the nooning. It would offer an excuse to ride with Cerys from the start. "Lady Cerys, there's been word of highwaymen just beyond the town walls. They've been striking during the day. Brazen and dangerous. Would ye like more men to accompany ye?"

Cerys nodded without looking at her guards. She knew it would annoy them immensely. They deferred to her for all things while they were within the castle walls. But she obeyed them once they left. She knew they would loathe having to listen to Blake, but as a nobleman, he outranked them.

"Thank you. I accept the offer. I think it would be wise unless we don't go, and I really would like to escape the keep for a while." Before either of her men could disagree, she spun back toward her horse and pulled the bridle over the animal's ears. Blake appeared at the stall door, prepared to saddle the animal for her, but she noticed him grin as she moved around with experience. "Highlanders may have learned to ride before they could walk, but I learned to saddle a horse before I could even reach."

"Then I'll ready Torque."

"Your brother?"

Blake's laugh rumbled in the cavernous space. "Nay. Get yer horse ready, and I will explain once we're mounted."

The riders soon had their steeds ready. They clattered out of the front gate and swung to the right, following the barmekin around to where a meadow stretched out before them.

"Does your horse have the same name as your brother?"

"Basically. Apparently, it's become a family tradition." At Cerys's confusion, Blake laughed again. It made Cerys's sheath ache from arousal. "Ma father named his horse after ma uncle Tavish because he'd been his favorite brother at the time when he was a wean. A couple sennights later, and his favorite brother was ma uncle Callum. Except the horse refused to accept a new name. Apparently, it got to where any time someone called out for ma uncle Tavish, the horse came too. Eventually, ma uncle Tavish agreed it was easier for the horse to be his rather than ma father's."

"So your uncle Tavish rides a horse named Tavish?"

"Alas, nay anymore. The beast died several years ago. Uncle Tavish didna speak for a sennight."

"That's rather sad."

"Aye. It was. Ma da's auld horse now spends his days in the pasture with Uncle Alex's and Uncle Callum's favorites. They're all too auld to ride into battle, but ma da and uncles canna bring themselves to put them down. Ma grandda would never expect them to, so the beasts get the best apples and carrots and are spoiled rotten."

"Sounds like a rather fine life. But what aboot your horse?"

"Much the same as ma da. When I got Torque, I could only think of names that belonged to people I kenned. I was seven summers, so I went with something familiar. I wanted to name ma horse Maisie, for ma sister, but alas ma horse is a him, nae a her. So that left Torquil. Once Da warned me aboot what happened with Uncle Tavish, I called the horse Torque instead." Blake grinned at her. "Nae that it matters. The daft beast comes any time someone says Torquil's name. But I refuse to give him up. I put in too much hard work training him to give him away."

Cerys could hear the affection in Blake's voice as he rubbed his horse's neck. There appeared nothing daft about the animal. She suspected he was highly intelligent and well trained for battle. Her horse never grew large enough or showed the temperament for a warhorse, so he wound up a gelding. It suited her because he was fast, sturdy, and more dependable than most of the horses in her family's stables at home.

"What aboot yer lad? What's he called?"

"You'll laugh."

"I willna."

"I can guarantee you will."

"I promise ye I willna, lass. Tell me."

"Let me say, in my defense, I was five when I got him, and he was still a spindly colt that my father and uncles decided wouldn't make a warhorse."

"Come on, lass. Spit it out."

"Kitten."

Blake choked, and Cerys watched as he struggled to contain his mirth. To his credit, he didn't laugh, but his body shook, and tears leaked from his eyes. But a sound he did not make. She cocked an eyebrow and turned away in a pretend huff.

"I didna laugh, *leannan*."

"Not out loud."

"Tell me how yer giant beastie came to be called Kitten."

"Only if you promise not to make fun. He's sensitive."

"Sensitive and called Kitten? Lad, what has yer mistress done to ye? I think ye need to come out with the lads more often."

"Shh." Cerys giggled. "I don't need you tempting my horse to leave me."

"Ye can come too." Blake whispered for only Cerys to hear and winked. She pressed her lips together to stifle her own laughter and nodded.

"There was a litter of kittens in the stables, and I really wanted one. But my aunt explained that they weren't pets. They had work to do outside and in the keep. I cried and begged to no avail. I was heartbroken. The next day, my father came into the Great Hall complaining about how useless his colt was and that the animal was fit for neither plow nor war. He wanted to sell him. I was still moping around, so my uncle Mitcham suggested Father give him to me. Aunt Matilda agreed and said it was better than a kitten. I thought it was as good as a kitten, and that's how he got his name."

"How auld were ye when yer father taught ye to ride?"

Cerys shifted in the saddle, growing somber. "The stable master taught me."

Blake blinked several times and remained quiet. Cerys's tone didn't welcome more questions. He reminded himself that most noble families were not like his. Fathers rarely paid attention to their daughters, but the men in the Sinclair clan all did. They valued every member of the clan as a person, not just for what they could contribute to the clan. Women were always treated with respect, and there was no tolerance for mistreatment of women, children, or animals. They were rules that every clan member knew, and so there were rare occasions when his grandfather had to impose them. But when he did, it was with a swift iron fist.

"Where would you like to ride to, my lady?"

Cerys turned toward Lyle, who she could tell was growing more annoyed with each word that passed between Blake and her. She nearly told him to save his horse the effort and just ride back to tittle-tattle to her father. Rather than provoke the man, she smiled.

"To the river and then up along the ridge." It was the route Blake suggested before he knew she was already in the stables. It was one that she and her guards took often. With Cerys in the center, they charged across the meadow. Blake glanced back at her frequently from where he rode in the lead. Once they forded the waterway, they rode south in pairs. Blake maneuvered and gestured for his two guards to ride ahead. It forced Cerys's two guards to ride in the rear, when he moved Torque beside Kitten.

"We can ride harder for a few more leagues, then come back down to the river. It'll give us an excuse to water the horse. We can talk while we wait." Blake kept his head facing forward and his voice low. He didn't see the twinkle in Cerys's eyes before she pulled her right rein, making Kitten step around the Sinclair horses in front of him. With a whistle, she took off. Her guards knew the signal, and it only took a moment for the Sinclairs to catch on. She laid low over her horse's withers. She knew Kitten's name usually fooled people into underestimating him, especially when they learned her father rejected him as a potential warhorse. But his leaner physique allowed him to be more agile than the larger stallions and destriers, and it also gave him more speed than most.

Cerys heard hooves pounding much closer than she expected. She never got more than a furlong ahead of her guards, but Kitten could outpace both of the other horses. She should have known that the Sinclair horseflesh would easily keep pace with her horse. It was only another four strides before Blake and Torque were even with Kitten and her. Both animals sensed the competition and took off.

The horses grew lathered, and their breathing labored before either steed was willing to concede. It was their riders who finally had to call a halt to the race and declare it a tie. After the brief but hard ride, they allowed the animals to amble down to the river. Blake swung down from his saddle and was beside Cerys before she could kick her foot out of the stirrup. Large, warm hands wrapped around her waist, reminding her of the previous night. Blake was gentle as he lifted her down, and she felt like barely more than a feather when he did it with such ease.

"Ye might have warned me, *leannan*. I would have prepared Torque for being put in his place finally. I think it hurt his feelings that a wee beastie named Kitten nearly bested him."

"Nearly?" Cerys scoffed. "We were ahead, but I told Kitten not to embarrass your horse or its owner."

Blake squeezed her waist before releasing her. His eyes sparkled with merriment, and she suspected he would soon get his own back on her. They guided their horses to the river's edge and didn't need to encourage them to drink. They both laughed as all the mounts guzzled noisily. Blake led them to the shade beneath a tree. He looked at his men and jerked his chin in different directions. The Sinclair men stared at the Kerrs, who made no sign that they would move away from their horses. Cerys watched all three Sinclairs glare at her guards in disgust. She didn't understand why, since her men weren't doing anything different from usual. But when she watched the Sinclair guards patrol the areas Blake assigned them, she understood his men were far more diligent than hers.

"Are my men wrong not to walk around like yours? They've always stayed near me."

"Nay. They werenae wrong when it was just the three of ye. They should stay close. But I ken they heard ma warning aboot the highwaymen. I wasna spinning tales, and I'm sure they already kenned. With me to stand with ye, they should take up watch and patrol like ma men. It keeps us all safer if nay one can approach without warning."

"Should I tell them to help?"

Blake looked at Tyree and Lyle. Neither seemed inclined to help his men. He hoped they were more attentive than they appeared and weren't taking advantage of the Sinclairs' presence to enjoy an afternoon off. "Do ye usually give them orders?"

"No. Almost never. When we leave the castle, I follow their orders."

"Then leave be for today, *leannan*. Ma men are more than capable. Let yer men feel better by sticking close to ye. What did ye need to tell me?"

Cerys swept her gaze around her and shifted away from her guards. Blake guided her closer to the tree, so he was better positioned to see around them. His hands rested on his belt, his arms akimbo. It was impossible for Cerys not to see how his leine tugged across his broad shoulders and chest. She glimpsed the sun-kissed skin beneath the open laces at his neckline. It tempted her to run her fingers beneath the laces and discover if his skin was as warm as she sensed. She watched him peer around the tree at her guards before his hands went to her waist. He tugged lightly, giving her the choice to move closer. She took one, then two steps until their bodies nearly touched.

"I spoke the truth last night, Cerys. I willna take what isnae offered freely to me. But I will oblige aught that ye ask for."

Cerys twisted to look behind her. Neither of her guards looked in their direction, too busy talking to one another. "I'd like a proper kiss."

"Were last night's nae proper?"

"Not proper enough."

"I think most would say they were vera proper for a mon and woman who arenae courting." Cerys went rigid, and Blake's brow furrowed. "What did I say wrong?"

"Naught. But I told you last night, that naught can come of this. I may want you to kiss me, but I cannot agree to more."

"And I told ye that I would never take advantage of ye, then walk away."

"I didn't think you would. But my father and uncles would never consent to you courting me. This cannot and will not go further than this." When Blake's eyes narrowed, Cerys realized he'd taken it as a challenge, as though she'd just thrown down the gauntlet. "Don't chase me for the sake of your ego, Blake. That's not fair."

His hands dropped from her waist in an instant. She saw the same hurt and anger as she'd seen the night before when she doubted his character. She'd done it again without thinking.

"We dinna ken each other. Yet. Dinna judge me by two sentences ye heard me utter. I made them in jest, albeit a poor one. I am nae a womanizer or a debaucher. I may have enjoyed flirting with women in the past and even liked the chase, but naught aboot ye is like those women. And I dinna want to be aught like the mon I was. I'm nae declaring marriage just yet, but I do want to get to ken ye better. If we find we suit, nae yer father nor any other mon will keep me from ye if that's what ye want. If we dinna suit, if ye truly dinna want aught between us, then I willna push ye. But dinna turn me away, turn down the chance for us, because of someone else."

"That's easy for you to say, Blake. You'd get to keep your family and your clan. I would have to forsake mine. They would never forgive me for it, and you'd wind up with the Kerrs back at your family's gates. I've made mistakes in the past, for which I'm still trying to redeem myself. My family's patience isn't that long."

"Vera well." Blake looked anything but well. "Ye wished to tell me something."

"Will you listen to me as a friend?"

"Aye. Ma pride might smart, but if I wished to court ye, it's because I'm interested enough to want to be yer friend."

"I overheard two conversations I wasn't supposed to. One was between my father and uncles, which didn't alarm me. But I heard Home, Hannay, and Cunningham talking. Neither group knew I was there."

"I saw the latter three go into the stables. They came out awfully quickly to have tended to their horses."

"They didn't. I think my father and uncles happened upon the stables being empty, but I think the other three planned it that way. There was only one stable boy there. Blake, they were talking about Balliol. Hannay said he sent a messenger to his clan, and they would get word to Balliol. Hannay thinks he's with the Cliffords in Cumbria. It's no surprise that the Hannays side with the Balliols since they're distantly related. But the Cunninghams were loyal to the Bruce. I know little aboot the Homes."

"They were one of the few clans that survived the Bruce's decimation along the border a few years before I was born," Blake mused. "I dinna ken much either. I thought they were at peace with the Bruces, but mayhap they still hold enmity because of the threat they lived through. Mayhap they couldnae do aught to a powerful monarch like Robert the Bruce, but they can against a boy-king in a distant land."

"I think that might be it. Hannay talked aboot something happening in France, that it would no longer be safe for King David. I think he knows men who intend to invade or attack."

"Are ye certain? That seems like a far stretch. Mayhap he was posturing in front of the others."

"I know what I heard, Blake."

"Ye may be at court, but do ye ken of politics? Mayhap Hannay was testing Home and Cunningham. Mayhap he intends to bribe them if he threatens to share their secrets."

"I know plenty aboot politics." Cerys chafed at Blake's dismissive tone. Who was he to question her understanding when he lived on the farthest northern coast before dropping into the sea? She narrowed her eyes, offering him a glare that must have matched the ones she'd received from him more than once. "Do not pretend to know more than me because you are a mon. I spend my days hearing and seeing things you can only guess. I'm not a hen-wit. I understand perfectly what I heard. Don't patronize me, Blake. I won't have it."

Blake watched as Cerys's blue eyes sparked like the hottest part of a flame. Her voice held authority and demanded respect he'd failed to show. Her hands were now on her hips, matching how he stood. He was in awe and nearly forgot to listen to her actual words. When she stopped talking, he realized she expected a response. He was nearly too tongue-tied from desire to speak.

"I apologize, *leannan*. That was patronizing. I've already learned I shouldnae underestimate ye."

"Do you believe me then? If you don't, say so, and I won't waste my time."

"I do. There's naught I can see ye'd gain from lies and manipulating me."

"That's why you think I'm telling the truth? Not because it's what I really heard. Not because I'm trustworthy. Not because you say you wish to court me, which means you must think me at least moderately competent. You believe me because you think I don't want aught from you or I'm not trying to help someone else. Never mind, Blake. Forget I said aught. I'll find my father."

"And ye think he'd believe ye faster than me?"

Cerys sighed. She knew her father wouldn't even listen to her request to speak with him, let alone let her talk long enough to recount what she heard. Her uncles Mitcham and Michael might listen, but their reaction would be even more patronizing than Blake's. Marcas was likely to claim she spun stories, then track her down and accost her for more details. Her family wasn't an option.

"Mayhap not. But your father and uncles would. They can do more than you could anyway."

"Dinna be hurtful in return because I inadvertently insulted ye, lass. I should have thought before I spoke, but ye said that on purpose."

Cerys looked at their feet and nodded. "I did. But what you said was hurtful too, Blake. It felt like you think I'm just a dimwitted woman."

Blake lifted her chin and brushed a soft kiss on her cheek. "I never thought that. What ye shared surprised me. I didna respond well. I should have listened longer and considered ma words before I spoke. It doesnae bode well for me representing ma clan once ma father and uncles leave." Blake grimaced as he finished speaking. He was disappointed in himself.

"We both spoke out of turn."

"Will ye trust me again and let us think aboot this together?"

"Yes. I feel more comfortable talking to you than your family. They're intimidating, and they have plenty of cause not to believe me."

"*Leannan*, they ken ye arenae yer family. Ma da—"

56

Blake couldn't believe he felt himself blushing yet again around Cerys. "—understands ma interest and gave me his blessing."

Cerys's eyes became saucers. It shocked her that he'd spoken about her to his father, and it left her stunned that Magnus consented to Blake's pursuit. But as quickly as the wave of happiness washed over her, regret followed. She trusted him with this news and wished to hear his thoughts, but nothing had changed from the night before. Nothing could come of their flirtation.

"Who do you think Hannay meant? Who could be on their way to France soon?"

"Likely he kens mercenaries. Nay clan would dare send an army to France. Mercenaries arenae cheap, but if they're Gallowglass men, then they are good. They'd be in and out before anyone kenned what was happening. They work more like a small army than a band of misfits." Blake appreciated that their conversation no longer focused on his misstep. "Did ye hear aught else?"

Cerys nodded. The knot in her stomach eased now that they weren't having a disagreement. "It didn't sound like it was the first time they met. They intend to get information from you and Torquil, and they think you're little more than lapdogs to Murray. They're fools to underestimate you. I don't know how much they trust each other. Mayhap they were bluffing to one another or testing each other to see what they think aboot you. Your suggestion might not have been far off. But either way, I don't trust them alone, and I most definitely don't trust them together."

"Thank ye for telling me, lass. I ken ye were trapped inside, but I want ye to stay away from them. I ken I am nae in a position to tell ye aught, but I'm asking ye. This is twice in two days that ye've been far too close to them. Today may have been an accident, but I dinna ken if last eve was."

"It was, Blake. I didn't know they would be there. But I admit I didn't turn down the wenches when they whispered that they were trying to get you to talk more."

"Will ye tell me why ye were there, please?"

Cerys inhaled deeply and slowly exhaled. She could admit part of why she was there. "Not long after I came to Stirling, I was on my way to the haberdasher when a woman fell into the street in front of me. She was badly beaten and bleeding. It was clear she was in the midst of miscarrying her child. Tyree and Lyle tried to drag me away since it didn't take a guess to know she worked at a tavern. It was one of the few times I ordered my guards to do aught. Tyree carried her to the apothecary. The woman bled to death before the man or his wife, who's a midwife, could do aught. The midwife said something in passing that stuck with me. I go once or twice a month to the apothecary and pick up sachets of herbs that are too expensive for tavern whores to afford. But they've prevented any more unwanted bairns or women being beaten for carrying the wrong mon's bairn."

"Just The Wolf and Sheep or the other taverns?" Blake couldn't believe what he was hearing. His heart swelled with admiration that she cared about the other women, who most would believe were so far below her station that she shouldn't even see them. But it also made him fear for her safety if she went around alone at night once or twice a month.

"The three most popular ones."

"Did ye go to all three last eve? Or will ye be going out again tonight?"

Cerys looked at her toes. "Again."

"Then I come with ye. I'm nae stopping ye, but I dinna want ye out alone when I can help."

Cerys hesitated, then nodded. "Meet me in the music room this eve, an hour after they lock the gates."

"Vera well. And stay away from those three. They're—"

"Lady Cerys." Tyree walked toward them. "It's time to head back."

Blake clenched his jaw and glowered at the Kerr guard. It was one thing for her guards to advise her when she relied solely on them. But they were not in a position to command him.

"We're still talking, Tyree. I'm not ready to return."

"It's time, Lady Cerys. They can do as they please. We're going back."

"I—"

Blake stepped between the two Kerrs, placing Cerys behind him. He crossed his arms and spread his feet hip-width apart. It was like looking at a stone wall. Blake's back was so broad that she couldn't see anything in front of the giant, only what was to her left and right. She noted the Sinclairs were still patrolling.

"I dinna answer to ye, Kerr. I also dinna end ma conversations when a guardsman interrupts. Most are wise enough nae to do that."

"Look, Sinclair. If you don't like how I do my duty, then you can be on your way back up to your hea-thenous home."

"It'll be much faster for ye to go back to the keep. Ye can go politely. Or ye can go riding belly down on yer horse, knocked out."

"You don't command me."

Blake laughed, rocking onto the balls of his feet. He stood six inches taller than the Kerr warrior, and his physique made Tyree, who wasn't a small man, look like a sapling compared to Blake's mighty oak.

"But I think I do, and we both ken it. I willna argue with ye, so make yer choice. Ye mount yer horse and ride back with dignity. Or I put ye on it, and ye can explain to the castle guards when ye come to."

"Bast—"

"Say it, Tyree, and you will be on your way home before the sun sets." Cerys stepped beside Blake. Tyree's gaze swiveled to her, his eyebrows up to his hairline. "You will not speak to a nobleman like that. I don't care what clan he hails from."

"You'd side with a Sinclair?"

Cerys stepped forward, so now she placed Blake behind her. "Since you and Lyle decided you'd rather stand around and nashgab like fishwives rather than keep us safe like the Sinclair men, I don't think you're in a position to tell me what to do. I only listened when we were away from the keep because I trusted you to protect me. You not only embarrass me, but you make me doubt whether I can trust you anymore. Go back."

"Your father will have an apoplexy when I tell him."

"Go ahead. Tell on me," Cerys challenged, sarcasm dripping from her words. "That'll make me respect and trust you even more. I think it's time you visited your family. It's been too long. I'll make sure Uncle Mitcham knows you've earned time at home."

Tyree stared at Cerys, his glare enough to set a lesser woman aflame. But she merely raised her chin in challenge. Blake decided he'd said enough and willingly listened to Cerys stand up to her guard. He agreed with her assessment.

"Very well, Lady Cerys. Lyle and I will return."

Cerys knew he thought to force her into compliance if he threatened to take Lyle back with him.

"Good. It'll be safer for you to travel together. I'll be well protected with three Sinclairs. I'm certain my father and uncles will understand why you both left without me."

Tyree stormed away and muttered something to Lyle before mounting his horse and spurring it back toward the castle.

"Are ye all right, *leannan?*"

Cerys thought he would stop calling her that once she rejected his suit. She sighed, more from relief that he hadn't abandoned the endearment than because her guard angered her. It gave her a warped sense of hope she shouldn't have.

"I'm all right. But we should head back. My father will be in a right dither when he hears Tyree spin whatever tale he's going to tell."

Blake whistled and his men appeared, hastening their way back to the horses. Lyle handed her Kitten's reins once Blake lifted her into the saddle. "Stay between me and ma guard. Lyle can lead. Ma other guard will ride in the rear. Nay races, *leannan.*"

"If you say so, Blake." Cerys wheeled Kitten around and fell in among the men. They'd barely made it into the meadow when Cerys's heart leaped at Blake's bellow.

"Ride!"

CHAPTER 6

*B*lake heard the approaching horses at the same moment his peripheral vision caught movement to his left. He glanced toward the disturbance and knew immediately that a band of highwaymen approached. The exact thing that worried him and prompted him to have his men patrol now descended upon them like a hoard of locusts. There was at least a half-dozen men in ragged clothes and with dirty faces. He was certain he could smell them despite the distance that still separated them.

"Stay in the middle, Cerys. Nay matter what, ye dinna leave the circle."

"Yes, Blake. Who are they?"

"I dinna ken beyond them being lawless men. Can Kitten keep up?"

"Yes. He can keep this pace and make it to the castle. They came from the direction Lyle and Tyree could have patrolled. Were they watching us?"

"Likely. Worry aboot getting to the keep, Cerys."

Blake drew his sword, and so did the other three warriors. Cerys laid low over Kitten's withers, making herself as small as she could to remain out of the men's way if they had to swing their weapons. She glanced at the approaching men between steering Kitten and praying. Blake had been right. What would she have done if only Tyree and Lyle were with her?

The angle at which the men approached made it impossible for Blake and the others to avoid them, since they failed to outrun them. The first clash of swords rang in the air. As he swung, he was ever aware of where Cerys was. He trusted his men, Ray and Kenrick, but he didn't know how well he could rely upon Lyle. He felled the two men, who made him their target. He was certain they believed attacking together would allow them to overtake him. But he sliced through the first one and thrust his sword into the second.

"Blake! Behind you!"

Cerys's scream had him looking toward her, which almost gave the highwayman stalking Blake the chance to decapitate him. He only survived because Cerys reached over and tugged Torque's reins, making him veer to the right. When Blake twisted to see where his attacker was, he spied Lyle sprawled on the ground, his neck at an unnatural angle. Blake swung his sword, aiming for the man's head, but the awkward position only allowed him to cleave the man's arm from his shoulder. It wasn't the bandit's sword arm, but it meant he could no longer control his horse and wield his weapon. Blake thrust his sword into the man's heart.

He spun back to check on Cerys in time to see her hurl a blade past Ray and into an attacker's throat. She whipped out another and slashed at a man who was far too close. Blake placed the reins between his teeth, guiding Torque with his thighs. He pushed Cerys down with his left hand as his right arm swung, taking the man's head from his shoulders.

"Dinna look, *mo leannan.*"

He'd finally said it, but he'd done it without thinking. It wasn't the tender moment for which he'd hoped.

He wasn't even certain she noticed, and he didn't know if she understood. But when she straightened and looked him, he knew she did. But it wasn't happiness he saw. It was deep sadness, so much that it threatened to distract him.

"We're nearly there, Blake," Ray called out. The attack forced them to stop and fight, but they'd neutralized all their attackers and were once more racing toward the keep. They were close enough to see the guards pouring out of the postern gate on horseback. The king's men rode to their aid, but it was no longer needed. The riders separated and made way for Blake and the others to clatter into the bailey.

"What the hell happened?"

Cerys reined in and cowered. It wasn't often that her father grew this enraged, but she'd learned to fear it when she was a child. Blake noticed and felt another wave of bloodlust course through him. He wouldn't tolerate any man terrifying Cerys, especially not after what they just survived. He was beyond proud of her bravery and knife-throwing skills. Blake dismounted and came around to grasp Kitten's bridle. It kept Cerys from dismounting since he stood in her way.

"Lawless men set upon us." Blake kept his voice level despite the adrenaline still coursing through him.

"Where's Lyle?"

"Father, they killed him."

"Your whoring ways got another mon killed. Get down from your horse and go to your chamber. I don't want to see you again before I leave. You and your quim have disgraced yourself enough."

Blake took a long step forward until he was nearly on top of Muir. He leaned forward, emphasizing how much larger he was than the older man. "Do nae ever speak to yer daughter like that again. I promise ye willna live to say another word."

"What, Sinclair? Going to kill another of us?"

"Nay. I didna say I'd kill ye. But I will cut out yer tongue. A mon with any decency would ensure his daughter was hale, rather than spewing such vile things in public." Blake turned his attention to the other three Kerr men. He cocked an eyebrow at them, challenging them to defend their brother.

"Lady Cerys, go to your chamber." Mitcham didn't look at Blake as he issued his command. "You will be dealt with later."

Cerys finally slid from her saddle, her chest burning from exertion and fear for Blake. She didn't trust her family not to slay him where he stood. But she didn't think there was anything she could do.

"Sinclair, Lady Cerys, a moment, if you will." Cerys looked toward the royal captain of the guard, relief for a distraction washing over her. "What happened?"

"Highwaymen attacked. They came from the east. A half dozen. Their horses were good, better than they should have been. But the men were filthy and tattered." Blake focused on the new arrival to their conversation.

"How many men did you lose?"

"Only one."

"But I saw you ride out with Lady Cerys and four guards. Only two returned with you."

"Aye. One mon returned to the keep before us."

"You bluidy bastard. You threatened me. You kept Lady Cerys against her will and look what happened."

Tyree was backing her into a corner. He knew she couldn't safely claim she wanted to remain. He made himself the wronged party. Cerys looked at each of her family and decided she couldn't let Blake shoulder this. It could be his death warrant if his family didn't get there in time. She doubted anyone had summoned them.

"You refused to listen to a nobleman when he tasked you with keeping watch. You and Lyle both. Had you done so, Lyle likely wouldn't be dead, and they wouldn't have attacked. They came from the direction you should have scouted. Lyle's death is on you, Tyree. Blake gave you a choice. You could return on your own since you refused to obey a noble, or we could send you back. You should not have spoken to Sinclair or me as you did. It was impertinent and look what it caused."

"Caused," Tyree snarled. "You're blaming me because of a band of highwaymen attacked. That's a pile of shite."

Blake spun toward him. His hand was on the hilt of a dirk at his waist. "Ye dinna speak to yer mistress like that. Ye ignored ma signal to patrol. Ye issued orders to yer mistress that would have most certainly guaranteed her death, since it would have only been ye and Lyle riding with her. And ye've clearly been telling tales."

"Lady Cerys." It was the royal captain's turn to speak again. "Were you harmed?"

"No. The Sinclairs warned us aboot highwaymen. It's why they offered to accompany us. Lyle died at the beginning of the fight. If it hadn't been for the Sinclairs, I would likely have been ravished and killed. I'm alive because they defended me. I am indebted to them."

"Ye owe me naught, ma lady." Blake didn't turn to look at her. He kept his focus on the Kerrs, not trusting them for him to look away. "A lady's safety always comes first. Her clan doesnae matter. It's what warriors train for and what guards are tasked with doing."

"Very well." The captain left, and the tension rose once more. With that, Blake turned toward Tyree, Muir stepped toward his daughter. Cerys fought not to wither against Kitten's flank. The rage in her father's eyes, the desire to lash out at her, was maniacal. She knew he was already plotting how to punish her for this.

"You're naught but a whore," Muir hissed. "You were when you got the last mon killed, and you still are now. How many times have your lifted your skirt for this bastard since he arrived? Pack your bags."

"What? Why?" Cerys fought not to stammer.

"Your days as a lady-in-waiting are over. So are the days of being a laird's niece. You can make your home at the Picked Over Plum."

"You'd—you'd leave me at a tavern. How would I get home?"

"That is a whore's home. You'll fit in."

Blake's hand shot out and grabbed Muir's tunic. He lifted the man off his toes and shook him like he was trying to knock fruit from a branch. Without putting the older man's feet back on the ground, he pushed him as hard as he could. Muir flew and landed hard on his back. Blake stalked forward and lifted him by the throat.

"I warned ye, and ye didna listen. Ye should have." Blake brandished a dirk and brought the tip to Muir's chin. "The lass is under the Sinclairs' protection now. Dinna speak to her again. Dinna even look in her direction. Ye forfeited any right when ye threatened to defile a noblewoman, yer daughter or nae."

Blake slid the knife's tip along Muir's skin and between his quivering lips. He didn't press hard enough to even leave a mark. However, the threat was effective. He pushed Muir away again when the older man pished his breeks. Blake spun on his heels and strode back to Cerys, whose hand he took. She was unprepared for Blake's gentleness after what she witnessed.

"Ray, Kenrick, ye will stand outside Lady Cerys's chamber. Ye dinna let anyone who isnae a Sinclair pass. Come, Cerys." Blake didn't wait for a response, but he prayed Cerys would follow willingly. Or he would have just made the most monumental fool of himself. But he hadn't been able to see reason once Muir insulted his daughter a second time, and he barely restrained himself from killing Cerys's father when he threatened to turn her into a whore.

Cerys didn't hesitate to follow Blake. She didn't look at her father or uncles. The other Kerr men had done nothing to protect or defend her. They were as bad as her father. Any fealty she'd once felt dissolved when her father announced his intentions. She knew it was no hollow threat. He would follow through and not look back.

They entered the keep, and Blake looked around. He spied an alcove and guided Cerys toward it. He knew Ray and Kenrick would remain close but give them privacy. Once inside, with a tapestry hiding them, he pulled her into his arms. She didn't resist, going lax against him. She wrapped her arms around his waist and rested her head on his chest. Blake felt like he was all that kept her on her feet as she sagged more as she accepted his support.

They stood in silence, just absorbing the comfort they offered one another. It was several minutes before they pulled apart. Cerys's hands fisted Blake's leine as he cupped her jaw.

"I ken I didna ask what ye wanted, but I couldnae stand it. They arenae taking ye anywhere, Cerys. I meant what I said. Ye're under ma family's protection, but that doesnae mean I claim ye as aught more than a friend. Ye deserve men who are loyal to ye and put yer interests ahead of their own. Ye will get that in ma clan. Ye are welcome at Dunbeath, or I will take ye where ye wish to go."

"I haven't anywhere to go. I don't have a home anymore."

"Ye do, *mo leannan.* It can be with ma clan, or it can be where ye wish. I will help ye wherever ye choose."

"What would people say if I arrived at your home, having traveled with you for sennights, but we aren't married? I wouldn't do any better than what just happened."

"I ken ye only ken what ye've heard aboot us. That isnae how ma clan is. Women command the same respect as men. Aye, there might be gossip at first. But nay one will speak out against ye. Ma people expect the laird's family and every Sinclair warrior to defend those who canna do it themselves. It would disgrace me if anyone learned I left ye to fend for yerself. I dinna think ma mother, ma aunts, ma sister, or any woman in ma clan would forgive me. If ye arrive as ma friend, then that's how it will be. Nay one would gainsay either of us."

"And if I didn't arrive as just your friend?"

Blake's hands slid to cup her shoulders. They squeezed but not painfully. "Ye willna be ma mistress, Cerys. Nae ever. If ye wish for more, then it's as ma wife. I dinna believe in having them."

Cerys's brow furrowed. It wasn't that she assumed all men had them. It was the vehemence in the proclamation.

"Ma uncle Callum and ma uncle Tristan both had leman before they married ma aunts. The women brought danger and harm to ma aunt Siùsan and ma aunt Mairghread. Ma uncles nearly lost the women they love because of their past. Ma uncle Tavish didna settle his attentions on only one woman before he wed. I ken that's embarrassed ma aunt Ceit over the years. All three regret their decisions. Ma uncle Alex had more discretion and thought aboot a future wife's feelings more than ma other uncles. Ma da fell in love with ma mama when he was six-and-ten. Once he declared himself, he never looked elsewhere. Nae even during all the years when most people would claim ma parents' handfast expired. Once married, nay Sinclair mon strays. It would be too dishonorable, and I would never hurt or shame ma wife."

"I'm not ready to agree to aught like marriage, but I'm glad you explained. I would have wondered. Thank you, Blake. I know this has complicated your life. You'll have to explain what's happened to your family. They might not approve or agree. If that happens, I will figure things out on my own."

"Ye have a bad habit of nae listening to me. I dinna ken what goes on in yer bonnie head, but ye dinna seem to hear me when I explain who I am. Or mayhap, it's worse. Ye dinna believe me."

"I have a hard time trusting, Blake. I don't have much experience with men. I only know what I've been warned aboot. I only know what I've seen. It's not that I'm not listening or don't believe you. I'm just —cautious."

"I understand, *mo leannan*."

"Why do you call me your sweetheart when I keep turning you down?"

Blake shrugged. "It feels right, so I guess it's stuck. Do ye nae want me to call ye that, Cerys?"

"I do. I just don't know that it's right. Or is it just something you—"

"Nay. Ye dinna need to finish. I dinna just call any woman that. I have never called another woman that. It fits ye only."

Cerys nodded. They locked eyes, and something stirred in them both. Cerys went onto her toes as Blake leaned forward. Their mouths collided with the passion that had simmered beneath the surface since they met. This was not the whisper of a kiss they'd exchanged before. This wasn't a hint that they both longed for more.

This was more. It was consuming. It was overwhelming. It was everything they both hoped it would be.

Cerys wrapped her arms around Blake's neck as he lifted her off her feet, bringing her to eye level and making it easier to draw out the kiss. He flicked his tongue against her lips, and after a moment's hesitation, she opened to him. He sensed her inexperience, then reveled in her excitement as their tongues tangled together. He moved one arm to rest beneath her backside, and he felt her shiver. The other arm slid up her back, between her shoulder blades, until he could cup her skull. Blake was grateful for his sporran, since it kept Cerys from feeling how hard he'd grown. He couldn't keep his mind from wondering what he would find if he eased his hand beneath her skirts. Then he couldn't stop picturing doing just that. He groaned as he thought about tasting her and slipping inside her. He'd never wanted a woman more than he did Cerys.

"Blake!" Magnus's voice boomed and startled them both. Cerys gasped, and Blake nearly dropped her. He placed her back on her feet, and she ran a hand over her hair before running both down her skirts. Even in the dim light, Cerys's lips were swollen and entirely delectable. They veritably screamed what they'd been doing. He pressed a kiss to her temple before he moved the tapestry aside and faced all four members of his family and the entire Sinclair retinue of warriors. Cerys's hands clenched the back of his leine as she tried to hide behind him. He wrapped his arm back around her and eased her to his side.

"Explain, because what we heard was damning, nephew." Callum didn't look at Blake but stared at Cerys. Regretting his action, Blake pushed her back behind him and crossed his arms. His father and uncles laughed, but there was little mirth.

"Ye're only making it worse for the lass, son."

71

CHAPTER 7

Cerys followed Blake and his relatives to the Sinclair suite, but she hung back when the men entered. "I can't go in there with all of you, Blake. If anyone found out, everyone would believe I'm what my father said."

"Nay, they wouldnae. There is nay one in this life or the next who would believe ma father and uncles would betray their wives. If they wonder if ye're with Torquil or me, they will see ye have three chaperones."

"Lady Cerys, ma brother speaks the truth. Our family is too well known for anyone to believe any of them would stray. There isnae one among them who's interested in anyone but their wives. If naught else, everyone kens ma mother and aunts would run any gossip monger through if they even thought aboot it. Ma father and uncles may be large men, but dinna be fooled aboot who runs our family." Torquil grinned, lightening his words, but it didn't make it any less true.

As protective as the older Sinclair brothers and their brother-by-marriage, Laird Tristan Mackay, were toward their wives, the women were just as fierce. The five women would never stand by and allow anyone to question their husbands' honor or fidelity. Cerys hadn't lived under a rock, so she was familiar with the stories. She followed Blake and the others inside.

"We came belowstairs to look for ye. It was growing late, and we wondered what kept ye. We entered the bailey and had Kerrs bellowing at us and threatening God only kens what. We didna stay to get their version of the story. We wish for the truth."

"Magnus, may I speak?" Cerys addressed his father, but she looked up at Blake. He nodded, his hand going to the small of her back. Nothing too overt in front of the others, but it was a sign to everyone and reassurance to Cerys.

"Aye, Lady Cerys."

"Your son and guards saved my life. Blake warned my guards that there was talk of highwaymen in the area. Blake offered to accompany us, and I didn't let my guards decide. I accepted. We enjoyed a race along the southern ridge before stopping to let our horses drink. We chatted while your men patrolled. Mine ignored Blake's silent command, even though I'm certain they understood. Tyree antagonized Blake on purpose and was inexcusably rude. He issued orders to both of us and interrupted our conversation. Blake gave him a choice aboot how he returned here. He opted to ride back of his volition. But it left us missing a guard. Blake, blessedly, spotted the lawless men. He and your men fought and won, but Lyle died in the process. They brought me back with barely a hair out of place."

Tavish stepped forward and held out two knives. Cerys once again glanced up at Blake, uncertain what to say. "Lass, we were in the bailey long enough for one of the king's men to give these to us. I ken for certain they arenae ma nephew's, but the guard said one was in a mon's neck, and they found the other bloody on the ground."

"They're Lady Cerys's. She threw the one that

landed in the mon's throat when he nearly overpow-
ered Ray. She used the other to cut a mon who got too
close."

Cerys didn't know what to make when all five Sinclairs grinned at her. Their reaction didn't suit the conversation at all.

"She'll fit right in." Torquil clapped his brother on
the back and laughed at Cerys's confusion. Blake ignored his brother.

"Uncle Callum, I offered Lady Cerys our clan's protection. I told her she is welcome at Dunbeath, or I will
help her settle wherever she wishes. Things went vera
poorly once we entered the bailey. Her father said
things that nay mon should ever say to his daughter
and made threats I couldnae ignore. I ken I did this
without yer permission, but I believed ye would understand."

"What did Muir say?" Callum looked between his
nephew and the young lady to whom he was clearly at-
tached. When her face paled and Blake slid his arm
fully around her waist, he wished he hadn't spoken.

"Lady Cerys doesnae need to hear it repeated. I will
tell ye later. I'd like to send her back with ye."

"What?" Cerys spun toward Blake. That wasn't the
arrangement to which she considered agreeing. She
didn't even know Blake that well, but she felt like she
knew him well enough. She only had the rumors and
curses spewed about the other men by which to go.
Traveling without Blake scared her.

"Ye'll be safe, Cerys. They willna let aught happen to
ye, and ma mama will welcome ye."

"What aboot Brighde?" Cerys's voice barely came
out as a whisper, and Blake saw fear and shame in her
gaze.

"I dinna doubt she will welcome ye and protect ye

just as she would anyone who sought sanctuary with ma clan. She will understand better than anyone."

Cerys shook her head and tried to back away, but Blake still had his arm around her. "I can't."

"Lass, I have to stay here, but it's nae safe for ye. I will follow ye back in a fortnight."

"No. I can't leave with them while my family is here. They will not let me go with your family. And I—" Cerys shook her head. She wouldn't admit in front of everyone how upset it made her to think Blake would send her away. She needed time to reason why it bothered her so much, and she was too embarrassed.

"Lady Cerys, we will gladly escort ye to Castle Dunbeath. Ye would be our guest while ye wait for Blake. If ye wish to become part of the clan, then we would help ye make a life for yerself. Ye could have a croft if ye wish it." Magnus's paternal smile nearly made Cerys burst into tears. It was so kind and so foreign to her. She appreciated he didn't assume she and Blake would marry. But she felt Blake's hand rest heavier against her waist at his father's suggestion. He didn't like it.

"I still can't leave while my family is here. They won't allow it. You might not be able stop them from—" Cerys swallowed. Blake had tried to protect her from sharing the truth, but she couldn't hide it if she were to accept their offer. "From turning me out and leaving me to work at the Picked Over Plum. If it comes to that, I would rather the Merry Widow or The Wolf and Sheep."

Cerys watched a transformation that was enough to make her heart stop. Callum, Tavish, Magnus, and Torquil seemed to grow beyond their six-and-a-half-foot height. Their chests broadened as they sucked in whistling breaths. The look that settled on their faces was that of a warrior's nightmares. Gone were the kind and welcoming men who encouraged her to come home with them. What was left were men ready to go to battle against her father and uncles.

"Da, ye're scaring her." Blake pulled Cerys against his chest and turned her away from the ferocious men. He pressed her head against him, and his arm shielded her view. She inhaled Blake's scent. The blend of pine, fresh air, and soap was heady. Much like she had in the alcove, she sagged against him. He tightened his embrace until she sighed and wrapped her arms around his waist.

"Our apologies, lass." Magnus's voice was soft, and it almost tempted her to run into his embrace for a fatherly hug. But she was content to remain with Blake, unwilling to worry about appearances.

"Da, Torquil and I will bring Cerys if she decides to come with us. Uncle Callum, can ye leave two more men than ye would have? I want two guards outside Cerys's chamber any time she's within. I want men with her any time I canna be."

"Aye. We can do that." As clan tánaiste, it was Callum's decision. The Sinclairs numbered close to one hundred as they fought alongside Andrew Murray. The wounded were already on their way home. The barracks housed the rest, or they camped outside the castle walls. They would return home with threescore men, so sparing two more would be no hardship. Five would already remain behind to ride home with Blake and Torquil. Seven made Blake feel more comfortable, since he was determined to bring Cerys to Dunbeath, be it as a bride or a friend.

"Thank you." Cerys turned in Blake's arms, relieved to find the men once more at ease. She hadn't dared look up at Blake's expression for fear that it would have mirrored the other men's. But now she did, and she found reassurance there. There was a softness to his gaze that melted her heart. She wanted nothing more than to be alone with him again. They hadn't had nearly enough time in the alcove. She knew her desire went against her better judgment, but this Highlander was peeling away every layer of defense and resistance she had.

"Does that mean ye'll come with me in a fortnight, *mo leannan?*" Blake whispered against her ear. She fought to hide the shiver that shimmied down her spine, not wanting anyone to see how Blake affected her. His warm breath made her breasts tingle. His sporran had shifted when he abruptly pulled her against his chest. She could feel his steely length against her mound. She itched to rub herself against it. An ache took root in the bottom of her belly. She understood what it meant, even if she'd never experienced it before.

"Yes, Blake." If only they were alone. She wanted to capitulate and enjoy what Blake wished to offer. But she knew it was a blessing that they weren't. Her growing feelings for him wouldn't change things in her life that were never under her control and would always keep her alone. No matter how he tempted her, she would remind herself that no future with them as a couple existed beyond their time in Stirling.

"There's time for me to send for a bath before the evening meal. Would ye like that? And would ye join us for the meal?"

"The bath I will gladly accept." *And I'd accept you washing my back. Could we both fit? Cerys!* "But I don't think it would be wise for me to sit with you. It will only make people talk."

"Aye. I ken. I want ye beside me because I want ye. But sitting with us will show everyone I meant what I said. Ye are under our protection. Ye are untouchable." *I wouldnae mind touching ye every day for the rest of time—this life and the hereafter.* Blake waited for Cerys's decision. She nodded, but he wasn't certain if she was agreeing to both offers or just the bath.

"I'd like to sit with you." Cerys smiled before she turned back to the others. "I apologize in advance. Wilma doesn't have the sense God gave a gnat. It isn't entirely her fault. Her father never educated her, and she never left her home except to come here. In many ways, she's little more than an overgrown child. What comes into her mind comes out of her mouth. She'll have plenty to say."

"Seems like a family trait. Her aunts Margaret and Sarah Anne werenae any better." Tavish named two women who'd once been among the most hateful ladies-in-waiting ever to grace Stirling Castle. They'd arrived after Deirdre and Ceit left, but they were infamous.

"We'll deal with Lady Wilma when we must, ma lady." Magnus smiled, then nodded to Blake.

"Come. Let's get yer bath ordered." Blake led Cerys into the passageway and spoke with two men she didn't know. "I'll send Ray and Kenrick to the barracks to rest. Two other men will come with us. When ye're ready to go to the Great Hall, they'll escort ye. One walks in front of ye, and one behind."

"All right. Thank you."

"Ye dinna need to thank me, *leannan*."

Cerys stopped herself before she argued. She would appreciate what Blake offered without disagreement. He was taking care of her in a way her family never had. Even when she was newly arrived, the guards she had at the time never ensured her safety within the keep. Even now, she only saw her guards at meals or if she wished to leave the castle walls.

Blake stopped a servant and requested the tub and hot water. When they reached Cerys's door, she looked behind her at the two new Sinclair warriors. She smiled to them and appreciated their respectful nods.

"My family won't be pleased to see me with you."

"Unless they wish for a worse scene than before, they will keep away." Blake signaled the men to come closer. "Lady Cerys, this is Paden and Quinn. They'll be yer guards until morning. I will assign two others to take ye to Mass and as ye go aboot yer day."

"Thank you." Cerys once more smiled at the men.

"Ye're welcome, ma lady." Paden spoke with a heavy Gaelic accent, and Cerys nearly didn't understand him.

"They speak Scots, but not fluently. If ye need aught, speak slowly."

"All right. I will see you soon."

"Dinna hesitate to come to me, Cerys, if there's aught ye need. I willna make the same mistake as I did before. I willna ever discount what ye tell me again."

"I know I can, Blake. I'll see you in the Great Hall." Cerys opened the door wide as servants arrived to prepare her bath. She appreciated the blessed silence once she was alone and soaking in the near scalding water. It eased all the tension that had settled in her during their breakneck ride back to the castle, then her confrontation with her father, and having to explain to the Sinclairs. Once her hair was clean and she'd scrubbed herself nearly raw, she prepared for the evening meal. She rarely cared which kirtle she wore, but she wished to look particularly nice for Blake that evening. He was staking a claim, one way or another, so she wished to make him proud. It also gave her confidence a boost, since she knew the meal wouldn't be peaceful. She wondered just how disastrous it would be.

79

CHAPTER 8

"*S*he'll be along shortly." Magnus watched his son try to hide his fidgeting. Blake wasn't prone to nervousness, and when he was, he rarely showed it. Magnus glanced at his brothers, who forced themselves to hide their mirth. All three men recalled when they courted their wives. Magnus, Tavish, and Alex found love matches on their own. Callum's marriage had been arranged, but he and his wife fell in love before they exchanged their vows. None of the older generation of Sinclair siblings had an easy time during their courtship, each facing obstacles and danger. But none of the brothers or their younger sister allowed circumstances to defeat them, and now each had spent more than two decades with their soulmate.

"I dinna doubt that. I worry aboot her family accosting her on the way. If they do, there's four of them against our two men. Cerys would be in the middle. I dinna like it."

"Breathe easier, brother. She's just walked in." Torquil nudged Blake, who'd been looking at their father. Blake's head whipped around as he spotted Paden and Quinn. There was someone in between the towering guards. He knew it was Cerys, even if he couldn't see her yet. He rose and crossed the Great Hall. Silently, he took her arm and wrapped it around his. When they reached the table, he glared at his brother. Torquil pretended not to understand, taunting his older brother. Magnus tsked, and Torquil finally relinquished his seat, moving to the other side of the table. Blake guided Cerys to sit between Magnus and him.

He considered how diminutive she appeared at a table of Highlanders. While she looked out of place among the rugged men, it also cast no doubt that they would be formidable foes to anyone who threatened her. He withdrew his arm, but he felt her hesitation before she let go. He wanted to wrap his arm around her and assure her that there was nothing to fear. But he could do neither of those things. He couldn't display any affection, and he couldn't make false promises. Instead, he pushed his trencher between them. She looked up at him in surprise. That was what betrothed and married couples did.

"People will think you're bedding me. I should have my own."

"Or they will think we're betrothed. Once we leave, nay one will be the wiser that we arenae. For now, they will ken that ye have someone watching over ye."

Cerys remained unconvinced that it was prudent, but she didn't want to argue. And if she were honest with herself, she liked the idea that someone was watching over her. Her aunt Matilda had done that when she was a child, but it had been years since she felt like anyone specifically cared about her wellbeing.

"I seem to say thank you a lot today, but I am thankful."

Blake's gaze met hers, and she offered him a soft smile. She couldn't miss the heat that flared in his eyes. She felt it all the way to her toes. But Blake's next words were like being thrown into an icy loch.

"It'll still be light after we finish the meal. Will ye walk with me in the gardens? I would understand what yer father meant by his accusations."

"I—" Cerys's tried to work down her gorge that rose into her throat and threatened to choke her. This was the last thing she wished to talk about, but she knew Blake deserved an explanation, since he took the risk to defend her. The best she could do was nod.

Blake noticed the tears Cerys fought not to let fall. There was the same pain and misery he'd seen earlier. Gone was the smile from a moment ago or even the trust she exuded when they talked to his family. There was reticence and, dare he say, shame. He wondered if he had overstepped and wished he had said nothing.

"Ye dinna have to tell me all, Cerys. Just enough so I'm prepared if I must defend ye."

"No. I'll tell you all of it." Cerys swallowed as she watched the food set before her. The servant's arrival relieved her from saying more. The meal kept her occupied, and she listened to the Sinclairs banter. She couldn't help but notice how the woman served Blake the best pieces of meat, but he casually moved them to her side. His arm brushed against her shoulder throughout the meal, and it was torture. She nearly jumped out of her skin when he placed his hand on her thigh just above her knee. It was there only long enough to give it a soft squeeze, but she nearly melted right there on the bench.

She needed his silent strength when her relatives entered the Great Hall. Shock turned to anger when her father and uncles spotted her among the Sinclairs. Muir's eyes narrowed with a hatred Blake never imagined a parent could feel for their offspring. It was like a weight that descended upon him, and he could only imagine how Cerys felt. When she gripped the bench on each side of her, Blake covered her hand with his.

He used a finger to pry hers loose before entwining his with hers. His thumb brushed the underside of her fingers until he felt her relax, but it was only temporary.

"You want her, you can have her." Muir's statement didn't surprise Cerys, but that lack of shock didn't stop the words from cutting deep.

"Muir, Marcas, find us a table." Mitcham waited until his younger brothers walked away, appearing unconcerned by their censorious expressions. When they were out of earshot, Mitcham looked at Cerys. "You have made your choice, Niece. You have chosen who you wish to make your bed with. But that doesn't change that you are a Kerr. It's your blood. You won't find a warm welcome, but you can always return."

"To what end, Uncle? To be judged and sentenced without question?"

Mitcham narrowed his eyes and shook his head. "You are our blood. You'd be wise to remember that and appreciate it more. People haven't forgotten, and they aren't likely to forgive this, but you can still return to Kersland."

He didn't spare another look before he marched away. Cerys breathed easier until she noticed Wilma watching her. There was a look of speculation on her face that made Cerys want to groan. The encounter with her family was bad enough. She could tell Wilma was trying to contrive a reason to approach the Sinclairs. Cerys knew the moment Wilma devised a plan.

"Lady Cerys." Wilma barely looked at her as she approached. She ran her gaze over Blake before focusing on Torquil. At least, Cerys knew she had no reason to be jealous. Torquil was as handsome as any of the other Sinclairs, but he held no appeal to her. Only Blake drew her like a moth to a flame.

"Lady Wilma."

"The other ladies and I are planning an excursion to

the almshouses tomorrow after the midday meal. Mayhap you will join us?"

An excursion indeed. They make charity work sound as if it's as much a pastime as sewing. They care not for the people. It's a means to while away the time. She knows I go at least once a sennight, even if she doesn't know what I do for the tavern wenches. She makes it seem like it's her idea, when they would accompany me.

"If you don't mind spending as much time as I do each sennight. If you wish to be done sooner, I won't keep you."

Wilma's lips tightened to a purse, making her appear haughty. But she smoothed her expression and offered a smile, her eyes back on Torquil as she nodded.

"Mayhap your friends could accompany us and ensure our safe return."

"Ma lady," Torquil chimed in. "We leave in the morning. I can see ye've survived in the past without us, so I am certain ye shall survive in the future."

"But I heard aboot those highwaymen from today. What if they should try to accost us?"

"Then dinna venture onto a highway, ma lady." Torquil grinned.

"But—"

"I will accompany you after the midday meal, Lady Wilma. I will join you for Mass in the morning. I wouldn't want your meal to grow cold now, so I won't keep you." Cerys hoped Wilma took the heavy-handed hint from her since she didn't seem inclined to take Torquil's. The other lady-in-waiting turned in a flounce of skirts and stalked back to her seat with the other royal attendees.

When the meal ended and everyone rose, Blake whispered something in his father's ear. Cerys watched as Magnus nodded with a smile, but a look of warning passed over his gradually aging face. Blake returned the nod and offered Cerys his arm. He led her onto the terrace and out to the gardens. The mid-June evening was still bright, since it would be late before the sun set so far north. They walked in silence until they reached the center of the hedge maze. With so few people in attendance, Cerys's nervousness about people watching eased.

Cerys took a seat on the bench at the heart of the maze and watched as Blake moved to stand in front of her. Blake's size had never intimidated her before, but it did now. Not because she feared he would ever hurt her. But it made her feel vulnerable, and she knew she would only feel worse as she told her story.

"Will you sit, please?"

"I thought to give ye space, *leannan*."

"But it's uncomfortable to crane my neck to see you, and you—you're—well, just very large."

Blake's eyebrows shot up as he chuckled. "Ye say that as though it's a bad thing, lass."

"It's not. It's just a little overwhelming right now."

Blake's laughter halted, and he offered her a rueful expression as he lowered himself beside her onto the bench. He watched her fold her hands in her lap, and she looked straight ahead.

"When I was four-and-ten, Uncle Mitcham arranged a marriage for me to a local baron's son. As the daughter of a fourth son, there weren't aspirations for me marrying a laird or an heir. And that was more than fine by me. I don't want to be a clan's lady. I will run a household, but I don't want the attention and scrutiny of being a laird's wife. I met Alfred when he and his father came to sign the documents. He was so handsome." Cerys offered a soft smile as she remembered that day. Blake forced down the spike of jealousy that burned behind his ribs. "He was quiet but kind. At seven-and-ten, he seemed so worldly to me. His family stayed for a fortnight, and we spent as much time together as we could. We suited better than I could have ever hoped."

Cerys looked at her lap as she knotted her fingers and loosened them over and over. The wound was being ripped open, having to recount what happened, but she couldn't overcome the sensation of how wrong it felt not to tell Blake about her past.

"We sent missives back and forth for eight-and-ten months until it was time for the wedding. I was so certain I was in love and him with me. We'd hinted at it in the missives, but neither of us made a declaration. His family arrived, and along with them was their neighbor who'd been Alfred's friend since childhood and the man's wife. Everything felt so natural, and I was blissfully happy. I overheard some maids talking aboot how fortunate I was to have such a handsome and virile betrothed. They joked aboot what I could expect on my wedding night."

Cerys closed her eyes and pressed her lips together. She fought not to cry, but the tears leaked from under her lids.

"Ye dinna have to tell me, Cerys."

She turned to look at Blake. His concern for her was nearly palpable, and it only made her cry harder. He pulled her against his chest, a place she wished she could always remain since it was now her favorite. He stroked her back until she felt composed enough to sit back.

"The night before the wedding, I thought to sneak into Alfred's chamber. I didn't think we'd fully anticipate the wedding. I knew we had to have the sheet the morning after. But I thought I could learn something, maybe even impress him. I was so focused on drumming up my courage to open his chamber door that I didn't see my father and Uncle Marcas coming up the stairs. I pushed open the door and was greeted by the very clear sound of two people coupling. Both voices were very deep."

Cerys watched Blake to see if she would have to be any more explicit. She feared what he would say since everyone else she knew thought the act was unnatural and ungodly, but Blake didn't seem fazed. He merely raised his eyebrows, waiting for her to continue.

"My father slammed me against the door in his hurry to enter the chamber. I tried to get out of the way, but I was too slow. My father and Uncle Marcas dragged them out of the chamber, uncaring that they were both naked. There was so much bellowing, I could barely make heads or tails of what was happening. I was too naïve and inexperienced to understand what I stumbled upon. I couldn't fathom how it was possible until the accusations began flying. Uncle Mitcham ordered them taken to the bailey, where they we locked in the stocks. They weren't allowed any clothes. At that point, the humiliation was the greatest punishment. But it got so, so much worse."

Cerys rested her elbows on her thighs and buried her face in her hands. She could see every moment of those twelve hours as though it were still happening.

"I tried to talk to Alfred, apologize, get an explanation. But he refused to even look at me with aught but vehement disgust. It was Aunt Matilda who explained why they'd been forced to receive the public shaming. When morning came, my uncle had guards surround me and force me out to the bailey. He demanded I tell everyone gathered what I'd seen. But the chamber had been dark. I hadn't actually seen aught. I said that, and it was the first time I'd ever been truly terrified of my father. He grabbed my hair and shook me, demanding that I tell what I saw. I kept repeating that I hadn't seen aught. He wanted me to sign their death warrant, bear false witness against them. When I wouldn't, he had me chained to the pillory pole and lashed me."

Blake sucked in a deep breath before lifting Cerys onto his lap. She was unprepared for it, but when his brawny arms wrapped around her, she felt like she'd finally found her home. He said nothing, and she didn't need him to. She just needed his silent strength and to know he wasn't passing judgment on her.

"They were convicted of sodomy, a mortal sin and crime against nature. Uncle Mitcham and the clan council never gave them a chance to defend themselves. Uncle Mitcham and the council sentenced them to death. I know now that it was the first time anyone discovered or accused either of them. Castration or even dismemberment would have sufficed by the law of many lands. But as laird, Uncle Mitcham's word is law. He ordered them stoned, then burned. He constructed the pyres, so they faced each other, the pillory post between them. They watched each other burn, and I had nowhere else to look."

"Cerys, I'm so vera sorry ye had to witness that. All of it was so vera unnecessary. That was mon's pride ruling the day. Yer family was humiliated, and they wished to exact revenge. What did Alfred's family do? Did they say naught?"

"I think some of them knew, but it shamed them. They stood by, and some even condoned what happened. The neighbor's wife was one of the loudest, bewailing how it affected her more than anyone, that she was married to a sodomite. Through it all, they blamed me for being a whore who went to Alfred's chamber to join them. That I was lured by carnal sin, and had I possessed more restraint, none of it would have happened. Some even claimed I bewitched them into their acts for my own carnal pleasure. Others claimed I did it because I didn't want to wed. I thought I was in love with him."

Cerys's uttered her final words with such anguish that Blake's heart broke for her. He held her tight as she sobbed once again. While he had known no one like the couple Cerys spoke of, he was aware of common opinion and beliefs. They weren't ones he or his family shared. As a warrior forced to be away from home for long stretches, either on patrol or for war, Magnus explained to Blake and Torquil that it wasn't unusual for people to grow lonely on patrol or aroused after a battle. He told them about how people often remedied their needs. He explained that for some people, it was a natural part of them, regardless of circumstances. He'd told his sons that it was none of their business how that happened. As long as people were consenting adults, they were to allow others their own choices. No one in the Sinclair family was God, or even St. Peter, so it wasn't their place to pass judgment or dole out punishment for something like that.

"That's what yer father meant by ye'd already caused one mon's death from being unchaste."

"Yes. When you found me in the antechamber, it was because my father reminded me—as though I could ever forget—that it was the anniversary of the day I was to wed. What he really meant was it was the anniversary of the day my choices sentenced two men to death."

"That was nae yer fault, Cerys. Mayhap ye shouldnae have been out of yer chamber or entering someone else's without knocking. But ye didna force them together. They were aulder than ye and clearly more experienced. They kenned the danger to begin with, let alone in another clan's keep on the eve of Alfred's wedding. That was their decision."

"It doesn't make me feel any less guilty, especially

since my feelings for Alfred faded faster than I expected. It feels like such a waste since I don't even love him anymore. I don't think I ever really did. I think I loved the idea of being a wife and of someone caring aboot me. That I would escape my family and be welcomed by a mon who wanted me. The worst thing is, I would have willingly and without reservation kept his secret. It could have been prevented if I hadn't been so wanton."

"Nay. Ye were a young woman, and it was natural for ye to be curious. Especially since ye thought he would bed ye for the first time the next night. Ye did naught wrong wanting to ken more. I ken why a lass's maidenhead is so precious among noble families, but I think it's ridiculous to believe that lasses dinna have the same curiosity and interest as lads. And what is it aboot noblewomen that God supposedly made so different that they shouldn't enjoy intimacy like a common woman does? Ma mama and aunts talk to their daughters aboot relations between a mon and woman. I dinna ken exactly what they say, but I ken it's none of the lay in bed like a dead fish nonsense. It's clear ma parents, and ma aunts and uncles all love each other. Ye can see it when they talk to and aboot each other. Ye can tell by watching them together. And ye can most certainly see it from how large ma family is."

Cerys didn't know what to say. Blake had left her utterly speechless. No one had ever said, not even her aunt, that it wasn't her fault. She hadn't thought that it was, but eventually she accepted the blame because everyone piled it upon her from all directions. As for how open-minded Blake was, that stunned her into silence. She'd never imagined a man as rugged and masculine at him would be so accepting. Though, from what she'd learned and witnessed about the Sinclairs in the brief few days they'd been at court, it shouldn't have been so shocking. They were a family unlike any other.

"Is this why ye've said we canna be together? That we dinna have a future?"

"In part. Blake, my father has already paid a convent my dowry. Once my tenure ends here, I'm to take the veil. My family believes it's the penance I must pay. I took away two lives, so I must give up mine. His threat today was only because I chose to ride out with you."

"I dinna think ye wish to be a nun, *mo leannan*."

"I don't, but they have already given my dowry to the nunnery."

"Cerys, ye ken yer aunt Brighde married ma uncle Alex. She didna come with a dowry. Ma grandda didna think twice aboot it. Ma aunt Siùsan came with a pittance that was more an insult than a dowry. Ma grandda kenned and still sought her as a bride for ma uncle Callum. Ma mama was forbidden from being with ma da. She didna come with aught but the clothes on her back, same as Aunt Brighde. Ma aunt Ceit was a Comyn before she became a Sinclair. She had naught either, and just like the others, ma grandda welcomed them. He loves them as much as he does his only daughter, ma aunt Mairghread. A dowry is always useful, but it isnae what makes a woman valuable or even ensures she's good for the family. Ma family kens that. We always have."

"Not all families are like that. Mine isn't."

"I ken. But other families arenae who we're talking aboot, *mo leannan*. Let the convent keep the dowry if yer clan already paid it. Ye nae being there to work isnae what will matter to them with the coin already in hand. Yer father and uncle dinna have to come up with another. Or let them squabble with the abbess to get it back. But ye dinna need one to join ma family, Cerys."

"Are you asking me to marry you?"

"I dinna think ye're ready to answer that yet. Mayhap in a fortnight we'll realize we dinna suit. But if we do, then I dinna want ye believing ye arenae acceptable to ma family. And I dinna want ye believing yer life is already determined."

"How auld are you?"

"Twenty summers. Why?"

"You're very wise for someone so young."

"Ye've met ma father and uncles. I've had good tutors on life. What aboot ye?"

"Nine-and-ten."

"Give thought to what I've said. If ye've decided by the time we arrive at Dunbeath, or if ye need more time than that, then I will accept yer choice. But nay matter what, ye are welcome among the Sinclairs."

Cerys didn't move. She kept her head pressed against Blake's chest, her ear over his heart. The steady rhythm nearly lulled her to sleep as she let the guilt and fear slip away for the first time in three years. It was a burden that lingered with her always. Not ever-present in the forefront of her mind, but a nagging sensation that made her think about it. Her family's presence only made it worse.

"Thank you, Blake."

Blake kissed the top of her head. "Are ye ready to go inside? It's growing cool now that the sun isnae so high."

"Yes. Will your family leave at dawn?"

"Aye."

"I'm an early riser, but not always that early. I'd like to see them off. Would that be all right? Would one of my guards knock and wake me?"

"I'll come to yer chamber. I'll knock thrice, and if ye dinna stir, then I'll leave ye to sleep. If ye're awake, then I'll escort ye to the bailey."

Blake stopped them in a recessed corner of the castle, out of sight of anyone passing by. He wrapped his arms loosely around her waist, and she rested her hands on his biceps. Understanding and mutual respect were what they found in each other's gaze. Cerys slid her hands to his chest, and he cupped her jaw in one hand as their mouths came together. It began with the soft whisper of a kiss, like outside The Wolf and Sheep. But it combusted a heartbeat later. The arm around Cerys's waist slid lower until his hand rested on her backside. She moaned and pressed herself more firmly against Blake.

He squeezed, eliciting another moan. Her hands roamed over his chest and over his shoulders before slipping beneath his arms to reach his back. Blake's hand continued to squeeze and knead the plump flesh while his other hand slid to cup her throat.

"Blake." It was an entreaty.

"What do ye need, little one?"

"I don't know. I just want you to touch me."

"Tell me if ye wish me to stop, and I will. Always."

"No. I want more, not less."

Blake chuckled before he shifted his hand from her throat to her breast. His massive palm and long fingers spread to cup the lush mound. His thumb swept over it until he could feel her nipple pebble. He pinched it lightly, and her nails dug into the muscles in his back. The kiss deepened as her hands found his chiseled buttocks. She'd never felt something so firm on herself. It mesmerized her as the muscles bunched and relaxed in her hands as he rocked his hips.

"I wish to touch more of ye, Cerys."

"Mmm." She could only moan her agreement as she nodded. She felt the cool air waft around her ankles, then calves, then the back of her thighs. Before she knew it, two warm hands covered her bottom, kneading it without layers of fabric in the way. She pressed her hips away enough to try to move his sporran, but Blake didn't budge.

"I want ye, Cerys. More than I've ever wanted another woman, but I dinna want to frighten ye."

"I felt you earlier, when you kept me from seeing the anger in your father and the others when they learned what happened. It didn't scare me. It—it —made me…"

"What did it make ye, *mo leannan?*"

"Ache." The confession came out on a breath, but it was laden with desire and heat. Blake obliged and pushed his sporran away, but he didn't stop there. He lifted her and guided her legs around his waist. He stepped as close to the wall as he could, ensuring anyone who walked by and saw a couple couldn't see Cerys's face or distinct dark hair.

Cerys tightened her thighs around Blake's trim waist. She could feel his rod pressing against her sheath, and she wanted to rock against him, but she didn't dare. She burrowed her face into the crook of his neck when he swept a finger along her seam. It made her shudder, encouraging him to go further. He inched a finger inside her as his free hand guided her to rise and fall against his shaft. It was just what she wanted. The most arousing feeling grew from her pearl into her core as it mingled with the biting ache of wanting more of him inside her. She needed more of what he was doing. It was like she'd found an oasis after roaming a desert. One sip wasn't enough. Every moment she shared with Blake only made her want more. Sip after sip, but she didn't think she could ever quench her thirst for him.

Blake was drowning in his need for the woman in his arms. He had enough experience to know what he was doing and to be more than competent. He'd experienced lust many times without slaking it. But what was happening with Cerys was beyond his wildest imaginings. It felt like the craving to pleasure her, to merge his body with hers, was a wild animal. A beast he could control, but he wasn't certain he wanted to. He wanted to join their bodies, have them claim each other, and never let go. He wanted to have her beside him, be inside her, for the rest of time.

As they moved together, Cerys felt a tightening in her core. A second finger joined as he worked her sheath. Her pleasure nub continued to rub against his pelvis, and the friction brought her need to a head. It coalesced into a burst of pleasure that made her go rigid as she felt waves of bliss roll over her. She felt Blake's cock twitch beneath her. Then there was something moist against the wool. She wasn't certain if it was him or her, since she felt her dew coating her inner thighs.

Well, that hadn't happened before. While Blake rested his forehead against Cerys's as they tried to catch their breath, he wondered if she had any idea that he'd climaxed with her. Neither of them had even touched his bare rod, but just as the friction had been enough for Cerys, it had been enough for him, too.

"What aboot you?"

Blake kissed her temple and grinned. He leaned his head away so she could see his face. "That was the best release I've ever had."

"You..." Cerys's brow furrowed as she raised her head. Her confusion was adorable and made Blake chuckle.

"Aye. Feeling ye against me, touching yer sheath. I got a wee too excited."

"Oh."

"Aye, oh." Blake smattered kisses on her cheeks and the tip of her nose before their lips fused. It was tender in the aftermath of their desire.

"Do you think it would be like that if we…" Cerys's face flushed, and her ears burned.

"If we what, lass?"

"If we did that again. Do you think it would be like that if we did it again? Or is it just because it was the first time? Or because today's been rather fraught?"

"I pray it's like that for years to come. I think it could be, Cerys." Blake lowered her to the ground. "So aye, I think it would be like that next time."

"You want there to be a next time?"

"Aye, *mo leannan*. Vera much. I willna take yer maidenhead unless ye offer it to me as ma wife. But I would like to touch ye and kiss ye whenever I can. I want all of ye, Cerys. Body and mind."

"I want you too, Blake. Mayhap we don't love each other, mayhap we will grow to love each other. But mayhap not. Either way, we know we suit in at least one way. An important way. You've asked me to consider marrying you. It would give us both what we want."

Blake shook his head. He entwined their fingers as their arms hung down between them. "*Leannan*, ma parents have promised ma sister, ma brother, and me the right to find love matches. I dinna have to marry for an alliance or for ma clan's coffers. I dinna want to marry ye for convenience. Ye have the protection of ma sword, even if ye dinna have the protection of ma name. If ye consent to being ma wife, it's because of how we feel for one another. Nae because we lust for each other or because ye fear I willna care for ye as I promised."

Cerys nodded, rejection stinging and clogging her throat. She knew he wasn't really pushing her away. His reasoning was sound, and she respected it. But it had been hard to suggest, and it felt wretched not to have her feelings reciprocated. Or at least having them deferred.

"Lass, look at me." Blake waited until she lifted her chin, but she looked over his shoulder. He tilted her chin, and, with a light touch, he held it in place. "I am nae turning ye away. I dinna want ye to act in haste, then regret it. If it's pleasure ye wish to explore, then I happily oblige. If ye wish to marry, let it be because that's what ye really want. I willna walk away regardless of whether we wed."

"You spend a lot of time reassuring me." Cerys blurted what came to mind, and it resulted in Blake blinking at her as he stared. "I mean, I really don't like that I make you feel like you have to keep proving yourself to me. You don't. I trust you, Blake, in a way I trust absolutely no one else. I can't explain it, but I don't think I'm wrong aboot doing it. It's like everything in me and around me is telling me I should be with you. I don't know why. And that scares me as much as it reassures me."

"I'll keep doing it if that's what ye need."

"I don't want it to be like that. From now on, I won't question you when you tell me things. If I don't understand or I'm unsure, I'll ask you to clarify. And I think we agree that we both want a future, but we're going to take time to be certain. I didn't think that was possible before this evening. It's all a little overwhelming. But naught aboot you says you'd play me false. If for no other reason than I think your father and uncles would beat you witless. And if you haven't exaggerated aboot your mother, she'd skelp you to an inch of your life."

"That's exactly right, *mo leannan*. I wouldnae play ye false regardless, because ye are too dear to me, Cerys. I want naught but to make ye happy and have ye at ma side."

"I want that too, Blake."

They sealed their agreement with a kiss that felt as natural as breathing. While they returned to their blissful bubble, where nothing mattered beyond being together, they both knew life wouldn't let that be true. Plenty more would matter soon enough.

CHAPTER 9

$\mathcal{C}$erys waved goodbye as the sizable Sinclair entourage mounted and rode under the portcullis. She'd received fatherly embraces from Magnus, Callum, and Tavish. She'd wished to cling to each of them. She hadn't realized how bereft of affection she'd been until they freely offered it to her. She wanted to bottle it and carry it with her. Her own family departed only minutes before the Sinclairs without acknowledging her in the slightest, riding south rather than north. It relieved her that they wouldn't travel in the same direction, forced to share the road.

Blake wrapped her arm around his and kissed her temple, seeing the longing in Cerys's gaze for the easy affection his family so openly shared. He knew he often took it for granted but seeing it through Cerys's eyes gave him a new appreciation for the blessings he'd received throughout his life. He guided her to the kirk but had to release his hold on her as she moved farther down the aisle to join the other ladies-in-waiting.

"Ye seem to have come to an agreement," Torquil whispered as they slipped into their pew. Blake nodded as they both lowered to their knees. After they'd each prayed, they took their seats and waited for Mass to begin. "Are ye courting?"

"Aye. She kens ma intent, and I think she shares it. But we agreed to let this take its course and see if we suit before we enter a betrothal. I want her to be sure. I believe I am, but I dinna want to make a mistake and trap us into an unhappy life. I want what Mama and Da have, and she deserves the same. If it isnae with each other, then we'd do well to take our time. With barely anyone here, I hope it makes it easier to court her."

"Mayhap it will be. But what happens if Murray rides out, and we have to follow? There's always the chance that we'll be riding off to battle rather than riding off to Dunbeath."

"I ken. I think aboot it every time I see her. I dinna ken what to do. I've sworn to protect her, and I want her as ma wife. But I canna ignore our duties, and I canna pretend like there is naught that could complicate this. I just pray we are given a chance. If I must leave without her, I'm coming back. I am nae giving up. If I survive whatever happens next with Murray and Balliol, then I'm taking her home with me."

"And if ye dinna suit? If she doesnae wish to marry ye?"

"I will be heartsore. But it willna change what I've promised. Uncle Callum agreed she can come home with us. I ken Grandda would say the same without reservation. If she still wants that, even if she doesnae want me, then I willna renege on ma word."

"What do ye think Murray plans? Do ye think he will allow us to go home before the next campaign?"

"I dinna ken. I need to seek an audience with him, though. Cerys overhead something yesterday that alarmed her. She went to the stables before me and got trapped in her stall when her father and uncles came back from their ride. Before she could escape, Cunningham, Home, and Hannay came in. I saw them go into the stables, but they werenae there long. They didna enter or leave with their mounts."

"What did she hear?" Torquil swept his gaze over the gathering congregation, ensuring no one paid them attention.

"They were talking aboot how they got nay information from us the night before, but they would continue trying. She also heard them talk aboot Balliol being across the border. Hannay said something aboot the king nae being safe in France anymore. From what she said, it sounds like the Hannays may be involved with mercenaries."

"What do ye think Murray will do?"

"I dinna ken. I canna lie aboot how I came to learn this, but I fear he willna take it seriously when he learns it came from a woman."

"Do ye really think he would ignore something like that because Cerys heard it and nae ye?" Blake cocked an eyebrow. "And I suppose ye canna say ye canna reveal how ye learned that."

"Ye ken him."

"True."

"I think—"

The bell signaling the beginning of Mass rang, cutting Torquil off. Blake disliked feeling so unprepared and unresolved about his upcoming audience with Murray. He didn't know if Murray would even grant Blake his attention that day. He might have to petition more than once. While he and Torquil represented one of the most powerful clans in Scotland, he was still young enough to be Murray's son and younger than most of the delegates remaining at court from the army that fought alongside Murray. He hoped their military leader would take him seriously. He would have to wait and see.

As the brothers rose from their pew at the end of the Mass, they spotted their cousin once removed. Thomas Fraser was their mother's cousin through her father--Deirdre's uncle's illegitimate son. When Deirdre's cousin, Elizabeth, married Robert the Bruce's adopted brother, Edward, Thomas and his half-sisters moved in with his other half-sister, Elizabeth. Before that, Thomas had served as a page in the royal household for several years until he grew too old, and his father refused to acknowledge him. But he was now a well-respected member of the king's counselors who'd opted to remain in Scotland to help Andrew Murray, who served as the Guardian of Scotland.

Blake looked toward Cerys, who watched him. It was clear she recognized Thomas, but he could see she tried to work through his connection to senior advisor. When it dawned on her, she offered an understanding smile. As she filed up the aisle with her peers, she dipped her chin to Blake and continued out of the kirk. He wondered if he would speak to her before his meeting in the Privy Council chamber. He doubted it since he and Torquil intended to grab some bread and fruit to break their fast rather than sit to eat a bowl of porridge. They wished to be among the first in the chamber when Murray arrived.

"Cousins." Thomas extended his arm, and Blake, then Torquil, grasped his forearm in a warrior handshake. "I wondered who I would find here when I was on my way. I passed your clansmen just outside the town gates. It's good to see you lads too."

Thomas's amused grin reached his eyes as he looked at the two strapping young men, both of whom were several inches taller than him and much broader. Closer to their parents' age, Thomas had known the Sinclair brothers since they were bairns.

"Thomas, what brings ye to court?" Blake clapped

him on the shoulder as the three men left the kirk and made their way to the Great Hall.

"I'm to meet with Murray. I would hear his account of the battle, and we will discuss our next course of action."

"We're headed to the Privy Council chamber for a meeting with Murray. He's having all the clan representatives convene there. I dinna ken if it's to discuss what happened or to plan for the future, but we're eager to learn." Torquil passed through the doorway first, talking over his shoulder as Thomas, then Blake, followed him into the keep.

"Do ye have any thoughts on what that future might be?" Blake wondered if he should share with Thomas what Cerys overheard. He trusted the older man's council, but he was apprehensive about the information reaching too many ears.

"I do, but I can't be sure they will come to fruition. I can only advise, not decide." Thomas waved to a Clan Dunbar representative. "I shall be a moment, then I will join you to break our fast."

"We intended to take bread and fruit with us to the Privy Council chamber," Blake explained.

"Murray is over there aboot to eat. You have time. We don't need to listen to your stomachs growling all morning." Thomas chuckled before walking over to the man he greeted.

"Do we tell him?" Torquil asked the burning question.

"I dinna ken. I trust him, but I fear too many people kenning, especially since it involves Cerys. She has Jimmy and Calvin with her today, but I worry aboot her safety if too many people learn it was she who overheard those bluidy Lowlanders."

"Aye. But I think we should. It might be better if

someone in his position kens before we try to approach Murray. He might secure us an audience."

"But what if it angers Murray that we didna come to him directly?" Blake glanced at the man in question.

"Then we tell Thomas just enough to get him to help us gain that audience."

"Vera well. I think ye're right. But if he asks aught too direct, I willna lie."

"Good."

The brothers found a table and waved over a servant, who laid five bowls of porridge on the table. The Sinclairs knew Thomas was right. Their stomachs would growl on just bread and an apple or two. They'd both have two of the bowls while they left one for Thomas. They kept their eye on Murray, gaging how quickly he ate. They would still try to arrive in the council chamber when the leader did.

"I noticed you watching Lady Cerys." Thomas didn't hesitate with his bluntness as he took a seat. "I saw her smile as she left the kirk."

"Aye. I'm courting the lass."

"Are you sure that's wise? What will your father say? And wasn't that rather quick?"

"It is. He kens. And it was." Blake glanced at Cerys, who sat among her peers and laughed. "There's something aboot her that draws me. There was an incident with her family after we met, and I didna feel she was safe with them as her guardians. I offered the Sinclairs' protection, which ma father and uncles agreed was the right thing to do. We're seeing if we suit."

"Sounds like what Edward says aboot how he fell in love with my sister."

"It's probably similar. I'm glad to see ye here. I have something I would ask yer advice aboot."

"Yes?" Thomas said before swallowing a spoonful of porridge.

"I learned there are three courtiers here who are trying to gain information aboot Murray through Torquil and me."

Thomas scanned those present, nodding to some. But when his eyes rested on someone behind Blake, they hardened.

"Who do ye see?" Torquil sat beside Blake, so he couldn't tell who caught Thomas's attention either.

"That bluidy Hannay. Was it him? They're still holding out against the Bruces' claim to the throne. Balliol descends from the same Galloway prince as they do, and suddenly they're the closest of kin. That ruddy British arse-licking pretender plays to that shared ancestry just as his father did. The aulder Balliol didn't even like his mother, and it was Lady Devorgilla who connected her son and grandson to the Hannays. And distantly at best. Bluidy excuses if you ask me."

"Aye. He was one of them. Domnall Cunningham and Stanley Home are his confidantes, it seems."

"That's surprising. Clan Home is connected to the Douglases, who are ardent Bruce supporters. Everyone knows that. Even their connections with Clan Dunbar should have them loyal to King David. The Dunbars may have wavered during the first war, but they've been loyal since Lady Isabella served the auld queen. How is she, by the way?"

"She and Dedric, along with the twins and their sister, are all well. Despite her being a Lowlander and Dedric being raised in England, they're as much a part of our family and clan as they would be if they were born at Dunbeath."

"That's good to hear. Are either of the twins wed?"

Kirk and Keira Hartley were a year older than Blake, and their sister, Sarah, fell between Blake and Torquil in age. Their parents were Lowlander Isabella Dunbar and Scotsman Dedric Hartley, who English warriors kidnapped from his Lowland home as a child and raised to be a knight at the court of King Edward I. They made a home in the Highlands after their married life at the border proved too dangerous because of Dedric's past in England. He'd sent back his spurs, but former allies refused to accept Dedric had returned to his roots and his people.

"Nay. Though it wouldnae surprise me if it were soon. I think Kirk might have his eye on our sister." Blake grimaced as he thought about one of his oldest childhood friends looking at his younger sister with a romantic bent.

"He'll do well to remember that Maisie is still too young. I warned him that if it isnae Da who gelds him, it'll be me if he thinks to touch her." Torquil's chest flexed as he leaned back and crossed his arms. He didn't hold any serious fears for his sister, but he felt it his duty as an older brother to remind any man not to get too close until a ring resided on his little sister's finger.

"Ye'll have yer turn after me, little brother." Blake grinned, an expression boasted by an older brother.

"Och, ye willna do aught to him. Ye're too close."

"All the more reason. It would be the worst betrayal." Blake was more resolved to the idea than Torquil, but he'd warned his friend, too. It didn't hurt to err on the side of caution, especially if the couple's feelings were anything like what he'd discovered with Cerys. "Anyway, Hannay is someone I wanted to talk to ye aboot, Thomas. I learned something that troubles me."

"What's that?"

"Hannay, Cunningham, and Home were in the stables yesterday discussing Balliol. Hannay believes he's with the Cliffords in Cumbria, but he also spoke of the king nay longer being safe in France. It sounded like he might ken aboot or be involved in mercenaries going after King David."

Thomas straightened and swept his gaze around the Great Hall. Blake had whispered, but a castle like Stirling had ears. Satisfied no one could overhear them, he leaned forward.

"Are you sure of what you heard?"

Blake's lips flattened. "I didna hear it, but I trust the person who did. That person has nay reason to lie."

"Who was it?"

"I dinna think it's safe to say."

"You must do better than that. I assume you plan to tell Murray. He will want to know."

"I dinna doubt it. But I would protect this person."

"Protect?" Thomas's gaze shot to Cerys, who chose that moment to rise from her bench and look straight ahead, which meant she looked at their table. Her previously relaxed expression tightened as she looked between Thomas and Blake. "It was Lady Cerys."

Blake took a deep inhale before he sighed. "Aye. We were going for a ride, and she got to the stables before us. She was in her horse's stall when the men came in. They didna see her, but they were just beyond the stall wall. She heard everything. She told me when we stopped to water the horses."

"Is that why she's under your protection?"

"Nay. That had to do with her father threatening her. But I will protect her regardless of whether it's aboot her family or this."

"Her family left this morning, didn't they?" Thomas watched Cerys as she and the ladies left the Great Hall. Blake wondered where they would spend their morning. It frustrated him that he hadn't had more time with her between the bailey and the kirk.

"Aye. That's why she has Sinclair men guarding her

now." Blake nudged his chin toward the two Sinclairs following the women out the door.

"Two won't be nearly enough if anyone learns it was she who overheard the treasonous bastards."

"I ken. That's why I dinna want anyone to ken she was the person to overhear what I told ye."

"Murray is going to demand to know, unless you lie and say it was you."

"I dinna want to do that. That's why I wanted yer advice. How can I tell him without giving away Cerys?"

"The way you told me, but hold fast when he demands to know. Be prepared for him to threaten you."

"Do ye think his threats will be a bluff? Or would he follow through?" Torquil would support his brother no matter what, but he worried about his sibling. He knew Blake would put Cerys's wellbeing above his own. The only thing that could force Blake to give in was a threat to their clan. He wouldn't put hundreds of people's lives and safety ahead of what he wanted. But Torquil didn't doubt Blake would whisk Cerys away the moment his admission endangered her. If he couldn't be free of his obligations to Murray and the army, he would find somewhere safe for Cerys. Blake confirmed that when he spoke again.

"Thomas, if I canna get away, but Cerys needs to flee, I'll need yer help. Can ye take her to Elizabeth?"

Thomas's eyebrows rose before he nodded. It was clear Blake was earnest about his concerns, and it surprised Thomas to see such maturity in the younger man's eyes. He'd known Blake since he'd been in raggies, but he was looking at a man ready to start a family of his own.

"Yes. I'll be certain she makes it to Elizabeth. But would she come with me?"

"I think so. If I explain it to her. If I dinna come back, then I hope Elizabeth and Edward can get her to ma family. She belongs at Dunbeath, with or without me."

"Very well. Murray is aboot to leave."

The two Sinclairs and one Fraser followed Murray into the Privy Council chamber, leading the man's retinue. As the elder of the two brothers, Blake took a seat at the massive wooden table. Torquil stood behind Blake's right shoulder. Thomas took a seat to Blake's right, not just as a family member, but in a show of solidarity. Blake watched as members from other clans filed in. There were men from Clans Sutherland, Mackay, Fraser, Cameron, Mackenzie, and MacLeod of Lewis and of Assynt. Blake and Torquil were related to each clan's laird's family, either directly through the Sinclairs or indirectly through the Sutherlands. The Gordons, Grants, Rosses, and Munros had delegates who represented clans allied with the Sinclairs and Sutherlands. The brothers' grandmother, Kyla, had been a Sutherland before she married Laird Liam Sinclair. The two clans were tightly bonded and, between them, were connected to almost every clan in the Highlands. The Douglases, Elliots, Dunbars, and Kennedys represented the Lowlands. The Kerrs were notably missing.

Blake watched as Shaw Hannay, Stanley Home, and Domnall Cunningham entered the chamber and looked for seats, but they'd arrived too late, forcing them to stand behind their fellow Lowlanders. They kept a wide berth from the Highlanders. When not on the battlefield, the Lowlanders and Highlanders rarely trusted one another and generally avoided each other. Never had that been truer than now that Blake and Torquil knew the three late arrivals were conspiring against the crown.

"We chased the fucking pretender back to where he belongs." Cheers met Murray's booming voice. "But we know from the past that he will not stay away. We may not be fighting now, but it is only a reprieve before the next onslaught. We must remain committed to bringing back our one true king, David, son of the Bruce."

As fists pounded on the table, Blake shifted his gaze to keep Home, Hannay, and Cunningham in his peripheral vision. He wouldn't blatantly stare, but he wished to watch their reactions. They appeared as determined as the other men, but Blake wondered for what their determination was. Was it as Cerys heard? Were they determined to undermine Murray's mission? Or were Home and Cunningham secretly still on King David's side? Was Hannay testing them?

"Do we dare let them hear what's planned here?" Blake whispered to Thomas, keeping his face forward.

"I thought the same thing." Thomas shifted his gaze from Murray to the three Lowlanders. "We need them out." He signaled a royal guard who approached. He gestured for the man to lean down and whispered in his ear. The guard straightened and moved around the table to stand beside Murray. When the Guardian of Scotland noticed the man, he shot him an aggrieved glance, but listened as the guard spoke in low tones.

"Since there are so many here to support King David, I will discuss our plans in groups. The Highlanders will remain for now. Their use will differ from the Lowlanders since their homes are farther away. I will summon the rest of you when I'm ready."

With confusion, the men looked around. The Lowlanders reluctantly moved toward the door. It still left more people in the chamber than who departed. Murray looked at Blake, then Torquil before locking gazes with Thomas. He signaled the three men to follow him across the expansive chamber. He waved away his own guards and crossed his arms.

"What's this?"

"The Sinclairs learned of something that could threaten any plans discussed today. It's best if you hear this without an audience and without the Lowlanders." Thomas spoke up.

"What did you learn?"

"We're aware of three men who met yesterday to discuss the recent campaign," Blake explained. "These men sat and drank with us the night before at The Wolf and Sheep. They attempted to glean information from us aboot the future. We told them naught, but yesterday they agreed to continue trying. They spoke aloud support for Balliol and alluded to a plot against the king. France may nay longer be safe for our sovereign."

"How do you know they agreed to keep trying or that they might be plotting? Did you hear this?"

"Nae directly. But I trust who told me, and that person heard it directly."

"Who?" Murray's single word was a demand.

"I canna say. It wouldnae be safe for this person, and they told me in confidence."

"I take it I cannot interview this person with the big ears."

"I dinna think it wise for their sake."

"Are you that person, Sinclair? Or your brother? Are you hedging to save your own arses if this goes astray?"

"Nay. This person happened to be in the wrong place at the wrong time. They entrusted me with this information. I gave ma word they would be safe."

"Did you offer them your protection?"

Blake's mind fired a warning shot over the bow. The keyword was protection. Murray must suspect Cerys since it was no longer a secret that the Sinclairs were guarding her. He didn't want to give away Cerys's identity yet if he could avoid it, so he repeated himself. "I gave ma word they would be safe."

"How convenient." Murray glanced at the chamber doors through which the Lowlanders passed. "Who are these three men?"

"Shaw Hannay seems to be the leader, and Stanley Home and Domnall Cunningham are with him. It was Stanley and Domnall who tried to loosen our tongues. Hannay spoke of the threat in France."

"When?" Murray's dark gaze bore into Blake, unrelenting and unbelieving.

"I dinna ken an exact date. Hannay said a messenger was already on his way to his clan. The rider should arrive tomorrow. From there, they would take a message to Balliol."

"And you didn't bring this to my attention yesterday when there might have been a chance to catch the messenger. Why?" Blake opened his mouth, but Murray hadn't finished. "I know why. You were too busy playing Sir Galahad to your Holy Grail. The greatest knight to live may have captured what he sought, but he didn't live long after that."

Blake knew the Arthurian reference, and he didn't appreciate it. It was but a myth, while Cerys was a living and breathing woman who needed his protection and for whom he felt a great deal already.

"Mayhap you wish to prove yourself worthy of the Holy Grail, young Sinclair. You are, after all, the son of a fourth son. Warrior or a monastery. I understand why warrior appeals more, knowing your lusty family. Mayhap you wish to impress me. Or mayhap it's the young lady. Mayhap it's even the king. But unless you offer me more, why should I believe you?"

"Why should ye nae? I'm a Sinclair." Much like Blake assumed it explained everything to Cerys when they first spoke, he assumed it would suffice with Murray.

"There can still be one bad apple in an otherwise perfect barrel," Murray mused.

"Andrew." Thomas was unimpressed with his long-time friend. "You insult Blake and his clan. You know, just as everyone else in this court, that the Sinclairs—all of them—have unimpeachable integrity. If Blake says he knows of a conspiracy, then he knows of one."

"Mayhap she wishes to ingratiate herself since her family branded her a whore and left her here."

Blake clenched his fists behind his back, the only way to keep from swinging at Murray. "Ye ken ma family, so ye ken we dinna take to women being called such. Since ye seem so aware of the goings-on in ma life, ye can imagine how I feel aboot ye speaking of her that way."

"And what will you do, Sinclair?" Murray turned to face him fully. Lines and creases marked his harsh face from a hard life spent mostly in battle. His gaze was unapologetic, even verging on taunting. "You cannot merely storm out like a wean. You cannot strike me, even though from your fists behind your back, that's what you wish to do. You cannot refuse to serve since you are not here of your own volition, but to represent your grandfather and clan. So what now?"

"I may nae have a choice aboot staying, and ye are right that I willna leave, but that doesnae mean I'll hold ye in as high esteem as I did yesterday. It doesnae mean I willna relay this conversation to ma grandda when I tell him aboot ma time here. It doesnae mean ma uncle Tristan and great-uncle Laird Sutherland will nae hear. In fact, mayhap I will speak to ma relatives here now who can tell their own lairds. Ma cousin Hamish represents the Mackays, and ma cousin Graham MacLeod represents the MacLeods of Lewis. He will surely share what he hears with his grandda, Laird Sutherland."

"I don't take well to threats, *lad*."

"I dinna issue threats, ma laird. I merely shared ma thoughts. Letting them ken what abounds is much faster than having to send missives once I return home."

"You play a dangerous game that you are not winning. You will cease before you shame your family and your clan."

"Andrew," Thomas tried again. "I believe him. Why would he lie? His family helped your brother-by-marriage gain the throne and keep it. They were there in every battle you fought. They are among the most loyal clans you have fighting alongside you. Why is it so preposterous that he heard this?"

"Because he is the son of a fourth son. He wishes to make a name for himself since he is so far from inheriting the lairdship."

Thomas leaned forward until his nose nearly met Murray's. "And I'm the bastard son of a once-publicly disgraced courtier, but here I stand on my own merit. I think being the son of a fourth son is more desirable than being a bastard. You accept me and always have. You look like a fool to question a Sinclair."

"A fool?" Murray squinted at Thomas, and the latter wished he hadn't shared his last thought. "I will banish you from court and strip you of your position, Thomas, if you're wrong. Sinclair, I will deal with this as I see fit. You will listen and speak only when spoken to."

Murray walked back to the table, leaving Blake, Torquil, and Thomas staring after him.

"If I didna ken better, I might suspect Murray didna care that there was a potential conspiracy. I would think he'd take this more seriously." Torquil was aghast at the exchange he just witnessed. He credited his brother with patience and forbearance he wasn't certain he possessed. He couldn't imagine hearing a woman he courted called a whore and not running the man through.

"Mayhap he wishes to make this seem unimportant

to us, but among his top advisors, he'll take it to heart."
Blake mentally crossed his fingers.

"Blake, I'm among those top advisors." Thomas
sighed. "I think he is just as prejudiced against your
place in your family as he sounds. He was at court
when your father discovered your mother here. He
witnessed everything, and he sided with your Fraser
grandfather. He may respect your father on the battlefield, but he thinks little of him as a fourth son. Only
Callum and Alexander were of consequence to him before Thormud was born. Now Alexander is of lesser
importance since Callum has his own heir. His position
as Guardian and as husband to the dead king's sister
swelled his head. He's a powerful leader and experienced warrior, but he's always been an arse."

The three men returned to their seats and listened
as the conversation continued around them. Thomas
joined in as the senior advisors discussed their plans.
Blake watched them carefully, studying body language,
tone, and what they said. It surprised him when
Murray suggested sending the Dunbars and Kennedys
back to the western border. That would place them
near their homes, but also Clans Hannay and Cunningham. It heartened Blake to think Murray might consider what he shared, even if he refused to
acknowledge Blake.

When Murray dismissed the Highlanders, Thomas
and the other members of the Privy Council remained
to discuss matters with the Lowlanders. Blake and
Torquil sought their cousins. Hamish, Mairghread and
Tristan Mackay's second son, greeted them with bois-
terous claps on the back. Graham, Maude and Kieran
MacLeod's oldest, was more circumspect. Graham's
mother was the older Sinclairs' cousin. She'd been a
Sutherland before she married Laird Kieran MacLeod
of Lewis.

"Bluidy good to be in a bed again, with a hot bath," Hamish grinned. "I dinna ken how yer da and uncles slept on the ground for so many nights. I'm getting too auld for this."

Graham was the same age as Blake, and Hamish was a year younger. None of them were so old that they should complain of the discomforts. It was a jest they'd heard before. One they'd all made when in truth they marveled at how their fathers and uncles still camped under the stars and spent weeks, even months, sleeping without a bed. None ever appeared worse for wear.

Torquil poked his finger into Hamish's abdomen, which was solid muscle, just like the rest of them. "Ye're a wee softie, Cousin. Dinna let yer da hear ye. He'll send ye out to sleep in the woods for a sennight, just like he did Liam when he made the same complaint."

"Looks like we willna be going home to our beds any time soon," mused Graham.

"I ken." Blake wondered where Cerys was. There were no immediate orders for them to leave, but it didn't appear likely he and Torquil would return to Dunbeath in a fortnight like they'd all hoped.

"Shall we share an ale this eve after the meal? Merry Widow?" Hamish grinned.

Blake was hesitant to agree since he hadn't spent any time with Cerys, and he hoped to steal kisses like he had the previous night. But perhaps he could have a pint or two once she retired. Torquil answered for him.

"Aye. We'll join ye."

The cousins parted ways, and Blake went in search of Cerys.

CHAPTER 10

Cerys sensed someone behind her as she returned to her chamber after an afternoon at the almshouses. She'd accompanied the other ladies-in-waiting as they made their rounds, encouraging them to spend more than a few moments at each place. She spoke to women and made a list of items they needed, mostly clothes for the children. She passed out sweets to the young ones. But she was blessedly free of the other women when she stopped at the apothecary. She hadn't finished her visits to the other taverns since meeting Blake, and she wanted to resume her routine. She knew he wouldn't agree to her going alone or even with Sinclair guardsmen, so she hoped he would take her.

As she approached her floor, Cerys glanced at Jimmy, the guard who walked behind her. He nodded, and she was certain he sensed what she did. She continued on, trusting her guards, relieved that Blake insisted upon them. The four Sinclair men who had already rotated through two shifts were far more diligent than any of her previous Kerr guards. However, despite feeling safe with Jimmy and Calvin, something still felt amiss. As they approached the stairwell leading up to the ladies' chambers, she found Stanley and Domnall waiting at the bottom. With them stood two guards from each of their clans. The six men forced them to stop since they couldn't pass.

"Lady Cerys."

Cerys turned to find Shaw approaching with one of his men. It was now eight men against two. Jimmy and Calvin positioned Cerys behind their backs, so hers was against the wall. She was barely visible behind the two behemoths. But it did little to reassure her since her guards were so outnumbered. Jimmy and Calvin rested their hands on their belts, but it was obvious they reached for their dirks. Swords weren't allowed in the keep, except for the royal guard. All the men had relinquished them when they passed through the gates. It only mildly reassured Cerys that there might not be a bloodbath.

"Hannay."

"I'd have a word with you, my lady."

"You've already had two. I must prepare for the evening meal. Cunningham, Home, please move aside." Cerys hoped her voice sounded stronger than it did to her ear. Her stomach knotted as Shaw, Stanley, and Domnall all stepped forward, crowding her guards and her. Calvin and Jimmy broadened their stances, elbows out and feet wider, effectively blocking Cerys from anyone's view. She prayed no one could see her cowering.

"I noticed you left the stables yesterday with your guards and the Sinclairs. Yet I never saw you go inside." Shaw tried to peer between the Sinclair guards, but it was useless. "I saw your relatives go in and come out, and I saw the Sinclairs go in. But you seemed to just appear like a fae. Tell me, did you fly into the loft and rest amongst the hay?"

"Do I look like I can fly, Hannay? Last I checked I

have no wings. And I've never lived inside a tree. A fae I am not."

"Ah. Well then, as a mortal woman, you must have hidden while you heard two conversations that didn't include you. As a lady, I assumed your mother taught you manners."

"My mother died the day I was born. I'm afraid she didn't have the chance to teach me aught." Cerys didn't bother modulating the sarcasm in her voice.

"No wonder you're so uncouth. It's most unfortunate that you eavesdropped, my lady. But we shall hope your memory is as poor as your etiquette."

"Good day, Hannay. I have no time for this, and unless you wish for all the ladies to descend upon us, you'd do well to let us pass. You'll have far more than me to worry aboot when it comes to eavesdroppers. Unless of course, you wish to talk to Lady Morag again."

Cerys rose on her toes to peek over the Highlanders' shoulders. Morag Gunn was the oldest lady-in-waiting in residence, and she was desperate to snare a husband. She'd set her sights on Shaw and was unrelenting in her quest. Cerys watched Shaw grimace before he took a step back.

"I wouldn't wander alone, Lady Cerys."

"As you can see, I am not alone. Good day, Cunningham, Home. Thank you for moving aside." Neither Stanley nor Domnall had moved, nor had their men. But Cerys pressed between Calvin's and Jimmy's shoulders until she could twist and look at the other two Lowlanders. She met Domnall's gaze and refused to look away first. He glanced at Shaw before signaling for his men to step away from the stairs. With her once more between them, Jimmy and Calvin escorted her up the stairs.

Cerys wasted no time washing her face and neck

before changing into a kirtle better suited for the evening meal. She finished tying her laces, which she now had to do alone since her maid left with her family, and slid her feet into her slippers. She pulled open the door and found Blake on the other side with his fist raised. She noticed a moment later two different men stood with Blake. Jimmy and Calvin no longer guarded her door. Blake stepped forward, forcing Cerys to step back. She gasped and tried to look past him.

"We're alone, Cerys. Are ye all right? Calvin told me what happened."

"I'm fine. You can't be in here. Blake, if someone sees you, you'll have no choice but to marry me."

Blake smirked and waggled his eyebrows, but he grew serious a moment later. "Cerys, they may have figured out that ye were in the stables, but I fear they may also ken I told Murray what ye told me. I never said yer name, didna even hint at it. But Murray guessed without a hint. I dinna ken what he said to the Lowlanders since he met with them after he spoke with the Highlanders. I dinna ken if he let on that he kens aboot the conspiracy. If Hannay and the others figured out ye were in the stables, and Murray said something aboot the plot, it might be why they dared approach ye."

"How could you, Blake? I told you in confidence."

"How could I nae? Ye kenned I would have to tell Murray."

Cerys sighed. He was right, but she was still shaken by the confrontation. She hadn't expected the Lowlanders would waylay her with so many men. She thought she was calm after a few minutes to herself, but she felt jittery again. She slid her arms around Blake's waist and pressed her head to his chest. His arms went around her immediately. The steady heartbeat gave her something to focus upon, calming her.

"Wheest, little one. I willna let aught happen to ye."

"I know, but it was terrifying. I was more scared of what would happen to Calvin and Jimmy if those men attacked. It was eight to two."

"But that was eight Lowlanders to two Highlanders. I pity those fools. They wouldnae have come out alive."

"Are you really that arrogant to think that being outnumbered didn't matter?"

"It's nae arrogance when I've seen what ma men can do. I dinna fear them losing. But I dinna like kenning it would have taken both of them fighting, which meant leaving ye unguarded. I am adding an extra guard to yer detail. If it comes to it, two fight and one always stays with ye."

"Do you have that many men?"

"Aye. Torquil and I had our guards before I asked Uncle Callum for two more. I'm taking nay chances with yer safety, *mo leannan*. But I must talk to ye aboot something else. We must plan in case I canna stay with ye."

"Not stay with me? That's what you promised."

Blake heard the waver in her voice, and he hated knowing that he worried her. But there was nothing for it. He wasn't in control of where he went or when he went there. "Cerys, ye ken I represent ma clan. Most went home, but those of us who remain must follow Murray's orders. He hasnae issued any, but if he says we must travel with him, then we must. I pray it doesnae come to that, since there are so few of us here. The Sinclairs, Sutherlands, Mackays, and MacLeods sent men to fight first. That's why ma clan left. We've fulfilled our time for now. But that doesnae release Torquil or me since we still represent the clan."

"Where will you go?"

"I dinna ken. Murray excused the Highlanders without telling us any of his plans for us. He spoke to the Lowlanders separately. Once he kenned Thomas wanted to speak to him privately, he dismissed the Lowlanders. I'm nae certain he believed me, but I think he did. He sent some clans home to the western border, which puts them near the Cunninghams and the Hannays."

"Dunbars and Kennedys?"

Blake hesitated to share the specifics, but he figured Cerys would soon know once those clans' armies left. "Aye. The Kennedys have been staunch supporters since the Bruce's early days. The Dunbars have become loyal since the Bruce took the throne. They're trustworthy, so I feel a wee better kenning that. They're both influential and formidable, so I hope that makes the Hannays and Cunninghams reconsider. I doubt it will, but I can hope."

"I can hope too. But what aboot Shaw, Stanley, and Domnall? I know you said you'd post three guards. But what if they try to do more than just intimidate me?"

"Ma men ken ye're to be defended above all. They're trained to protect, and they ken that's their duty. They pledged to do just that. Even if ye werenae ma—important to me, they would because ye're vulnerable to trained warriors. They wouldnae turn a blind eye to any woman in danger."

Cerys wondered what Blake had been about to say before he caught himself. They still embraced, and Blake ran his hand up and down her back. When he stepped away, the air suddenly felt chilled. She immediately missed the contact. He guided her to the window embrasure and gestured for her to take a seat.

"You said you might have to leave. What will happen then?"

"Thomas Fraser will take ye to his sister, Elizabeth. She's King David's aunt-by-marriage. Her husband was adopted by the Bruces. She and Thomas are both ma mother's cousins. She and her husband, Edward, will ensure ye make it to Dunbeath."

"That's a lot of being passed off among strangers. Mayhap staying here is better."

"Nay. I willna be able to leave any men behind, Cerys. I willna have anyone who can guard ye. Mayhap if they hadnae accosted ye, but I canna trust that Shaw willna do aught to ye. He worries me the most, and nae just because he seems to lead the conspiracy. He strikes me as a mon who doesnae have limits when it comes to what he wants. I've kenned Thomas, Elizabeth, and Edward ma entire life. They're family."

"But I can't just travel with Thomas and his men. I don't have a maid anymore. She left with my father. I have no chaperone."

That gave Blake pause. He had to admit a chaperone wasn't something he usually had to consider. When his sister or female cousins traveled, his parents and older relatives arranged the guards and chaperones. It was Cerys's concern when he recommended that she travel with his family or him. The fact that Thomas was married, his own children Blake's and Cerys's ages, wouldn't matter. People could still gossip. It also meant he had to trust men he didn't know around Cerys. Blake wasn't acquainted with all of Thomas's guards. However, he didn't feel there were many more choices.

"I ken, *leannan*. But one option is the danger of gossip. The other is a danger to yer life. If ye're leaving court and going to Dunbeath, then the gossip willna hurt ye. Nay one at Elizabeth's home will speak against ye. They wouldnae dare since they would be speaking against her brother."

Cerys nodded. She wasn't convinced Blake was entirely correct, but his point made sense. "I trust your judgment, Blake. It's frightening, but I know you wouldn't endanger me on purpose."

"Never." Blake cupped Cerys's face, lifting her chin as he leaned forward. The kiss began soft, much like theirs usually did. But within a heartbeat, it consumed them. Cerys rose and pushed Blake's sporran to the side before she went onto her toes. With an arm beneath her backside, Blake lifted her off her feet, leaving them to dangle against his calves. Their tongues mated as they both wished they could. Cerys's hands cupped his neck before sliding into his deep chestnut locks. The strands were silky and soft, making Cerys wonder if they were freshly washed, or if they were always like that. Blake pulled back, but Cerys could tell that wasn't what he wished to do. "We'll be late to the evening meal. People will notice."

"I've already sat beside you, and you escorted me to Mass. Now that your family is gone, it will be even more obvious. So I care not aboot being late. I don't care if we miss the entire meal. I'd rather be with you. Gossip be damned at this point if I might travel with Thomas."

"I want the same, but I dinna want to create it while we're here. It willna harm ma reputation, but it will yers."

"Can we stay just a little longer?"

Blake couldn't refuse her because he didn't want to. Once more their mouths fused as Blake kept her pressed against his body with one arm while his free hand roamed. When he slid it over her pert breast, she arched her back and moaned. The sound echoed in his head, urging him to do more, take more. But he didn't want to take. He wanted to give. He wanted to introduce Cerys to ways they could enjoy one another and share their feelings without having to put them into words. Words neither was ready to articulate.

Cerys's fingers knotted in his hair as her desire grew. Her body felt like a coil ready to spring loose. She didn't know if she wanted him to keep massaging her breast, or if she wanted to rub her body against his like a needy kitten. But she knew she wanted him to touch her more and preferably without so many layers of clothes in the way. She tugged at his leine, pulling it loose at the back. Her hands slid under the fabric and met scorching skin that rippled over muscles that flexed with every breath Blake took. She reveled in the feel of such a monstrous man who touched her with such gentleness, even when she felt his desire. It made her feel precious and petite, knowing he restrained the power that came so naturally after years of physical training. He could snap her in half, yet he touched her with tenderness, even though it was driven by lust.

"Cerys, I wish to taste ye, lass. Do ye ken what I mean?"

Cerys tried to clear her mind enough to understand Blake's request. She couldn't work her way through his words while she hungered for more contact, more intimacy. But his meaning broke through her haze when she realized he offered what she craved. She considered what he alluded to and recalled what she'd overheard the maids talk about all those years ago. She nodded as she peered over his shoulder at the bed. He looked back before meeting her gaze. When Cerys nodded again, he carried her there and laid her down. He brought his body over hers but propped his weight on his forearms and knees, keeping some space between them.

"Ye ken how ma fingers made ye feel. I would do that with ma mouth."

"I understand, Blake. I've never done it before, or rather had it done to me. But I know what you mean. I want that." Cerys searched his dark chocolate eyes and wondered if she'd just painted herself the whore her father accused her of being.

"I dinna think less of ye or believe ye to be without

125

morals because ye wish to share this with me, *mo leannan*. Do ye think me a rogue or a rake for asking?"

"No."

"Is that because I'm a mon, and ye expect that of me?"

"No. I know you have more experience than me. But I don't think I mind. I suppose one of us should know what we're doing."

Blake eased to Cerys's left side and tucked hair behind her ear before pressing a soft kiss to her lips. "I'm nae a virgin, but neither am I a mon who's been with barrows full of women. I ken what I'm doing, but I am nae a womanizer. I dinna seek whores or wenches when I'm at home or here. I dinna accept offers from camp followers when I'm on campaign. There are a few women at home who live in the village, but they're widows. I dinna go often, and ye ken I dinna believe in lemans. Even if I did, ma family would skelp me alive. I've always been careful and discreet. I'm more bluster than aught else. Male pride."

"You don't owe me an explanation, Blake."

"But I wish to offer ye one. I dinna want ye to wonder who ye might meet when ye arrive at Dunbeath. I dinna want ye to be uncomfortable and wondering if ye're talking to a woman I've bedded. I've heard how that's hurt ma aunts over the years. Mostly when we've come here or visited other keeps. Ma father and uncles have been faithful from the beginning, so it doesnae seem to pain ma aunts as much since they all married close to two decades ago. But I remember looks and comments that I didna understand when I was younger, but I do now. I dinna want that for ye. I've never wanted that for any bride. The men in ma family have warned the lads against making the mistakes they did. I admit I've flirted and teased with more women than I should have, but I havenae bedded as many as most might guess."

"Thank you for explaining, but I really don't want to think aboot that right now. I only want to think aboot us."

"I understand. I'm only thinking aboot us, too. I only want us, Cerys."

"I only want us, too." Cerys ran her fingertips over his cheekbone then over his bristled jaw. "How do you say my darling?"

Blake's eyes widened. It surprised him that she wished to use a term of endearment since she'd never hinted at one before and that she wished to learn a Gaelic one. "M'eudail. It's ma dear or ma darling. Or ye can say mo ghràidh."

"M'eudail." Cerys repeated it in her head thrice before speaking it aloud. She knew she didn't sound exactly like Blake, but she thought she'd gotten close. The happiness that radiated from his eyes and his smile made her wish she'd asked sooner. She hadn't thought such a small sentiment would mean so much to him, but she chided herself for underestimating him once again. She knew how much she reveled in hearing him call her his sweetheart.

Blake rolled back, so his upper body draped across Cerys. But that didn't satisfy her. She wanted him over her like when they first moved to the bed. He shifted and rested between her legs. But he was in the way once he tried to raise her skirts. He pushed up onto one forearm, and Cerys marveled at the strength she saw as his leine strained against his chest and bicep. It made her mouth water.

She never imagined seeing a man's muscles bunch and flex could arouse her to such heights, but she wished to run her tongue over all of him. He looked too delicious to ignore, which made her think about what he asked to do. That only made her think about how she could reciprocate. Her eyes flew to his plaid trapped by his thigh, where she could see the outline of his rod now that his sporran was out of the way. She'd felt it against her mound when they stood and then a moment ago.

Once her skirts were out of the way, Cerys pressed Blake's lower back, urging him to settle his weight on her again. She could tell he offered her only a fraction of it, but it made her want to latch onto him and never let go. Her knees bent and bracketed his hips as his still-free hand ran along the back of her thigh. Their mouths came together as Blake wrapped her leg over his hip and rocked against her. He swallowed her moan, but he voiced his own sound as her back arched and pressed her breasts against him. He slipped his hand under her back and tugged at her laces, untying them, and loosening them enough to draw the sleeve down one shoulder. He untied the chemise ribbon and revealed one of her breasts. He dipped his head and laved the nipple.

"Blake." It was said on a sigh as she moved restlessly beneath him. As much as he wished to lavish attention on her breast, Blake knew that if he didn't get his cock away from her, the friction would result in the same unprecedented ending as the night before. He suckled until her nails bit into his back before he eased away and moved down the bed. His long legs dangled off the end as he settled his shoulders under her thighs.

Cerys watched Blake's every move, intrigued and nervous. She felt a moment of mortification when he pushed her skirts over her waist, and she watched him catch his first glimpse of her mons. But his ravenous look as he feasted his eyes put her at ease. When his tongue swept across her seam, she stifled her moan, not wanting to admit how much she liked the feeling. He ran his flattened tongue along her from bottom to top twice before dipping his tongue inside of her. His masculine groan made her core clench. She nearly bucked off of the bed when his teeth grazed her sensitive pearl. She clutched the bedcovers when he flicked it with his tongue, then sucked. She squeezed her eyes shut as she struggled to breathe. The sensations were unlike anything she imagined and so intense she wasn't certain she could endure it. But nothing would incite her to stop him.

"Ye taste better than the sweetest honey or the freshest fruit tart. I could make a meal of ye every day, leannan."

St. Columba's bones. I'd let you too. How the hell does something that seems so untoward feel so bluidy good? Does it feel this good for every woman? With any mon? Or is it Blake? I think it's him. I want it to only be him. I don't think I would react this way to another mon. And it's not just because he's the handsomest mon I've ever seen. It's because it's him.

Cerys felt the urgency increase with each pass of Blake's tongue. When he slipped a finger inside her, she shuddered. It offered her momentary relief from her neediness, but it soon compounded her desire. When the tip of his tongue joined his finger, and his thumb circled her nub, she felt the same wave of pleasure crash over her as it had the night before. She swallowed her scream as her body undulated beneath Blake.

As the wave crested, and her body pushed through to the other side of her climax, she clawed at Blake, urging him to move back up to the bed. She cupped his face and pressed her lips to his, her tongue darting into his mouth, uncaring that she could taste herself. As he adjusted his weight, her hand dove beneath his plaid and wrapped around his sword. She froze for a moment, uncertain what to do, before she recalled how he rocked his hips against her. She imagined him doing that inside her, and it dawned on her that she should stroke him.

Blake thought he would come out of his skin when he felt her hand wrap around him. He tried to calm himself, but the moment Cerys stroked him the first time, all reason flew away. He grunted as he thrust into her hand. She worked him as she strove to give him the release she'd just experienced. As they moved together, their clothes shifted. The tip of Blake's cock rubbed against Cerys's entrance. Temptation seized them. Blake pressed forward as Cerys guided him toward her. As the head of Blake's rod slid past her netherlips, they both froze. For several heartbeats they looked at one another, both debating whether they should dare continue.

But reason got the better of them both. Blake pulled back, and Cerys didn't stop him. She still stroked, hoping to bring him to climax with the same ease he'd done to her. She suppressed her grin when only a few more glides of her hand had his cock twitching and his body shuddering. She looked down for the first time, seeing much of his length. She watched a viscous cream jet from him and splatter the inside of her thighs. Without thought, she swiped her index finger through a droplet and brought it to her mouth. It was a strange, but not wholly unlikable, flavor. She'd now tasted herself and him, and she was certain she would enjoy doing both many times to come.

With labored breathing, Blake kissed her temple, nose, cheeks, and finally lips. He rested his forehead against hers as they both struggled to catch their breath. Cerys tilted her head and kissed the tip of his nose before pressing a kiss to his lips.

"Are ye all right, *mo leannan?*"

"Far better than all right, *m'eudail.*"

"Lass, ye dinna ken what it does to me to hear ye say that. To hear ye speak Gaelic and to ken ye call me that. Ma heart already races, but I fear it might beat right out of ma chest. It feels too big to fit."

"That's how you make me feel. That's what it's been like for me since the first time you called me sweetheart. Even then I wanted you to call me *your* sweetheart."

"Always, Cerys. Always."

They gazed at one another before sharing several more soft kisses. However, a knock at the door made them both freeze. Shock filled their eyes as they both remembered two men stood outside Cerys's chamber. How easily they'd forgotten about the rest of the world. There was little need to speculate what the couple had been doing locked away for so long. It would only be a question of how far they'd allowed passion to carry them away. Their foreheads pressed together again. Reality had returned far too soon.

CHAPTER 11

*B*lake opened the bedchamber door after they adjusted their clothes. As a maiden, Cerys wore her long tresses loose, so she only needed to run a hand over her hair to smooth it. Blake found his brother on the other side. Torquil wasn't looking at him but over his shoulder to Cerys, who struggled to maintain a neutral expression. Torquil's gaze told her that neither she nor Blake fooled him. When his eyes darted to the bed, Cerys's eyes flew there. The bedding was still made but rumpled.

"Blake, ye're missing the evening meal. Ye wouldnae wish for Lady Cerys to starve after such a long day. What would people say?" Torquil's voice held a warning, even if his expression was amused. Blake scowled, issuing his own warning. He didn't want his younger brother embarrassing Cerys any more than the situation already would.

"Cerys kens she'll travel with Thomas to Elizabeth and Edward if we canna go to Dunbeath."

"Is that what she kens?" Torquil whispered, a smirk playing at his lips. But it dropped when he noticed Cerys blush and look nearly in tears. Blake turned back and spied Cerys's expression before she could hide it.

"Arse," Blake hissed. He reached out his hand, but Cerys hesitated. She shifted to peer out to the passageway. She could only see one shoulder from each guard. She suddenly wondered how much they'd heard. She'd tried to be quiet, but she couldn't recall if she had been. It mortified her. Blake took a step toward her. "Cerys?"

"Yes. I'm coming." She accepted his hand, gripping it out of discomfort. He leaned over and kissed her temple.

"Wheest, little one. Nay one will say aught. Ma men wouldnae dare, and nay one else kens."

"It's bad enough some of them do know."

Blake grinned and shook his head. "Ye'll understand when ye meet ma mama and the rest of the family. We're a large brood, and nae by accident."

"They're married!"

"They werenae always."

Cerys squeezed her eyes shut as she passed over the threshold. When she opened them, she kept them straight ahead since the guards now walked behind her, Blake, and Torquil. The brothers bracketed her. She wasn't certain if it was having four men with her that made her feel invincible, but she suspected it was Blake at her side. She couldn't reason through why her trust was implicit. They didn't know each other well, but it seemed so natural. She knew other dependable and honest men, but none made her feel like Blake. He and Torquil were so similar that people might mistake them for one another, but the younger brother held no appeal for her.

When they reached the Great Hall, Blake released her hand, but it took her a moment to follow suit. She didn't want to. He wrapped her arm around his, just like he did whenever they were in public. The meal progressed without any confrontations, for which Cerys was grateful. However, she didn't miss how people stared even more now that Cerys remained with the Sinclairs, despite most of them leaving. No longer did she have the paternal Sinclair men as a shield. It was clear she was involved with Blake since they shared a trencher again, and now Torquil sat on her other side rather than Magnus. Just as he had the night before, Blake discreetly moved the best pieces of meat to her side.

"You don't have to do that." Cerys glanced at Blake from the corner of her eye. "You're the one who needs more than I do."

"I have plenty."

"But—"

"I want to, Cerys." Blake's voice was tender but resolute.

"Thank you, m—Blake." She'd nearly slipped and used the endearment in front of his men.

"Ye can call me what ye wish, *leannan*. They're all too busy clishmaclavering to notice, and Torquil has the good sense nae to say aught." Blake shot his brother a glare over Cerys's head. But his attention whipped around as he sensed someone approaching their table. He stiffened when he saw it was Murray. Cerys sensed the tension, making her nervous.

"Lady Cerys, Sinclair." Murray greeted them both, but his attention was on Cerys. She offered a serene smile and dipped her chin. "I would have a word, my lady."

Cerys wanted to look at Blake, but she didn't dare. Their hands were beside one another's on the bench. She pressed her little finger against his, and he covered it with his.

"Good evening, Sir Andrew. What do you wish to speak to me aboot?"

"Not here, Lady Cerys. It would be better in the antechamber."

Cerys didn't want to go. She trusted nothing about this situation, and the thought of being shut in a room alone with the man terrified her now that it was clear he knew she was the eavesdropper. When Blake rose, she felt marginally better, but it didn't last.

"Not you, Sinclair."

"Lady Cerys was threatened today. She doesnae go anywhere without a guard." Blake remained standing.

"You believe I would do her harm? Or do you believe I'm incapable of protecting a lady?"

"Neither. I'm merely overprotective of what's mine." Blake knew what that declaration meant. He would sort it out with Cerys later, but for now, he would be clear with Murray about where he stood on the matter of Cerys going anywhere without him.

"Are you betrothed now? I hadn't heard."

"Yes."

Both men looked at Cerys, who stood beside Blake. She didn't look at him, keeping her gaze on Murray.

"My felicitations on the auspicious occasion. When did this happen?"

"Yesterday." Cerys knew she was digging herself into a hole from which she couldn't climb out, but she didn't want the senior warrior to believe Blake asked because of his unsatisfying audience with Murray.

"You didn't mention this, Sinclair, when we spoke this afternoon."

"But now ye can understand why I wished to protect ma betrothed's identity." Blake rather liked saying that. He knew it was only pretend, but it was what he'd wanted since he'd spoken to Cerys outside the tavern two nights ago. He'd met plenty of women since he came into his manhood, but never had he encountered a woman he wished to marry. It was impulsive at best and ridiculous at worst, but his very marrow told him that Cerys was the right woman for him.

"Why didn't your father or Callum announce this last evening before they left?"

"Who is there to announce it to?" Blake looked around the Great Hall, which looked vacant compared to how it once teemed with people. He shrugged as he turned his gaze back to Murray. "Whose business is it? We canna get the king's permission to marry, and we canna get the queen's permission to discharge Lady Cerys from service. Since it isnae possible, there is nay one to consult."

"Without permission, there is no wedding," Murray countered. Blake kept his expression impassive, but his eyes bored into the older man's, and it made Murray realize that he'd underestimated the young man. He'd found him jovial and lighthearted when they were in camp. He seemed to have few cares in the world beyond staying alive and the next ale. But he knew him to be ferocious on the battlefield. He was discovering that behind the easygoing appearance laid the famous Sinclair stubbornness and conviction. Murray concluded he would have to tread more carefully, lest he wished to see Blake follow through on his earlier warnings about telling his family. He wouldn't discount this Sinclair again.

"Sir Andrew, I will speak to you. But it would only be appropriate if my betrothed and a guard accompanied me."

"No guard. This is not for everyone's ears."

"He waits outside," Blake interjected. "And ma brother comes, too."

"No."

"If aught happens to me, Torquil must ken what's transpiring."

Murray's lips pursed, but he nodded. The trio followed him from the gathering hall and into the antechamber. A Sinclair guard posted outside the door.

They found Thomas awaiting them. The man's face was grim as he watched them enter. Blake's stomach sank, and Cerys felt sweat at her hairline above her neck. She sensed Torquil was on edge, but he remained behind Blake and her.

"Lady Cerys, I would hear from you what was said yesterday."

Cerys looked at Blake, not entirely because she sought his permission, but because the reassurance helped. She wanted Murray to see that she would defer to him just as a wife would. They couldn't afford for him to doubt them. She'd already been brazen to agree to the meeting without waiting for Blake's permission. He nodded, then she turned back to Murray.

"I planned to go for a ride with my guards. While I was within the castle walls, my guards didn't follow me. I arrived at the stables alone and went to my horse's stall. I wondered why it was so quiet, since there are usually a handful of stablehands working. I only saw one, and he soon disappeared. I heard my father and uncles talking as they came inside. I admit I avoid them when I can, so I thought I could wait in the stall until they left. They stopped to talk while they tended their horses. They spoke aboot returning home and that I would remain here. I don't remember there being aught else."

"Then what?" Murray's impatience was clear.

"I was aboot to tack my horse when more voices entered the building. I recognized those, too. It soon became clear why there was no one besides the now-absent stable boy and me inside. I assume they paid off the other hands to give them privacy. Cunningham and Home said they'd tried to get information from Blake and Torquil the night before at The Wolf and Sheep but to no avail. They sounded frustrated. They agreed to try again. They wanted to know what your plans are.

137

Hannay expressed his support for Balliol and said the true king wouldn't be safe in France any longer."

"Aught else?"

Cerys thought for a moment, running the conversation she heard through her mind. "Hannay said that he'd sent a messenger to his clan when you and the army arrived. He said another messenger would be dispatched to the Cliffords in Cumbria, since he believed Balliol went there. I don't remember aught else. I don't think there was aught else."

"And you told Sinclair this during your ride?"

"I did. He and his guards arrived in the stables just after Hannay and the other two left. Blake was concerned aboot the threat of highwaymen. He offered to join my guards for the extra protection."

"A Sinclair protecting a Kerr." Murray's skepticism rang in the air.

"Lady Cerys is still ma aunt's niece. Just because our clans dinna get along, doesnae mean I can ignore that connection or that I should willingly stand by when a lady might be endangered."

"Rather close connection for a betrothal," Murray mused.

"Ye ken ma aunt Brighde is related to me by marriage. We dinna share any blood. It is more coincidence than aught else, but the connection and duty remain."

"How very noble, Sinclair."

"Aye. That is what a nobleman should do." Blake knew that wasn't what Murray meant, but he would turn his words on the man since he didn't care for how he spoke to Cerys. His tone was patronizing. "We talked and while we were out, I asked her to marry me."

"Ah." Murray made the sound as though he suddenly understood everything. "You offered to marry her to protect her. It wasn't such nonsense as the rest of your family."

Blake inhaled, broadening his chest to its full expanse, and pushed his shoulders back. It was obvious Murray thought his family ridiculous for making love matches, but it told Blake a great deal about the man's own marriage to Christina Bruce. The warrior might have come to her defense, but he really protected the castle she held.

"The protection of ma sword and ma name comes with me. I'm marrying Lady Cerys, nae ma weapon." He was careful not to say sword or blade when he mentioned marriage, since he was certain Murray would take it as a euphemism. Blake didn't trust the man not to say something vulgar in front of Cerys.

"Another love match then." Murray spoke with scorn, but his face registered surprise when Cerys slid her hand into Blake's.

"Yes." Cerys nodded before leaning against Blake. He released her hand and wrapped his arm around her waist, drawing her closer. They took comfort in each other. Blake wanted to steer the conversation away from their supposed romance and pending nuptials.

"Why didn't you tell me yesterday afternoon or evening, Sinclair?" Murray crossed his arms, but he still wasn't nearly as intimidating as Blake now that his full girth was clear.

"I kenned we were to meet this morning." Hoping that would suffice, Blake changed the topic. "Hannay and his partners still intend to wheedle information from me. I have none I could give away, but I ask ye now, is there aught ye wish for me to tell them?"

"Plenty, but none of it has to do with any plans." Murray scowled, but for once neither Cerys nor Blake felt it directed toward them. Blake looked at Thomas, who'd remained silent during the entire exchange. The latter shrugged. That didn't help. "You will return to the tavern tonight. When they join you, share that the

Dunbars and Kennedys are the next to return home, but they will be riding the border from the Solway Firth to the Murrays. Missives have already been sent to the Maxwells and Gordons to inform them."

"And if they ask for how long?" Blake would try to anticipate the other men's questions and have answers at the ready.

"Until I summon them back."

"That crosses both of their lands. What do I say when they ask if ye'll inform them?"

"That it isn't any of your ruddy concern what courtesies I might extend."

"What aboot—"

"Enough, Sinclair. Spin whatever tales you need, then tell me in the morning. I expect information from you after Mass."

"Aye. Vera well."

"You may return to your meal."

Blake once more looked at Thomas, wondering why he'd been there if he never spoke. His answer came a moment later. It made his blood run cold, but he feared steam might come out of his ears.

"By the by, if you fail, Lady Cerys will marry Fraser's oldest son."

Blake cocked an eyebrow, refusing to reveal how that announcement made him feel. Instead, he adopted an amused expression, as if to say Murray could try. He would make sure the councilman's son didn't come near his supposed betrothed. He'd run from court with Cerys before she married another man. They filed out of the antechamber.

"Cerys?" Blake worried about her now that no one watched. Torquil slipped back into the Great Hall while they moved farther down the passageway until they found an alcove.

"I'm all right, but I'm scared and angry."

"Nae so all right then." Blake engulfed her in his arms when she stepped into his embrace.

"Would he really marry me to another mon?"

"Aye. But it willna happen, Cerys. I wouldnae ever threaten Thomas's son, but that doesnae mean I wouldnae kill anyone who tried to take ye against yer will. If ye dinna want to marry him, then ye willna."

"What we said in there…"

"Naught has changed, *mo leannan*. If we suit and wish to marry, then we will. But if that's nae what ye want, then ye return to Dunbeath with me, free to marry as ye wish."

"Do you think we should? What if Murray questions you since we have no betrothal contract."

"Murray kens how ye and yer family parted. I doubt he expects them to dower ye. Besides, ma clan doesnae need it and has a history of accepting brides without one."

"You didn't answer my question. Do you think we should?"

"It would give ye more protection, and it would grant me the right to punish anyone who harmed ye. But it would be for a lifetime. When this is over, and ye're safe again, I dinna want ye to regret it. It might nae be so convenient anymore."

"And if I don't think I'll regret it?"

"It's still aboot convenience."

Cerys could tell that was the furthest thing from what Blake wanted. He'd made it clear often enough that he wished to marry her if they were compatible, but he wanted to do it with genuine affection. She wanted to argue that they would likely develop that genuine affection regardless, so why not marry. But she wouldn't push it upon him.

"I need to visit the other taverns, Blake." Cerys

changed the subject, knowing they wouldn't make any headway talking about marriage.

"I dinna like it because it was dangerous before this, but I respect yer reasons. Will ye let me go with ye?"

"I'd hoped you would." Cerys frowned. "You can't. Murray expects you to go to the tavern and drink with those men."

"I can do that after ye make yer rounds and I'm certain ye're safe in yer chamber."

Cerys wasn't fond of the idea that Blake would purposely put himself in Hannay's and his confidantes' path. But she was certain he wasn't thrilled about her going to the taverns, even if he was with her.

"We can go earlier since you're escorting me. The news of our betrothal will spread since I doubt Murray will keep that to himself. It won't be scandalous if I'm with you, especially if we go before it's dark."

"Let's gather what ye need, then Torquil and I will accompany ye."

They went back to the Great Hall, where they found Torquil. Blake dismissed the men, except for those he assigned to Cerys. He ordered them to stand watch outside her door while they were away, and they would have the night shift once she returned. The trio walked through the castle gates twenty minutes later. The brothers walked with Torquil leading, and Blake following behind Cerys. She didn't like not having him walk beside her, but she understood the strategy. She did need someone to guard her back.

142

erys breathed easier as she slipped out of the Merry Widow's kitchens. She'd already stopped at the Picked Over Plum and three other taverns that were less infamous but with whores just as in need of the medicinals Cerys gave away. Besides the woman who'd died in the street in front of her, she saw how unwanted and abandoned children lived in the almshouses. When she first started buying the herbs that prevented pregnancy, the apothecary gave her a derisive look. But his wife, a midwife, soon learned of Cerys and asked why she bought such quantities. Cerys was honest, and in return for her charity, the midwife secretly discounted the price by three-quarters.

With so few people at court and no one to impress, Cerys could save nearly every coin her family gave her. But she knew her time helping the women would draw to an end soon, even if she didn't leave with Blake. Cut off from her family, Cerys was certain she would no longer receive an allowance for her living expenses. That meant she would have no coin to purchase the herbs. The little she had left, she would have to stretch.

Finished with her rounds, Cerys once more fell into

step between Torquil and Blake. The men were prepared to take her through the front door of each establishment, but she insisted on using the kitchens. She argued that it was best for her reputation if not too many people observed her, and she pointed out she couldn't hand out sachets to the women with patrons watching. It was easier for the women to come to her in the kitchens.

When they arrived at Cerys's door, Blake didn't linger, much to their mutual disappointment. They knew he needed to return to The Wolf and Sheep, and spending time alone with Cerys once while it was daytime had been risky. Doing it twice, and when it was nearly dark, was pushing their luck too far. One of the other ladies-in-waiting could still spy them. With a chaste kiss, Blake wished her goodnight. She watched him walk away before shutting her door. Alone, she suddenly felt exhausted. She looked at her bed, remembering the pleasure she and Blake shared there only hours earlier. She knew it would feel lonely climbing into bed alone now that she'd had a hint of what it was like to have a man share it with her. But once she undressed and burrowed under the covers, she was soon asleep.

Cerys woke to something crashing against her door. The portal shuddered before there was another thump. She heard muffled voices as she rose, tossing back the covers and nearly falling out of bed. It took little effort to realize there was a brawl outside her chamber. She hurried to pull her kirtle back on and find her boots while she pulled up her stockings. A loud moan made her pause as she wondered if it was one of her guards. Against her better judgment, she crept to the door and put her ear to it. She heard grunts but no words. It sounded like a small army was outside her door. Then it was silent.

The unexpected cessation of noise gave Cerys pause, but she scrambled to grab her cloak when someone rattled the door handle. Her guards would never enter without permission, and Blake would have announced himself. This could only mean it was one of the unknown nefarious attackers. She had no hesitation now. She darted to the fireplace and stirred the embers until a flame leaped alive. Another sound at the door made Cerys suspect whoever it was tried ramming into it.

When the flames steadied, she pushed a stone near the fireplace that released the latch to a hidden door. She pushed the portal open and reached for the torch she kept on the ground just inside the tunnel. She pushed the end covered in burlap and oil into the fire. As soon as it caught, she pulled back. She slipped into the tunnel and shut the door just before an almighty crash signaled whoever was there had succeeded in breaking through the barrier. Voices flooded the chamber. They weren't raised, so some were hard to decipher. But none sounded happy.

"Where is the bitch?" Cerys was certain it was Stanley. "We saw him bring her back. He didn't fuck her this time."

Dear merciful God, they've been watching. They know Blake stayed in my room earlier. What else do they believe is going on?

"I don't know. I've watched her door for the past two hours. No one has come or gone. They were the same guards as when he left."

Were? Are they dead? Who is that? I don't recognize his voice. Is he one of Stanley's men? Does that mean Shaw and

Domnall are at The Wolf and Sheep distracting Blake? Or did they attack him, too?

Cerys held her breath and turned her back to the secret door when she heard footsteps approach. She shielded the flame, ensuring no light could accidentally shine through a sliver between the stones. Whoever it was didn't linger nearby.

"She didn't jump, that's for sure. We're on the third story. She'd have died." Cerys didn't recognize this third voice either. "Besides, I checked."

"Could there be tunnels?"

How many of them are there? That's another mon I don't know. And I can't linger much longer if they're going to search for the door. I can't risk them finding it.

"Search the walls. Braiden, tell the others to go to the Sinclairs' suite. Break in if you must. No one should be there. Search the chambers." Cerys listened to Stanley issue the order, and once again she wondered how many men were there. She'd heard at least four men, which was double the men guarding her door.

"Do you think we need all six to go? Should we have some search this passageway?" It was the third voice she heard speaking again. Ten men. How much of a fight had the Homes believed her guards would put up if they needed ten against two? She doubted there was much chance either man survived. Guilt flooded her as she imagined them having families and people grieving for them.

"It must be this wall or the one behind the bed. There can't be tunnels along the outside wall or the one along the passageway. Help me look. The bitch knows too much. She isn't going to know aught when I'm done." Stanley's words made Cerys flee.

As much as she wished to hear what else they might reveal, she couldn't linger. If they found the way in, she couldn't risk them seeing her torch's shadows. She lifted her skirts with one hand while holding the torch out with the other. Normally, the rats made her skin crawl, but she cared not as she wound her way through the warren. She smothered the torch when she reached the door that would take her outside. She eased it open, inch by inch, waiting for someone to sound the alarm. When nothing happened, she burst out, slamming it shut in her wake. She sprinted to the tree line and followed it until she reached the path that would take her into town. It was only a ten-minute walk. She just needed to make it to The Wolf and Sheep, but she didn't know if she would.

Blake watched Domnall and Shaw. Something felt off. First, it surprised him that Shaw arrived at The Wolf and Sheep instead of Stanley. He was certain they knew he'd learned of their waylaying Cerys and his men, but neither appeared to care. They'd been sitting together for two hours, going around in circles as Domnall and Shaw fished for information. He wished they would merely ask, but it was clear they weren't going to. He would have to drop hints if he ever wanted to enjoy his whisky in peace. What he really wanted, though, was to return to the castle and check on Cerys. It bothered him that Stanley wasn't there.

"Alasdair must be eager to return to Barsalloch Point. I heard his wife is expecting their sixth bairn." Blake raised his mug in mock toast.

"Bah. Probably a fourth lass. He better hope it's a son, since the one he has is sickly." Shaw shook his head, but Blake caught the glee. The Hannays and Dunbars had been on foul terms for more than a decade. They'd aided the Earl of Salisbury in capturing Laird Dunbar's youngest daughter, Blythe, and his Aunt

Siùsan's cousin, Michail MacLeod. Blythe's oldest sister, Isabella, lived among the Sinclairs. They feuded until recently, when fighting Balliol became more important than fighting each other. At least, it had become more important to the Dunbars.

"I dinna doubt Innes Kennedy is ready for Jamie to return. His nephew is the only heir he has until Jamie's son isnae a bairn anymore."

"The Kennedys are headed home too?" Domnall interjected. His clan and the Kennedys were neighbors. They were peaceful, and Blake guessed Domnall wished it to stay that way. When he inherited the lairdship, Domnall wouldn't want to face Innes or Jamie. Innes had been a mercenary before he became laird. It was no secret that he still went on missions into enemy camps to kill without being seen. The man was as old as Blake's grandfather. Liam still rode out to battle, even in his sixth decade. He had remained at Dunbeath with Alexander because not all of the clan's leaders could go. Blake would never want to face either of the older men on the battlefield.

"Aye. Soon too," Blake added.

"But you're still stuck behind," Shaw mused.

"I didna expect to leave before a fortnight." Blake watched Shaw, his unease growing as the man kept darting his eyes to the door.

"You have someone to keep you here."

"Ma betrothed will travel home with me." Blake shifted, allowing him to see Torquil now talking to Domnall.

"Betrothed," Shaw scoffed. "That won't last beyond your time here. It's just an excuse for rutting with her. Her reputation is already ruined since she's a soiled dove. It doesn't matter that she's not chaste."

Blake drew his longest blade and placed it on the table as he glowered at Shaw. "Ye are nae long for this world, Hannay. Ye are a fool to speak aboot a mon's bride to his face. Ye dinna value yer life to do so to a Highlander. And ye have a death wish to do it to a Sinclair."

"Are you going to gut me right here?" Shaw howled with pain after his taunt served as a challenge. Blake's blade cut across his chest, not so deep as to kill him, but deep enough to leave a massive gash.

"Since ye didna heed ma words of warning, I hope for yer sake that ye heed the warning from ma blade."

"Murray shall hear aboot this."

"Go tittle-tattle like a wean. He'll appreciate being disturbed in the middle of the night." Blake held his blood-covered dirk pointed at Shaw. "Apologize."

"I will not," Shaw blustered, but he howled again as Blake cut another line across his chest, marking a long and wide "X."

"Reconsider." He tilted his head toward where Torquil held a knife beneath Domnall's chin.

Shaw glowered but relented. "My apologies."

"Dinna speak of ma betrothed like that again. Ye ken, just like everyone else, that her father lied aboot the past, and I wouldnae dishonor any maiden. Especially nae ma own betrothed. Ye'd do well to consider yer words before ye speak. I willna be so forgiving again." Blake watched the expression in Shaw's eyes. He saw pain from the wounds, but there was a smugness. It was as though he knew something Blake did not. He was certain now that something was happening to Cerys while he was away from the keep. He dropped coins on the table, signaling the Sinclairs were leaving. "Mind ma words, Hannay. If ye do aught to Lady Cerys, ye will find yer grave that day."

"You talk a lot for a Highlander. I liked you a lot more when you grunted."

"Ye may have only seen me in the lists, Hannay. But

dinna doubt what ye saw because it's only a hint of what I'm like in a real fight. I didna get to this size by licking arses and sitting in pretty clothes." Blake ran his eyes over Hannay, insinuating his disdain. He didn't wait to hear anything else. He led his men out of the tavern. Once they were out of sight, he picked up his pace.

"What goes, brother?"

"Something's happening to Cerys. I dinna ken what, but Hannay hinted at it." Blake broke into a run. The castle gates would close soon. He'd assumed he'd be forced to stay at the tavern most of the night and planned to sleep on a bench. As he rounded a corner, he spied a small figure running toward him. He would know it anywhere. He sprinted until he reached Cerys and caught her in his arms.

"Blake." Cerys's chest burned from running, but she hadn't slowed since she left the tunnel. As his woodsy scent filled her nostrils, she inhaled. After several breaths, she felt her heart slow. The fear subsided from her mind, but her body was still on high alert. She shivered as her initial instinct to flee wore off, and reality set in.

"What happened, *mo leannan?* Why did ye leave the castle?"

"I think your men are dead. There was a fight, then Stanley and his men broke into my chamber. I was already in the tunnel when they came inside. They guessed there must be one. I don't know if they found it or not because I ran. He said I know too much, but I won't know aught once he's done."

Blake's arms draped over her shoulders, shielding her from the world. He looked over her head at Torquil, who stood close enough to hear. The other men fanned out and made a circle around them. The guards gave them room to speak but not enough for anyone to reach them.

"Stanley brought nine men with him. He sent six to raid your suite. Four came into my chamber. I don't think your men survived." Cerys couldn't get that thought out of her head.

"I ken, little one. Ye told me. We will check on them and decide what needs doing. Let's go back. If they ransacked our chambers, Murray must learn of this."

Cerys shook her head against Blake's chest. She was too scared to go back. She didn't want to go anywhere near the keep. She wanted to get on Kitten's back and ride far away.

"I can't stay here. They want me dead. They'll find a way since they know I heard their plans. They said I already talk too much. I don't want you or any more of your men dead because of me. Blake, it won't take them long to know I've left. They'll assume you took me north, back to Dunbeath. Let them go that way. I can go to Kersland."

"Ye'd have us run to yer family?"

"My grandfather fought alongside Wallace. My father and uncles fought for the Bruce." Cerys pulled back and looked up at Blake. "I've been feeding them information since I arrived. It's why they wanted me to stay. I'm certain since they didn't want me at home. It's the only reason they've let me stay here rather than sending me off to the nunnery. I've never had news aboot battles, but I tell them what happens at court. I tell them who's getting along and any gossip. I know what I've told them has made its way back to Murray and his advisors. It's changed their strategies and alerted them to attacks. They will want to know aboot Shaw, Stanley, and Domnall. My father may not care aboot the threats to me, but Uncle Mitcham might. He reminded us that I'm still of their blood. An attack on me is an attack on a Kerr. He won't stand for it."

"I'm nae so convinced ye're safe there, but ye are right aboot them likely heading north. Mayhap we travel toward Kersland, but we dinna cross into yer clan's territory. Or at least we dinna go to yer family's keep. I dinna think it wise for them to see us together. They're already livid that I intervened. I dinna trust them if they believe we're betrothed."

"Married. We must tell them that we're married. That can't be severed like a betrothal. It's a four-day ride from here. We'll pass through Edinburgh. We can do it there. It's only a day and a half from Stirling. They will demand to know which parish registered it."

Blake listened to Cerys, and he saw the sense in what she said. But he hated the idea that they were marrying out of desperation. He felt horrible that his family wouldn't be at his wedding. "We could handfast, lass. It's the same as a marriage, but if ye wish it to end in a year and a day, it can."

"Do you want it to end?"

"Ye ken I dinna. But this is vera rushed."

"Our families could have arranged marriages where we didn't meet the person until we both reached the kirk steps."

"True."

"And we already like one another. We've talked aboot marrying, and we both want it."

Blake knew why he wanted it, and he believed Cerys had sincere feelings for him. But he disliked knowing she also wanted it because she needed his protection. He wasn't convinced she felt as deeply for him as he did for her, but perhaps it would grow into something more for her over time. Before Cerys, he never imagined how much he would want his wife to love him or how much he thought he could love a wife.

His demonstrative relatives made more sense to him now. Even his cousin, Wee Liam Mackay, who married a few months ago had tried to explain how he felt about his bride, Elene. But it had just been words and a vague notion. Now it made sense.

"If that's the case, then we marry before we leave."

"Brother." Torquil stepped forward, his voice a whisper. "Ye both seem to have forgotten ye havenae had the banns read even once, let alone thrice. How are ye going to marry without them?"

Blake looked down at Cerys and swallowed. "We lie."

"To a priest?" Cerys and Torquil said in unison. Blake gestured for them to continue making their way to the castle before the gates closed.

"Aye. Even if we waited until Edinburgh, we'd encounter the same problem. Rather than lie there and claim the banns were read somewhere else, we tell the priest in the town's kirk that we handfasted three months ago. We wish to marry now since ye are expecting a bairn."

Cerys stared at Blake for a long moment before she nodded. Her mind raced with ideas of waking up to Blake beside her, of making love to him, of carrying their child. She saw them walking together into what she imagined was Dunbeath's Great Hall. She pictured them in his chamber—or rather their chamber—in their home. An unbidden thought came to her, and she couldn't believe this was what she wished to know.

"How do you all fit in one castle?"

"Lass?"

"Your grandfather, four couples, and probably a score of weans. How do you all fit?"

Blake chuckled. "Tightly." But his laughter faded as he looked at Torquil. He shared a chamber with his brother. He wouldn't be able to do that if he had a wife.

He hadn't thought about that. "Would ye accept a croft if it were yers to set up as ye wish? Or would ye prefer the keep?"

"Croft." Cerys answered without hesitation. She'd spent her life with people watching her, never having privacy. A croft sounded far better than a castle any day of the week and twice on Sundays.

"We could have one inside the barmekin or in the village. If we lived in the village, I might be able to build ye a larger one. But there are a couple with nay one living in them within the walls."

"Can we decide when we get home?"

Blake loved hearing Cerys say the word, knowing she meant Dunbeath. "Aye, *mo leannan.*"

"Nae to interrupt again, but nay priest is going to marry ye in the middle of the night. Lady Cerys's chamber has already been broken into, and it's likely they've been through ours. We need to figure out where to stay." They arrived in the bailey as the bell clanged and the portcullis lowered. They hurried toward the doors. "We check on Roddy and Ben, then we have to decide what to do."

Torquil didn't speak aloud what hung over the group. They might have to arrange two burials. They'd walked quickly back to the castle as they talked, but they hadn't mentioned the possibly dead guardsmen again. Blake hadn't wanted to upset Cerys, but he had nowhere safe to send her while he dealt with his men.

"Blake!"

Blake and Torquil whirled around. Blake's arm around Cerys's waist brought her in a half circle with him. "Roddy?"

"Aye." A man with one eye fully swollen shut and the other eye mostly swollen shut hobbled toward them gripping his ribs. His other arm hung limply from his shoulder. Bruises mottled every inch of visible skin.

"Bluidy hell, mon." Torquil rushed forward to help support the large warrior's battered body. "Where's Ben?"

"Passed out in the barracks. There were ten of them. Knocked us both out. Must have thought they killed us. Gone by the time we woke. Couldnae find the lady." Roddy labored to breath between sentences.

"Lady Cerys is here. She's hale," Blake said. It was clear Roddy's vision was next to nothing. He must have recognized Blake from his size.

"How?" The beaten guard looked toward Blake's voice.

"Dinna fash aboot that." Blake wouldn't reveal the secret tunnels. "She's safe, and we're relieved ye're alive. We didna ken what we would find. How'd ye make it to the barracks? Ye can barely put one foot in front of the other."

"We both woke to women screaming the bluidy roof down. I thought ma head might cave in. Every mon within the walls must have swarmed that passageway. Hamish and Gordon and a few of their men carried us to the barracks. If I never hear that Lady Wilma's voice again, it will be too soon." Roddy turned his head in what he assumed was Cerys's direction, but he looked into an open space. "She was in a right dither over ye nae being there, ma lady. Said she wouldnae sleep for a sennight. She claimed her chest hurt her and that she feared fainting. She begged guards to stand outside her chamber lest the attackers return."

"She would make it aboot herself." Cerys shook her head, and Roddy turned his head with a groan when he realized he'd spoken to only air. "She'll be in a fine mess until she sees me. Everyone else would do well to let me calm her down, otherwise we all suffer. She does like the attention."

"I couldnae have guessed," Torquil quipped before his brother rolled his eyes.

"Tor, see that Roddy and Ben have all they need. The rest of ye come with us. We're going to Lady Cerys's chamber." Blake glanced down at Cerys. "Pack aught ye need for a fortnight. But it must fit in two satchels."

"Away from court, I can make do with two or three kirtles for that long. I don't need much."

They and the remaining guards with them moved through the keep until they reached the floor that housed the ladies-in-waiting. There was blood splattered on the walls and floor outside Cerys's door. He tried to shield her from it, but she stood and stared. He watched her swallow twice before she reached for her door. She gasped as she found her chamber in shambles. Clothes were strewn across the floor and furniture, many slashed to rags. The room smelled of every toilette bottle she had. She saw the glass on the floor. The chamber had been ransacked.

"Lass, I'm sorry. Are ye all right?"

Cerys could only nod as she took in the disaster. She walked to her chest and looked inside. A pair of stockings and two chemises had survived. She withdrew those and laid them on the bed. She moved to her armoire and pushed back the door hanging from a single hinge. None of her kirtles had survived. Even the three still hanging had rips and cuts. She ran her fingers over them, judging which ones might be salvageable. Only one held any promise. She placed that on the bed with her sewing kit next to it. She looked around on the floor, but there was nothing worth trying to mend. Moving to the table that once held her fragrances and hair ribbons, she found her jewelry box tipped on its side but still closed. She opened it and breathed easier. None of her pieces were harmed or missing. The few items she had were from her mother.

After she placed her jewelry box in the bottom of a satchel, she packed the few clothes she had and the sewing kit. She kneeled beside her bed and reached beneath. She felt around underneath the mattress until she found the coin pouch. She withdrew it and rose. She walked over to Blake, who'd remained quiet and given her space. He'd been the silent comfort she needed.

"This is what I have left from years of saving. The midwife gives me a discount and doesn't tell her husband. I rarely buy clothing or trinkets, so I have most of the allowance my family's sent me since I arrived. It's not much, but it's something."

"Hold onto it, *mo leannan*. That is yer money."

"But it becomes yours the moment we marry. You should know how much there is."

Blake covered her hand with his, keeping the pouch clasped in her palm. "Nay. It was always meant for ye. Keep it to do with as ye wish, lass. I have coin to travel with, so we willna go without."

Cerys knew no man whose wife or daughters could consider the money they were given as freely theirs. It was always an allowance they were permitted to spend, but the money was always their husband's or father's. Blake didn't even peek or try to estimate the contents by holding it. He released her hand and moved to pick up the satchel. Cerys hurried to gather everything scattered on the floor. Habit had her folding the items and stacking them on her bed. There seemed little point in placing anything in the trunk since the clothes were barely better than scraps of fabric. They were likely to end up as rags or in a fire. She wished she could have given them to the almshouses, but they required far more than darning. Once the room was as tidy as she could make it, since she had no means to sweep up the glass, she looked around a final time. She felt nothing.

Blake held the door open as Cerys passed through the doorframe. She looked toward Wilma's chamber and considered checking on her friend. But after the draining experience of weeding through her belongings, she couldn't manage her friend's tendency toward histrionics. She was simply too tired. Blake guided her to the Sinclair suite. It shocked her to find Torquil already there and the chambers untouched.

"Hamish and Gordon said they saw Home trying to shove the door open. When he spied them, he retreated rather than have a confrontation. They were waiting outside the door when I arrived. They've gone back to their chambers, but they said they would return if we needed them."

Blake carried Cerys's satchel through to where he'd slept since they arrived. Their family suit consisted of four bedchambers and a central room. He would prefer to sleep by the fireplace while Cerys took the bed, but he would accept sleeping outside her door if that arrangement made her uncomfortable. She followed him into the room and looked around before her gaze settled on the bed. He couldn't guess what she was thinking.

"I'll sleep on the floor by the fireplace. I'll wait for ye to call me when ye're settled in bed."

"You can't sleep on the floor, Blake. We'll both be riding for the next few days. That doesn't make sense."

"I'll move a chair to yer door and be just on the other side if ye need aught."

"No. You are not sleeping on the floor or in a chair."

"I'm nae comfortable being in a chamber across from ye. I'm a light sleeper, but I dinna want to miss any threat. I canna stand the idea of anyone getting closer to ye than they already have."

"Blake, share this bed with me. It'll be your right to-morrow night as my husband. What does one day matter?"

Blake fisted his hands, the temptation so all-encom-passing that he struggled to remember he had any honor. Despite his cock arguing with him and calling him a fool, he shook his head. "I willna treat ye as a wife until ye are ma wife."

Cerys's cheeks reddened when she realized what he assumed she meant. She stepped close to him and pried his fingers open before she entwined them. She bent their arms and guided his knuckles to her lips. She smattered kisses over them.

"Blake, you are the finest mon I've ever met. I didn't mean we would couple, though I don't think I could turn you away. I merely wish to sleep in your arms. I'm doing everything I can to hide how scared I am. I don't want to look weak in front of the others. But I'm on the verge of sobbing. I just want you to hold me."

"Och, little one. Come here." Blake opened his arms to her and engulfed her. Before she knew what was happening, he scooped her into his arms and carried her to the bed. He sat on the edge and pulled her boot laces free. When the shoes were loose, he pulled them off. He shuffled a little until he could loosen his boots and toe them off. He adjusted his position, so he sat with his back against the wall and his long legs stretched out before him. He eased Cerys against his chest and stroked her hair. His deep voice rumbled in his chest as he hummed to her. She didn't recognize the tune, but it eased the tension consuming her body. It was only moments later that Blake felt her body go lax. He pulled down the covers and tucked her in before going in search of Torquil. He found his brother in his chamber.

"We leave here in time for Prime in the town's kirk.

As soon as the prayer service is over, we convince the priest to marry us. Then we ride."

"To where?"

"Ye to Dunbeath. Cerys and me to Kersland."

"Are ye barmy?"

"Vera likely, little brother. Vera likely."

CHAPTER 13

Cerys looked down at her rumpled kirtle that she'd slept in. She hadn't felt Blake move her or rise from the bed. She'd shifted closer to him in her sleep when he returned and laid down beside her on top of the bedding. She woke to the massive furnace spooning her, a bulky arm wrapped around her waist. It pinned her against him like a steel band. She'd reveled in the feel and noted that she couldn't remember the last time she'd slept so well. But now they stood in their pew in the Stirling kirk. The prayer service drew to a close, and they would soon ask the priest to marry them.

She wished she were marrying in something better than her disheveled gown, but she reminded herself that it was the man she married, not her clothes, that mattered. She'd done what she could to freshen her appearance before they left the keep. She'd run her fingers through her hair before she recalled she had a bejeweled comb among her belongings. She drew it through her long, dark tresses before scrubbing her face and chewing on a mint leaf.

Blake stood beside her in a fresh leine and plaid. He

looked presentable, which only made her feel more discomforted. But she'd seen his expression when she emerged from their shared chamber. There'd been hunger in his eyes as she'd walked toward him. Torquil was still in his chamber, so Blake had seized the opportunity to ravish her mouth. His hands had cupped her bottom, pulling her onto her toes. It was a hint of what was to come once they married. If only they could return to the keep after the ceremony rather than mounting their horses. She knew which stallion she wished to ride.

As the congregation filed out of the church, Blake took Cerys's hand and steered her toward the sacristy. As he often did, Torquil followed on their heels. The door was open, so Blake released Cerys's hand and stepped into the small chamber.

"Father?" The priest jumped at Blake's voice. "I beg yer pardon, but I hoped ye might help me and ma bride. We wish to marry."

"I can post the banns on Sunday. Come back then." The priest barely spared Blake a glance.

"Nay. Today, please, Father. Ma bride and I handfasted four moons ago, but we learned yesterday that she carries our bairn." Blake feared lightening who strike him, and God would smite him for lying in church to a holy man, but he continued. "It will be several sennights before we return home. We wish to marry before she gets any further along."

"You're a Highlander. You're as good as married in your people's eyes." The priest spoke as though Blake were some foreigner, not as though he merely lived in another region of their shared homeland.

"I am. But ma bride isnae. We met here at court, but with—" Blake caught himself before he named David as King, unsure of with whom the priest's loyalty laid.

"Nay monarch in residence, we couldnae ask permission for a formal marriage. But now that ma bride is expecting our bairn, I dinna believe we need anyone's blessing."

The priest looked past Blake to where Cerys stood with Torquil. His gaze dropped to her middle and narrowed. Cerys knew she didn't look pregnant, but she hoped the man would realize it would have been too early for her to show. He looked back at Blake and nodded. The trio moved to the altar with the priest, who kissed his stole before placing it around his neck. The couple turned to face each other and were married in less than five minutes. It felt wholly anticlimactic. Cerys welcomed Blake's kiss, which she thought felt like it lasted longer than the vow exchange. By the time they pulled apart, the priest had disappeared. That left Blake, Cerys, Torquil, and their guards. Roddy and Ben slumped in the last pew while the other men stood guard at the doors.

"What now?" Cerys realized something shifted in her while she said her vows. She'd promised to obey, even though she doubted she'd be any good at that. But now that she'd committed herself to Blake, she found that deferring to him in this came naturally and felt like a relief.

"We gather the horses from the town stables. Tor and the others ride for Dunbeath, and we ride south. In a fortnight, we'll set off for Dunbeath. By then, Shaw and the others will have likely called off the search, and it will be safe to travel north. Tor will be home by then and will explain everything. If the weather holds and they ride long hours, they might even catch our family along the road."

"Are we taking any guards?"

Blake pressed his lips together. He'd run this question through his mind for most of the night. He'd fallen asleep just as the sun peeked over the horizon. He could have laid on the floor or sat in a chair for all the rest he got, but he'd enjoyed having Cerys curled against him too much to think twice about the other choices.

"Nay. It'll be dangerous to go without, but we'll draw less attention if we don't look like nobles."

"Our horses will give that away. They're too fine."

"I ken, but ma hope is that nay one will pay that close attention to us if we dinna have a retinue."

"Mayhap one guard?" Cerys didn't feel as secure as she had a moment ago.

"That's another mon and horse to feed and shelter. If we have only one guard, we look like weak targets. I dinna wish for anyone to look that closely."

It made sense to Cerys, even if she felt uneasy all over again. As she gazed at her new husband, nothing about his size made him look approachable. Few would guess how kind and gentle he could be when he looked like a mountain. She supposed that would protect them, and if anyone was foolish enough to beset them, she nearly pitied them in advance. She didn't doubt Blake's ferocity if he had to protect her. She nodded and smiled as he slipped his hand into hers before they walked to the stables.

She accepted Torquil's well wishes and smacking kisses on the cheek when he lifted her off her feet. She knew he did it to irritate Blake, but the brothers exchanged warm embraces with plenty of back pounding. The group rode out of the town's gates together, but they soon parted ways. Cerys looked over her shoulder as Blake did the same. They waved thrice to Torquil, who also looked back and waved. Then they were on their own.

"It's still early, so we should make it a fair way before nightfall, but I dinna think we can make it to Edinburgh without running the horses into the ground. We can stop at Linlithgow for the night. There we can be Blake and Lady Cerys Sinclair. We should be able to secure a chamber since neither the king nor queen are in residence. The keeper is an abbot, so I hope he wouldnae turn us away."

Cerys nodded. It relieved her that their wedding night wouldn't be spent on the ground. Any other night, she wouldn't mind. But she'd hoped they might have somewhere nice for that night. Then she considered whether Blake intended to consummate the marriage. It was a union she'd pushed for out of convenience. The church's blessing made it permanent, but she wondered if he still felt like they needed to get to know one another better.

"Cerys, I wish to make ye ma wife in truth tonight, but if ye dinna feel up to it after a day on horseback, or ye arenae ready, then ken I'm nae rejecting ye but trying to keep ye hale."

That resolved Cerys's uncertainty. "I want to be your wife in truth, Blake. I—" She paused, uncertain if she should speak her desires aloud. But she figured they would have a long life together, and never had Blake made her feel that she should pretend disinterest. Just the opposite. "I wish we didn't have to wait until tonight."

Blake groaned and shifted in his saddle as his cock came to full attention. It had settled to a semi-aroused state after their kiss, but now it was at full mast. "*Mo leannan*, ye tempt me like the devil. I would find a place in the shadows and have ye right now, but I willna make love to ma wife for the first time the same way some men…"

Cerys didn't need Blake to finish his thought when he trailed off. She knew he meant he wouldn't consum-

mate their marriage the same way some men took a
whore. She appreciated the respect, but it did nothing
to quench her desire. She looked at his strong profile.
The smooth brow, the straight nose, and the chiseled
chin. His cheekbones were angular without being too
prominent. His neck was thick and corded with muscles that ran into his shoulder and disappeared under
his leine. His sleeves were rolled back to show his forearms as his hands held Torque's reins with ease. The
hem of his plaid revealed the end of his powerful thigh
before his boots covered him from midcalf down.

He was as handsome as sin incarnate, and she
wouldn't mind if he took her against a wall or a tree, as
long as he took her. But he was also a hidden romantic.
She wouldn't steal the occasion from him by insisting.
She knew he wished their wedding had involved his
family, even if he never said it aloud. She knew he
wished it could have been more of a celebration for
them and that she'd been able to have a fine kirtle to go
with it. Beneath his brutal appearance laid a soft heart.
One she was rapidly falling in love with.

"I know, *m'eudail*. Linlithgow will be perfect. I worried you might not want to do it so soon."

"Soon?" Blake chuckled. "Ye ken how many times
I've had to walk away from ye since we met. It doesnae
feel nearly soon enough, lass."

It seemed like they'd lived half a lifetime in the past
couple of days, not like they were virtual strangers. His
family believed that sometimes God put the perfect
match into someone's life. They knew it didn't happen
for everyone, but they counted their blessings that
they'd each found the other half of their soul. Blake
knew he'd found his with Cerys.

"It has been rather hard." As soon as the words left
Cerys's mouth, her cheeks flamed. She choked as she
tried to stifle her giggle.

"Aye. Vera hard, lass. Ye have tonight and a lifetime to ken just how hard, *leannan*."

"Promise?"

"Och, aye. And when we stop to water the horses, I shall give ye a hint."

Heat surged through Cerys as she squeezed her thighs, trying to ease the ache in her core. She hadn't been thinking, and Kitten thought it was a signal. Her mount increased his pace, and Torque kept up.

"Trying to make the horses thirsty sooner, lass? I like how ye think."

They rode for a couple hours before they came to a loch's shady shore. Blake lifted Cerys from her horse, sliding her along the length of his body. He was already kissing her by the time her feet touched the grass. Impatience clawed at them both, but Kitten's own impatient snort drew them apart. Blake hobbled both horses, allowing them to drink and graze a patch of high grass near the water's edge. With their hands clasped, the newlyweds walked to the gnarled oak tree that provided the shade.

Cerys and Blake came together in a tangle of arms that were uncoordinated and frenzied. She pulled his leine from his belt, her hands diving beneath and gliding over his smooth skin. Blake hiked up the back of her skirts and grasped her bare backside. Cerys's hip nudged his sporran out of the way before he pressed her backward against the tree trunk. Their hips rocked together. Their mouths were fused, both pulling in air through their noses, unwilling to end their tongues' mating.

Blake's hand released one bottom cheek before he trailed his fingertips over her hip and along the inside of her thigh. Cerys shivered as he teased her, but her knees practically gave out when his fingers brushed along her seam. His hand released her bottom and drew one of hers from his back before he pressed it against his engorged flesh.

"This is mine, Cerys." He dipped his fingers into her opening. "Just as this is yers." He pressed her hand around her cock. "There will be nay others. Never question that I will only ever want ye. Dinna hold back yer desires from me. If ye wish to couple, dinna fear telling me that. But I need ye to be clear that if ye dinna wish to couple, dinna fear telling me that either. I willna ever force ye. Ye must want it too, or it willna happen. And it's always all right if ye dinna want to."

"And if you don't want to?"

Blake chuckled. "I canna imagine an instance where I wouldnae, but if it ever happens, it's nae because I dinna want ye. It'll never be because I want or have someone else. Ye're ma wife to cherish and honor evermore. I meant ma vows. I will be beside ye in all things this life brings. But what the vows didna mention is that I promise that ye are ma equal partner in this marriage. I didna get to ask ye properly. *Am pòs thu mi?*"

"What does that mean?"

"Will ye marry me?"

Cerys chuckled as she gazed at the ring on her finger. They'd used one of her mother's that she'd been given before she arrived at court. She had no memories of a mother, who died the day she was born, so the jewelry was all she had that connected them.

"Ye're a few hours late asking that."

"I ken. But I dinna think the church vows are as special as ones Highlanders exchange when they handfast. I would tell ye ma own promises."

"Will you say them in Scots so I can understand?"

"Aye, sweetheart."

168

Blake unpinned the extra length of plaid at his shoulder and wrapped it around their joined hands. Their gazes met, and Cerys saw the earnest expression she'd come to know, and she saw the tenderness that she felt when he held her. She didn't doubt that whatever he would say, he would mean it from the depths of his soul.

"Ye are Blood of ma Blood, and Bone of ma Bone. I give ye ma Body, that we Two might be One. I give ye ma Spirit, 'til our Life shall be Done. Ye canna possess me for I belong to maself. Ye canna command me, for I am a free person. I pledge ma loyalty to ye, and everything that I own. I promise ye the first bite of ma meat and the first sip from ma cup. I pledge to ye that yers will be the name I cry aloud in the night and the eyes into which I smile in the morning. I promise to honor ye above all others. Our bond is never ending, and we will remain, forevermore, equals in our marriage. This is ma wedding vow to ye."

Tears slid down Cerys's cheeks as she nodded, her throat too clogged with too much emotion to make a sound. Blake brushed his thumbs over her cheeks, a soft kiss following each swipe. He tasted the salt on his lips before he pressed his mouth to hers. She pulled away when she was certain she could speak again.

"I've never heard aught so beautiful."

"We arenae the savages Lowlanders think we are."

"I've never thought that. I don't know aught sufficient to say back." Disappointment filled Cerys since she wished she had such moving words to share.

"I dinna need ye to say aught, *mo leannan*. Ye've trusted me with yer life since the beginning. Ye're willing to follow me now, wherever we go. Ye were willing to come to Dunbeath with me, even when the future was uncertain. Ye have faith in me to protect ye and to be a good husband to ye. That says more than any words could."

Cerys smiled softly. "I think my only fight with your family will be that I have the best husband, and they're all wrong if they think theirs is better."

"That's a fight often had, but it's usually the men arguing over who has the best wife. I already ken I've won that." Blake had replaced the word love twice in his vow, once with loyalty and the other with bond. He wouldn't say an untrue word in his pledge, and he wasn't certain Cerys was ready for any declarations of such a deep sentiment. But he suspected it wouldn't be long before he felt that emotion. He guided Cerys to the ground where they sat for a moment, their hands still bound.

Cerys look around, enjoying the serenity of the spot they'd found. There wasn't a hint of anyone nearby. The horses were content as the grass quivered beneath their noses with each of their exhales. She ran her eyes over Blake before sweeping her gaze across their surroundings again. "Linlithgow will be a welcome place to lay our heads tonight, but there will be other people around. This spot is just ours. Somewhere we can share something that is only between us."

"Are ye saying ye wish to make love here?" Blake wished for the same. He marveled at bucolic scenery, and how it felt like they were in a world where only they existed. He didn't want anyone around who might hear them make love for the first time. He didn't want to share something so intimate with anyone else. He wanted each of his wife's moans and whimpers to be for him only. He didn't want anyone else to hear how his wife brought him incomparable pleasure.

"Yes."

They stood and undressed one another until they stood naked. Cerys had never seen a man in the flesh before, and certainly not a fully aroused one. While she had no one with whom to compare, she suspected Blake's cock far exceeded average. She'd caught a glimpse when she stroked him to release in her chamber, but this was an entirely different view. She ran her fingers over his chiseled abdomen before sweeping her palms over his chest then down his ribs and around to his backside. As she stepped closer to reach, Blake's rod twitched between them, and he groaned. She looked down, and an idea percolated in her mind. She recalled how sensuous and erotic the feeling was when Blake had his mouth on her. All she would need to do was bend forward, and she could take him in her mouth. She wondered if that was something women did.

"Ye look as if ye have a question, *mo leannan*. What do ye wish to ken?"

"Can I—" *Don't be a hen-wit. He's your husband and just swore you could ask aught of him when it comes to our love play. Spit it out.* "Take you in my mouth like you did for me?"

She was mortified. She couldn't believe she'd spoken her question aloud. She was certain she'd lost the last shred of being a well-brought-up young lady. But part of her taunted herself that she didn't care if it meant she pleasured her husband. She watched Blake's face, a moment of surprise, then longing, then caution passed through his eyes.

"Ye can, but I dinna expect it. Most ladies arenae—" *How the bluidy hell do I say this without making it sound like only whores take a mon in their mouth? Shite. 'Most.' That sounds like I ken a great deal aboot what ladies will and willna do with a mon.* "Hell." Blake ran a hand through his hair. He couldn't figure out how to salvage what he wanted to say.

"What? Most ladies aren't what?"

He heard her honest curiosity and saw her confusion. "Ladies who ken aboot such things often dinna wish to do what they consider to be—" Blake tilted his head back. He was making a hash of this. His father had explained to him that he might marry a woman who was adverse to such an intimacy and that he was never to push his wife to do anything she didn't want. Now he had a wife who was curious. He should stop talking while he was ahead. "How do ye ken aboot such a thing?"

"I don't." Cerys shrugged. "I just thought of it. But now I want to know what you were aboot to say. You've stopped twice. Just spit it out, Blake."

"Ladies often think only whores take a mon in their mouth." There. He'd said it. He watched embarrassment fill her eyes, and he loathed that he'd done that. "Cerys, it's nae true. Being a lady has naught to do with what a mon shares with his wife. If it's something ye wish to try, I willna lie and say I dinna want it. But if ye dinna want to or dinna like it, then we find other things to share. But it doesnae make ye aught one way or another. Ye're still ma wife. A woman I adore."

Blake held his breath. It was as close to a declaration of love as he'd ever made. He wasn't ready to profess love, since he still wasn't certain how he felt. But he knew he wasn't lying. He did adore his wee wife.

"I adore you, too." Cerys's voice was little more than a whisper. "I want to try."

"Then ye can. Whenever it feels like a natural part of our lovemaking. It doesnae have to be now." Blake had been admiring Cerys's body since the moment her last stocking fell to the ground. Her breasts were pert and full. Her belly was slightly rounded, and her hips broad. He already knew what her buttocks felt like. Two soft pillows upon which he loved resting his hands. He'd never seen a woman whose body enticed him more. His limited experience had afforded him an opportunity to bed women of different sizes and builds. Cerys was the most perfect he'd ever seen.

He hurried to spread his plaid on the ground, grateful that his height necessitated extra yards of fabric. It gave them plenty of room. They laid on their sides facing each other. Their hands drew lazy patterns as their kisses began quick and short. As they deepened, their hands gripped each other's backsides. Blake eased Cerys onto her back before he kissed along her neck to her collarbone, which he nipped. He moved back up to the tender flesh behind her ear. He pressed a kiss there before he flicked, nipped, then suckled her earlobe. Her breath tickled his skin as her fingers pressed into the divot along his spine.

He eased her arms from around him and held them over her head in one hand. The other kneaded her breasts, alternating with his mouth as he pulled on her nipples. He rolled his tongue over them before grazing his teeth on the distended flesh. He wished to taste her again, but he wasn't ready to abandon her breasts, so he spent several more minutes feasting. He continued to massage them as he eased down her body. Finally forced to release her hands, he slid his forefinger into her sheath, marveling at how her dew pooled between her legs, making the top of her thighs sticky. He licked each drop from her inner thighs before sweeping his tongue over her entrance. He delved his tongue in, following the motion of his finger.

Cerys writhed on the plaid, savoring each touch as Blake made her body come alive. Having no clothes as a barrier or worrying about someone overhearing them, freed her to enjoy every moment of their lovemaking. She moaned without reservation, discovering each sound drove Blake to elicit more. His lips encased her bud as he drew it into his mouth, his tongue doing wonders as the bundle of sensitive nerves pulsated. She didn't know how long they'd been on the plaid when she felt the hints of her climax. It could have been mere minutes or hours. She had no concept of time in a world made up of only Blake and her.

Blake felt Cerys's core tightening around his fingers as he moved them within her and along her netherlips, varying where he spent his focus. As he knew she drew close, his thumb replaced his mouth as he rubbed circles over her button. He feasted on her breast, squeezing it with his hand to allow more into his mouth. Her body undulated beneath him as she moved her hips, seeking the release he would bring her. When it crashed over her, Blake eased his cock between her legs.

"Look at me, *mo leannan*. I would see ye as we claim each other."

"Mine." Cerys breathed the single word, and Blake could no longer wait. He thrust into her, wincing when she went rigid. He hated causing her pain, drawing away any of her pleasure. But he'd waited until the moment she went lax but still felt the euphoria from a climax. He'd hoped it would lessen the pain. She shuddered and squeezed her eyes shut, but with the next breath, she sighed.

The sense of fullness wasn't one to which she had a comparison. It felt odd and uncomfortable to a certain degree, yet she craved it and never wanted it to end. She noticed Blake's worried mien and how he held himself still. She knew he did it out of consideration for her, and her heart swelled. She hadn't exaggerated when she told him how she felt. She adored the boyish charm she'd seen glimpses of. She adored the decisive warrior. She adored the devoted husband. And she adored the attentive lover who waited for her to be ready. She tilted her hips in what she hoped was an invitation for him to move. He slipped deeper into her, and their combined sounds of bliss filled the air.

"I never want to leave ye, *mo leannan*. I never imagined something could feel so divine. But I'm sorry I hurt ye."

"Shh. I know, Blake. You didn't do it on purpose, and it's passed. I feel like I need to move, like I want you to move. I'm restless." Cerys's brow furrowed as she tried to make sense of demands her body was making that she didn't understand. Blake drew his hips back before pressing forward. He was slow, drawing out their need, but also mindful not to hurt her. Not only had she been a virgin a moment ago, but he was a large man everywhere. He knew he could injure her if he wasn't careful.

Cerys lifted her hips to match each thrust, urging Blake on as she grew more familiar with the sensations. It wasn't long before she begged him for more. At first, she didn't know if she wanted it faster or harder, then she realized it was preferably both. Each time he surged into her, she pressed his buttocks, holding him in place for a moment before he withdrew and did it again. Over and over, they moved in tandem as sweat dripped over their bodies. They both sought release, but neither wanted their first time together to end.

Cerys grabbed his jaw and drew him close, pressing her mouth to his as another wave of pleasure crashed over her. Her movements, including her kiss, were frenetic until the climax crested, and she eased over the peak. Blake continued to thrust, circling his hips, making Cerys moan again. The sound made him piston his cock into her harder. He felt compelled to dominate her body until she surrendered. As if she intuited his need with a shared one of her own, she held onto him and closed her eyes. She let his movements carry her away, as though she soared into the clouds rather than pressed against the ground. She followed his lead until she felt the now-familiar sensations.

"I'm so close again, Blake. It feels—oh, God. Blake!" She cried out as the most powerful climax she'd experienced yet held her in its grips. "I want you to feel the same thing."

"I am. I'm there. Cerys!" Blake thrust once more and held himself inside her, deep within, all the way to his bollocks. His cock pulsed with each jet of his seed. It seemed to go on for forever, and he relished every moment. Whether with another woman or by his hand, he'd never had such a momentous climax. His arms shook as he held himself over Cerys as the last sparks of pleasure ebbed.

"You won't squash me." Cerys tried to draw his body down to hers. He lowered himself, giving her some of his weight but ever careful not to hurt her. Her knees bracketed his hips as she clung to him. He felt her contented sigh as she lay beneath him. He looked at her face and found her eyes closed as she panted. Despite her labored breathing, her expression was serene. "That was amazing, Husband."

"Say it again."

"That was—"

"Nay. The last part. Say that."

"Husband."

"Good God, Wife. Naught has sounded sweeter to ma ears."

"Say that word again." Cerys wanted to hear it again as much as Blake had wanted to hear her.

"Wife. Ma wife."

"I am." Cerys grinned as Blake peeled away hair plastered to her temple. "That was perfect. And now I could sleep for a moon of Sundays. I ken we need to go, but can I just hold you for a little longer?"

"Aye, *mo leannan*. I wish to hold ye, too."

"*M'eudail*, I will remember this always. No first time could have ever been better."

They rested in each other's arms after Blake rolled them, so he laid on his back. Cerys rested her head against his chest, wondering if one day they could fall asleep together just like this.

inlithgow Castle loomed before them as the
sun set, casting rays of soft light against a red
and orange backdrop. They'd rested along the loch's
shore for another half an hour after they coupled.
They'd been tempted to join again, but both accepted
Cerys would already be sore, both from riding and
their first time. They didn't want to make it worse,
which was wise because Cerys wound up riding with
Blake, her legs over Torque's left flank. She'd winced
one too many times, so Blake plucked her from her
saddle and nestled her against him between his mus-
cled thighs. They'd ridden into the wind, so he
wrapped the extra length of wool around her, then he'd
encircled his arm around her, and she melted against
his chest. The cocoon, his heat, and the horse's gait
lulled her. But she fought to stay awake, reveling in the
feel of being tucked against her husband. Now they
would seek shelter for the night, and she prayed a bath.
Hot water would ease her discomfort since she intended to make love again.

"Abbot Casters, we seek shelter for the night. Would
ye have a chamber ma wife and I could use?"

"A chamber?" That single question announced the

abbot recognized them as nobles, despite their dust-covered clothing. A noble couple often occupied separate chambers, whereas peasants or gentry would share without question.

"Aye. We dinna wish to inconvenience ye, and I would feel better kenning ma wife is with me."

"Do you not believe you are safe here?"

"I believe I'm a newlywed." Blake hoped that would suffice. When the priest's eyebrows flew to his hairline, then a knowing smile plastered across his face, he figured it did.

"Felicitations. Where do you head?"

"South." Blake was still gaging what he could reveal to the priest. He seemed like a friendly man, but he was still a stranger. Being a man of the cloth guaranteed nothing.

"Where did you come from?" The abbot canted his head. "Besides from north."

"Stirling. We're going to visit ma wife's people before we return to our home in the Highlands."

"Yes. You're a Sinclair. We don't have many in these parts." Blake couldn't deduce anything from the man's tone. It was clear he knew plaid patterns since he hadn't introduced himself yet.

"I'm Blake, and this is ma wife, Lady Cerys Sinclair."

"Lady Cerys? As in Lady Cerys Kerr?"

Alarm bells rang in both Blake and Cerys's heads. Why would he know who she was? Why would it matter?

"Yes, Abbot. I was until I became a Sinclair." Cerys said it with pride, and Blake's heart filled to bursting.

"You're an unlikely pair. A Sinclair and a Kerr. Does that mean there's a truce between your clans?"

"We werenae feuding." Blake wanted to cross his arms and widen his stance, but being defensive would get them nowhere. "We've been at odds."

"Och, that's one way to put it. The Kerrs who passed through here a few days ago weren't of the opinion that it was merely being at odds. Lady Cerys, your father and uncles oppose this union, though they didn't describe it as marriage."

Cerys's cheeks burned at the indignity. "I can assure you Stirling's kirk has us registered, and its priest performed the ceremony. I am at odds with my family."

"I see you're both given to understatement. Well, we can't stand out here all day. You're in time to join us for Vespers." The abbot didn't wait for them to follow but made his way to the keep's kirk. Blake wrapped his arm around Cerys's waist as they entered the small structure. They slipped into a back pew as the small congregation filed in. The castle employed a sizable staff, but with no laird or other noble in residence, the kirk felt half empty. With no one paying attention to them, the couple went through the prayer service with their hands clasped. There was an air of uncertainty after their conversation with the abbot, and both felt more confident with the contact as a sign of solidarity.

When the evening service concluded, they trailed behind most of the people until they reached the Great Hall, where the meal was ready to be served. Blake guided Cerys to a lower table, but a middle-aged woman approached.

"I heard we had nobles joining us. I've set a trencher on the high table for you. My lady, a bath will be in your chamber when you finish."

"My thanks. I'd hoped for such a luxury." Cerys's appreciation was genuine, and the older woman beamed.

"I heard you're newlyweds. Don't fear. This won't be a long meal." The woman winked at Blake before spinning on her heels. They made their way to the raised dais and took the steps. The abbot already sat in the center seat, the one usually reserved for royals or lairds. He looked at home presiding over the castle's occupants. Cerys steeled herself for whatever would come next. She doubted the man was finished prying.

"Lady Cerys, if you are at odds with your family, then why do you travel south?"

"The Kerrs arenae the only clan south of here," Blake interjected. "We are bound to the Johnstones and the Dunbars. Ma father's cousin is married to a Johnstone, and Lady Isabella, who lives among us, is still close to her Dunbar family."

"But is that where you head?" The abbot was persistent.

"Aye." Blake shoveled a bite of food into his mouth, his knee nudging Cerys to do the same. They couldn't speak if they kept their mouths full. Each time the abbot opened his mouth to speak, they took another bite until they were both nearly to the point of discomfort. Cerys noticed servants carrying the tub and buckets abovestairs.

"Abbot, your housekeeper arranged for a bath. It looks like they're preparing it. I wouldn't want to keep them waiting or for it to go cold."

"And I havenae seen the chamber yet. Ma wife doesnae go without me."

"Back to thinking she isn't safe?"

"I'm a possessive mon with a beautiful wife. I trust ma wife, but I dinna trust anyone else."

"You are a Sinclair."

Blake tried not to glower. The men in his family were not possessive so much as devoted and protective. None kept their wives from doing anything they wanted or going where they pleased with whom they wished. He'd said it as an excuse. He didn't appreciate the derision in the abbot's voice.

Bluidy Lowlander. So much for welcoming all sheep into his flock.

Cerys and Blake excused themselves and made their way abovestairs. They found their satchels were already placed at the foot of the bed, and the servants soon filed out of the room. Once Blake was certain the door was secured with the lock and bar, he moved to Cerys's back and pulled the laces loose. He'd tied them for her with ease, and he knew it had made her uncomfortable. He'd told her about his younger sister, Maisie, and how she did everything Blake and Torquil did, including exploring a sea cave in the cliffs beneath Dunbeath. It meant he'd tied her gowns countless times. He'd told the truth when he said he'd never dressed another woman.

Now he pushed the gown over her shoulders and down her arms until it rested at her waist. His hands slid around to her breasts as he pulled her back against him. He kneaded the mounds, tweaking the nipples until they pebbled. He kissed beneath Cerys's ear as her hands reached back and fisted his plaid. She tugged on the fabric before reaching back and fumbling with his belt. Blake released her long enough to whip off his clothes and shuck off his boots. When he was bare, he slid his arms back around her.

"That tub is far larger than I expected, *mo leannan*. I've had a fantasy since I met ye. Can ye guess?"

"I think it's large enough for two, husband. Will you wash my hair if I scrub your back?"

"I will wash all of ye, wife." Blake closed his eyes as he continued to enjoy the feel of Cerys's breasts in his hands. He felt the chemise fall loose and cover his wrists. He pushed it and the kirtle to the floor, where it pooled around Cerys's ankles. She kicked off her boots and drew down her stockings. He resumed his ministrations until he could wait no longer to suckle. He turned Cerys and wrapped an arm beneath her backside, then lifted her high enough to bring her breast to his starving mouth. She rested her hands on his shoulders, not for balance since she didn't fear falling, but because that's what she could reach.

The head of Blake's cock rested against her mons, making her want to shift until she could take him into her. She wrapped her legs around his waist and tried to press her weight down. Blake loosened his hold, and her sheath enveloped his sword. She thought her moan sounded like one of pure pleasure, but Blake froze.

"I'm all right, Blake. You didn't hurt me. It feels so good. Would that I could stay in your arms just like this all day, every day. I could go aboot my day pointing to things and asking people to help, so I could keep my husband with me."

"That would be a sight in the lists. The men would envy me, but I wouldnae be able to train. And I dinna wish for anyone, especially any mon, to see what we share."

"That would be unfortunate. I wouldn't want any woman seeing what we share, either. I find you're not the only possessive one. I trust you, husband, but I trust no one else." Cerys grinned, her words teasing.

"Mayhap I should show ye just how possessive I am, wife."

"Yes, please."

Blake walked them to the tub and climbed in. He was cautious not to trap Cerys's legs as he sat. They shifted and found a comfortable position. The hot water eased their weary muscles, but it added a layer of eroticism that hadn't been there when they coupled under the oak tree. Immersed, with steam rising around them, the lapping sensation urged them to move. They were in no hurry. Each thrust and roll of the hips was slow and drawn out. Blake's hands settled once more on her bottom. He was certain her backside had been made just to fit his palms and fingers precisely. His mouth craved her breasts just as his hands longed to hold her buttocks.

Cerys's fingers wove through Blake's hair as her other hand cupped his jaw. She raised his chin and claimed a kiss, eagerly leading this joining. She rose and fell on his rod, clenching with each descent. It elicited one groan after another from Blake, and the sounds made her hungry for more. She circled her hips twice, before Blake let go of his control. He gripped her flesh as he drove her down onto him over and over, his hips rising in unison with her movement.

"Tell me if I hurt ye, *leannan*," Blake panted.

"Don't stop. This feels too bluidy good to hurt." Cerys tugged his hair to reinforce her command. Blake growled, making her giggle. But they soon made only sounds of pleasure as she pressed her mouth to his, their tongues twirling.

"*M'ionmhas*," Blake murmured as his hands cupped her jaw. The feeling as they kissed was incredibly intimate and arousing to Cerys. As she cupped his jaw, she wondered if he thought the same. She had her answer when Blake spoke again. "I've never felt a connection like this to anyone. I never imagined such intimacy. It's ye, Cerys. It's always been meant to be ye."

"My heart was only meant to be yours, Blake."

"Ye already have mine, *m'ionmhas*."

"What does that mean?"

"My treasure. What we have is a rarity, and ye're priceless."

"How do you say my heart?"

"*Mo chridhe*."

"That's what you are. *Mo chridhe*." Cerys's kiss was passion filled and needy, and Blake met it with equal measure. Blake surged into her, pinning her to his pelvis as he ground against her pubic bone. It sent Cerys up in flames. Her moan filled the chamber as her head fell back, and her eyes closed in bliss. The sight was too much for Blake. His cock erupted, and he was certain his fingers would leave bruises on Cerys's ivory flesh, but he couldn't let go, couldn't ease his hold until the last drop left him. Cerys's sagged forward, her head against his shoulder as he wrapped his arms around her.

They hadn't declared their love, but they'd both felt it. They'd shared desire and lust since they met, but their lovemaking under the tree and now were manifestations of much longer lasting emotions. They'd bound their lives with their words, but they bound their souls with their bodies.

Cerys lifted her head and pressed her forehead to Blake's. They exchanged tender kisses as the euphoria wore off. Affection replaced passion as Cerys stroked his temple, and Blake feathered his fingers along her spine.

"Is it always like that?"

Blake understood Cerys's question. He knew it was both curiosity and self-doubt. "It's never been like being with ye. I kenned it would be different. It would mean something. A person can couple for the physical release and enjoy it. It can be satisfying in the moment. But it doesnae compare to being with someone who makes yer heart happy."

"Do I do that?"

"Vera much, lass."

"That's why I wish to call you *mo chridhe*. You make my heart happy, too."

"Ma generation is vera different from when ma uncles were ma age. Ma brother and the aulder male cousins and I have some experience, but really just enough to ken what we're doing. Ma uncles didna have the foresight to understand what ma grandda tried to teach them. Uncle Tristan isnae a Mackay, so he didna have ma grandda to guide him. But Uncle Callum thought to enjoy himself before he one day becomes laird. Uncle Tavish planned to remain unwed because he feared loving, then losing, a woman like ma grandda did with ma grandmama. I understand what they've said for years. Ye can dally with someone and enjoy the moment, or ye can love someone and enjoy the lifetime."

Cerys and Blake locked gazes as she nodded. He still hadn't professed love, and neither had she responded. They both needed more time for the emotions to continue to develop. But they shared the optimism that they had found their match.

As they washed each other, they laughed about how they avoided answering more of the abbot's questions. It led to them learning more about each other's favorite foods, which led to favorite colors, holidays, animals, and various childhood memories. They remained in the water until it grew cold, and their fingers and toes pruned. They dried each other as they continued to talk, then they sat before the fire while Cerys's hair dried. They learned things about each other they supposed couples who chose one another would usually share before they married.

Blake told tales of his family, and Cerys grew more eager to meet them with each story. Some were funny and some were heartbreaking, but every one shared the same theme. A family bound by a deep and abiding love and loyalty to each other and their clan. Cerys could never describe her experience with her clan of birth like that. She supposed others might, but as a child without a mother and with a disinterested father, she'd felt alone when she saw how her cousins were as siblings. She'd been close to them, but it had never felt the same as being siblings. And Blake had so many cousins, where Cerys only had five. She pictured roaming bands of children of varying ages tearing across Dunbeath's bailey and out into the rolling hills that surrounded the castle. She imagined them swimming when Blake shared how they often picnicked as a family and everyone enjoyed being in the water, even if it was nearly always freezing. By the time they climbed into bed, she felt like part of the family.

Blake woke to the sound of hooves clattering into the bailey. He glanced at the fire, which was still burning as brightly as when they went to bed. He touched his hair and found the ends still a bit damp. He realized they must have only retired an hour ago if that. They'd both fallen soundly asleep once Cerys wrapped her arm around Blake's abdomen and rested her head on his chest. He'd encircled her with his arm, and they'd drifted off.

The sound wasn't what he expected and was out of place, even if the night was still young. He extracted himself from Cerys, but she stirred and opened her eyes.

"What's wrong?"

"I dinna ken. Someone's arrived, and it's an odd hour. There must be nearly a score of whoever's come." Blake made his way to the window embrasure and stood against the wall, pushing back the hide covering just enough to peek out. "Shite. We need to go."

"What? Who's there?"

"All three of them and their men. Hurry. Dress and we slip down the servants' stairs. We wait until they're inside before we go to the stables. We canna dally. They'll close the gates soon, and they'll hear we arrived before they even get their own chambers."

Cerys was half dressed by the time Blake finished

talking. Watching Blake pleat his plaid with ease and speed threatened to distract her, but she forced herself to do her laces while she watched. Fortunately, neither had unpacked their satchel, so they were soon sneaking out of their chamber and down the passageway.

"How'd they know?" Cerys whispered as they entered the stairwell.

"I dinna ken. They may just be on their way home and passing through. Poor coincidence." Whether it was or not, Blake didn't intend for them to remain long enough to learn. They reached the first floor near the kitchen. He carried both satchels crisscrossed over his chest. He took Cerys's hand but kept her behind him. His much-larger frame would shield her from anyone who approached from their front. They slipped along the passageway until they reached a door that led outside. They could hear the swell of voices from the Great Hall and knew the men were entering.

Blake looked around, but given the hour, the bailey was empty except for stablehands tending to the newly arrived mounts. He guided Cerys across the expanse until they reached the stables. They didn't speak as they saddled their steeds and walked them to the doors. Most of the horses were now in stalls. No one said anything to them, and it relieved them how quickly the servants retired. But it made Blake worry that the gates were already closed. There were no secrets tunnels they knew about to smuggle them out.

They entered the bailey just as a guard began cranking the portcullis shut. Blake tossed Cerys into the saddle before swinging into his. They hurried forward and laid low over their horses. They ignored the guards calling out a warning, barely making it beneath the deadly teeth of the lowering gate. They were soon free and back on the road. None of the guards tried to stop them once they were outside the barmekin, so they galloped until they could no longer see the keep.

"Domnall and Shaw will head west soon, but Stanley will follow us. His home isn't more than a couple day's ride from where my clan lives."

Blake noticed she didn't say her own home. He liked that she already considered Dunbeath home. Or at least he wanted to think that was it. It could be she merely no longer considered herself a part of the Kerrs after what her father did.

Blake surveyed what he could see, which was very little. The moon was behind a cloud cover, which was likely what brought the men to Linlithgow if they weren't following them. It wasn't safe for their horses to remain on the road in such conditions. They risked injuring their mounts. But he also didn't feel safe stopping so soon. He needed them to put more distance between them and their nemeses. He considered having them dismount and lead the horses, but that wouldn't get them away fast enough if the men learned they were nearby. He slowed Torque from a canter to a trot, and Kitten followed.

"It's too dark to go any faster, but we need to get farther away before we can stop."

"Do you think they'll come after us tonight? They must know by now that we were there. I doubt the abbot kept that a secret."

"I doubt it too. We'll ken if they're tracking us if they do follow." Blake once again looked around. They approached a meadow to their right. It swept back around to a forest that lay behind them. An idea struck Blake, and he prayed he was doing the right thing. "We turn off here and go back to the woods. We hide there until we see them go past. Rather than lead, we follow. They may continue home without a care aboot us, or they will think they're chasing us."

"All right."

"The grass is too tall for the horses to see where they're placing their hooves. We walk them." Blake dismounted and prepared to help Cerys down. But she was on her feet just as he landed on his.

"I'll gladly accept your help when we aren't in a hurry."

"Ye just like having me touch ye, dinna ye, lass?"

"Yes." Cerys's teeth shone in the dark as she grinned. They each took hold of their horse's bridle and led the animals into the pasture. The ground was uneven in places, so they were grateful Blake was cautious. It took them half an hour to cross the field and enter the trees. They stayed back from the road far enough not to be spotted but close enough that Blake was confident they would hear if a score of horses rode past. They didn't dare unsaddle their steeds lest they be unprepared to flee. Blake looked at Kitten as he drew Cerys onto his lap and wrapped his plaid around her. He knew Torque was trained not to make a sound, even if he smelled other horses nearby. He wasn't certain Kitten would know not to nicker or whinny. They would have to wait and see.

CHAPTER 15

Cerys watched Kitten's ears flicker before her gaze darted to Torque. The horse's eyes shifted, but he didn't move. It was as though the mighty beast held his breath. Kitten's head swung in the direction of the approaching riders. But he made no noise. He turned as still as Torque. They'd only been hiding for about ten minutes before Blake squeezed her and put his finger to his lips. He pointed to the ground and shook his hand palm down. She knew he meant he felt the vibration. She couldn't hear anything until a couple minutes later. Then it sounded like an entire army. She kept watching Kitten. Her steed didn't even flinch. She would feed him every apple and carrot she could find.

It felt like forever before the last horse was audible. Blake moved Cerys to sit beside him before he crouched and drew his sword. He turned in a full circle, not because he sensed anything but in case he didn't. He made a gesture for Cerys to stay before he crept toward the road. He wouldn't go far enough that he couldn't sprint back to his wife in a few steps, but he wanted to ensure none lingered.

It was as he feared. Two men with swords drawn inched toward him. He saw their outlines and moved

191

behind a tree. When the men's pace didn't increase and neither cried out, he figured they hadn't seen him. He waited until they stepped past him before he moved. He came around from the back and cleaved one head, then the other, from the men's shoulders. Blood sprayed him, and he regretted that he would return to Cerys with evidence of what he'd done. He felt no guilt since they would have harmed her, but he didn't want to frighten her. He felt around the men and found two dirks on each of them. Her dirks had been missing from her chamber when they left. She didn't realize it until after they'd departed Stirling. She had no weapons of her own, so he felt better arming her.

He wiped his blade on one man's chest. He leaned over the other and cut a swatch of fabric from the doublet. He used it to wipe his face, neck, and hands. There was nothing he could do about his leine. He would change it as soon as he could. When he returned to where he'd left Cerys, he found her mounted on Kitten with Torque's reins in her hands. She swung down and ran to him. Uncaring about his stained leine, she flung herself into his arms.

"I heard two thuds and feared one was you. I was ready to ride if it wasn't you who came through the trees, but I don't know if I could have left you." Cerys squeezed her arms around Blake's waist, uncaring that his sword hung in the way.

"Wheest, little one. There's naught to fear among the trees anymore. But we canna stay. They'll notice when their men dinna return. They'll send someone back. We move farther into the trees before we cross the meadow again."

As they moved deeper into the forest, it was so dark they had to walk with an arm stretched out, sweeping from side-to-side and glide their feet along the ground to avoid tripping. When they finally went far enough that Blake felt comfortable entering the exposure of the meadow, it was so dark he could barely see Cerys or the horses. They walked between the mounts, so he took her hand, not wanting them to get separated.

They'd walked halfway across the meadow when Blake squeezed her hand and stopped. She turned to look at him and could barely tell he stood beside her. It was the darkest night she could remember. When she turned to look forward, she squinted and jutted her chin out in disbelief as she saw something flicker. It was surely a campfire. She swept her gaze away from the flame she spied and spotted two more. The very people they'd tried to allude, they'd stumbled upon. Blake tugged on her arm and led them back to the road. She tried to stop, not understanding why he would bring them closer, but he tugged again. She deferred to him, pushing aside her fear, and trusting Blake would do nothing to endanger her.

They inched their way across the meadow, cautious not to make a sound. Blessedly, the horses seemed to sense the dire situation and remained silent except for the soft crunch of the grass beneath their hooves. When they reached the road, Blake led them across to a hill. They wound their way around it until they were once more in front of the other riders. With no safe place to hide, and since it remained too dangerous to stay close to Shaw, Domnall, Stanley, and their men, they walked all night. They arrived at the outskirts of Edinburgh before noon. They'd mounted at dawn and ridden hard.

❧

Cerys inhaled the meat pie Blake bought her. She'd wolfed it down despite how it burned her tongue and the roof of her mouth. She hadn't cared about the crumbs dropping from her lips. Her stomach started rumbling nearly two hours outside Edinburgh. Blake had laughed, but she felt badly when he offered her one of his. He'd bought three for himself and one for her. She worried they'd both be hungry if he shared. He'd assured her he would feast on the tastiest honey that night, so he didn't worry about being hungry now. She'd flushed and accepted half the meat pie, insisting he kept the other half. It proved enough to fill her.

Blake knew Cerys and their horses were exhausted, but they couldn't stop when they reached the town. He bought food for Cerys and him, but he urged them to continue walking until they passed Holyrood and approached the Firth of Forth. He prayed that any pursuers wouldn't cross the town to search for them. It was market day and took them nearly an hour to get to the firth's shore. Blake spotted a stream, but he wasn't certain if it flowed into or from the firth. He strode to the edge and scooped up a handful and dipped his tongue into it, relieved to find it was freshwater. He spied a spot near the water where there was nothing but grass, so they led the horses to where they could drink and graze.

"How do ye fair, *mo leannan?*"

"All right." She wouldn't complain about the blisters on her feet. She wouldn't complain about the bruise that formed on her calf when she'd banged it against a fallen tree limb. She wouldn't complain about her thirst. She wouldn't complain about any of the myriad aches and pains she had from walking and riding for so long. She knew it would only worry Blake more and make him feel guilty. She knew he was doing his best, and none of it was his fault. Even if they'd traveled with all the Sinclair guards, the Hannays, Cunninghams, and Homes outnumbered them. They were likely luckier to only be a couple. They could hide easier and blend in.

Blake had hated it, but he'd slipped into a pair of breeks just before they reached Edinburgh. He explained he had them with him for this reason, to blend in with Lowlanders. It had shocked her when she heard Blake speak to the food vendor. Gone was his Highland burr, and in its place was a modulated Lowland accent. He'd winked at her when the vendor turned his back. He told her he was always proud to be a Highlander, but there was a time and place for showing that in the Lowlands. That didn't happen to be now.

"How aboot you?"

"I'm well, *mo leannan*. Dinna fash." Cerys much preferred his brogue now that they didn't fear anyone hearing them.

"It's a little late to tell me that. You shouldn't have married me if you didn't want me to worry aboot you."

"Och, ma bonnie bride. Will ye minister to ma needs, so ye dinna need to worry?" Blake's eyes sparkled as he waggled his eyebrows.

"Get us out of this town and get back into your plaid. Then I can see aboot ministering to your needs." Cerys swept her tongue over her top lip in what she knew was an overly suggestive move. Blake pounced and pressed her against the ground.

"Cheeky. If we werenae in public, I would be inside ye already. Ye tempt me too much. I will remind ye of yer teasing later. I shall have ma own back on ye."

Cerys didn't think she liked the sound of that. She feared she might combust if he ever decided to tease her when they were intimate. She shook her head before twisting to look around. Satisfied they were alone, she drew his face to hers and kissed him. She felt his rod thicken against her hip. The breeks left nothing to the imagination, which was why Blake pulled away with a woeful sigh.

"I know we can't stay here too long. What do we do next?"

"We're going to see if we can get a boat to Lamberton."

"Lamberton? That's practically England."

"Aye. We'll be closer to the Sassenach than I like, but yer family's keep sits on the border. It'll be a day and a half's ride to Cessford Castle."

"You think we should go to my father after all?"

"I think we get close enough that it gives us protection if anyone continues to pursue us."

Cerys looked skeptical, but it had been her idea to flee back to her family. She'd hoped they could follow Blake's earlier suggestion, either not enter the territory at all or not get that close to her former home. From the sound of it, Blake intended to take them practically to the keep's doorstep.

"You can't wear your plaid anymore, and I need something to cover my hair. It'll be too recognizable to anyone on Kersland." Her nearly raven tresses were darker than the hair of anyone she knew. She'd inherited them from her mother, and she stood out among the nearly white-blond hair her family mostly shared. "I wish I'd known my mother's people."

"Who was she before she married?"

"A Johnstone. She was your father's cousin's wife's cousin. She and Arabella grew up together. When my mother died after Arabella married Lachlan and went to Dunrobin, there were no ties left to her clan. My father never took me there, and no one came to visit. If we showed up there, I doubt we'd receive any warmer a reception than a pauper."

"What was her name?" Blake's voice was soft, uncertain if talking about her mother specifically was painful for Cerys.

"Eleanor," Cerys whispered. "She'd been barely six-

and-ten when I was born. She was a few years younger than Arabella, but they'd been close from what my aunt Matilda told me. It was my aunt who raised me. Her husband died in the first war, and she was barren, so she never had to remarry."

"It must have been hard to leave home for court."

"Yes and no. I still miss Aunt Matilda and my cousins, but it was hard having no siblings when everyone else had brothers and sisters. It was hard not having a mother, and only Aunt Matilda took interest in me. My uncles' wives never did. They were busy with their own children. Even before what happened with Arthur, my father was distant. He remarried twice while I was a wean. Both women died giving birth to stillborn sons. After his third wife died in childbed, he swore off marriage. He didn't need an heir anyway."

They continued talking about their childhoods until Blake was certain the horses had enough rest. They went to the harbor and tried to find a boat that would take them south. All but one captain refused to take a woman aboard their vessel, claiming it was bad luck. With several coins in hand, the final captain agreed. They boarded with their horses and sat in the bow. Cerys had her cloak, but Blake had nothing to shield himself from the wind and spray. His plaids were in his satchel, but he couldn't pull them out unless he wanted people to recognize he was not only a Highlander but a Sinclair. The one great danger to Blake's plan was they would land in the heart of Home territory.

Several hours later, they disembarked in Lamberton. It was late afternoon, and once more they were hungry. They made their way to the public stables, where Blake paid for hay and stalls for their horses. They wandered to the tavern closest to where they left their mounts. Cerys hesitated, but Blake assured her.

"It took us only a few hours to get here. It will take

Stanley nearly three days to get here from Edinburgh. That's assuming they went there. We will be on yer clan's land before he reaches his."

Cerys nodded and walked through the door when Blake held it open. Warm air blasted in their faces, and they were greeted by a noisy crowd. It was the last thing Blake wanted. More eyes on them, but he hoped they could blend in until he secured a chamber for the night. He wrapped his arm around Cerys's shoulders, and she gladly pressed against his side as they walked to the bar. A harried woman poured ale and barely spared them a glance.

"A chamber and a meal, please." Once more, Blake's Lowlander accent was in place.

"You're not from here."

Blake wanted to say what local asked for a chamber in an inn if they had a home nearby. Instead, he nodded. "On our way north and just stopping for the night."

"And where'd that be?"

"Dunglass."

"So you're a Home, then, are you?"

"We are." Blake just wanted a key and a meal. He didn't need this nosey woman asking questions. He pulled out coins and placed them on the bar, hoping it would hurry the woman along. It didn't.

"Where did you come from?"

"Dun Laws." Blake named the only two places he knew other than Lamberton in Home territory. He didn't even know where they were, only which direction they lay in relation to Lamberton. He prayed he made good choices. When Cerys relaxed beside him, he assumed he had.

"Very well, lad. Your woman looks aboot ready to drop. I can't offer you a bath, but I can give you a clean chamber and some food." The woman made good on her offer. While they waited for their meal, they both scrubbed what they could with the soap and linen square laid beside a ewer and basin. They ate and were soon in bed. Both were exhausted after a night of no sleep. However, neither wanted their second night of marriage to be a chaste one. They made love, in no hurry despite their tiredness. When they shuddered their release, Blake rolled onto his back, bringing Cerys with him. She lay draped over him with his hand laying at her waist. His steady heartbeat had her drifting off just as she felt Blake twitch then go still.

Morning came, but neither Cerys nor Blake stirred. It was close to midday before they emerged from their chamber. They felt recuperated from the rest, even if they regretted not getting on the road sooner. It shocked Blake that he slept so long. He assumed it was having his bride curled around him that made him slumber so well. But he hadn't minded because he worried about Cerys falling ill from exhaustion. She was unaccustomed to such long, physically arduous stretches. It reminded Blake of being on campaign.

"What do you think Murray thinks aboot us disappearing together?" Cerys asked as their horses cantered west.

It was as though Cerys read his mind. "I had the same thought. He's probably dispatched a furious missive to ma grandda."

"Will he punish your clan?"

"He might threaten to, but he canna afford to lose our support politically. We will always fight for Scottish independence, but that doesnae mean ma grandda and Uncle Callum will continue to support him as Guardian. He needs the Sinclairs because without us, he willna have the Sutherlands or the Mackays. That also means the MacLeods of both Lewis and Assynt would withdraw their support, along with the Camerons and the Mackenzies. It could be his downfall to alienate us. We have more alliances through blood and marriage than he can accomplish with money or words."

"Your family really is powerful."

"Aye." Blake grinned. When he was at home at Dunbeath, he rarely considered the influence his family held. They were merely his family. But when he considered their role in Scotland, it still amazed him that his kindly grandfather who used to carry him around on his shoulders and still taught him in the lists was an earl twice over, a renowned warrior, and a political force. His great-uncle Hamish Sutherland was the same way. He'd taken Blake for rides on his horse when the family visited Dunrobin, and he'd slipped sweets to Blake, Torquil, and Maisie along with their cousins when his wife, Amelia, or their parents weren't looking. The man was the Earl of Sutherland and brother-by-marriage to the Earl of Ross. He was just another grandfatherly man to Blake.

"I suppose we can't worry aboot what we don't know."

"Aye. We have enough to fill our minds right now. I would get us to Kersland then decide what to do." Blake prayed they encountered nothing more to derail their escape from Stirling. His wish was granted until the next evening when they arrived on the border of Kerr territory. Then all hell broke loose.

"Lady Cerys!"

Cerys twisted in her saddle and uttered, "Bluidy bleeding hell."

"Who is that?"

"My cousin Stewart. Mitcham's auldest and heir. He's an arse but don't underestimate him. He makes me uncomfortable like my uncle Marcas does. I don't trust him. Please don't let him near me alone."

Blake's gaze swung to the man riding toward them before he looked back at Cerys. He'd just learned two men in her family were a danger to her, and he suspected it wasn't just words that they wielded. He reigned in his temper just as he reigned in Torque. He kept his posture loose, but he replayed in his mind how fast he could reach for his sword or a dirk. He watched Stewart approach with two other riders. He assessed what type of threat they presented. He knew, if it came to a fight, he could likely best them. But it wouldn't be easy, and Cerys might be harmed in the process.

"Lady Cerys, what are you doing here?"

"Stewart, you're still family." Cerys watched as the two guardsmen snickered, but Stewart held up a hand, stopping them both immediately. It was clear Stewart already knew what happened at court. Her family must have barely arrived. They were approaching from the northeast, so not the route her father and uncles would have taken. It was possible Stewart had been on patrol and encountered them, or he'd just started his rotation riding their land.

"Who's this?"

"My husband." The three Kerrs laughed until they realized Cerys wasn't smiling.

"Your husband? Last I heard—"

"Which was when? Are they back?"

"Yes. Yesterday. You aren't welcome here, Cerys." Stewart dropped the formality, which had sounded ridiculous to Cerys, since they were cousins.

"That's not what your father told me before they left Stirling. I'm still your blood."

"Who are you?" Stewart looked at Blake.

"Lady Cerys's husband."

"Hiding behind her skirts, are you?"

"Do I look like I would fit behind my wife's skirts? She has a mind of her own, and you're family, so why wouldn't I let her speak? And why wouldn't I be proud to say I'm her husband?" Blake's arms were crossed at the wrists, making it appear as though he sat casually on his horse. But when he learned forward and Torque took a step, it made him look as threatening as he was. None of the three Kerrs pressed the issue. He kept his Lowland accent, wanting to give them no cause to call him a savage or barbarian.

"Stewart, I have information for the laird. That's why I've come." Cerys would tell her family what happened in exchange for safe harbor for a fortnight. It would be miserable, but she was confident her family wouldn't turn her out.

"Very well. We'll take you." Stewart wheeled his horse around and led the way. Cerys and Blake rode in the center with the two guardsmen bringing up the rear. They rode in silence for two hours. It was uncomfortable, but at least Cerys didn't have to do mental jumping jacks to keep from saying anything upon which Stewart could pounce. She would have enough to contend with when she met with Mitcham.

As they passed through the gate, she spied her uncles leaving the lists. She knew the moment they spotted Blake and her. They charged forward, swords drawn.

"What the devil are you doing here, Sinclair?" Mitcham demanded.

"Sinclair?" Stewart parroted. "You might have mentioned that."

"So you could keep us from coming? So I would be a widow already? I think not. You might be fool enough to kill a Sinclair, but I know your father isn't. And since he isn't that great a fool, he won't let any of you do it either." Cerys swept her gaze across her uncles and cousins before bringing it back to Mitcham. "He's my husband, and I have news."

Cerys held up her hand with the ring on it. Then she swung down from Kitten's back, handing the reins to a stable boy and thanking him. She waited until Kitten and Torque were led away before taking the arm Blake offered.

"You may enter, but he doesn't."

"Very well. Robert! Bring back the horses. We aren't staying." Cerys looked over her shoulder at Mitcham now that she faced the stables. "You'd best hope the Homes don't show up."

"What are you talking aboot?" Mitcham asked.

"My husband and I are given the clan's protection. We stay in my chamber. And no one harasses my husband."

Blake listened to Cerys. An air of command he'd never heard before filled her voice, and he found it far too enticing for the situation.

"And why should we do that?" Muir joined the conversation, having come from the keep.

"Because Stanley Home chased me after I left court. He and his friends shall bring the battle back to the border, and it won't be to keep our independence."

"How do you mean?" Michael asked. He stepped forward and offered his arm to Blake, who studied him a moment before accepting. They grasped each other's forearms and shook. It was a bold move on their part, especially Michael's, since Mitcham hadn't seen fit to greet his guests so warmly. When Michael released Blake, he held out his hand to Cerys. She was hesitant

203

but laid hers on his. He leaned forward as if to kiss her cheek. "Be careful," he whispered. "Trust no one." Michael straightened. "Niece," he said for everyone to hear.

"What say you?" Cerys locked eyes with Mitcham.

"Fine. But he leaves his sword at the gate."

Cerys looked at Blake, who lifted his sword from his back. He waited to see if they would demand he hand over his knives. When they didn't, he smothered his smile.

Fools. The sword might mean I have a longer reach. But I willna hesitate to gut ye with ma dirks if ye do aught to ma wife. I can promise ye that I carry more dirks than any of ye.

Blake's hand rested at the small of Cerys's back as they entered the keep. A middle-aged woman with papery skin and sun-bleached hair approached. He watched Cerys smile and accept the embrace offered to her. He figured it must be her aunt Matilda.

"Cerys, what're you doing here? And who is—" Matilda paused as she finally looked at Blake. "Merciful saints. You've married one of them, too."

"Lady Matilda, I've been told I resemble the other men in my family. It must be true." Blake reached out his hand as Michael had done to Cerys, expect he took the older woman's and brought it toward his mouth. He kept it a respectful distance from his lips as he bowed his head. "It is a pleasure to meet you, my lady. I know Lady Cerys has missed you."

"You have?" Matilda shifted her gaze from Blake to Cerys as he released her hand.

"Every day, Auntie Tildie." Cerys kept her voice low, reverting to what she'd called the woman when she was a child and couldn't say her full name, and using the childhood honorific.

"Aw, lass." Matilda pulled her in for another embrace as she glanced up at Blake. He could see the warning in the woman's eyes, but he wasn't sure what it meant. He watched her murmur something in Cerys's ear. "Trust no one but Michael."

Cerys stepped back, fighting to keep the surprise from her face. Matilda was born between Michael and Marcas, making her older than Cerys's father, but only by two years. Her uncles, aunt, and father had been born in rapid succession, one year in between each birth. She'd noticed as a child that Matilda was closest to Michael. She usually kept a wide berth from her other brothers. Her warning made Cerys wonder if she could tell her uncles and father what she knew.

"Cerys, come to my solar. Sinclair, have an ale or something."

"No." Cerys wouldn't budge as the four Kerr men turned away. "My husband comes with me."

"He's not one of us," Muir sneered.

"According to you, neither am I. I am not here to see you, Father. Uncle Mitcham, my husband comes with me, or I go nowhere, and we have the conversation here."

"Do you not trust us, lass?" Marcas's gaze skimmed over her before moving to Blake. Now Blake understood what Cerys didn't like. There was something lurking beneath the surface that made Blake want to push Cerys behind him and shield her from Marcas's sight. It wasn't the look an uncle should ever give his niece. Blake glanced at the other Kerr brothers. Only Michael watched Marcas, the look of disgust clear for anyone to see.

"Why should I? Only Uncle Mitcham said I was welcome to return. The rest of you would have let my father abandon me at a whorehouse. Your father tried to kill his own daughter, then he tried to kill my husband's uncle when he saved my aunt. Your sister."

"If we're that wretched, why come here, daughter?"

"I asked for a place for my husband and me to stay for a fortnight in exchange for information I have."

"Your husband comes," Mitcham declared. "We aren't doing this out here. Matilda, arrange for Cerys's chamber to be made ready. They will take all their meals there. They will remain there unless summoned by me."

Blake listened to the laird give his commands. Part of him was content to while away the days locked in a chamber with a bed and Cerys. But without his sword, being in an enclosed space made him uneasy. He didn't feel either he or his wife was safe. His hand remained at the small of her back as they entered the solar. Cerys took a seat at the oblong table in the center of the chamber. Blake stood behind her, his hands resting lightly on her shoulders. Cerys sat up straight, her back stiff and chin raised. She waited until everyone else sat.

"After you talked aboot me in the stables, Home, Hannay, and Cunningham came into the stables."

"After we talked aboot you? When was that?" Michael asked.

"I don't know which other times you spoke aboot me there, but it was the day my father accused me in the middle of the royal castle's bailey. The day my husband swore to protect me."

"Cerys," Mitcham warned. Blake pressed his right hand against her shoulder, offering the same warning. But she knew what she was doing. She would paint them into a corner by reminding them of their dishonor. The only way to redeem themselves was to help her.

"Yes, Uncle. I was just making sure I was clear aboot when this happened. The three of them came in just after you left. I was in Kitten's stall during both conversations. They said they were going to keep trying to get Blake and his brother, Torquil, to share Murray's plans.

The Guardian doesn't trust them. He's sending the Dunbars and Kennedys back to patrol the border, which will have them crossing both Cunningham and Hannay lands until they reach Murray's own clan."

"Why doesn't he trust them?" Mitcham wondered.

"Shaw Hannay is still in league with Balliol." Cerys kept her hands clasped in her laps, her fingernails biting into the back of her hands. She looked at Mitcham, but she kept Michael in the corner of her eye. He appeared speculative, but she couldn't guess what he was thinking. "Shaw, Stanley, and Domnall discovered I heard their conversation. They tried to accost me in a passageway, but my Sinclair guards protected me. Stanley and his men broke into my chamber to take me, but I wasn't there. They destroyed my clothes and toiletries. They tried to break into the Sinclair suite, but Blake's cousins stopped them. They followed us from Stirling."

"We only arrived yesterday. How did you get here so soon? You must have left right after us."

"Not long after you. We sailed from Edinburgh to Lamberton, then rode inland."

"You sailed right into Home territory when you claim they're chasing you." Muir turned his nose up at his daughter.

"This clan doesn't live near the sea. It was the fastest and safest way to put distance between us and them." Cerys was careful not to use a possessive pronoun to describe the clan, since she didn't think either "your" or "our" would be well received. "I may not be a welcome member of this clan anymore, but when they tried to intimidate me and when they left my chamber in shambles, I was still a Kerr. Their threat to me is a threat to you. They were willing to kidnap and harm a woman bearing the Kerr name. A trustworthy neighbor that does not make."

"How do you know that they weren't merely headed home, just like you?" Michael questioned.

"They assaulted the Sinclair guards outside my door and left them to die before they forced my chamber door open. They were there to take me because of what I heard. If they were willing to do this, do you think they would just let me walk away? Do you think they would just let me go to the Sinclairs with what I know?"

Muir's visage was mocking as he looked at Blake. "Left for dead, were they? Not such the incredible warriors the Sinclairs pose as. So much for being adequate guards if they got into her chamber."

"I didn't say they were dead. I said they were left for dead. It was two against ten, and they still live to tell the tale. And I wasn't in my chamber when they entered."

"I suppose you were with him." Muir nudged his chin toward Blake.

"We were getting married," Blake stated. They would be none the wiser that it didn't happen until the next morning.

"And where did these nuptials purportedly take place?" Muir sneered at Blake.

"Stirling's kirk. You can check the parish register the next time you're there. You will find Blake and Cerys Sinclair recorded there for posterity." Blake grinned. He knew it would irritate the man, and it did. Muir's nostrils flared as he bared his teeth.

"Do stop, Father. Will you froth at the mouth next?" Cerys turned back to Mitcham. "They know I heard Hannay affirm his loyalty to Balliol. He made it clear his clan shares the same sentiments as him. Cunningham and Home agreed with him. I'm not so certain their clans agree with those two men, but if they do, your neighbor may soon harbor Balliol or his men. That will be on your doorstep."

"You've given me much to think aboot. Retire to your chamber for the night. Take your husband with you. Aggie will send up a tray." Mitcham dismissed them with barely a wave. Cerys was glad to go. She disliked Aggie, the housekeeper, and had since she was a child. But Maeve, the clan's head cook, was kind. She didn't doubt the tray would have ample food for them both. As she rose, she dared a look at Michael, who watched her. When the man lifted his gaze, she knew he and Blake were staring at each other. A moment later, Michael's gaze returned to her with a dip of his chin.

"Later," Michael mouthed.

CHAPTER 16

*L*ater turned out to be a fortnight. They locked Cerys and Blake into her chamber from the outside. Servants delivered trays thrice daily and were the highlight, since Maeve sent copious amounts of food, having spied Blake as he passed the kitchen on the way to Mitcham's solar. Aggie begrudgingly sent up a bath each evening. However, the newlyweds minded not at all. When they weren't sleeping or coupling, the latter taking up much of their days, they talked. They continued to get to know one another, talking about what they'd envisioned their adult lives being when they were children. They talked about Blake's duties and Cerys's time at court. They skirted any further mention of emotions, but now as they lay on Blake's plaid in front of the fire, their conversation moved to a family of their own.

Blake's arm draped over Cerys's back as she lay on her side against Blake. His fingers skimmed along her back, creating periodic shivers. Her top leg coiled around Blake's right thigh. He kissed her forehead as her hand swept over his abdomen and chest in gentle circles.

"*Mo leannan*, obviously I ken how strained things

are with yer family, but they are who ye ken. I dinna want ye to feel alone or like a stranger when we arrive at Dunbeath. Ma mama and aunts willna give ye a chance, but I ken they can also be a wee overwhelming. The more they try, the more I fear ye will feel out of place. I saw it with ma cousin, Liam, when he returned from Orkney with his wife. Elene doesnae speak Gaelic and isnae fully fluent in Scots, so that was part of it. But her family wasna a happy one, either. Her father died years ago, and her mother was too fond of the drink. She has a younger brother and sister to raise. Her situation's a mite different than yers, but I saw how nervous it made her. I dinna want that for ye. If it gets too much, find me, tell me. If ye canna do that, excuse yerself. They willna think ye rude. They'll understand without ye saying aught."

"What will your mother think of me?"

Blake heard the apprehension, so he pressed her closer to him and kissed her forehead again. "She will be thrilled to meet ye. She isnae the type to feel like ma wife is stealing me from her. She kens I'm a mon and of an age to marry. She will see ye as a second daughter. What ye should worry aboot is Maisie. She will talk yer ear off, and before ye ken what's happening, she'll have ye riding too fast and whatever other stunt she tries. She's wild."

"She sounds perfect." Cerys grinned and tickled Blake's ribs.

"Och, aye. Perfectly naughty."

"Naughty? She's not a wean."

"Nay, but she isnae quite wicked." Blake grinned.

"Were you wild?"

"Och, aye. Truth be told, most of ma cousins are a wee wild. But it's because there's so many of us. There's always someone suggesting something because we're also a wee competitive. Liam, Hamish, and Alec are the worst among the lads. Ainsley is probably the worst of all of us. They're ma aunt Mairghread's. She's the most competitive of all ma da's siblings. Ainsley is like ma aunt. She's observant and reads people far too well. She strategizes, so she vera nearly never loses at what she does. Ma aunt is like that too. Drives her brothers barmy."

"She sounds wonderful. When can I meet her?" Cerys giggled and waggled her eyebrows.

"I dinna want ye to feel rushed to find yer place among the clan, and I dinna want ye to fear what people might expect."

"Expect? As in when they might expect me to be expecting?" Cerys already wondered if she might be carrying their first child. They'd certainly coupled enough to nearly guarantee it.

"Aye. But I dinna want ye to fash aboot what duties to take on. Ye dinna have to do everything at once. I'd like ye to take time to get to ken people and find what ye like and want."

"Besides being in bed with you?" Cerys winked, but her good humor was cut short by a knock at the door. It wasn't mealtime, nor was it time for a bath to be brought. Cerys exchanged a look with Blake as they rose. She hurried to slip her chemise back on and donned her robe. She still had clothes in her armoire from before her time in service. Blake wrapped his plaid around his waist, not bothering to pleat it. When he was certain Cerys was presentable, he responded to the person who continued to knock.

"Enter."

The couple listened to the key turn in the lock before Michael entered. He looked at Cerys, then Blake, then the pillows in front of the fire. Neither Cerys nor Blake was embarrassed. They were certain that people heard them coupling since they'd seen guards outside the door at times. They knew other people moved along the passageway, and Cerys's family had chambers on their floor. They were married and refused to feel ashamed, especially since they hadn't chosen to be sequestered.

"Cerys, Sinclair." Michael smiled at his niece and nodded to Blake before he glanced back into the passageway, then closed the door.

Blake noticed no one else was outside the door. He shifted his gaze back to Michael, uncertain how to interpret the man coming alone. He had a dirk strapped to each of his thighs, so he felt prepared to protect Cerys.

"Uncle Michael, you made me think you wished to talk to me. It's been a fortnight."

"I couldn't follow on your heels, and I've had other matters to settle."

Cerys watched her uncle. He hadn't been the clan's tánaiste in nearly ten years since Stewart ascended to the position. However, he was the clan's captain of the guard, so Cerys wondered what type of matters needed settling.

"You're here now. What is it?" Cerys did what she could to sound hospitable.

"Stanley Home approached Stewart three moons ago, happening to meet him along the border during their patrols. He intimated Balliol was gathering more support from the English. He tried to gage our position. Stewart, with his usual lack of tact, laughed and reminded him that our clan fought alongside Wallace. Rather than gain more information, Stewart rode away."

"Not surprising." Cerys crossed her arms and sighed. She noticed Blake had positioned himself to stand between them, facing the gap. He could easily reach either of them. It was subtle, but she was certain Michael understood.

"It's not. Hearing your account reaffirms that Stanley is up to no good. But it would have been useful to have more information to prepare for whatever he, Cunningham, and Hannay are planning. I believe you know more than you shared."

"What more could I know?"

When Michael took a step forward, Blake crossed his arms, making the muscles in his chest, biceps, and forearms ripple. His feet were already hip-width apart. Without a shirt on, he looked even more impressive. From the glance Michael cast him, Blake sensed he terrified the older man. It was just how he wanted it.

"Why did you come here instead of going to your husband's home?"

"Those men likely assumed we were going to *our* home. We chose to go in the opposite direction from which we thought they would guess. Mayhap they started out headed north and spied my brother-by-marriage traveling without us. Mayhap they got word of which direction we traveled. Mayhap it was a coincidence until they learned we stopped at Linlithgow. They arrived after us at Linlithgow, yet they were soon on the road after we left. Why stop there for the night then leave again, especially since it was exceedingly dark? They were after us."

"You must have heard more than Hannay saying he supports Balliol if they're willing to chase a woman all the way to her clan's land."

"Mayhap they have given up the chase."

"They haven't. They were spotted at the northern border. Hannay and Cunningham are with Home. They passed where they should have turned east to go to the Homes' keep, and there is no reason for Hannay or

Cunningham to travel this far east if they're headed to their homes. What do you know?"

Cerys shrugged. "Hannay thinks Balliol is with the Cliffords, which means Westmoreland."

"They have four keeps that he could have fled to. Did any of them mention which one?"

"No. It could be Appleby, Brough, Pendragon, or Brougham for all I know. He could be wrong, and the usurper isn't at any of them."

"What of Murray's plans?" Michael abruptly changed the subject, and it made Blake wary. He wanted to know how he thought Cerys would know such things. He wasn't asking Blake.

"I know naught of that. No one spoke aboot them. You would do well to ask Blake." Cerys looked at her husband. She knew he wouldn't share anything if he knew it. Since he hadn't been told any of the plans, that would save him from lying one way or another.

"Murray is aware of their conversation. He's keeping his plans only among his senior advisors. I know naught of his next move." Blake continued to use his Lowland accent as much as he disliked it. He'd spoken Scots his entire life and could hide his burr with ease. But it never felt as natural as Gaelic. It was a reminder of how Lowlanders thought themselves superior to Highlanders since none of them learned Gaelic. He hated that Highlanders had to bend to Lowlanders lest they snap and be left asunder. Then what would become of Scotland? It would already be England.

"Neither of you know any more than that?"

"No, Uncle. But I suspect there is more afoot." Cerys wanted to look at Blake, praying he would be able to tell her by his eyes alone if she should share the threat to France and the true king. But she didn't dare look at her husband. She couldn't afford Michael thinking they were hiding more. Matilda said they could trust

Michael, but he'd said to trust no one. Did that include himself? Was she reading too much into that? Cerys didn't know, so she would err on the side of caution. "What will Uncle Mitcham do if they come here for us?"

Michael hesitated as he looked at Blake, then back to Cerys. "Your father said to turn you both over since we know all you have to share. I reminded our laird that he gave you his word, so he cannot go back on it." That was what Cerys relied on. For all her oldest uncle's faults, he valued his honor, since his father had none. His family nearly lost the lairdship because of his father's scheme to murder Brighde and the conspiracy with Randolph de Soules. "You may remain, but you are to continue to stay in here. In ten days, you will leave and not return. What happens once you are on the road is your cross to bear."

"How gracious," Cerys muttered. "Uncle Michael, why can't I trust anyone else? Is it merely that you all despise me for something I didn't even understand until after? Or is there more?"

"Not all of us despise you, Cerys. Matilda has pined for you since you left."

Matilda. Not you. Not my cousins or other aunts. Just Matilda. Remember, it's a roof over your head and food in your belly while you are here. Be gracious.

"I missed my aunt, too. It wasn't easy to leave her. But why can't I trust anyone else?"

"You know how your father feels aboot you. Marcas and Stewart are as much a danger to you as they are to any lass. And our laird and Stewart do not think enough steps ahead to be real strategists. They would have turned you out without hearing aught. But I warn you, Cerys. If you know aught else, now is the time to tell me. If you think holding onto information will make your life more valuable, it will not. You're more likely to receive better treatment, maybe even some freedom to leave this chamber, if you prove you're still valuable."

Cerys listened to her uncle, and it tempted her. But she still wasn't convinced telling them about the threat was wise. They could do little beyond having the satisfaction of knowing. Murray knew, and that was who mattered. He was the only man in Scotland with the authority to do anything. Unless Mitcham decided to kill Stanley, Shaw, and Domnall, knowing more would do little. It might give them something with which to bribe the three conspirators, but what did the Kerrs need from any of them?

"There is naught else to tell you, Uncle. Murray knows what happened. I came to tell you that Home is involved since he's a neighbor. If his clan offers safe passage or harbor, then it brings Balliol and his forces to this keep's doorstep. Since the Kerrs stand with the Bruces, I thought you should be warned. The people here deserve to be prepared and protected."

"You're very careful not to call yourself one of us."

"Everyone has made it clear that I'm not, which is fine because I'm a Sinclair."

Blake listened to the ongoing exchange. When Cerys announced her new fealty, he wanted to beam and twirl her in the air. She'd said it before, but he was hardly tired of hearing it. He was proud of his wife. He'd admired her fortitude to live at court and to endure what she did at Stirling Castle. But her bearing and tone proved she was not a pushover. He'd seen her cower in front of her father in the royal bailey, but that fear seemed to have disappeared. He wondered if it might be because of him, but he suspected that it came from her finally feeling free of her family. Perhaps it was both.

"Very well. Give my best to Brighde when you meet."

Blake's mouth pursed, his mood shifting drastically. There was a flippancy to Michael's voice that concerned him. If it had been scorn or sincerity, he might have accepted it. But the dismissiveness made him wonder how he really saw Cerys, since his niece's situation was similar to that of his sister. The wariness in Cerys's gaze made him think she shared his concern.

"I will."

The bells chimed for the evening meal, bringing their conversation to an end. Michael took his leave, and the door locked behind him. The couple waited several minutes before they moved to the window embrasure and kept their voices low.

"I'm so vera proud of ye, *leannan*. Ye were confident and judicious."

"I was confident because I'm no longer scared of him or anyone else here. That's because I have you with me. I know I'm safe, and I know you'll support me. I couldn't have done that without knowing you'll always be at my side."

"Always, Cerys." Blake tucked hair behind her ear before brushing a kiss against her lips. "Why didn't you tell him aboot the threat to the king and the mercenaries?"

"What can they do aboot that? Murray knows, and that's what mattered. They have naught to tell him that can influence the outcome of a battle or dictate strategy. I gave them enough for us to stay here. The rest they don't need to know, so I didn't need to tell them."

The couple paused their conversation when a maid arrived with their evening meal. Seated at the table in the center of the chamber, they continued to talk in quiet tones.

"What do ye think they're doing at the border? Does yer clan get along with the Homes?"

"They do for the most part. There haven't been any problems that I know aboot. I think the patrols will allow them safe passage since those men won't know what's gone on here. My only fear is them coming here. I don't want to think my family would turn us over to them, but I'm not convinced. Mitcham and Michael might, but Marcas, Stewart, and my father probably would. I don't trust any of them not to turn you over."

Blake looked into his chalice. Something tasted off about his wine. He swirled the drink and tipped the goblet sideways to see the bottom and how it coated the metal sides. He sniffed it, but there was no odor.

"Dinna drink anymore, Cerys."

"I've already finished mine. What's wrong?"

"I dinna ken that aught is wrong, but I thought I tasted something bitter." Blake looked toward the bed then toward Cerys. "We should dress."

"Why? Do you think someone's poisoned us?"

"I dinna ken if it's that or a sleeping draught or naught at all. But if it is something, I dinna want ye in just a chemise and robe. If someone has tampered with our drinks or our food, they're likely to come in here once we're incapacitated. We should dress now while we can. Put yer boots on too."

"You're scaring me, Blake."

"I ken, *leannan*. I wish I werenae. I dinna trust yer family, but I trust ma tongue. Hurry. Ye drank all of yers, and ye're much smaller than me. It will affect ye sooner." Blake rose from the table, and the chamber spun. He gripped the table as he swallowed down the nausea.

"Blake?"

"Hurry, Cerys. Whatever it was is strong."

The couple hurried to dress, but Cerys had barely

pulled on her second stocking before her head bobbed. She pulled her kirtle on with her eyes closed. She tugged at her laces, but her fingers wouldn't cooperate to tie the bow. She looked at Blake, who donned breeks instead of his plaid. She wanted to complain, noting she didn't like him in the Lowlander garb, but her tongue felt too thick.

"Blake, I don't feel well." Cerys climbed onto the bed and laid down. "I'm so sleepy, and I feel ill. Am I dying? I don't want to die. I just married you."

"I don't think we're dying, *leannan*. But I think we will sleep for a long time." He gathered Cerys's boots and slipped them onto her feet, tying them then her kirtle's laces. He struggled to pull on his boots as his head bobbed. He checked his knives. One in each boot, one on each wrist, two in his belt that anyone could see, and one tucked into the belt at his back that his leine hid.

"Blake, I hope we're only sleeping, but what if we aren't?"

"Wheest, *mo ghaol*. Dinna fash. We will be right as rain come morning. Now let me hold ye while we sleep."

"What does that mean? *Mo ghaol?*"

"My love. I love ye, Cerys."

"I love you, Blake."

As their eyes closed against their will, both wondered if that would be the only time they'd speak those words. From the way they felt, they were certain it was.

❖

"Do you still think she's lying?" Mitcham sipped his whisky as he sat at his desk. His brothers and oldest son sat around the table in his solar.

"Of course she is," Muir barked.

"No. I don't think she's lying so much as holding back one more thing." Michael imparted most of what he learned while he talked to the couple, but he hadn't told everything. Granted, there had been little to say anyhow.

"It won't matter once she's on the boat, and we've given the savage to Home and his allies." Mitcham took another swig.

"Are they really allies or merely strange bedfellows?" Stewart looked between his father and Michael. He ignored Marcas and Muir like usual. He emulated his father, but Michael left him in awe. He marveled at the man's astuteness and how he always seemed to know the right answer. For the life of him, Stewart was always too slow on the uptake when it came to matching wits with Michael. He'd felt the same way about Cerys, so he'd been glad to see the hind end of her horse when she left for court.

"Either way. They'll both be gone. But she'll do well to remember her duty to this clan. She'll be a widow by dusk tomorrow. She'll be a Kerr once more." Mitcham turned his piercing stare at Muir. "You will not say another word to your daughter. Disowning her nearly proved a mistake. Had she not come to us, we wouldn't know what we do, and we wouldn't be several pounds richer. Home paid good coin for us to turn Sinclair over. We wouldn't have her to send to court as our informant. She hasn't been dismissed from the queen's service, so the queen she shall serve."

Mitcham raised his mug in salute to his brothers and son before raising it toward the door and the general direction of Cerys's chamber abovestairs.

"When do we move them?" Marcas inquired.

"In a half an hour. Stay away from her." Marcas's predilections weren't a secret among the brothers, but it turned Michael's stomach over to think of incest. If no one else would keep his brother from his niece, he would. He didn't dislike Cerys, he didn't even believe she was guilty of what they'd accused her of two years ago, but she had outlived her usefulness at Stirling. Now she would do as she was commanded and be useful once more. She couldn't do that if she fell victim to Marcas. If that wouldn't be bad enough, he was certain Stewart would have a turn, too. That didn't suit the plan he devised. No, he needed Cerys in one piece and able to travel.

CHAPTER 17

*B*lake woke to cold air against his face and something moving beneath his belly. He kept his eyes closed as he assessed the situation in which he found himself. His tongue felt swollen, and his mouth was dry. His head pounded from whatever had been in the wine and from being stretched across Torque's back. He was certain it was his horse without looking. The beast wasn't merely a means to travel. He was an extension of Blake in battle. They moved as one, knowing how each other thought and moved.

He strained to hear anything in his surroundings. He was certain it was still night since he heard an owl hoot, but he didn't hear any other animals. Not fearing anyone noticing if he opened his eyes, he did so slowly. He could see little other than Torque's flank and the ground beneath him. He turned his head slightly, keeping his lids nearly shut and spotted two horsemen following him. He turned his gaze in the other direction and recognized Stewart leading them. He tried to tell if there was anyone else on the other side of him, but he heard nothing to convince him there was.

"How much farther?" Blake slid his gaze back to the

riders following him. He didn't recognize either of the men.

"Aboot another hour. They're camped halfway to the keep. If they refuse to pay when I meet with them, kill him and leave him for the animals. We don't need him, but I won't let them have him without the coin." Stewart looked over his shoulder, glancing at Blake, who appeared to still be unconscious.

"What if one of them kills us for doing it?" The other rider behind Torque sounded less confident than the first rider.

"You'll know to kill him because I'll shake my head as I return. You'll be behind the knoll waiting. We're not taking him near them until we have the coins. "

Blake listened as he flexed his feet. He felt the dirks at his ankles, the tip of the handle sticking out of his boots. He shifted and felt the dirk at his back and the two pressing against his belly. The only ones he couldn't feel were the ones that had been in his wrist bracers.

Where's Cerys? She isnae with us, and they havenae said aught aboot her. What have they done to her? It must be at least two or three hours since we drank the wine. If it was enough to knock me out for this long, what's it done to ma wee wife?

Blake forced himself to breathe in a steady rhythm as worry turned to panic. He needed to learn what became of her, and he needed to figure out how to get away from his three captors within the next hour. Before that, preferably, since each step took him farther from Cerys and was more ground for him to cover. Deciding it was time to make them aware he was awake, he groaned and shuffled. Neither his wrists not ankles were bound. A rope tied across his back and passed underneath the saddle was all that kept him atop of Torque.

"He's waking," Stewart announced. "Reign in and let's get him sitting upright. I want him to watch every league pass by while he's unable to get to her side. She's already aboard the boat in Berwick."

Berwick? What the bluidy hell are they doing going to England? And where the fuck do they intend to take her? Let them untie me long enough to get me upright. I'll take the favor, ye bluidy eejits.

Blake didn't move until Torque stood still. Stewart came to stand by his head and slapped him twice. "Wake up, you heathen."

"I'm awake." Blake wanted to say more, but he bit his tongue. He felt someone come around to his back. Hands plucked at the rope knotted across his back. The moment it came free, he pushed his weight backward and dropped from Torque's back. He knocked over whomever stood too close. He rolled over and grabbed a blade from his boot, slashing it across the unsuspecting man's throat before anyone knew what was happening. The other horseman who'd been behind him rushed forward. Blake hurled the knife, embedding it in the man's throat.

Stewart rushed him, having run around Torque's head, with a sword raised.

"Ye fucking bastard. Ye would kill me with ma own sword." Blake recognized the weapon as the moonlight reflected off the steel. The Damascus steel had an "S" smithed into the center of the blade. All Sinclairs had it on their swords. Blake barreled forward, his shoulder plowing into Stewart's middle. He tackled him, hunching below where the man had held his sword. The blade flew into the air as the two warriors crashed to the ground. Blake wrapped his massive hand around Stewart's throat and squeezed. "I will strangle ye. I will make it slow and agonizing as the last of the air in yer lungs slips from ye. Tell me what I want to ken, and I will show ye mercy. I will make yer death quick."

Stewart tried to speak, tried to buck Blake off of him, but his efforts were futile. Blake easily weighed four stones more than Stewart. He shifted his weight forward, trapping Stewart's arms under his knees and pressing down on the man's throat.

"Ye arenae saving yerself by trying to fight. We both ken ye are little more than a gnat that I will squash. Why is ma wife going to Berwick? Tap the ground if ye will answer. Say aught but the truth, and I will drive this through yer eye. It willna kill ye, but it will hurt like the devil." Blake held up a wickedly sharp *sgian dubh*. The dirk had a short blade, but it could be deadly. Stewart's hand slapped the ground twice. Blake eased the grip on the man's throat.

"France."

The single word was all Blake needed. It meant Cerys was being sent to King David's court. Her family was sending her to even more danger. It gave Blake pause to wonder if they should have told Michael everything after all. But realization nipped at Blake. They likely would have sent her there regardless. It gave them the opportunity to hand him over to his death, or so they thought. And it got her away from Scotland and them. She wouldn't easily return to Kersland once in France. It also gave them the opportunity to gather information and secrets from another royal household.

"Thank ye." In one swift move, Blake released Stewart's throat, drawing back his left hand as his right hand swept the *sgian dubh* across his throat. He leaped to his feet then wiped his dirks before he grabbed his sword. He dragged the sheath over Stewart's head and placed it across his own back. He was sliding the sword into its home as he mounted Torque. He swung his steed around and squeezed the beast's flanks. "Ye made friends with Kitten, and I want ma wife. Let's go, lad."

Cerys's head ached with a pain she couldn't describe. It was a combination of pounding and searing. She'd been awake for what she estimated to be an hour. She was on horseback behind Michael. Her wrists were bound around his waist, forcing her to lean against the older man. They rode in the dark with four men and Kitten. She'd remained still when she woke, but it was Kitten who gave her away. He nickered as she returned to consciousness. Michael told her she could pretend to be asleep, or she could enjoy the midnight ride. Neither appealed, but she took the opportunity to look around. It didn't take long to realize they headed southeast. As they continued to ride, the scent of sea air increased. They were riding toward the North Sea. She couldn't tell where Michael intended to take her, but they'd already crossed into England. Of that she was certain. The landscape was similar to the Scottish side of the border, but the Kerr men were extra attentive.

"I will tell you only this one, Cerys. Behave yourself when we reach the port. If you put up a fuss or try to get anyone's attention, I will knock you out again. And this time it won't be painless."

"There's naught painless aboot how my head feels right now." She'd drunk her entire chalice when Blake hadn't drunk all of his. She wondered if he was awake yet and whether he was as miserable as she was. She could only imagine what he would do when he discovered they'd been separated. "Who has my husband?"

"Stewart and two guards."

"You know they aren't going back to Cessford. You guaranteed their death," Cerys warned.

"Hardly. Stanley won't kill the Kerr heir, no matter how much he might not want to leave anyone alive."

"Stanley isn't who you need to fear. Blake will not go willingly, and he will not forgive anyone." Cerys could imagine how Blake would react. "He'll be awake by now. That means Stewart and the other two are already dead."

"Hardly. He'll sleep until after they turn him over. They're meeting halfway between the keep and our border."

"I'm the one who drank the full chalice. If I'm awake already, then Stewart is likely already dead." Cerys felt Michael suck in a breath. They'd assumed Blake drank more than her. They counted on that when they found an empty goblet. She closed her eyes again, shutting out her surroundings and the men with her. She prayed over and over that she was right, that Blake would learn where they took her. She prayed that Torque had the endurance to ride hard for at least two hours. She and her captors were riding at a trot, so she tried to convince herself that Blake would catch up. "Where are you taking me?"

"Berwick."

What? Why? The only reason to go there is for the ships. Why not take me to a Scottish port town? What awaits me there?

"You're going to hand me over to the English?"

"No. A French merchant."

"What?" Cerys didn't need an answer. She deduced they were sending her to King David and Queen Joan. She was the daughter of the English King Edward II and Isabella of France. David and Joan married when he was four, and she was seven. He was now three-and-ten, and she was six-and-ten. Cerys didn't look forward to serving the younger woman. Not even if she weren't a captive.

"You will make yourself useful again. By the morrow, you will be a widow. That means you will be a Kerr once more. You will go to France and gather information for us. The captain who's taking you will ferry missives for you. I expect a report every fortnight to a moon. If you go longer than that, you will be punished."

Cerys didn't want to imagine what that punishment would entail. She was certain it would be horrid. But the thought that Blake might be dead made her not care. Without her husband, who she'd fallen love with so easily, she no longer saw anything bright in her future. She didn't doubt the royal couple—or rather their advisors—would decide to whom she would marry. If not, her father would eventually order her to the convent. Both could issue her orders, but she would not have any husband but Blake. She wondered if they might have already started a family. Lord knew they'd made it highly probable with how they'd passed the hours during the past three days.

CHAPTER 18

*B*lake arrived on the outskirts of Berwick exhausted and still suffering the lingering aftereffects of the drug he'd ingested. But his determination to find Cerys far outweighed his desire for rest. He dismounted Torque to better disguise himself. He was already an impressive sight with his height and girth, but atop his horse, he was impossible not to notice. He wished to blend in as best he could. As he drew closer to the docks, where he expected to find his wife and her wastrel family, he unsheathed his sword with his right hand and pulled a dirk from his belt with his left. He was careful not to slice Torque with his knife as he led the trusty steed to a vantage point.

Cerys was easy to spot as the only lady on the docks, her attire setting her apart from the fishmongers and whores. She huddled within her cloak, appearing small compared to the men who surrounded her. Blake recognized Muir from his body language. He leaned toward a sailor while gesturing toward Cerys. It was obvious he was trying to force the captain into taking Cerys aboard. He inched forward until he was within hearing distance but hidden in a warehouse's shadow.

Muir confirmed his suspicions as Blake listened to him issue orders to a man who looked unconvinced.

"I have more than enough coin to cover her fare," Muir insisted in French. "You need to deliver her to Calais. How she gets there once aboard your ship isn't my concern."

Blake felt his anger spike once more as he listened to the man's dismissal of his daughter's safety. He was ready to charge forth, but he was more likely to get himself killed than rescue Cerys. He tempered his eagerness to have his wife back in his arms with the strategic mind of a warrior. He assessed the men with Cerys, deciding who he should aim for first. He would ensure none interfered again. His bloodlust urged him to slay Muir as well, but he couldn't ignore that the man, for the worse, was still Cerys's father. However, that didn't mean the conniving scoundrel wouldn't leave Berwick bloodied and battered. Urgency coursed through him as the captain accepted the purse, and a dockhand led Kitten aboard the ship. Once he'd observed long enough to have a plan, he mounted Torque. With his sword and knife raised and a battle cry on his lips, he surged forward.

Cerys glowered at her father's back, understanding her father's meaning. She would be damned if she let any man touch her. In fact, she was determined not to board the ship in the first place. She scanned her surroundings for any means to avoid being forced onto the boat, but she saw no options. She could either run to the end of the dock and plunge herself into the water, or she would have to battle her father's men. While they'd known her all her life and never harmed her in the past, she didn't doubt they wouldn't hesitate to restrain her with whatever methods they needed. She might survive, but she would be far worse for wear.

"You can glare at me all you want, Cerys. I care not. Once you're in France, you will make yourself useful. You will befriend the king and ensure you are at his side. You will hear what he says and see what he writes. He need not know that you can read, but he will know that you're a talented companion. From what everyone heard while you rutted that barbarian, you have the skills now to make a fine mistress."

Even if Cerys weren't in love with Blake and would never consider being unfaithful, the thought of bedding an adolescent barely out of boyhood made her want to retch. She couldn't imagine doing something so vile. It would make her no better than Marcas, and a predator she would not be.

As her gaze shifted toward the wharf, intuition told her Blake was nearby. She darted her eyes across the buildings and people on shore without turning her body in that direction. It only took her a moment to spy Blake and Torque. She watched him release Torque's reins as they stepped out of the shadows. She held her breath as he raised his weapons and spurred his mount. Despite knowing he prepared to charge, his roaring battle cry made her jump. Her father's men swung around, startled, and scrambling for their weapons.

Muir shoved Cerys toward the gang plank, but she dug in her heels, trying to stop the forward propulsion. But her father was far stronger than her, so her refusal did nothing to thwart him. He issued orders to the captain to get underway, and a moment later he hefted Cerys off her feet and tossed her onto the ship's deck. She landed hard, knocking the air from her lungs. She laid dazed for several heartbeats before she scrambled to her feet. She watched Blake clash with the first Kerr warrior, but he felled the man with a quick swipe of his knife across the man's throat.

Her attention wavered when she realized that the French captain obeyed her father's command. The ropes tying the ship to the dock landed with a thud on the dock as men scrambled to leap aboard as oars dropped into the water. She watched her hope for freedom inch away. She turned around, considering jumping from the boat on the far side from the dock. She gathered her skirts and prepared to make a dash, but an arm wrapped around her waist and hauled her backward. She banged into the center mast before a meaty hand forced her to sit. She was soon bound to the wooden beam, unable to enact any type of escape. She turned her attention back to the fight on the dock.

Blake cut a swash through the men trying to keep him from his wife. Torque was as much a weapon as his sword and knife. The animal reared and kicked out, striking a guardsman in the head. The force was enough to crack the man's skull and kill him before he landed on the ground. His faithful steed bared his teeth and nipped at a man who drew too close. The Kerr warrior howled in pain as the horse's teeth sank into his arm. Blake and Torque continued to press forward. He caught sight from the corner of his eye of the men releasing the moorings. He knew time was not his ally. If he didn't end the battle immediately, he wouldn't reach Cerys.

"You're too late," Muir taunted as Blake maneuvered Torque with his knees, making slow progress toward the end of the dock where Cerys's father gloated. Realizing Muir would be right if he waited another minute, he left two men alive. He raced Torque down the dock toward the departing ship. He noticed they hadn't yet replaced the open rail with the missing strip of wood. He turned his attention back to Muir, making a decision. When he was close enough, he slammed the pummel of his sword into Muir's temple. It wouldn't kill the man, but it would incapacitate him, making him a threat no longer to Cerys's rescue.

As Blake raced toward the end of the dock, he judged the distance to the ship's open rail. He sheathed his sword but held his dirk as he squeezed Torque's flanks. He had faith in his steed, having ridden him when the animal took flying leaps. He just prayed the animal would be as confident over water as he was on land.

Cerys watched with her heart in her throat as her husband approached. She realized what he intended, and she thought she might faint. The ship's sails had caught the wind, and it was increasing speed. She feared she would watch him plummet into the water with Torque, and she could do nothing. Her chest burned as she watched Blake come even with the ship, then over-take it. He swung Torque around, so they faced the ves-sel. He bellowed a command, and the horse's hooves ate up the short distance to the edge of the wooden plat-form, then propelled man and best into the air.

Blake and Torque landed on the ship's deck with a clatter of horseshoes. Men rushed forward and sur-rounded Blake. He raised his right hand as he returned his dirk to his belt, then raised his left hand.

"All I want is my wife," Blake explained in French. "I have no interest in fighting anyone. But if you try to keep me from her, there will be bloodshed, and it won't be mine." With his hands still raised, he swung his right leg over his saddle and slid to the deck. When no one approached him, he hurried to Cerys. He drew his knife and reached for the ropes binding her to the mast.

"No." The captain rushed forward.

"We are too far from the dock for me to escape with my wife. I don't intend to make my wife and my horse swim. We are stuck aboard your ship until we reach Calais. I've already sworn not to fight. There is no reason for my wife to remain confined. I'll cut her free, then give you my sword and knife."

"Very well," the captain said with a heavy accent. "I am René Saint-Michel." The man didn't linger after announcing his name,

Blake didn't fear being unarmed, since he had knives hidden. When no one moved to stop him, he severed the restraints around Cerys, displeased to see rope burn on her wrists. He ran his thumbs over the underside of her wrists before tossing his knife behind him. He pulled her into a brief but heated kiss.

With regret, he pulled away, but only long enough to hand his sword to the captain. He noticed a deckhand already had Torque by the reins. The horse looked to Blake as if asking permission. When Blake nodded, the animal allowed the man to lead him to the hold where the crew stored other animals for the journey.

"I have never been so terrified in my life," Cerys whispered.

"Did ye doubt I would come for ye, *mo chridhe*?"

"Of course not. I was terrified that you and Torque wouldn't make the leap, that you would miss the ship completely, or worse, slam into the side and be knocked out."

"There was nay way I was letting ye leave without me, wife. Where ye go, I go. Nae even the devil himself could keep me from ye." Blake sat beside Cerys and drew her into the space between his legs. Their kiss was much slower and languid than the one from a moment ago. Beneath Cerys's cloak, his hands roved over

235

all he could reach. "I'm nae letting ye out of ma reach until ma last breath."

"Promise?"

"Och, aye. Ye shall be sick of me before I let ye go."

"I doubt that will be anytime soon. I love you."

"As much as I love ye?"

"Mayhap even more."

"Nae possible, lass."

They sank into another kiss as they reveled in their relief. Cerys rested her head against Blake's chest, finally feeling at ease since the moment they realized someone had drugged them. His arms tightened, creating a shield to protect her from the world. Despite the hours in a drug-induced stupor, she suddenly felt weary.

"Sleep, little one," Blake whispered before kissing her temple. She tried to shake her head, but he squeezed. "Rest. Ye still arenae used to this type of strain. Ye will fall ill if ye dinna. Listen to yer body."

"If I did that, I'd be coupling with ye in front of this entire crew." Cerys shifted, pressing her hip against Blake's arousal. She'd felt it the moment she moved onto his lap. It had only swelled further as his hands roamed over her. His touch made her core ache, and she wasn't sure she could sleep without satisfaction.

"Ye dinna half tempt me, *mo ghràidh*," Blake murmured ruefully. "But I dinna want anyone to see us sharing our passion. That is for us alone."

"I know. I don't want anyone watching us either, but that doesn't mean I don't want you."

"Tonight. When it's dark. I'll ease that ache when I'm certain nay one can see." Blake was true to his word. Once night fell, he slid his hand beneath Cerys's skirts and worked her heated flesh. She turned her head into his chest to silence her moans as she climaxed. It necessitated more logistics to free Blake's cock, so she could stroke. But Cerys was determined, and Blake appreciated every moment until his seed spilled over her hand. It wasn't long before Cerys slept soundly against him. He only allowed himself to doze in fits and starts, trusting no one who had the cover of darkness to strike. Besides their love play, the night was uneventful.

They arrived in Calais, and men hurried them off the ship before dock workers and the crew unloaded crates and barrels. Cerys and Blake watched as the captain talked to another man, gesturing in their direction. They couldn't hear the conversation, but neither looked pleased. They bore a strong resemblance, so the couple assumed the men were closely related. Eventually, René dropped a coin purse into the other man's hand, and they both approached the couple.

"This is my brother, Jean-Philippe, and those are his four sons," the captain explained in French as he gestured to a group of men standing across the dock from them. "He will take you to Château Gaillard."

No one could ever describe the man as verbose. Cerys and Blake turned their attention to the sailor's clearly displeased brother. He barely spared them a nod before he called out orders to his sons. He said nothing to the couple before he stalked off.

"I thought you were to convey me to the château. My father paid you to do that."

"Your father paid to ensure you arrive there. I cannot be away from my ship for that long, and my brother lives in that direction." René shrugged. "By the by, he only speaks French."

Cerys and Blake were soon left staring at the captain's back before turning toward Jean-Philippe and his sons. Cerys couldn't imagine traveling with the five men alone. She inched closer to Blake, ever grateful that she had a husband, especially one who struck fear in most men's hearts. Without another word, they mounted their horses and departed Calais, following Jean-Philippe, who drove his wagon, and his four sons on horseback.

CHAPTER 19

*T*he first day of their journey in France, the weather was fair and lulled Cerys and Blake into thinking it would be milder than Scotland. The second day and the next five proved otherwise. The constant downpours threatened to wash away roads and made mud come up to the horses' fetlocks. It was slippery and dangerous. Blake wished Cerys could ride with him the entire time, but it was precarious enough for one rider per horse. He wouldn't risk Torque or Kitten. But he insisted she wrap his plaid around her head and shoulders. He taught her how to fold it into a Highland arisaid, then produced one for himself. He kept his breeks on and covered himself in it.

It surprised Cerys how warm and dry it kept her. She had her own Kerr plaid that she'd left at Cessford before moving to Stirling, but it was something she almost never wore. Most Lowlanders didn't unless they attended an event where they wished to distinguish themselves among many clans. She understood now why Highlanders preferred them. Despite being sopping wet, the wool somehow insulated her from the cold and rain. She huddled under it as she sneaked peeks at Blake, who seemed unfazed by the foul weather. The Frenchmen appeared like drowned rats. No one complained, but she could tell the French wished to. They probably would have had they not been in Blake's company. They refused to appear weak before him when his only acknowledgment that the weather was against them was to pull his plaid over his head.

On their final day of travel, the sun peeked out from behind the thinning cloud cover at last. The cold wind was gone, and the rain was more a mist than a deluge. On Jean-Philippe's insistence, they'd slept in proper beds at inns each night. It was also at Blake's expense. Jean-Philippe claimed the coins René gave him were merely to get them to the château, not to ensure they had food or shelter. He demanded Blake provide those things. The Highlander wanted to argue that the man and his sons would have faced the inclement weather regardless of whether Cerys and Blake traveled with them. But it was a small price to pay to get Cerys a hot bath and hot meal each night. It gave them privacy to make love slowly and enjoy their time alone.

As they spotted the royal estate, neither knew what to expect. They parted ways with Jean-Philippe and his sons, which suited them both. But it meant there were only the two of them as they approached the armed guards. The warriors were all French and distrusting of the foreigners. But once Blake spoke his clan's name, one of the guards nodded vigorously, firing off an explanation in rapid French to his comrades. The man explained that the Sinclairs were one of the most famous clans in Scotland and were known for their prowess with swords and women. The latter made Blake scowl, but Cerys chuckled.

The guards admitted them, and a servant pointed to the estate's main doors. Stablehands appeared to take their mounts before they walked up the stairs to the entrance. They looked at one another, uncertain whether they should knock or wait. A man who pulled open a massive door answered their unspoken question. He ushered them in and told them to remain in the entryway. An efficient-looking woman, who introduced herself as Madame Remier, led them abovestairs to a chamber that overlooked a sprawling garden.

The massive bed looked more inviting than any Blake or Cerys had ever seen. There was an opulence they'd never before experienced. They looked at each other as the housekeeper explained a bath would be sent to them, and the evening meal would be in three hours. She offered to send up a tray now, which they both eagerly accepted. Once they were alone, Blake put his finger to his lips. Cerys's brow furrowed, but Blake shook his head. As Scots, the guards at the gate hadn't collected any of Blake's weapons, so he still had his sword on his back. Instead of withdrawing it, he pulled a *sgian dubh* from his boot. He moved along the wall with the fireplace, methodically running his hands over all the stones. He brought his eye close to the wall, stooping several inches to be at a more average height. He found what he sought and glowered. He pulled his leine from his breeks and cut a strip of cloth, which he stuffed into the spyhole. He would have no one watching him with his wife. He wondered if anyone occupied the chamber next to theirs and if there was someone who would attempt to make use of the tiny hole. Once he finished his search of that wall, he moved to the one along which the bed sat. He began close to the window and worked his way across. He found nothing in that wall.

By the time he finished his search, Madame Remier returned with an army of servants who rolled in a copper and wood tub. Maids lined the tub then dumped buckets of steaming water into the massive basin. She offered to launder Cerys's gown, but the younger woman politely declined. It embarrassed her to admit she only had the one kirtle. The housekeeper tsked and assured her that she would find something suitable for Cerys while she saw to the noblewoman's gown. Cerys wanted to ask from whom she would borrow clothes, but she opted to graciously accept the woman's second offer.

Blake waited to undress until after Cerys ducked behind a screen to remove her gown and gave it to Madame Remier. They didn't dawdle once the older woman left. They yanked their clothes from one another with an urgency that ripped Cerys's chemise and nearly snapped the laces to Blake's breeks. They chuckled but were not deterred. Blake backed Cerys against the bed poster, hooking one of her legs over his hip. He nipped at her neck before trailing his tongue over the dip between her collarbones. She tunneled her fingers into his hair, relishing the feel of his hands and mouth on her skin. She moaned and arched into him when his tongue laved her nipple. His teeth tugged it into a puckered dart. When his mouth took in as much as he could and suckled, Cerys feared her legs would buckle. He alternated breasts as Cerys reached down to wrap her hand around his cock.

Blake was certain he'd go cross-eyed if his eyes weren't already closed, reveling in the feel of Cerys's breasts in his hands and mouth. They weren't overly large, nor were they small. They were exactly what Blake wanted. His broad hands could cover most of the flesh, but they were ample enough that they left Blake wishing he could suckle more. His fingers found her sheath after he'd trailed them over her belly and elicited a shiver. He ran them along her seam, once more drawing a moan from Cerys. He dipped one, then two, then three, fingers into her entrance. Temptation gnawed at him when he discovered how damp his wife was for him. He wanted to plunge into her over and over, but the more consuming need was to taste her. He lowered her leg and dropped to his knees, but he soon had the leg hooked over his shoulder.

Cerys reached over her head and gripped the wood pole, bracing herself as her body quivered with need. Blake roused a fire inside her belly unlike anything she'd imagined as a girl wondering what it would be like to couple with a man, hotter than she'd imagined when she met Blake. His tongue flicked her nub over and over as his fingers parted her netherlips. He drew his tongue along her seam as her hips undulated against his face. When his tongue finally slid inside her, she was panting.

"Teach me how to do this to you," she begged.

Blake shook his head, refusing to cease his ministrations. But he pulled back long enough to look at her when he felt her stiffen. He realized what his response meant to her. "Nae now, lass. Later. Right now, I'm busy feasting on ma wife." He returned his attention to her quim. When he swept his tongue over his lips, clearly savoring her taste, Cerys thought she might collapse. Then his tongue touched her, and she was certain of it. She shifted, needing to sit on the bed to keep from falling. Blake's hands came around her waist and lifted her onto the bed farther. He remained on his knees and worked her nub until she cried out. As he came to his feet, he watched the rapid rise and fall of his bride's chest, pride humming within him.

But he didn't expect her quick recovery or how she'd snatch his hand and yank him toward the bed. He was unprepared for her speed as she pushed him onto the mattress and rolled to her knees. She examined his cock as her hand wrapped around it again. She leaned forward and lapped up the pearl of fluid that leaked from his tip.

"Teach me." This wasn't a request but a demand.

"Lick and suckle like I do with yer breast, but dinna bite." Blake finished with a chuckle as Cerys shot him a glance that clearly said, "obviously."

Cerys swirled her tongue over the head of Blake's shaft before licking him from stem to stern. She stroked him twice before taking a breath and lowering her mouth onto him. He grabbed handfuls of bedding to keep from thrusting into her mouth. The tentativeness and hesitations only drove him crazy. He'd enjoyed this experience before, but it had only been with experienced women, who were paid to make it quick and satisfactory. His wife's inexperience was a tease she didn't realize she created. He wanted to squeeze his eyes closed as waves of pleasure and need coalesced. He knew she didn't know how her exploration was more erotic than any wenches' previous actions.

"Cerys, ye're getting me too close. I dinna want to climax like this. Nae in yer mouth." He tried to sit up, but Cerys pressed against his chest with surprising force. When he tried to lift her away, she clamped her mouth around him and redoubled her efforts. She gagged as she tried to take all of him into her mouth. She forced herself to calm, breathing through her nose and relaxing. When the head of his cock slid against the back of her throat, Blake's mind had no control over his body. His hips surged upward, nearly choking Cerys. But she refused to relent. With a groan that surely came from his soul, Blake climaxed and shuddered.

When Cerys no longer felt waves of Blake's seed hit her throat, she eased back, licking his rod as she retreated. She watched him as he screwed his eyes shut, tremors still running through his body. But his sigh wasn't blissful like hers had been. It was frustration. When he looked at her at last, her brow was furrowed in confusion and anxiousness.

"Ye didna do aught wrong." Blake took her hand and tugged her to lie alongside him. He drew her arm over his waist and held her tightly. "I didna want to finish like that because I feared it would scare ye, make ye regret it."

"Why would I ever regret bringing you to release? You didn't stop any of the times you've tasted me while I climaxed." Cerys stilled. "Wasn't I supposed to do that? Is that what only whores do?"

Blake rolled onto his side and nudged Cerys's chin up until their gazes met. "What we share as husband and wife has naught to do with what anyone else does. We may enjoy the same acts as a mon and his—companion—but it is nae the same. We share this because we love each other. This is nae a transaction. I dinna want ye to think less of yerself for doing it or fear I will think less of ye. But I dinna want ye to do aught ye dinna enjoy."

"I did enjoy it," Cerys whispered.

"I'm glad to hear that because I certainly enjoyed it too." Blake grinned.

"None of it scared me, Blake. It was new and strange at times, but I liked watching you. I liked knowing I was giving you pleasure. As for your release, I didn't know what to expect, but it wasn't bad."

"Wasna bad." Blake chuckled. "I'm relieved of that, lass."

"I meant, I didn't consider what that much would—taste like." Cerys felt her cheeks heat. But if she couldn't talk openly to Blake about this, then they wouldn't be as close as they believed. "I didn't dislike it. I just need to get used to it."

"Ye wish to do that again?" Blake tried to keep the

eagerness from his voice, but she must have seen it in his gaze because she giggled.

"Yes."

"Ye might be the death of me, *leannan*. Come. Let's bathe. The water shall grow cold soon."

They climbed into the bath, finding the water the perfect temperature. They wouldn't have been able to get in any sooner. As Cerys ran the soapy linen square over Blake's body, kneading his tight shoulders and back, then teasing the cloth over his rippled abdomen, they grew aroused once more. They kissed as they washed one another until neither could wait any longer to join. Blake eased Cerys onto his rod as she kneeled over him. They both sighed at the feeling of Blake entering her, a sense that they'd both come home.

Cerys rocked slowly, just enough to keep them both on edge as they washed each other's hair. When all the suds were gone, Blake wrapped Cerys's mane around his hand and tugged gently. She tilted her head back, exposing her throat to his ravishing kisses. Their movement increased, water sloshing against the sides. They'd discovered how much they both enjoyed making love in water. Neither had taken a bath alone since they married. Each occasion grew more sensuous. Their movements were languid, both wanting to make the moment last. When neither could hold back their release, they crested together, their arms wrapped around one another.

Blake lifted Cerys from the tub, her legs wrapping around him before he draped a drying cloth over her. But their post-coital bliss was interrupted by a knock at the door. Blake lowered Cerys to the floor and handed her the drying linen. She ducked behind the screen as Blake tied another around his waist. He bid whoever was at the door to enter. Cerys peeked around the screen and watched a pretty young woman enter the chamber. She carried clothes for Cerys, but her eyes feasted on Blake. He appeared not to notice, but he hastened to put on a fresh leine. The woman drew too close. He took a step back, but she followed.

"Mademoiselle, arrêtez. Vous apportez des vestements à ma femme que je vais habiller. Vous allez partir mantenant." Miss, stop. You bring clothes to my wife, who I will dress. You will leave now. The command and annoyance were clear in Blake's voice. The woman blinked several times before dropping the clothes on the bed and spinning on her heel. Blake pressed his lips together as Cerys's voice carried from behind the screen.

"Vous pouvez regarder, mais si jamais vous essayex de toucher, je vous couperai les mains et vous arracherei les yeux comme un corbeau." You may look, but if you ever try to touch, I will cut off your hands and pluck out your eyes like a crow.

The woman flew to the door, slamming it behind her. Cerys gave an exaggerated huff as she emerged from her hideaway. They wrapped their arms around each other, and Cerys rested her head against Blake's chest.

"I know I'll have to get used to women appreciating how you look, but I will not accept one trying to touch you. Thank you for sending her away."

"I dinna want another woman to touch me. It's annoying. But do ye ken now why I dinna like other men leering at ye?"

"Yes. I shall protect you from those brazen women just as you protect me from those uncouth men."

"Protect me, will ye?"

"Aye. I will protect ye from pushy lasses who think I share. I dinna."

Blake laughed heartily at Cerys's attempt at a Highland burr. It wasn't half bad, but it was endearing to watch her concentrate more on her accent than the claim she made. He lifted her off her feet and gave her a smacking kiss before giving her backside a playful smack. They dressed and sat before the fire to let Cerys's hair dry. She'd just finished braiding it when another knock sounded.

It was too early for the evening meal, so the couple glanced at one another before they rose. Blake drew a dirk from his boot. Though the person at the door had knocked, he wouldn't trust that meant the person wasn't a threat.

"*Entrez.*" Blake called once Cerys tucked herself behind him. He'd given her the dirks he'd taken after killing the men in the woods and then Stewart and his men, but she didn't feel as though she needed them with Blake there. A guard opened the door and stepped aside. Cerys felt Blake relax, then put away his knife. She peeked around her giant husband and breathed easier.

"*Mon cousin!*" A young male voice greeted them.

"*Mon cousin.*" Blake's deep timber rumbled compared to the higher pitch of their guest. Blake and the new arrival clasped arms in a warrior handshake before embracing. When Blake stepped back, he bowed. "Yer Majesty."

Cerys stepped around Blake and dipped into a low curtsy. It was only then that she spied Queen Joan, who looked less-than-delighted to see the Scottish couple. She remained just inside the doorway. Blake straightened then bowed toward the queen. He wrapped Cerys's arm around his once she rose.

"Sinclair, what brings you here?" King David wasn't related to the Sinclairs by blood, but Blake, his siblings, and his cousins-by-blood considered the king to be an extension of their family. Many members of the family had never met him, but they all knew the long ties between the Sinclairs and Bruces. "Who is this?"

"Yer Majesty." Blake saw no reason to sound anything but his normal self, but he could tell the queen wasn't impressed. At least not with his accent. He wondered if she knew of the familial ties. As she cast an unimpressed gaze over him, then Cerys, he doubted she did. "Ma wife, Lady Cerys, and I made an unexpected voyage here."

"Lady Cerys?" Queen Joan stepped forward, suddenly taking an interest. "You are one of my ladies, are you not?"

"I am, Your Grace. I've served you for two years." It felt odd to say that, since she'd never once met the queen and had never been a true lady-in-waiting.

"I believed you unwed." Queen Joan cast a speculative gaze at Blake. The young woman was barely more than a girl, but it was clear she already took a healthy interest in men. Cerys glanced at the king, who was tall for his age and already beginning to fill out. He would likely inherit his father's stature, but he was still more child than man.

"My husband and I wed only recently, Your Grace."

"My felicitations." King David grinned at Blake but offered a more circumspect smile to Cerys. Queen Joan came to stand beside her husband, but her attention was still riveted to Blake. It tempted him to take up Cerys's offer of protection and step behind her. The young woman's inspection ran from his roots to his toes. When he looked at the adolescent girl, it was as if he looked at his sister. When he gazed down at Cerys, his cock threatened to come back to life, and his heart fluttered.

"Thank ye, Yer Majesty. I met ma bonnie bride at court and kenned the moment I saw her that I found ma match."

"Och, one of those Sinclair matches, then." The young king chuckled. "Your Grace, you can cease eying my cousin like an Epiphany goose. He won't stray. He won't even flirt."

Cerys and Blake fought to keep the shock from their expressions. The king spoke to his queen as though she'd already made a habit of infidelity, and he seemed not to care. The queen glowered at the man-child before casting another assessing look at Blake. It was clear she took it as a challenge, disregarding Cerys or the way Blake's hand covered hers on his arm.

"It is such a match. I couldnae help but fall in love with ma wife. She's as close to perfect as I will ever find. Dinna tell ma father, but she's a wee more perfect than ma mother. I ken now how Da feels aboot Mama. Cerys is everything to me. That's how I came to be here." Blake hoped his assertion would deter Queen Joan, but the stubborn woman appeared to redouble her interest. "Yer Majesty, Lady Cerys discovered a plot against ye. Murray kens. The men conspiring against ye learned that ma wife overheard it. We went to the Kerrs, but they still havenae resigned themselves to our familial ties. Having a second marriage between them and ma clan didna sit well. They looked to make ma wife a widow and tried to send her here alone. I have at least another three-score years before I'm willing to leave ma wife's side."

"Cease with the 'Your Majesties,' Blake. It grows tiresome." David scowled jovially.

"As ye wish, Davie." Blake's teeth shone as he grinned. The king pretended to growl but nodded heartily. "This is a matter to discuss with yer council-men. But I would prepare ye first."

Blake cast a brief but speaking glance at Joan. David sighed but nodded once more. This one was more re-luctant.

"*Leannan*, do ye wish to tell David and Her Grace?"

"What does that mean? *Leannan?*" Joan interrupted, her English tones harsh as she spoke the Gaelic word.

"Sweetheart." Blake's voice softened as he looked down at Cerys. He sensed how uncomfortable the queen made Cerys. He knew she didn't fear him straying, but it clearly embarrassed and annoyed her to watch the woman's eyes devour him. But she made no outward sign of how it bothered her. He'd seen David notice his wife's beauty. It was impossible not to. But the adolescent either wasn't of an age to appreciate Cerys's appearance, or he had the good graces to understand how inappropriate it was to ogle the wife of someone who was virtually a family member.

"Your Majesty, I—"

"It's David to you to, my lady. I'm not related by blood to the Sinclairs, but I may as well be. I assume your husband has already told you my parents were the Sinclair children's godparents. His grandfather is my godfather. I've known Blake and the aulder Sinclair cousins since I was born. You are my family now too. As such, whatever you tell me, you will be under my protection."

"Thank you—David." Cerys wasn't certain she would get used to it, but she wouldn't slight him by disobeying the monarch, exiled or not. "I was in the Stirling Castle stables when Shaw Hannay, Stanley Home, and Domnall Cunningham came in. They didn't know anyone could hear them. Shaw avowed his support for Balliol, and the other two didn't disagree. Shaw said he'd dispatched a messenger to his clan upon Murray's arrival with your army." Cerys was careful not to make it sound as though Murray held his own army, even if that was reality. The men who fought alongside Blake while on campaign with Murray were technically King David's army. "He said another messenger would be dispatched from there to the Cliffords. He assumed

Balliol is hiding among them in Cumbria, but I don't know at which keep. He stated clearly that you are no longer safe in France. He made it sound as though mercenaries are on their way."

Joan gasped, but it was for show. She leaned toward Blake, as though he might protect or comfort her. David made an annoyed sound in the back of his throat, and Blake didn't take his eyes off Cerys. But she was no longer willing to ignore the young woman's slight. She locked eyes with the exiled queen and stared. Her gaze was unwavering, daring the English teenager to challenge her further. She raised her chin in defiance, almost taunting the queen. She felt Blake's arm come around her waist and draw her against his side, but she didn't break her focus. Joan blinked first. She leaned away from Blake, and her shoulders slumped slightly. Cerys wasn't fooled. The younger woman thought she would elicit pity from Blake, as though Cerys meant to harm her rather than warn her. But her face turned red as Blake kissed Cerys's temple and squeezed her waist. It tempted Cerys to stick her tongue out in victory.

"Mercenaries?" David spoke up to ease the tension. He knew he had no control over his young wife. At least not yet. He knew she saw him as little more than a child, but he was more patient than Joan. He would bide his time, but there would be no doubt in the coming years who led their marriage. When he came to an age where she would have no choice but to take him seriously, he would rein her in and ensure she remembered her place.

"Yes. I don't know who or when. But he sounded completely convinced that his plan would work."

"Has there been any trouble here of late?" Blake asked.

"None. We are left alone for the most part. Philip

visits from time to time, but there is little excitement beyond the occasional hunts. We should speak to my council. Joan," David finally acknowledged his wife. "You may retire now that you've met our guests. Blake and Lady Cerys will accompany me. We will see you at the evening meal."

Joan's jaw clenched, displeased at her dismissal. But she left without fuss. Cerys was certain Blake's sigh matched hers. But David's next words shocked them both.

"She knows better than to take her curiosity too far. I'm young enough to have ten wives before I die. If she wishes to remain queen, be it in exile or not, she won't break her vows. But that doesn't mean she isn't provocative. Lady Cerys, you did well to stake your claim. Don't relent, or she will latch on and not let go until you ride through the gates."

Cerys didn't know what to say, so she merely replied, "Thank you."

CHAPTER 20

$\mathcal{D}$avid led them from the chamber to a larger one belowstairs. When they entered, men were already there. They examined parchments or spoke in clusters of two and three. But the conversation ceased when they entered. Blake was uncertain whether it was deference to David, surprise at the newcomers, or shock that Cerys was there. Men bowed to David as he moved to a chair at the center of a long, oblong table.

"This is Lady Cerys and Blake Sinclair. They are my guests. They're newly arrived from Stirling. Blake is Magnus Sinclair's son and the grandson of Liam Sinclair, the Earl of Caithness."

The chamber was filled with Scotsmen who turned toward Blake. Each man sized him up, some with suspicion, others with recognition.

"I knew you to be a Sinclair the moment you entered. I should have known you were Magnus's lad." A burly man with a tinge of Highland burr to his accent approached. He sounded like Blake when the younger man spoke like a Lowlander. The man stuck out his arm to Blake. "Eliot Mackintosh."

Blake grasped forearms with the man before he

bowed to Cerys. Other men followed suit. When they were done greeting nearly everyone, Blake guided Cerys to a seat and took the one to her right.

"Blake and Lady Cerys bring startling, but not entirely surprising, news."

Blake wondered how something could startle without surprise, but he wouldn't contradict the young king.

"What news do you bring?" Eliot asked.

"We're aware of a plot to send mercenaries here." Blake didn't prevaricate, but he did revert to his Lowland accent, much to Cerys's disappointment. By the look of annoyance on more faces, he came to understand what the king meant. It surprised no one that the threat continued against David. But they were unaware that there was one so immediate. "We don't know when or how. But I suspect Gallowglass men. I don't think it will be a lone mon or two. I think it will be an orchestrated attack since there are French and Scots warriors here."

"When did you hear of this?" A Lowlander demanded. Blake turned his gaze to the man, who seemed to deflate under Blake's attention.

"Aboot a three sennights ago." Cerys spoke up, testing how the men would respond to her participation. Most ignored her and waited for Blake to answer. A few gave her thoughtful perusals, most in a nonleering manner. But Blake's arm around her shoulders made most catch themselves before being too obvious.

"Why come here yourselves?" Eliot wondered.

Blake stroke Cerys's shoulder as he answered. "My wife was a Kerr." He ignored the shocked expression from the men old enough to remember the scandal that his uncle Alex and aunt Brighde's marriage was after the former Laird Kerr tried to kill his own daughter but died by Alex's hand instead. "Her family isn't as accepting as mine. They wished to end the marriage, and since annulment isn't an option, they planned to make her a widow. Since Lady Cerys hasn't been officially dismissed from service, and her family no longer sees her as useful at Stirling, they tried to send her here alone."

"You married while she was still in service to the queen?" Another man chimed in, censure in his voice.

"We didn't plan to visit at the time. Securing permission could have taken several moons. While my clansmen have been dismissed from Murray's service for now, I was still representing the Sinclairs. I wished to marry my wife before I risked being sent on campaign again. Our plan had been for her to travel to Dunbeath with my father and uncles, but that changed." Blake wouldn't offer more than that.

"The Earl of Caithness knows his family does not require my permission to wed as they wish." David spoke with authority that belied his young age. It was clear that he wasn't held in equal standing to the more experienced and aged men, but neither was he an inconsequential child. He might not control his wife well, but he was already proving he would be a formidable man when he grew into his role fully. "Let us turn our attention to the threat. We know it's the Hannays who lead this, which is unsurprising. They never accepted my father, and they continue to support the Balliols. They are so far up each Edward's arse, they could climb out the Sassenach's mouth."

"Without any clue to when—or rather if—mercenaries will arrive, there is naught we can do." Yet another Lowlander spoke. Blake watched Eliot and the other three Highlanders in the chamber roll their eyes. He didn't know the other three, but their size and bearing gave them away.

"Spoken like a mon who hasn't sharpened his sword

in years." A Highlander grumbled before turning to Blake. "Patrick MacDonnell."

"Adam MacPherson," another man said.

"Angus Ogilvy," said the final Highlander. The Ogilvies were neighbors to the Sinclairs. Blake had known the man most of his, but he hadn't seen him in years. He knew the older warrior married Lady Margaret Hay, which indirectly connected him to Cerys and Blake through scandal. It was Margaret's now-dead uncle, Archibald, who had an affair with Cerys's now-dead aunt, Mary. It was also Margaret's uncle who was supposed to marry Blake's mother when her parents forced her away from Magnus after they handfasted. But Blake begrudged the man nothing. Instead, he felt rather sorry for him after what he'd heard about Margaret. He didn't blame Angus for scarpering off to France to live among the exiled king's court. He wasn't an heir, so he had no need to remain with his wife or clan.

"We double the watch each night and have the men spend two more hours in the lists each day," Adam MacPherson announced.

"We need to add at least one more patrol and shift the others," Angus Ogilvy said after nodding his agreement.

"I'll oversee the men in the lists," Patrick MacDonnell offered.

"This seems a little excessive," the Lowlander who still hadn't introduced himself spoke up again.

"Nonsense, Johnstone." Adam shot him a look of contempt.

"Johnstone?" Cerys blurted. "My mother was a Johnstone."

"I know." The man looked at Cerys with disinterest. "She was my sister."

"Your sister?" Cerys's ears rang. She'd never met the

man, since she knew none of her mother's people. She didn't even know she had an uncle, let alone one who served King David and lived in France.

"Yes. Eleanor was my twin."

Cerys felt tears threaten as her gorge rose. The man barely looked at her, taking no interest in her. It cut deeply that she sat before family, and it stirred no loyalty or hospitality in the man. He could have spoken up sooner. He could have inquired about her safety while she was in Stirling and when they traveled. Instead, he treated her as though she were an insignificant nuisance.

"Johnstone, you're an arse. You could have told the lass when she was introduced," Eliot chastised.

"She knows where her kin lives. She's made no effort to know the Johnstones, and our efforts were rebuffed since my sister left our home."

"You tried?" Cerys choked.

"Do not pretend not to know. You saw us."

"When? I did not."

"We came to your first wedding." The man sneered. "I saw you looking at us when we were turned away."

"Merciful saints. I didn't know who you were. That —that was the worst day. I—" Cerys looked up at Blake, who pulled her into his embrace as he glared at the man.

"There was no wedding that day. In its place, Cerys was abused. She was forced to witness two men murdered. If you'd stayed, insisted on your right to watch your niece marry, you might have protected her. To my ear, you gave up far too easily. You can remove that expression before my wife turns around, or I will remove it. You will not speak to my wife with that tone either. She was a lass of six-and-ten that day, with no control over who her uncle admitted through the gates. You were a grown mon who could have tried harder." Blake rose to his full height, bringing Cerys with him. Despite his arms wrapped around Cerys, he kept his shoulders back. The full expanse of his chest was impressive, but with Cerys pressed against him, the contrast made him look even larger.

"What are you talking aboot?"

"Steven," a Lowlander warned. The man looked at Blake and Cerys. "I am Edward Johnstone. I am Steven's younger brother. I was there that day, too. I was too young to insist on aught, but Steven, you could have tried harder. I think you were glad to leave. You still haven't forgiven Muir for how he treated Eleanor when she was carrying. I haven't either, but that was hardly our niece's fault."

Cerys looked over her shoulder at the man who'd just spoken. He looked so much like Cerys that the familial connection was uncontestable. She knew they looked more alike than she did with Steven, who had been her mother's twin. She deduced Eleanor and Steven must not have resembled each other despite sharing a womb at the same time.

"Lady Cerys, we know what happened that day. We didn't learn of it until a year later, but we know what you were accused of, and we know them to have been ridiculous assertions made to protect your father's pride. But it was not long after that Steven and I journeyed here. I am sorry for what you've endured, niece. We should have done more."

"Thank you—Uncle." It felt strange addressing a man as such who wasn't her father's brother. She didn't feel any compulsion to call Steven that. But Edward struck her as kindly. He seemed to share the same disposition that Matilda said her mother had possessed.

"If the lass is your kin, then all the more reason to increase the defenses," Adam chimed in. "We have the king and queen, and you have your niece, Steven. We make the changes." As if it were an afterthought, he turned to David. "If that suits your wishes, Your Majesty."

"Don't simper, MacPherson," David said. "You know I will defer to you. You've distinguished yourself more than once in battle. I'm still learning to wield a sword. If you think we're best protected to increase the watches and patrols, then make it happen. Johnstone, when we're attacked, you face as much of a threat as I do. You'd do well to remember that it's your niece who warned us. I, for one, am grateful that we can prepare. I do not think it is an if. I'm certain it is a when."

The king's prediction proved correct.

Cerys froze as she entered the château's Great Hall. Wilma sat on the dais to Joan's left. She squeezed Blake's hand, who continued to walk into the gathering area, seeming not to notice.

"Dinna stare, lass. I see her." Blake nodded to the men they'd met earlier that day as he guided Cerys to the dais. Two seats remained open, and Blake knew they'd been saved for them. It was a privilege afforded him through birthright as a Sinclair. But he knew it would make Cerys uncomfortable with so much attention. There was little he could do. "Let us take our seats. We'll figure it out soon enough."

Soon enough came immediately. Wilma spotted Cerys and waved, calling out to her. "Lady Cerys! Lady Cerys!"

"Lady Wilma." Cerys's voice was far more modulated than the magpie Wilma sounded like. "I didn't realize you were here."

"Oh, yes."

Cerys waited for a lengthier explanation, but none

was forthcoming. It surprised Cerys, since she'd never heard Wilma be so succinct. "When did you arrive?"

"The other day." Wilma waved her hand in a vague gesture. "There was naught to do once you left. Where did you go? Why did you leave? Why didn't you tell me?"

As Wilma rattled off one question after another, Cerys felt more at ease. Annoying as it was to be bombarded, it felt familiar and predictable. Little had been predictable in the past moon, so it relieved some of Cerys's nerves.

"My husband and I," Cerys beamed at Blake. "Went to my clan after we left Stirling. We thought to announce our marriage." That statement wiped the smile from Cerys's face and left a bitter taste.

"Husband? So the rumors are true. At least some of them."

"Rumors?" Cerys was certain she didn't want to know, yet she felt like she needed to know.

"Some people claim you married in the Stirling kirk. Others say you merely ran off with Blake. Plenty say he abducted you as Highlanders are wont to do. Bride stealing and all." Wilma once again waved her hand in a vague gesture. Blake bristled at the comment. While it wasn't unheard of, the Sinclairs did not steal women. They had no need to.

"We married in Stirling and set off for Cessford, where we spent nearly a fortnight."

"What brings you here?" Wilma persisted. Motion caught her eye and shifted her gaze for a moment. But in that brief flash, Cerys saw something harden. There was a gravity there that she'd never witnessed in Wilma before. Cerys twisted to follow Wilma's line of sight, but she couldn't tell at whom Wilma glanced. Then the lady-in-waiting was once more staring at Cerys.

"King David is like family to the Sinclairs." Blake intervened, his hand on Cerys's shoulder. He didn't appreciate Wilma's questions since he'd seen her hardened gaze, but he hadn't discerned at whom she flicked her gaze. He didn't care for the woman while they were in Stirling, and something seemed amiss. However, without Torquil or the other Sinclair men, Wilma clearly took little interest in him.

"You must have left court not long after we did, Lady Wilma. When was that?" Cerys wanted an explanation to the coincidence that brought them together. Wilma had never hinted before that she wished to come to France or that she had the means to make the voyage.

"I believe it was a sennight after. I thought to go home, but I couldn't just leave the queen's service without notice." There was a chiding element to Wilma's tone. Cerys's eyes shifted to Joan, who smirked but was otherwise silent. "I decided France was the better choice. There were still too many warriors lurking in Stirling to feel safe with all the honorable ones gone."

Wilma finally settled her full gaze on Blake and smiled. It was coy and flirtatious, which made Cerys want to draw her talons and rake them over Wilma's face. She also wanted to look up and see her husband's reaction, but the soft sound of disgust told her everything.

"You feared for your safety and thought traveling to France alone to a court in exile was a wiser choice. Who chaperoned you, Lady Wilma?" Blake's burr was once more gone. His tone sounded convivial, but Cerys already knew it well enough to recognize the edge.

"My guards of course." Wilma offered a single shoulder shrug, brushing off the question. She ignored the rest of Blake's comment. Servants began winding among the tables, platters of food in their hands. It gave

Blake and Cerys the excuse they needed to take their seats. Blake sat directly to David's right, and Cerys sat to Blake's right.

"A friend, Lady Cerys?" David leaned past Blake after the priest blessed the evening meal.

"Yes. Lady Wilma and I arrived in Stirling to serve your wife at the same time. There weren't many of us, so we became friends."

"Interesting. She didn't mention you when she spoke of her time there." David cast a speculative glance at Cerys before looking at Blake and raising an eyebrow. "And she talked a lot."

Cerys wished to look down the table, but Blake's broad shoulders blocked most of her view. What he didn't hinder, David and Joan did. Cerys wondered what Wilma said and whether that might have contributed to Joan's icy reception. Then again, it was the queen's interest in Blake that soured things for Cerys; Wilma merely didn't help. Cerys heard the women's voices raised in laughter, sounding like old friends. She doubted she would find a place for herself in the queen's retinue since Joan already didn't like her, and Wilma found a better person onto whom she could glom. When Wilma's voice floated to Cerys, a ridiculous compliment to the queen flowing forth, never had it been clearer that Wilma was a social climber, and she'd climbed right over Cerys.

"My lady," Madame Remier called out in French as she ran toward Cerys, who sat beside a fireplace sewing. She'd found a chamber that the morning sun filled each day. She'd taken to sewing to fill her time while Blake was in the lists. She had nothing else with which to occupy herself. The housekeeper arrived at Blake and

Cerys's chamber the morning after they arrived with four bolts of fabric. Now a fortnight later, Cerys was finishing her fourth kirtle. She wore one of her new creations since the one in which she arrived was only suitable for travel. Albeit a sparse one, she was still at a royal court and felt compelled to dress the part.

"*Oui, madam,*" Cerys responded. She sensed the urgency in the woman's voice, then watching her lift her skirts and increase her pace as she spied Cerys, made the younger woman toss aside her sewing. Cerys stood and met the woman as she entered the chamber.

"Your husband sent me. Men have been spotted to the west. He told me to take you to the undercroft with the other women. Come." The housekeeper held out her hand. Cerys grabbed her sewing and hurried toward the woman, but rather than following her toward the stairs, she turned toward her chamber. "My lady, we must hurry."

"I know. But I have to go to my chamber first. If they find my clothes or my sewing, they will know there is another lady in residence. If the other ladies are not yet in hiding, they should get their clothing out of sight. If these attackers make it to our bedchambers, they will know there are more victims to search for. And it won't be just killing that is on their minds." Cerys burst into the bedchamber. She flung open the armoire and pulled her new kirtles from their pegs and stuffed them into her chest at the foot of the bed. She shoved everything in, uncaring that they were a tangled heap. She slammed the lid shut and locked it. She put her hands the front and shoved, grateful the chest wasn't tall. It slid beneath the bed. She kneeled and shoved it again, sliding it into the dark recesses. She moved to the door and looked toward the bed. The container wasn't visible.

As she left the chamber with Madame Remier, they

heard women screaming. Cerys looked at the house-keeper. There were no sounds of a fight, just hysterical women. Then there was a Scottish-accented voice bel-lowing in French.

"Cease your caterwauling. You will lead them to our door with your squawking. Why not throw the gates open to them, you hen-wits?"

Cerys suspected it was Eliot Mackintosh, but she wasn't certain. She rushed to the landing and peered down as she heard the click of women's shoes on the stone floor. She leaned forward and spotted the queen surrounded by her attendants. Almost all were French. It was clear none of the women were used to having their homes besieged. Living along the border, it was impossible not to experience it at least once in a life-time. Highlanders still fought one another, despite how the Bruce unified the clans, so Cerys was certain no Scottish woman would descend into a case of the fits at such a threat.

"Cease!" Cerys's voice filled the air. "Go to your chambers and hide your belongings now. Leave no trace that there are women here. Then follow Madame Remier's instructions on where to hide. Do it now."

Cerys watched as the queen shifted her attention and looked up at Cerys. Animosity continued to simmer between the women. Joan had made no further attempts to attract Blake's attention after her failed at-tempts the first week they were in residence. She for-bade Cerys from joining her or the other ladies. That suited Cerys, since she had no aspirations to rise in the queen's favor. Wilma filled that void if it had ever ex-isted. Cerys's former friend watched Cerys as though she was ready to serve her as the Christmas dinner. She clearly valued Joan's attention more than their friendship.

"Where are the servants?" Joan demanded. "They shall tend to that."

"No, Your Grace," Cerys countered. "They will be seeing to the livestock and the food stores. They cannot be taken from that task. If you don't wish these mercenaries to know how many ladies are here to rape, you'd all do well to hide any trace that we're here."

That thought had the panicked women racing up the stairs to follow Cerys's directions. She rattled off instructions, then shooed women to follow Madame Remier in waves to the storerooms and undercroft. Joan refused to come abovestairs to tend to her own belongings. Rather than do as the other women, she demanded the housekeeper lead her to safety with the first group of women. It sorely tempted Cerys to leave the queen's chamber as it was. A vindictive wave washed over her as she thought that it would serve Joan right if the mercenaries tore through her chamber first and directly went in search of her. She chided herself for such an unchristian thought. And she reminded herself that wherever the queen went, the rest of them were sure to follow. That would only mean the men would find them faster.

Cerys raced up to the third floor, where the royal chambers laid. She burst through the door and looked around. For a woman who lived in exile, she also lived in relative grandeur. Cerys found an armoire teeming with clothes and several trunks with undergarments and cloaks. There were rows of shoes. With no time to sort through anything, Cerys gathered the shoes and tossed them into the first unlocked chest she came across. She shoved it under the bed. The next was locked but also short enough to push under the bed. The chest that fit half the kirtles had a rounded lid that made it too tall to hide beneath the furniture. The best she could do with that one and another four was to snap the locks shut. She prayed the mercenaries wouldn't take interest once they found nothing in the armoire. If they were curious, she hoped they wouldn't spend the time to break the locks.

Once she'd done as best she could with the clothes, she found a sack in the bottom of the armoire. She swept her arm across the queen's dressing table, pushing jewels and toiletries into the bag. She drew the strings and closed the bag. She scanned the chamber a last time before running down the two flights of stairs.

"My lady, your husband searches for you." A maid ran to Cerys's side just as a tremendous roar filled the air.

"Cerys!" It sounded like an enraged bear, and Cerys was certain Blake would resemble one when he found her.

"I'm belowstairs!"

Blake stormed down the stairs, leaping over the last five, sword drawn. He looked around as he grasped her arm. Despite how he appeared, his touch was still gentle when he took hold of Cerys. "Why arenae ye hiding, *leannan*?"

"I was hiding the queen's belongings. I hid mine and told the ladies to do the same. I don't want the attackers to know how many ladies are here. They will search harder for us if they know."

Blake pressed a quick and hard kiss to her forehead. "Lass, ye've taken years off ma life, but I am so proud of ye. Come, *mo ghaol*." He led her to the undercroft, where he'd searched for her once he'd helped assign men to different posts throughout the castle and its grounds. He'd panicked when he found the other ladies, but no one knew where Cerys was. He'd wanted to choke Joan for her dismissiveness. Now that he knew Cerys sought to protect the queen and other ladies, he really despised the young consort.

Cerys followed her husband as they wound through the castle until they reached the underground storage area. Five guards stood in front of the door. Cerys pulled on Blake's hand before they reached the men.

"Tell me what's happening."

"Gallowglass men. There's at least three score. They're more an army than a band of cutthroats. It will nae be an easy fight to defeat them, but we have enough men. Cerys, ye dinna let any of the women out of that room unless it is me or a Highlander who comes for ye. Dinna let even these guards open the door. Push barrels and crates against the door and barricade yerselves in."

"Blake." Cerys wrapped her arms around his neck as he lifted her off her feet with one arm. "I love you. Come back to me."

"I will, lass. Ye canna be done with me. I willna let anyone near ye. Ye're mine to love for years to come. We have a family to make together."

Cerys touched her belly as he put her back on her feet. Blake's eyebrows flew to his hairline, but she shook her head. "I have no way to know yet. But it's certainly possible. I want a life with you and a family. Don't do aught foolish, Blake. Stay alive. That's all I ask."

They both knew this was not a promise that Blake could make. He would do all he could to make it back to her. But he wouldn't cease fighting until she was safe, or he drew his last breath.

"I love ye."

"I love you."

They spoke at the same time before exchanging an all too brief kiss. Blake guided her to the door as one of the guards opened it for her. She spun on her heels and watched Blake run toward the bailey as the door closed.

CHAPTER 21

*B*lake stood on the battlements as he watched the wave of mercenaries ride toward them. The organized band of warriors for hire originated in Scotland, but most Gallowglasses were now Irish or Norse. They'd relocated their operation to Ireland not long after they formed. But he suspected there were still plenty of Scotsmen in the approaching attackers. It galled him that his fellow countrymen would sell their allegiance to someone other than their true sovereign. They would fight their fellow Scots for coin, supporting Balliol and his minions merely for money.

"Bluidy bastards," Adam growled.

"Aye." Blake's gaze didn't waver as the other Highlander came to stand beside him. "They're a league away, I'd say." Both men could see the riders who appeared nearly three-and-a-half miles from the keep. The sky was clear, and the sun was behind them, giving them clear visibility. The riders were racing toward the downside of the rise from which they'd stopped to survey the castle. It didn't please Blake that the château was built on a flat stretch of land rather than having the benefit of elevation. But there was nothing anyone could do to change their location.

269

"We'll protect her, lad." Adam clapped a hand on Blake's shoulder. They both knew neither of them spoke of the queen. The Highlanders took charge the moment the patrol rode back to alert the watch. All the Lowlanders were experienced warriors who'd fought the English since they'd been old enough to ride off to battle. But the Highlanders' ferocity and tactics were renowned. Their guerrilla warfare would disorient and isolate the attackers, not allowing them to fight like an organized army. The Lowlanders acquiesced to the Highlanders, knowing arguing wasted time and would likely ensure their defeat.

Blake and most of the nobles had been in the lists with King David when the cry went out. He'd impressed the older warriors with his prowess, but he'd earned their respect when he worked with the thirteen-year-old king. He'd been patient and encouraging, but stern. They'd watched the orphaned king bloom under Blake's tutelage in a way none of the others had ever seen. The men who watched realized it was partially David's familiarity and comfort with Blake, but it was also the manner in which Blake taught. The Highlanders recognized the Sinclairs they'd fought alongside in this member of the younger generation. It made all the observers take notice, and each silently pledged to support the young Highlander, and in turn ensure his wife's safety. Obligations demanded they protect the queen, though Blake had noticed the men barely tolerated her. They would protect Cerys by choice.

"Thank ye." Blake nodded, only mildly more reassured than he'd been before Adam's pledge. The next hour passed with painful slowness. Then the scene erupted as grappling hooks and ladders landed against the retaining wall. They didn't have the oil or tar most keeps had to deter attackers. The archers picked off one attacker after another, but it wasn't long before the Gallowglass fired off their own rounds of projectiles. As men came over the wall, the Scots and French swung their swords, cutting the attackers down before their feet hit the wall walk.

But many survived the climb and clamored over the top of the wall. Blake's head dripped with sweat as he swung his claymore over and over. He'd abandoned his breeks the day after they arrived, and he was glad for it. He moved with ease in his plaid, his stance wide and agile with the material's freedom. Despite the exertion and the several nicks and cuts he took, he endured. Every time he felt the bite of a blade against his skin, or a sword swished too close to a limb or his head, it reminded him that he fought for Cerys. He found his well of energy and commitment was deeper than he ever imagined. He drew from it over and over as the time ticked by.

The attackers were well trained and worked together with obvious training to ensure their unified efforts. It took time for the Lowlanders, Highlanders, and Frenchmen to find a rhythm that supported one another rather than working at cross purposes. But once they came together, the tide turned in their favor. Blake fought until the last Gallowglass took his final breath. He was the one to slay him. He wiped the sweat from his brow with his sleeve as his other arm drew his sword across the dead man's chest, wiping his sword clean.

He inhaled, wincing at the stabbing pain in his ribs. He looked down to find his leine coated in blood. Most was not his, but the stain over his left ribs was his own. He was torn between getting clean then having his wound tended to and finding Cerys to ensure she was safe and to reassure her that he lived. He feared frightening her with his appearance, but his need for his wife won. He stopped at the trough outside the lists to dunk his head into the water. He scrubbed his face and hands to wash away as much blood as he could. There was nothing he could do to hide the blood on his clothing without getting changed.

He, Steven, and Edward made their way to the undercroft, where the men's wives also hid. The men all faltered a step, then burst into a run when they rounded the corner and found slain guards outside the door. The wood had been hacked at, but the door remained in its place. All three men pounded on what was left of the portal, calling out to their wives.

"Cerys! Cerys!" Blake cried in between his knocks.

"Blake, I'm here. Is it safe?"

Blake feared he might faint with relief. "Aye, *mo leannan*. Ye can open the door." He cared not that his burr returned.

"Just a moment."

The three men ceased rapping on the door and listened to objects scraping on the floor. Then the door opened. Blake's arms shot out and yanked Cerys forward. She slammed into him as Steven and Edward pushed past him. Blake spun around, and Cerys inched backward, tugging him with her, until her back hit a wall. Their hands roamed over each other until Cerys felt something sticky and wet on her hand.

"Blake," she hissed. She looked down to find her hand coated in blood.

"Aye. Have ye ever stitched a wound, lass?"

Cerys shook her head, going pale. Tears welled in her eyes as she looked at Blake's ribs, unable to tear her gaze away now that she could see the wound through the tattered fabric.

"Wheest. Dinna fash. It stopped bleeding, but it

needs cleaning and stitching. If ye canna do it, then dinna worry. I can."

Cerys shook her head again, finally meeting his gaze. Blake watched her inhale and press her shoulders back. She composed herself and took another deep inhale. "I can do it. You need to bathe, then I can tend to the wound. I'll call for the tub."

"Nay. There are others who will wish to bathe. I can go to the kitchens and wash there. I dinna need hot water."

Cerys wished to argue, but she swallowed her words. She looked at the other women emerging from their hiding place. Husbands and fathers came to retrieve their women. Those who had no menfolk gathered together with the queen. She watched King David approach Queen Joan. They appeared more awkward than ever. He bowed to his wife and asked how she fared. Assured that she was well, he dropped a perfunctory kiss on her cheek before stating he needed to see to the injured and find his advisors. He hadn't been allowed to fight, instead he had remained hidden away in a dugout hole in an outside storage building. But it was clear the young monarch understood his duties.

Cerys watched Joan's brow furrow as she opened her mouth, but the young woman snapped it closed and nodded. However, she didn't let David step away until after they embraced. David drew her into his arms, standing barely half-a-head taller than Joan. She cupped her husband's face and pressed a kiss to his lips. It was chaste, as was appropriate for a boy his age, but it was the first sign of affection Cerys had seen between the couple.

Blake led Cerys to the kitchens and toward a back corner. He pulled off his leine, and Cerys forced herself not to react. Her husband's body was covered in cuts and bruises, but the slash across his left ribs needed immediate attention. She hurried to bring two buckets of water to where he waited. As he stood still watching her, Cerys noticed how his face paled. She guided him to a stool when he trembled. She wasted no time running the soap over his arms and torso. She wished to argue when he pushed back to his feet, but he insisted. He stepped back into the corner, taking the soap from Cerys. He turned away and washed beneath his plaid. He felt no modesty in front of his wife, but they weren't alone. He did it more to save her the embarrassment than for himself.

By the time he finished, sweat beaded his forehead. Cerys doubted he would make it to their chamber, but he proved his will was stronger than even she suspected. She laid on her belly and pushed her clothes chest out from under the bed. Blake watched, puzzled, until she explained that was where she'd hidden her belongings. She soon had a needle and thread passed through a candle flame several times. Blake took several swigs from a whisky jug he'd brought into their chamber a few days earlier. Sitting in the window embrasure, where there was enough light for Cerys to work, she gritted her teeth and began suturing Blake. It took her a half-an-hour to mend his wound. The whisky tempted her when she thought she might need some fortification, but she worried the liquid courage would only make her hands shake more. By the time she finished, there was a neat line of stitches. Blake took another sip of whisky before kicking off his boots and climbing onto the bed.

"I need to sleep, Cerys. Come lie next to me, wife. I need to hold ye."

"Gladly." Cerys kicked off the slippers she'd been given and pulled off her kirtle. She climbed onto the bed in just her chemise. The day had both dragged and flown by. It had felt like every minute took four times as long as it should have to pass while she waited for Blake to come to her, but now it felt as though the battle had passed in just a heartbeat. It left them both exhausted. They knew the day was hardly over, but they would seize the chance to rest. Whatever was to come would surely require more energy than they had to spare.

A fever raged for three days, pulling Blake into darkness that he clawed at to reach Cerys. When it broke, he had no memory of those days. But a consuming need to touch his bride was the only thing that filled his mind. His eyes fluttered open, and she filled his vision. The fire flickered low in the hearth, but his wife sat watching him, a damp cloth in her hand.

"*Leannan*." Blake's voice rasped. Cerys brought a cup to his lips, chilled water slipped past his swollen tongue and down his parched throat. He wished to guzzle it all, but he knew it would make him ill. Cerys limited the amount, only letting him sip.

"I'm here, *mo chridhe*." Cerys watched Blake's lip twitch. She knew her accent still needed work, but she meant the endearment with every bit of her. "How do you feel? I mean, beyond just terrible."

Blake reached out and stroked her cheek, happy to see his wife smile. He noticed the exhaustion in her eyes and the way her shoulders stooped. He took the cloth from her hand and tugged her toward him, making her squeak because she wasn't prepared for his strength. He drew her from her chair until she sprawled across his chest. He winced when her weight pressed on his wound. She tried to scramble away, worried that she would make Blake worse, but his hand squeezed her backside. He brushed a kiss to her fore-head and tucked Cerys's head under his chin.

"How many days has it been?"

"Three-and-a-half days since I finished stitching you. It's nearly dawn."

"Have ye slept, little one?"

"Here and there. Your fever was powerful, but it wasn't as horrible as I'd feared. Your wound wept the first day, but a healer came and gave me a salve to put on it. It was a miracle. I think it helped bring down your fever because I couldn't get you to swallow the willow bark tea."

Blake winced again, but this time it was contrition. He loathed the taste of willow bark tea. He could only imagine how he'd reacted. "Did I hurt ye?"

Cerys looked away. She'd known he didn't control his reaction. He'd nearly swept her across the chamber when his arm swung out and pushed her away. She didn't want him to feel guilty for what was an accident, one for which he wasn't conscious.

"Cerys?"

"I know you didn't mean to." Cerys shifted her arm, trying to draw the sleeve over her wrist, but her move-ment only alerted Blake to what she attempted to hide. He lifted her arm gently, and she propped herself up on his chest with the other. He pushed back the sleeve and found a livid bruise in the middle of her forearm. "I banged my arm on the side table."

"Because I hit ye." Blake felt tears fill his eyes for the first time since he was three-and-ten and did just that to his mother when he was unconscious. He'd bawled unabashedly with shame and guilt at the time.

"You didn't hit me. You pushed me, but you didn't know what you were doing. It's not as though you could have warned me, and it's not something I thought to ask. 'Husband, I know we've only been married a moon, but do you react violently to willow bark tea?' We've never talked aboot what would happen when you ride out or if you ever got hurt. It's not your fault."

Cerys cupped Blake face with firm hands not allowing him to shake his head. She drew him in for a deep kiss that she infused with all the forgiveness she could. She didn't think there was anything for which Blake should feel remorse, but she knew he would.

"I am so vera sorry, Cerys. Ye're right that we havenae talked aboot what happens when I ride out or what to do if I fall ill. I hadnae thought aboot it, and to be honest, I suppose I assumed ma mother would tend to me, or ma aunts, as they've always done."

"There is much I don't know aboot the healing arts and much I wish to learn. But I hope you'll let me tend to you from now on. I..." Cerys shook her head and averted her gaze. She didn't want to admit how much Blake's fever and wound scared her. She'd spent many hours praying and crying while he slumbered.

"What, *mo leannan?*" Blake ran his hand over her back as he kissed her forehead once again.

"I don't want to be left out."

"I'm nae a vera good patient, Cerys. Ye may wish to take that back. But I ken I dinna want ye far from me when I'm poorly. I dinna remember aught from the past three days, but I can feel that I was fighting to get back to ye. I need ye as much as I want ye, ma bonnie bride. I willna turn ye away. And ma mama and aunts will understand. I'm certain they feel that way aboot their men."

"But you'll always be your mother's son. I don't want to get in the way."

"Ye willna ever be in the way. Mama will help and teach ye, but she'll understand as soon as she sees us together." Blake chuckled. "She'd better get a good gander because I'm locking us away in our chamber for a sennight once we're home."

"A sennight?"

"Aye. Seems it's a family tradition. The newly married couple has a honeymoon, or at least a honey sennight."

"Everyone will know what we're up to. And we already did that at Cessford."

"Dinna tell anyone." Blake put his finger to his lips and waggled his eyebrows. Before Cerys could argue, Blake flipped her on her back. With a grunt, he shimmied down the bed, pushing her skirts up along the way.

"You've been awake only a matter of moments. Blake, you're going to do yourself a mischief."

"Mischief is right, *mo ghaol*. I intend to get up to plenty of that with ma wife now that I'm awake. I have time to make up for." Blake tossed the ends of Cerys's skirts at her as he spread her legs wider. His side ached with a ferocity, but he wished to do something to make Cerys happy. He could see the toll caring for him took, both in her appearance and her tone. He knew he was healing, and the worst was over, so he wished to prove that.

Blake's tongue flicked out and tapped her nub before he grazed it with his teeth. Knowing already just what his wife enjoyed, he thrust two fingers into her sheath, feeling the dew around her petals. They slid in with ease, so he hooked them and stroked the spot that made her hips arch off the bed. He was relentless as his tongue and fingers worked in tandem. When his tongue joined his fingers, his thumb rubbed circles over the sensitive bundle of nerves. He alternated motions and methods until Cerys was insensate with need. He flattened her skirts, so he could watch her face as she flew over the precipice into her release. Before she returned to Earth, he rolled them again, pushing down the covers that hid his nakedness.

Cerys had tried to get her mind to focus as Blake created various sensations that drove her to the brink over and over before she finally tumbled. She wasn't prepared to find herself straddling her husband, but he guided her sheath to his sword and thrust it into the place it had surely been created to fill.

"You're going to hurt yourself. You just woke up. Blake—" Cerys moaned, cutting off her words.

"This is better for me than any medicinal. Ye are the only cure for what ails me."

"A sword wound. I'm the only thing that cures that?"

"Nay. The raging need and cockstand ma bonnie wife gives me just from thinking aboot her. It's pure torture when she's around, and I canna make love to her. Only she can cure that need."

"You're a fortunate mon to have a wife who wishes to minister to your needs." Cerys leaned forward as Blake pulled at her kirtle's laces. When her breasts were free of her gown and chemise, Blake kneaded both, alternating suckling each side. "Blake, I'm close."

"I ken. So am I. Let me watch ye find yer release again, *mo ghaol*."

Cerys's fingers clenched the bedding beside Blake's head as she rode his length, rocking, grinding, circling —everything until she felt her core tighten again. Her gaze met Blake's as he thrust into her. She could only imagine what he was doing to his wound, but neither could, nor would, stop their coupling. She needed and wanted him too.

"Blake!" Cerys cried out before burying her face against his pillow and moaning for only him to hear. "I'm—yes. Oh, sweet Lord, yes."

"Cerys!" Blake's cry filled the chamber as they climaxed together, his seed filling her as her inner muscles clung to him, milking him. He pulled Cerys's gown over her head and tossed it aside. She did the same with her chemise. She grabbed the covers and drew the material over them as Blake brought her body back to rest against his. They fell asleep still joined.

duction, and she could imagine the same unchecked desire
her passion incited and Blake's masterful restraint that hid in
her memories—

What do you do, you know—

CHAPTER 22

lake's convalescence was brief once the king's
advisors learned he'd regained consciousness. Against Cerys's wishes, which she made known to
more than just Blake, he found himself in the king's
solar each day. At first, Cerys joined him, both as his
nurse and as an informant. But the usefulness other
people saw in her faded quickly. The couple was reluc-
tant to spend any time apart, but Blake knew he
couldn't ignore the matter of the attack, and Cerys
knew she was unwelcomed. While Blake spent hours
talking, Cerys spent much of the time alone. She sewed
or walked in the gardens, since Wilma had deserted her
in favor of the queen, and Joan hadn't warmed to
Cerys.

On the fifth day after Blake woke, Cerys found herself wandering the gardens, enjoying the sunshine. She
wished she could take Kitten for a long ride, but no one
was allowed to leave the château, not even if they remained on the estate. The garden was the farthest the
women were allowed, and the men could venture into
the lists. Cerys wouldn't have wanted to go very far, but
a change of scenery would have been nice. She found a
secluded spot where the sun didn't beat down on her

directly, but she could enjoy its warmth. She'd brought her sewing, preferring the fresh air to another hour in her chamber.

"What are you doing here?"

Cerys froze. She looked to her right, prepared to answer Wilma's demand but uncertain why her former friend asked her anything. However, Wilma wasn't there. At least she wasn't beside her. She was on the other side of a tall hedge.

"I had to see you. I need word from you, which you have failed to send."

Cerys's eyes were so wide, she feared they would fall from her face. She knew that voice, and it was one that shouldn't have been anywhere near Château Gaillard.

"Shaw, how was I to send word without anyone growing suspicious?"

"Then what was the point of you coming here? You had no more news from Stirling, so you said you would gain more here. From what I can see, you dally with the queen and her other ladies, swanning around without a care, when the rest of us are fighting for our cause. Ours, Wilma. One you swore you were loyal to." Shaw Hannay's voice carried clearly to Cerys, who sat aghast.

"I am loyal."

"Mayhap. But you seem to only make an effort when you find it amuses you."

"Or when I don't fear having my head taken from my shoulders," Wilma snapped. "Besides, I did my part for that little failed raid. I arranged for the men and gave you the coin. I ensured the garden door was ajar for your men to get in. It's not my fault your men couldn't break down a door to get to Joan or Cerys. For the love of the saints, I'm the one who told you when Cerys and her brute arrived. I'm the one who told you they were likely to come here. If you'd checked the stables before yammering with Domnall and Stanley, you wouldn't need to kill them both."

Cerys smothered her laugh as Wilma berated Shaw for not being discreet, when she was the one guilty of broadcasting their conspiracy for anyone to hear. Though she supposed the inner depths of the garden was less frequented than a stable. Cerys had seen no one else here any of the days she'd visited. She kept herself still and tucked in the shadows.

"You make it sound as though you lead this campaign. I don't recall seeing you on a horse riding into battle."

Wilma snorted. "And I don't recall seeing you do that either. I sneaked away from all those blathering bitches and watched the bailey from my chamber window. You were not there either."

"How could I? Every Scotsman would have recognized me. But I was with those mercenaries until they rode over the last hill. I—"

"Enough, Shaw. I'm not interested in all the things you did or want to do to prove you're a hero. I already know how big your cock is. There's naught for you to prove. Did you get the medicinals I asked for?"

"Yes. How are you going to get it into Sinclair and his whore's drinks?"

"You let me worry aboot that. The men failed to breach the castle. They failed to kill enough guards. Your clan needs to start paying its share, Shaw. I cannot pay for it all."

"You're not paying for any of it."

"My dowry is. But it is not a bottomless chest. Between paying for the men and giving coin to Balliol, there will not be much left. What then? Are the Cunninghams and Homes going to contribute, or are they just all talk?"

"That's not your concern, Wilma. Those clans already have men fighting alongside Balliol. Take care of the Sinclairs tonight. Get Joan on her own tomorrow, and I will make it look like an accident. While everyone is in a panic over the queen's fall, Domnall and Stanley will take care of the usurper."

"That's such a ridiculous title. What is he usurping while living in exile?" Wilma muttered more to herself than for Shaw's benefit, but Cerys often wondered the same thing.

"Whatever you wish to call him won't matter after tomorrow because they only thing you'll be calling him is dead." Shaw gestured with his hand, catching his fingers on leaves that separated. He happened to look where he touched. It meant his gaze fell on Cerys, who scrambled to her feet, leaving her sewing behind. She gathered her skirts and lifted them to her knees as she ran. She knew from her position and theirs, she would reach the garden's exit before them. But Shaw was fit, with much longer legs than she had.

"Fucking bitch," Shaw hissed from far too close as Cerys hurdled a stone bench and flew out of the garden.

"He—" Cerys's call for help died on her lips with a strangled sound as Shaw's arm came around her throat, and a blade pressed against the side.

"You have a bad habit of being where you aren't welcome, Lady Cerys. I would have thought you'd learn."

"And you'd do well to check where you gossip. I was in both places first." Cerys stomped on his foot as she threw her head back. The top of her skull cracked against Shaw's nose. Stunned, his loosened his hold a fraction, and Cerys seized the moment. She drove her elbows back into his ribs and gathered her skirts again. She made ready to run, but she didn't make it two steps before she found herself at the tip of Wilma's *sgian dubh*.

"Cerys, you've outlived your usefulness a second time." Gone was the flighty intonation. Gone was the empty-headed husband seeker. In its place was a calculating woman who stared into Cerys's eyes. "First, you had a falling out with your family, which meant no more missives from you to intercept. Oh, yes. I steamed open every missive you sent home and read every little detail and secret you sent to your faithless father and uncles. Now, you run to tell your husband what you heard. I don't need that complication."

"All along, I thought I did you a favor by tolerating you. I'd befriended you out of pity." Cerys didn't break their eye contact as she took a challenging step forward, placing the lethal dirk's tip only an inch from her skin. "You used me, and I don't even care. What I regret is the wasted time and patience I gave you. You're just as pathetic as you pretended to be. You let a mon spend your dowry without even being wed. You made it sound as though you've already shared a bed—or whatever—mayhap a wall or horse stall for all I know or care. You will be naught by the time this ends. You will have no money to your name, no maidenhead, and no one willing to have you. If you think Shaw will marry you once your dowry is gone, then you're a fool. And that's assuming either of you live that long. Kill me, and you will be the first people my husband searches for."

"We're not killing you until we have your husband too. We're counting on him searching for you." Shaw pressed his knife to Cerys's kidney, pricking the skin. "In the meantime, taking your tongue will keep you from sharing secrets that aren't yours." Shaw made to step around Cerys. The moment he moved his blade from her back, her fist surged forward into Wilma's nose as her other hand went around the woman's hand.

Cerys ripped the *sgian dubh* from Wilma's hand and spun to her right.

Shaw lunged forward as Cerys turned toward him. His longer dagger slashed across her belly, eliciting a bloodcurdling scream. But the *sgian dubh* was even more deadly. The short blade forced Cerys to step closer, but she drove it up into the underside of Shaw's chin where it met his throat. His eyes widened in shock as he swung his blade again, catching Cerys in the arm. She pushed it harder until she thought it might come out the other side.

Wilma's scream was pure fury as she launched herself at Cerys, knocking them both to the ground. She pinned Cerys to the grass and straddled her. But when she stuck her hand over Cerys's mouth, she didn't think about Cerys's arms being loose. Cerys grabbed Wilma's little finger and wrenched it backward until she felt a pop. Now it was Wilma's turn to howl in pain. Cerys twisted, wrapping her hands around Wilma's upper arm, and dragging her off.

Cerys now straddled Wilma's chest, an arm pinned under each knee. She wrapped her hands around Wilma's throat and squeezed, watching the woman turn purple. Wilma thrashed, nearly knocking Cerys off more than once, but her determination to live didn't match Cerys's. When she no longer struggled, but Cerys was certain the woman lived, she released her former—what? Friend? Acquaintance? Peer? Cerys didn't know how to think of her as anything but an enemy and a traitor.

"Cerys!"

She looked up to spy Blake charging toward her, his plaid swishing around his athletic thighs. She watched his hair fly behind his shoulders as his leine stretched tight against his broad chest. He carried his sword in his right hand as his arms pumped beside his ribs with each step. He was St. George come to slay the dragon. Except Cerys had already done that. At least, she'd slain the dragon beside her. Domnall and Stanley still lurked.

Cerys tried to stand, but suddenly it felt as if every ounce of blood had drained from her body. She tried to make her legs cooperate, but they refused to move, to straighten or bear her weight. Her head felt like it weighed a ton, and her vision blurred. She knew it was Blake who approached, and it was he who pulled her into powerful arms. But none of the words that formed in her mind made it past her lips.

"Cerys, what happened? Where are ye hurt?"

Cerys turned a blank face to Blake, hearing the fear in his tone but unable to formulate a clear thought. She forced herself to breathe through the ferocious pain, and inhaling Blake's woodsy and soapy scent helped bring her back from the brink.

"My belly and my arm. He cut me."

Blake gazed as Cerys's abdomen, the fabric covering her silky skin completely saturated with blood. He felt it oozing on his hands from her arm. His wife was unnaturally pale, a blue tinge coming to her skin. He laid her back on the ground and unpinned the extra length of plaid from his shoulder. He pressed it against Cerys's belly, trying to staunch the bleeding.

"Get the king's physic now!" Blake bellowed as more people ran to them. He feared hurting Cerys with the weight he applied, but he knew she would likely die if he didn't. The wound was far deeper than he initially thought. With one hand still covering her belly, he examined her arm. The cut was also deep, threatening muscle and nerves.

"Blake?"

"I'm here, *mo leannan*. Do ye hear me? Can ye see me?"

"Yes. Don't go."

"God's angels and the Devil's minions couldnae get me to leave ye, wife. Let someone try." Blake leaned forward and pressed a kiss to Cerys's lips, which were also turning blue. "Get a healer!"

Blake looked around at the people gathering but none looked skilled at anything more than staring. He feared moving Cerys, but he couldn't keep her out here. Just as he was about to ask a lady-in-waiting to hold his plaid against Cerys's belly while he carried her to their chamber, the queen pushed through the crowd. Blake wasn't prepared for Joan to fall to her knees beside Cerys, a basket in her hands.

"If you don't know how to sew a wound or can't explain what happened, leave." Joan's voice rang with command that a young woman of six-and-ten rarely mastered. She no longer sounded like the petulant adolescent with a crush on Blake. She sounded like a leader and future ruler. People heeded her order and fell away, but most didn't leave the bailey. Joan's hand was gentle as she pushed Blake's away. "I need to look, Sinclair."

Blake hesitated before he lifted his hand. Immediately, blood gushed into the plaid. He moved to add pressure once again, but Joan shook her head. "In a moment. I have to see."

Joan peeled away the plaid and pulled apart Cerys's kirtle. The tear from the knife's blade looked inconsequential and practically unnoticeable, if not from the copious amount of blood pouring through it. Blake swallowed as he realized how long and deep the wound was. It hadn't punctured any organs, but it had cut through arteries and veins.

"Sinclair, we need to get her inside. The wound needs cleaning and closing." Joan looked down at Cerys, who'd passed out, then up at Blake. "Stitching this will likely kill her. She'll bleed to death before I can finish. It has to be a heated blade."

"I'll do it." Blake didn't look away from Cerys.

"It will leave a horrid scar."

"Ye think I would care aboot that? I dinna give a fuck what mars ma wife's body as long as she's alive to be ma wife."

"Not you. I don't say that to warn you or because I doubt you. I say it because it will be a hard reminder for her to accept. She will need your kindness and patience because it will matter to her, even if it doesn't matter to you. Don't dismiss that. She'll need you to understand that." Joan met Blake's gaze when he finally looked at her. She offered a soft smile, unfazed by the shock on Blake's face. "I think you and the king are much alike. He understood when I needed him to. I think you will do the same for your bride."

Joan offered no further explanation, and Blake wouldn't dare ask for one. But it left him curious and once more unable to reason through the complicated relationship he'd witnessed between two people far too young to be married, let alone rule a country.

He scooped Cerys into his arms and stood just as Wilma spluttered and gasped. He looked at the woman he'd seen his wife nearly strangle to death. He glanced at Shaw, then back to Wilma. The two of them together made Blake believe they deserved whatever Cerys did. Her eyes fluttered open as Blake lifted her. She glanced at him before looking at Wilma, who had a man holding her up and three women fawning over her. She struggled to raise her hand, but since it was her injured arm, she could do very little. Her good arm was pressed against Blake.

"They did it. Her dowry paid for it." Cerys wheezed as the pain threatened to steal her consciousness again. "Queen can't be alone. Accident coming. Poison you and me. King is next."

"Wheest, *mo leannan*. Ye can tell me once ye rest."

"No." Cerys shook her head once and howled in pain. "She plans to poison us. She's to get Queen Joan alone tomorrow. Shaw was going to make a deadly fall look like an accident. Stanley and Domnall are near. They were here before the raid."

Cerys's breathing labored, and her vision tunneled. She wanted to say more, explain everything she heard. But the pain overcame her. It was more than she could bear, and Blake felt so safe and comfortable. She let her eyes slide shut as she turned her face toward him. She feared she was dying. That made her resolved to whisper four more words.

"Kiss." She puckered her lips and accepted Blake's offer. "I love you."

Then it was as black as night.

❧

Blake would be forever grateful to Queen Joan. When they arrived at Cerys and Blake's chamber, Madame Remier already had a bath waiting. Maids and ladies-in-waiting milled in the passageways and in the chamber. It was he who was nearly chased from the room. Women with supposedly good intentions told him that it wasn't his place to be at his wife's side since she would need to be undressed. He stared at them, at a loss for words. He didn't think there was anyone at the château who didn't know they were a love match or how they expressed that love. Telling him he couldn't see his wife naked was beyond ridiculous in his mind.

Then women tried to convince him that he was too large and in the way. All he could think was that far too many of them served no purpose, and they were the ones to take up too much room. But when one overly concerned lady-in-waiting offered to distract him while he waited, he lost all restraint.

"Get the bluidy hell out of ma chamber. Leave ma wife and me to the healer. Cease yer nashgabbing and leave."

"Sinclair, you really—"

"You heard the mon. He wishes everyone to leave. Go." Joan's calm and quiet voice still filled the chamber. When she looked away from where she set out her medicinals, her expression once more hinted at the woman she would one day become. She spared only a moment's glance, but everyone but Blake, Madame Remier, a healer, and the queen left. Cerys groaned as the healer and the housekeeper cut away her gown. It was fortunate Blake insisted upon remaining because it would have been a struggle to get Cerys into the tub. But Blake set her into the giant basin with the gentleness of placing a bairn in a bassinet. It was he who bathed her. He thought of how she'd tended to his injuries only a few days earlier. This wasn't how he'd wished to reciprocate.

"You need to scrub harder than that, Blake." Joan offered him a sympathetic smile. She knew he feared making Cerys's injuries worse or causing her more pain. "You must get it as clean as you can. There can be no dirt or fabric left, or it will grow infected."

"I ken," Blake whispered in resignation. Every wince and moan tore at his soul. Cerys had never seemed so tiny as she did in that moment. He'd never felt like such a lumbering oaf as he did while trying to tend to his wife. He felt like he was all thumbs, and he feared his own strength. When he was certain that he'd done all he could, he lifted her from the tub, accepting the drying cloths Madame Remier handed him. He carefully toweled Cerys dry before carrying her to the bed. Her wounds still bled, but they no longer geysered.

Blake stood back as the healer and Joan worked. The old woman created a poultice from yarrow and some type of moss Blake hadn't seen before. Joan brewed willow bark tea, which Blake forced himself not to gag at when he smelled it.

"It's time for the blade," Joan said softly as she looked at Blake. "I can do it."

"Nay. I will." Blake drew a medium-length knife from his waist. He carried it to the table near the window, where a decanter of Scottish whisky sat. He considered taking a healthy swig, but instead, he took it to the basin beside the ewer where he and Cerys conducted their morning ablutions. He poured it over the knife, twisting it from side-to-side before he shook off the excess. He glanced at Cerys, seeing the healer place a strip of leather between her teeth. He turned away and thrust the blade into the fire. The remaining alcohol hissed and sizzled as the flames leaped and popped. Blake lowered the knife into the bluest flames until it glowed. "Are ye ready?"

Joan and Madame Remier stood on each side of the bed, holding Cerys's hands. The healer stood beside the housekeeper and pressed the wound closed. Blake crossed the chamber in four strides before climbing onto the bed between Cerys's legs. He drew in a deep breath and nodded. He focused all his attention on his mission. It shocked him to see how steady his hand was since nothing about him felt steady at all. He brought the flat side of the blade to Cerys's belly, laying it diagonally to cover all of the wound.

The smell of burning flesh filled the chamber, and Cerys screamed. Her eyes flew open and locked with Blake's. But they were glassy and unseeing. She bit into the leather strap as she tried to writhe. But Madame Remier and Joan kept her pinned in place as Blake continued to hold the scorching weapon to her skin. He felt sweat bead and drip along his temples. Tears filled his eyes, the pain of seeing his wife in such a condition and knowing he inflicted more agony upon her threatened to overcome him. However, he refused to be weak and fail Cerys. Not when she needed him.

The healer tapped his upper arm and nodded. There was empathy in her eyes as she looked at him. He pulled away, flinging the knife toward the fireplace. He looked at the angry, red, puckered skin from where he'd cauterized the wound. It would be a daily reminder to Cerys and him. Joan's words echoed in his ears. He was so immensely proud of his wife's courage. But he foresaw the invisible pain it would cause her. He pledged silently to ensure Cerys knew every day until death parted them that he loved her. Nothing about the scar made her less attractive to him. He knew he would loathe the reminder that she'd nearly died, but that wouldn't diminish the admiration he felt for her bravery.

"Blake, it hurts." Cerys's whisper brought Blake back to the present, keeping his mind from wandering again. He kneeled beside the bed, his enormous hand engulfing her smaller one.

"I ken, ma little lass. I'm sorry to make it hurt more before it can be made better." Blake watched as Joan held a cup to Cerys's mouth, urging her to swallow the tea. The healer stitched Cerys's arm, which would also bear a fierce scar, but it wouldn't be so easy for her to see.

"I killed him."

"I ken, *mo leannan*. Ye did what ye had to. I dinna doubt he would have killed ye. But ye can tell me later."

"No. I need to tell you now while I can. Wilma was behind this as much as the men. She's been conspiring all along. She would read my missives to my family. She came here to help kill the king and queen." Cerys turned toward Joan, sad to see the pained expression on the young woman's face. Cerys could tell Joan felt

293

betrayed. The adolescent no longer looked like a young monarch. She looked like a girl who'd been played for a fool by a woman she'd admired and trusted. "They intended to poison us tonight. I think Shaw was going to push you, Your Grace, out of a window or over the wall walk. During the confusion that would cause, they were going to go after the king. Shaw said the Cunninghams and Homes already fight alongside Balliol."

"How'd you learn this?" Joan kept her voice low and soothing, a drastic difference from how she'd addressed Cerys in the past. Confusion washed over Cerys's expression, eliciting a contrite nod from the queen. "I was foul to you. I'd listened to Lady Wilma speak aboot you before you arrived. She said you came to be my husband's mistress. I thought to take from you what you intended to take from me. I'm very sorry, Lady Cerys. You've risked so much many times over. You didn't deserve how I treated you."

"I understand, Your Grace. I truly do. You are not in an easy position both as queen and as a young woman navigating politics. Thank you." Cerys looked at Blake, trying to raise her free hand to him. He took it, helping her move it as she guided her palm to his cheek. "I was where I wasn't supposed to be again. I overhead them talking when they entered the garden after me. And once more, you came to save me."

Blake turned his lips to her palm. "Ye dinna need me as much as ye think. But I willna try too hard to convince ye otherwise." He grinned until he saw how tired Cerys grew. Her last vestiges of strength were sapped. Her eyelids grew heavy, and she was soon asleep. He barked a quick command when someone pounded on the door. Mackintosh and both Johnstone brothers peered around the door like weans spying.

"How is your wife?" Steven Johnstone asked.

"Weak but not dying." Blake hoped he was right. He

refused to look at any of the women, lest they contradict him, even by their miens. "Where is Lady Wilma?"

"Locked in her chamber," Eliot Mackintosh answered. "She refuses to speak other than to say Lady Cerys attacked her and murdered Hannay."

"And what say ye?" Blake looked at each of the three men.

"A maid saw what happened to our niece," Edward Johnstone said as he stepped into the chamber. He stared at Cerys, deep lines etched into his brow. "She looks exactly like her mother. It's uncanny."

"She does," Steven whispered. Blake noticed the haunted look in the man's eyes. There was great unresolved pain there from losing his twin.

"The maid was running to get a guard when you came charging across the bailey," Edward explained. "She saw Lady Cerys run from the garden and thought to see if my niece needed help. Before she reached Cerys, she saw Shaw grab her. She watched Wilma point a dirk at her. She couldn't hear much, but she saw Wilma and Shaw pin Cerys between them, so she had nowhere to go. Cerys fought Shaw and eventually shoved a dirk into his throat, but not before he slashed her twice. She came to blows with Wilma and could have killed the woman, but for whatever reason, she didn't."

"Likely so Lady Wilma can explain," Blake muttered. He doubted the woman would speak the truth without serious coercion. "What's to become of Lady Wilma?"

The three men looked at one another before looking at Blake. Eliot shifted his gaze to the women in the room and canted his head to the door. Not one of them budged. He scowled, but they remained rooted in place.

"Is Lady Cerys well enough for ye to leave and let me tend to her?" Blake knew the women wouldn't leave voluntarily, and the men wouldn't speak voluntarily as long as they were all in the chamber together.

"*Oui*," the healer said. "I will return to check on her in an hour. She must drink the tea throughout the night to avoid a fever. She won't do as well as you did. She doesn't have your constitution. We need to keep it from ever starting."

"I will watch her closely, *madam*." Blake watched the woman sweep her gaze over Cerys, resting the back of her hand against her patient's forehead. The healer then packed her arsenal of medicinals. She and Madame Remier moved to the door, but Joan remained. She shot a challenging gaze at the men, who didn't flinch. Neither did Joan. The two older women left, but Joan stayed.

"Your Grace." Steven's tone was nothing short of patronizing.

"Johnstone, we both know you think I'm naught more than a foreign-born wean. However, this woman nearly died to save my life, and yet my life is still at risk. You will not convince me to leave. But I will convince guards to remove you. We can have this conversation in the king's solar with him in attendance."

The men looked at her speculatively, respect burgeoning in their eyes as they considered the woman before them. Gone was the girl Blake met only days ago and with whom these men had lived for most of the past three years. In her place was a woman coming into her own, a force to soon be reckoned with.

"Very well, Your Grace. We have already spoken to His Majesty." Edward nodded before coming to stand at the foot of the bed. "Before Lady Wilma was shut into her chamber, my brother and I searched her belongings. The young woman thought she had a secure way to hide her most prized possessions—other people's correspondence. However, her chest is not that unusual. There was no false bottom, but rather a false back wall. I pulled it away and found dozens of missives that were written in the same hand. She'd copied each message that came through her hands. There were copies of missives exchanged between your wife and my brother-by-marriage. There were missives from your grandfather to Murray. And the *pieces de resistance* were the missives between Shaw and her. She kept all of them, even copies of the ones she wrote. It's all there."

"If Lady Cerys hadn't come here, and warned us of the plot, we wouldn't have been prepared for the raid. As much as I regret my niece's injuries, if she hadn't engaged with them today, likely more than four people would have wound up dead." Steven stepped next to his brother and stared at Cerys, who was still unconscious. "She is the very image of my sister. It used to pain me to look upon her. That's the real reason I didn't press to attend Cerys's arranged wedding. I miss my sister every day. But I missed so many years that I could have known my niece, could have found comfort in a small piece of my twin still among us. Now I am so grateful for my sister's sacrifice. She gave the world an incredible woman."

"What next?" Blake asked.

"The most recent set of missives are between Lady Wilma and Home. Unbeknownst to Hannay, the other two have been carrying on an affair. They were conspiring to kill Hannay once Balliol returns to Scotland. They would frame Hannay for killing the true king and queen and convince Balliol that Hannay plotted to kill Balliol's heir. If caught by us, Hannay would be blamed. If they succeeded, they would set Hannay up to look like he was ingratiating himself just to turn traitor."

"Sounds complicated and unrealistic." Blake wasn't certain if the plan was that fraught with things that could fail that it was ridiculous or if he was too exhausted to see the genius in the rationale.

"It was. From Hannay's missives, he had no idea of her or Home's duplicity. They are camped on the other side of Les Andelys. Macpherson and Ogilvy are investigating why none of our patrols reported a camp so close to the estate. They are taking some of their men to scout." Mackintosh grinned at the Johnstone brothers. "We decided it was best if Highlanders took care of this mission."

"What of Cunningham?" Blake wanted to know about the third conspirator.

"He's the least informed. He's being coerced into conspiring because he secretly married a peasant woman from his village. But as you might recall, he married Laird Fergusson's auldest daughter a year ago. He's a bigamist, and they are holding that over his head. He'd rather conspire to kill the king than have anyone learn that he loves a peasant and married her." Eliot's disgust was obvious. Domnall came across as a weak man who no one respected.

"He's the one they're looking for though. Ogilvy and Macpherson know he can be bribed, so they intend to make him work for them. They don't trust him, but since they know aboot his marriages and his role here, they believe he'll bend to them." Steven still watched Cerys. Blake wondered if the man would make amends once Cerys woke. He hoped the man showed this compassion when Cerys could appreciate it. She had no family of her own otherwise. "The Highlanders plan to learn how many men camp just beyond our sight and convince Cunningham to sabotage Home."

"When do they set off?" Blake would have ridden out on that mission to scout, but he wouldn't consider it while Cerys ailed.

"They already rode out," Edward answered.

"Cunningham might be able to explain what's already happened, but Home is the one who will decide what happens next." Joan looked toward the window. "There is a market in the morning, I will send my maids on the pretense that I wish for new hair ribbons. They will spread a rumor that Lady Wilma drank too much tonight. They'll say that she and Lady Cerys argued in the Great Hall, where Lady Cerys threatened Lady Wilma. They'll then whisper aboot how no one has seen Lady Wilma since the evening meal. Home will worry that either Lady Cerys learned more or that he lost his informant. It will draw him out. While he is here and the Highlanders lure Cunningham, our royal guards sweep through the camp and kill anyone they find."

"It could be a massacre." Eliot warned.

"Good." Joan met his gaze with unwavering conviction.

"Very well, Your Grace. We will inform His Majesty." Edward said as the three men bowed and left the chamber.

"What do you think?" Joan met Blake's gaze.

"I think there are a great many parts to these plots with plenty of places where the entire plan could fall apart. If one part falls, the rest should follow. But that also means that there's room for our own plans to fail. I would pray, Yer Grace. We will need the Lord's intervention to make this work. Regardless of what happens, ye and His Majesty will live to tell the tale."

"I shall hold you to that, Sinclair." Joan walked to the door but paused and looked back. "Do not hesitate to summon me if Lady Cerys worsens or you need sleep. I will sit with her."

"Thank ye, Yer Grace." Blake watched the queen leave, wondering what dawn would bring. He doubted it would be anything good.

CHAPTER 23

"*B*lake?" Cerys tried to raise her arm to rub her gritty eyes, but pain surged from her shoulder to her fingertips. She whimpered as she looked toward the cause. She inhaled deeply, trying to ease the agony, but that only sent a searing fire through her middle.

"Wheest, *mo leannan*. I'm here. Do ye remember what happened yesterday?"

"That was only yesterday? Bluidy hell. I feel like a bull ran me over."

"Ye look and sound better than I ever have after such wounds." Blake thought he sounded encouraging, but Cerys's wide eyes made him realize what he would have said to his brother or male cousins apparently wasn't what he should say to his wife. "Ye havenae had even a hint of a fever. Ye slept soundly all night."

Cerys lifted the sheet and spotted the bandage wrapped around her arm. Then she looked lower. Her gasp was the only sound she made, but her face told Blake everything. Joan's prediction was accurate. Blake eased onto the bed and slipped his arm beneath her neck. He eased her chin up and pressed a soft kiss to her mouth.

"What if I can't have any bairns?"

That wasn't what Blake expected. "The healer didna say aught aboot whether ye can have bairns."

"This scar. The skin won't be able to stretch. There won't be room for a bairn to grow."

"I never would have thought aboot that." Blake entwined his fingers with Cerys's. "I ken ye want bairns, and so do I. But I only want them with ye, *mo leannan*. That means I need ye alive and with me. I will make love to ye every day and night we can because I dinna think I'll ever get enough of ye." He brushed a kiss against her lips before flicking his tongue between her teeth. He pulled away sooner than Cerys wished. "If we dinna have any of our own, but I have ye, then ma life is full."

Cerys nodded, tears welling in her eyes. She continued to look at the scar, shocked and scared. "Blake." Her voice broke as the tears fell.

"Wheest, little one. Let's get ye healthy and on yer feet, then we'll worry aboot what comes next." Blake nipped at her ear as his hand massaged her breast. "Which will be making up for lost time."

"You don't mind the..."

"Cerys, I did that to ye." Blake swallowed, waiting for Cerys to pull away.

"I know, Blake. You saved me. I would have bled to death. I know that couldn't have been easy. I don't know that I could have done it."

"Ye dinna hate me for hurting ye? For marking ye?"

"No. Can you live with seeing this every time we couple? Or at least knowing it's there?"

"Cerys, do ye wish ye didna have to see ma scars when we make love?"

"They don't matter to me." Cerys accepted Blake's kiss with a hunger that nothing but he could satisfy. Their kiss grew heated, just as it always did.

"Then can ye believe me when I say it doesnae matter to me? I want ye right now just as much as I've wanted ye since the moment I saw ye. I love ye."

"I love you. I can't promise that I won't get embarrassed aboot it, and I'm scared I won't be able to have bairns because of it. But I won't hide from you. I won't turn you away."

Blake stared at his bride, trying to decipher what she wasn't saying. "Cerys, if we never couple again, I will still love ye. I will still want ye. I will nae forsake ye for someone else."

"When you married me, you believed I was a healthy woman who could bear you children. I might not be able to now. I may never give you a son."

"And we might have twenty weans, and they all be lasses. Having a son doesnae matter to me. Whether we have a score of bairns or none at all isnae what I care aboot. I love ye because ye're kind. Ye're intelligent and resourceful. Ye think of others before yerself. Ye make me laugh. Ye're braver than most people I ken. And ye dinna mind having a husband who people stare at and whisper aboot behind his back because he's too big."

Cerys grinned, pressing her lips together to keep from giggling. "There is naught aboot you that's too big. There's naught aboot you that's too small. It all fits just right. Like one of the bears the Roman gladiators used to fight. Except you're a Highlander, and you're mine. My Highland bear."

"I'll be whatever ye want, lass. But ye do make me roar." Blake flicked Cerys's earlobe with his tongue and squeezed her breast. "Mayhap I can make ye purr like a kitten."

"I hope you don't mean my horse. I'll worry if he starts purring."

"Cheeky, *mo leannan*. Rest and heal, then I will see what I can make yer body do."

"I recall what you could do when you woke after your injuries." Cerys raised an eyebrow, but it fell with the next breath when Blake shook his head.

"Nae yet, Cerys. I slept for three days. Ye've slept a few hours. Ma body is also used to healing from these kinds of wounds. Yers isnae. I willnae risk yer health for that. Let me hold ye while we sleep. But dinna fash. I will make up for all the lost hours."

Cerys's hand slid up Blake's thigh until her hand wrapped around his semi-aroused rod. "I shall hold you to it."

Four days later, Cerys sat in the garden on a bench beside Blake. He hadn't left her side since she was wounded. He'd attended to her, just as she'd done for him. Their scars didn't quite match, and it was a rather macabre thought when they pointed out the similarities, but both were healing from their injuries. Blake would return to the lists in the morning, but for now, they considered their situation.

"The scouts found evidence of their camps, but they still havenae found Stanley or Domnall," Blake explained. He'd attended a meeting in the king's solar while Joan kept Cerys company. The queen's plan would have worked, but it seemed someone forewarned them. The scouts hadn't found their newest camp. "We dinna ken if they learned Shaw died, or if they packed with haste simply because he didna return."

"Do you think they're still in France?"

"Aye. They've come this far. They arenae going to merely go home."

"Why not ransom Wilma to Stanley? He must have coin with him to pay mercenaries."

"I dinna think she's worth that much to him now. He willna believe she hasnae given away secrets. Or he willna put his own neck at risk to come get her."

"The queen spoke to her this morning. She's asked to see me. Do you think I should?"

"I dinna trust her within a league of ye. I dinna like the idea of ye being near her without me, but she willna say a word if she kens she has an audience. Whatever she wants to say, she wishes to do it while she's in control."

"How do we make her think she's in control while she's not?" Cerys giggled. "It's not like you could fit in the armoire and hide."

Blake tickled her uninjured side, and her laughter pealed through the air. But they both sobered when her uncles and Angus Ogilvy approached.

"Good day, my lady, Sinclair," Angus said, preferring Scots to French, and knowing none of the three Lowlanders spoke Gaelic.

"Angus." Blake nodded to the older statesman. He'd known the man since childhood and liked him, but something felt off as the Highlander looked at him. "What's happened?"

"It's Lady Wilma. Either she hid a dirk where no one found it, or someone slipped it to her. She slit her wrists this morning. A maid came to clear her morning meal and found her. She's still alive, but barely. She's asking for Lady Cerys."

Cerys and Blake exchanged a look before they rose. Despite her protestations, half-hearted as they were, Blake insisted upon carrying Cerys anywhere beyond their chamber door. She leaned against his expansive chest and enjoyed the coddling. When they arrived at Wilma's chamber, two guards stood outside. Blake lowered her to her feet, and she entered when one of the men opened the door. Wilma was deathly pale and sweat dripped from her brow. There was a sickly scent in the air, and Cerys knew it smelled like looming death.

"Cerys," Wilma rasped. "You finally came."

"You didn't have to go to such extremes to gain my attention." Cerys lacked any sympathy for the woman who would have gladly killed her. She noticed there were still livid bruises around Wilma's throat from when Cerys strangled her. She assumed that was what contributed to her altered voice.

"Always one to think everything is aboot you."

"When is it not? But you made it that way, didn't you?" Cerys drew closer to the bed, but she stayed well beyond Wilma's reach. She trusted her not at all, unconvinced that the woman was as frail as she looked, even if Cerys suspected she would be dead within a day. "What do you want?"

"A compromise. I will tell Stanley and Domnall to allow you safe passage to Scotland if you have me released."

"You're as daft as a hen without a head. You've committed treason. There is no letting you go. As for safe passage for me, have you not seen my husband? He is my safe passage. Besides, the Sinclairs know where we are." No, they didn't. "And they are on their way." No, they weren't. But Wilma couldn't know for certain.

"How can they know?"

"We didn't just blink and wind up here. The man who brought us here from Calais took a message back for us. His brother was the sea captain who brought us to France. So it seems like you have naught to offer me. In which case, I have naught I'm willing to offer you." Cerys turned toward the door, praying Wilma believed every part of her bluff.

"Wait." Wilma tried to sit, but she cried out in pain, coughing and retching. When she settled back against her pillow, her hair was plastered to her face and scalp, drenched with sweat. "Stanley and Domnall know Shaw is dead. A message went to them the day you murdered him. I—"

"I did not murder the man who would have killed me. Accuse me of such things, and I will leave. And when I do, I will be sure they throw away the key to this chamber."

"Fine," Wilma hissed. "They know he's dead. He was in charge of the mercenaries because he had the money. But Stanley is the one who planned the raid. They will have moved farther south and will come from the east."

"Why are you telling me this if I won't free you?"

Wilma sighed. "Because neither Stanley nor Domnall will come for me. Only Shaw would have rescued me. Since I know they won't think twice to abandon me because I am no longer convenient, neither is helping them still convenient. If I'm to die here without their support, they can die on the field without mine."

"Why did you even get involved? What did Shaw do or say to bring you into this?"

Wilma cackled, then coughed. "You still don't get it, do you? They didn't recruit me. I recruited them. I met King Edward—yes, Edward Balliol, the true king of Scotland—three years ago. I'm a little aulder than you, but not by much. He noticed me and took interest. A king made me his mistress." Wilma smiled but sighed wistfully. "I was at his side before the Battle of Culblean."

"You mean his defeat." Cerys crossed her arms.

"That was when he decided I should come to court and serve Joan. We both knew neither she nor the pretender were at Stirling, but Murray was. The bastard would rather bed down with his horse than a young woman. But you were there, too. And you were so eager to please your family that you wrote more missives than the Bible has psalms. Each piece of news you learned that I hadn't then became mine to barter. I sold it to Edward, and I sold it to Stanley and Shaw. I knew the Hannays leaned to Edward's side. It was easy to convince Shaw, and he brought me Stanley and Domnall. I took Stanley as my lover before I convinced my father to betroth me to him. I controlled Shaw and Stanley by keeping them in my bed, and I served Edward as best I could when I couldn't be in his bed. Domnall was—there, so why not?"

"Does Balliol know you best served him on your back?"

"It wasn't always on my back. Mayhap your husband isn't so virile if you think that's the only way to rut."

"I never said that I did. Mayhap your arse served Balliol as well as your quim." That took Wilma aback, making her pause before she cackled again.

"Not too far from the truth. Mayhap you aren't such a prim bride after all." Wilma sucked in several deep breaths, talking and laughing were stealing her strength. "With Shaw gone and my dowry spent, the Hannays will not care aboot me. Domnall is a mere puppet. Stanley will continue to fight for Balliol for his own reasons. I care not what those are now that Shaw is dead, and I am likely to share that fate soon enough."

"Then why tell me all of this? Do you merely want someone to know that you concocted all of this and led three men by their bollocks?"

"There is that. But I tell you this for one reason. I've hated you since the beginning. You blithely told secrets that weren't yours to share—though I thank you for that since it helped me. But you could do no wrong. Even with a family that loathed you, you were still respected at court. People told you things, confided things, or at least cared not if you overheard conversations. You only had to look in the Sinclairs' direction, and they accepted you. The bluidy Sinclairs. They might as well call themselves Bruces. So when you die tomorrow during the raid Stanley leads, know that it was me who really killed you."

Cerys laughed. She didn't have to pretend her humor. But she was laughing at, not with. "You are so utterly pathetic. I would rather be hated than pitied. You hated me but pretended to by my friend because it was convenient. It was far from convenient to be your friend, but you seemed so pathetic when we arrived at court. Ignoring you would have been like kicking a mangy pup in a storm. *If* I die tomorrow, it will be as a wife to a mon who acknowledges me and is proud of me. I am no one's dirty or inconvenient secret. I am no mon's mistress with naught but what's between my legs to offer the world. I am a Sinclair, and you are but refuse."

Cerys didn't wait for Wilma to say more. There was no need since she knew the woman would hang for treason. She turned on her heel and yanked open the door, making Blake jump back. She slammed the door, giving him a warning look not to ask questions. She didn't argue when he lifted her into his arms, and they remained quiet until they arrived at their chamber.

"It was her all along. She instigated it all. She was Balliol's mistress. She must have been barely more than a girl when she started bedding him. She recruited Shaw, and he brought on Stanley and Domnall. But Stanley was her lover before she added Shaw to her list of men. She said there will be another raid tomorrow from the southwest."

"Then we prepare for a raid. Do ye need to rest? Or can ye come with me to advise the king?"

"You are not leaving me behind, husband."

Blake walked along the battlements, his eyes scanning the morning sky to the southwest. He and Cerys spent several hours with David, Joan, and their advisors. Blake had kissed a sleepy Cerys and slipped from their chamber two hours ago. Now he continued to look for any sign of a raiding party or their returning French scouts. Better prepared this time, the mixture of French and Scots warriors awaited the signal. Their horses were saddled and waiting for them. They would meet their opponents in the meadow just beyond the château. They wouldn't allow their enemy close enough to breach the walls again.

As midday passed, and there was still no sign of an approaching foe, Blake wondered if everything Wilma said was a lie or if she wasn't as informed as she believed. He'd checked on Cerys and shared their nooning. But he was once more on the battlements.

"Regardez!" Look! A French guardsman pointed to shadows in the distance. The bells rang as the shadows appeared to shift. It was too far to see for certain, but Blake recognized a wave of horseman preparing to descend upon them. He raced down to the bailey, calling out in French and Scots. He swung onto Torque's back and drew a targe over his left forearm. He slid his sword from its sheath and pointed toward the gate as he wheeled his steed around. He and his comrades poured out of the gate, galloping toward their enemy.

The wind whipped across Blake's face, hair sticking to his lips and poking his eyes. He shook his head, undeterred by the inconvenience. As Torque's hooves ate up the distance, the mercenaries came into view. He had no trouble recognizing Stanley and Domnall at the head of their small army. Except, as the space between the two forces shrank, it was obvious this was more than just a small army. These were not just Gallowglass mercenaries. Blake recognized English knights' armor. These men dared to enter France when the two countries were already on the cusp of war. If King Philip discovered their presence, it would make the threat of war a reality. Part of Blake prayed it would happen. The English would have to focus their efforts on defeating France, which meant little to no support for Balliol and his quest for Scotland.

The clash of swords, grunts, and cries of pain filled the air from the moment the opposing sides clashed. Blake swung his sword and his targe, using them both as weapons. He maneuvered Torque with his powerful thighs. The steed and warrior became one, moving in synchronicity as they battled their foe. Torque was as much a weapon as any blade Blake carried. The horse's powerful hooves and legs were like battering rams when he reared and kicked. His teeth were ferocious and could rip man or beast apart. The animal fought as valiantly as its owner, taking on horses that drew too near or men who thought to cut the steed down from under Blake.

There seemed to be an endless onslaught of mercenaries and English. It was clear that they were going to overwhelm the French and Scots by their sheer volume. But the French and Scots had trained together for years during David's exile. They were used to one another, but the same couldn't be said for the English and Gallowglass. They fought like two separate armies that happened to show up to the same fight. They got into each other's way, and some of the knights cut down their own allies, not caring enough to distinguish between the Scots and the swords-for-hire. But their numbers were their advantage, and Blake knew it.

The English and French were accustomed to fighting one another, and eventually the battle broke into two parts. While the centuries-old rivals fought yet another round, the Scots faced the Gallowglass. Their strategies were similar, making their tactics predictable. This made the tide of victory ebb and flow for both sides. Blake watched as men fell around him. Many were English and French, several were mercenaries, but few were Scottish. However, there seemed to be an endless wave of opponents. For each one he struck down, three seemed to attack Blake. The targe he carried was splintered and dinged, but it saved his life several times. His arms ached, and his chest burned. He didn't dare stop swinging his arms to brush away the sweat from his eyes. He could take that moment of ease, but it would likely be his last.

As the fight continued, Blake heard something. At first, he thought it was the sound of his heart pounding in his ears. But as it grew louder, he recognized it. Warriors grew distracted and turned toward the approaching noise. Blake didn't need to see it to know the cause. It was the rhythmic thud of sword hilts hammering against targes. The sound of Highlanders joining the fight.

"Girnigoe! Girnigoe!" The Sinclair battle cry rang through the air, startling everyone but Blake. Never had he been more relieved to see his father, uncles, and grandfather than that moment as they led the charge over the nearest rise. At the head of the army rode Laird Liam Sinclair, Earl of Caithness and patriarch to one of the greatest Scottish families. The man's chestnut locks were peppered with gray, as was his bushy beard, but nothing else gave away his age. As he charged forward, his sword slashing across anyone foolish enough to find themselves in his way, he was just as powerful as he'd been the day he'd met his wife Kyla. He'd been a man in his early twenties then, full of vim and vigor. Life hadn't been easy, especially after losing his beloved when his children were still young. But those challenges forged him into the legend he was. It made him the man who raised four of the most renowned warriors in all of Scotland.

To Liam's right rode his sons Callum and Alexander, while Tavish and Magnus rode to their father's left. It was as though the great Cairngorm Mountains moved on horseback as the wave of Sinclair men descended upon the battle. Father and sons moved together like the many heads of Medusa's snakes. Each fought his own enemy, but they were a force together than no one could defeat. With a wave of clan warriors behind them, the Sinclairs plowed into the fray.

The Highlanders' arrival reinvigorated the French and Scottish forces. But it also made the English panic. No one needed to hear the name Sinclair to know who'd arrived. Experience and legend made the English desperate to flee. The Gallowglass knew no amount of coin was worth dying for at the end of a Sinclair sword. Death would be fast, just like it would be inevitable. The English fled as the clan's warriors chased them, cutting them down. The Gallowglass regrouped and came together to try to fight their way out of the battle and retreat.

"Ye were paid to fight, so fight!" Liam's voice roared over the clang of metal. He charged toward the mercenaries, his sons still riding alongside him. Blake spun Torque and leaned low as he raced to join his family.

"Son!" Magnus called as his sword swept a man's head from his shoulders.

"Da!" Blake took his place between Magnus and Tavish, just as he'd done when he first rode into battle and was still learning how different a real fight was from practicing in the lists. The field was becoming too choked with dead bodies, those of men and beast. It was growing hard to ride without the horses stumbling.

"Dismount!" Liam ordered. The men followed his command, even those who were not Sinclairs. It was as natural as drawing their next breath to defer to great warrior. They slapped their mounts rears, sending them away from the battlefield. "Blake, to me."

Blake moved to his grandfather's back as his father paired with Tavish; Callum and Alex fought back-to-back. The three pairs moved like a surge engine, never leaving anyone's back exposed but plowing through the remaining enemy. Time seemed to stand still for Blake as he moved as one with his grandfather, a man he'd idolized as a child and respected as an adult. He would fight to make his family and clan proud. He would fight to defend the man who always defended him. He would fight to ensure his wife remained safely hidden away in the château. He would fight to defend the rightful king of Scotland. And he would fight because he was a Sinclair.

The additional warriors ensured the Scottish and French victory. But it wasn't over while Domnall and Stanley remained alive. He spied them trying to retreat. He pointed at the men and whistled. Torque and the other Sinclair laird's family horses pounded back onto the battlefield.

"Those two," Blake yelled. "They did this."

Blake and his family mounted their horses and soon surrounded Stanley and Domnall. The men bumped into each other as they sought a way to escape. They didn't use the opportunity to defend one another's backs, to protect their own. Instead they jumped apart like scalded cats, which only brought them closer to the men who encircled them.

"Home, Cunningham, you stand accused of treason," Blake proclaimed in French, so everyone could understand. "Beyond your presence here, leading merce-naries paid to kill the One True King of Scotland, Lady Wilma confessed. A search of her chamber found stacks of missives detailing everything, including how you both are involved. You stand before Laird Liam Sinclair, Earl of Caithness, confidante to the almighty Robert the Bruce, and godfather to our king, King David. Make your confessions or plead your case. He will be judge and juror." Blake leaned forward, his arms crossed on his pummel. "And mayhap even executioner."

"Stanley Home, you stand accused of treason and conspiring with the usurper Edward Balliol. You also stand charged with conspiracy to murder my grandson. Och, aye. I've already heard aboot my grandson's and granddaughter-by-marriage's time with her clan. What say you in your defense?"

"God save the king. God save King Edward Balliol." Stanley spat, hitting Liam's boot. The older man sighed and shook his head. Without warning, Liam swung his sword, cleaving Stanley in half. His body crumbled like a tower of sand washed away by the tide.

"Domnall Cunningham, you stand accused of treason and conspiring with the usurper Edward Bal-liol. You also stand charged with aiding and abetting a conspiracy. It is clear you did not lead either conspir-acy, but you had knowledge of both. Your silence showed your complicity. What say you in your defense?"

"Whatever happens, keep my wives safe."

Domnall's response wasn't what anyone expected. Blake heard his uncle Alexander whisper "wives." Blake would explain that later.

"I cannot promise you that if your clan is involved."

"They are not. I acted of my own free will. I have disgraced my family and my clan by my choices today and in the past. I accept your judgment." Domnall raised his head and met Liam's gaze. The older man nodded. His sword moved swiftly again, sweeping the man's head from his shoulders, and sending it sailing through the air to then roll several feet once it landed. The body collapsed backwards.

"Blake!" Magnus practically ripped Blake from the saddle as he engulfed his son in an embrace that threatened to suffocate him. He tapped his father on the shoulder, hoping to signal that Magnus held him too tightly. But soon his uncles joined in.

"Easy, lads. He canna breathe. Ye'll suffocate him after saving him. I dinna think his bride or his mama will appreciate that." Liam chuckled and shook his head as three of his children eased away, but Magnus didn't release Blake. Liam couldn't blame his youngest son. He'd been in that position far too many times to count over the years. Never would it grow easier to send his sons and grandsons into battle. And never would the relief diminish to see them all survive. Magnus pounded Blake on the back again before pulling him tight against him.

"Da, ma ribs," Blake wheezed. "Still healing."

"What?" Magnus jerked away. Blake lifted the side of his leine to show where a new scar was forming where the stitches were placed only days ago. "What the bluidy devil?"

"It happened during their first raid." Blake looked back toward the château, an overwhelming need to get back to Cerys swept over him. Now that the battle was won, and his family and clan were there, he needed his wife.

"It's secure. We left men there."

Blake nodded at his grandfather. "How many did ye bring?"

"Five score in all," Callum answered. "Yer Great-

Uncle Hamish couldnae let the chance to thrash the English go by. He sent men to aid us."

Laird Hamish Sutherland, Earl of Sutherland, was a man as revered as Liam. His son and heir, Lachlan, might as well have been a fifth Sinclair brother. The two families were bound by marriage and by blood, but more importantly, by choice. Liam's marriage to Hamish's only sister, Kyla, ended a generations old feud and forged an alliance that created a web of alliances across the Highlands that few tested. And of those few, none survived. It warmed Blake to know that his extended family journeyed alongside his closest kin.

"What aboot Tor?" It hadn't escaped Blake's notice that his brother wasn't there.

Magnus looked up at the sky then turned toward the north. "He's likely eating yer mama's haggis and grinning ear-to-ear that he doesnae have to share with yer bottomless belly."

Blake nodded, but his father's quip did nothing to ease his now-growing worry. Had something happened along the way to Dunbeath? Was there a reason Torquil couldn't travel, couldn't fight?

"Fear nae, nephew." Alex clapped his hand on Blake's shoulder, tugging him close enough to drop a quick kiss on Blake's crown. One could have missed it if they blinked. It had been several months since they'd seen one another. No one would question Alex's relief to see his nephew after being apart for so long. "Yer brother is at home helping yer cousins. He's likely driving Thormud barmy, but he's helping."

Blake chuckled. Thor and Tor. They'd been a perfect storm of rabblerousing since they could both walk and talk. Both were aptly named for the Norse god. Their laughter and their bellows could boom and rattle just like thunder.

"He made it home safely then?" Blake looked at Magnus.

"Aye. But I think yer brother believes ye owe him, since he was left to tell yer mama and aunts all aboot yer bonnie bride. I heard him begging to come with us as I rode out of the gates."

"Bah. He'll be enjoying all of Mama's attention." For all that Blake teased his brother about clinging to their mother's skirts, even as an adult, he wouldn't trade the few moments alone he could snatch with his mother. No Sinclair child would ever outgrow the solace and strength they drew from the affection their parents freely lavished. But moments of undivided attention were difficult in a family so large. They were cherished.

"Nae for long. Maisie's already challenging him," Tavish chimed in as they began walking the battlefield, looking for their dead and wounded. Blake remained with them, even when Liam said he could return to the estate. He wanted to. He wanted to see Cerys. But he knew his duty, and he wouldn't shirk it. As a leader among his clan's warriors now, he couldn't put his personal desires above the needs of others. He would follow the older generation's example. It took three hours to triage the wounded and bury the dead. When they finally rode through the gates, Blake spied a flash of dark hair and tangling skirts. Cerys lifted the fabric to her calves with one hand while wrapping her other arm around her middle as she ran toward her husband.

"Cerys! What're ye doing?" Blake leaped down from his horse. He was unprepared for the whirling dervish that launched itself at him. Cerys knocked Blake back into Torque, who didn't appreciate being bumped. The horse swished his tail and sallied his hindquarters away, leaving Blake with no support. The couple tumbled to the ground as Blake tried to absorb the impact.

"I'm kissing my husband. *Sàmhach.*" It wasn't until

they were breathless and climbing back to their feet that Blake realized Cerys told him to be quiet in Gaelic.

"How'd ye learn that?" Blake asked as he swept Cerys into his arms, still not pleased to see her running.

"I asked two Highland servants I overheard speaking Gaelic. The women taught me a few words I realized I needed to know."

"Such as?"

Cerys grinned. "Mayhap I will tell you this eve." She playfully plugged both of their noses and winked. "After a bath."

"I'll make introductions this eve," Blake called over his shoulder as he sped through the entryway to the stairs, which he took two at a time to reach their chamber. With a bed and a bath awaiting them, they nearly didn't make it to the evening meal.

CHAPTER 24

They were headed home. At last. The strain took its toll on Cerys, who developed a fever the day after the battle. She'd paced their chamber once she knew Blake rode out with the other warriors. She'd heard the fight across the meadow and into the château. She'd never imagined the cacophony of noise. Steel against steel, cries of agony and death, horses' whinnies, and orders bellowed. She could see nothing, which only made the drifting sounds worse.

Then there'd been an almighty drumming from whence she didn't know. She leaned as far out of the window embrasure as she dared, straining to see. A tidal wave of mounted warriors poured over a hill, chanting a word she didn't know. They disappeared from sight once they entered the meadow, but the increased noise reverberated through her head and surely rattled the walls.

Each step pulled at her wound, but it gave her something to concentrate upon instead of picturing Blake slain and left somewhere on the grassy expanse. She'd nearly been ill when the bells finally rang, and cheers went up from the guards who'd remained to defend the château. Flinging open the chamber door, she ignored David and Joan as they called out to her. She nearly fell down the stairs when her skirts tangled around her legs. She spotted Blake immediately. He was all that she saw before she catapulted herself into his arms. Her exhausted and unsuspecting husband stumbled backward before taking them both to the ground. She cared not as a flash of searing pain ripped through her as they landed. All that mattered was Blake had returned.

However, soon much more mattered. They'd attended the evening meal, where Cerys met Blake's grandfather and Uncle Alexander. She'd charmed Liam, and he endeared himself to her. Alex was the most reserved of the older Sinclair siblings, tending toward brooding. But he was warm and welcoming. Cerys realized that Alex was her uncle too, albeit by marriage rather than by blood. He'd seen her expression grow pensive and deduced her worry. He assured her Brighde was desperately anxious to meet her niece and was eagerly awaiting her arrival. The meal progressed, but by the end, Cerys suffered the cold sweats, and the headache from earlier only grew worse. By the time Blake carried her to their chamber, her fever raged. Her misery was compounded by being awake during the entire ordeal. Unconsciousness never claimed her, and there was no reprieve from the pain.

Blake refused to leave Cerys, and none of the Sinclair men dared suggest it. They knew and understood where Blake's new loyalty laid. None could blame him, since they were much the same with their wives, even after more than two decades of marriage. But it was Liam who assured Blake there was nothing about which to feel guilty when he prioritized being with Cerys. The men talked in the passageway in low tones whenever Cerys slept. Blake recounted all that happened since his father and uncles left Stirling, from accepting his feelings for Cerys and marrying her to their time locked in her former chamber at Cessford and their plight there to their stay at Château Gaillard.

Liam and his sons met with King David several times. The boy king seemed to grow taller and wiser under Liam's guidance and attention. The four Sinclair brothers were like surrogate uncles to the thirteen-year-old monarch. He was on the cusp of manhood, forced to mature far faster than most his age. David emulated the four brothers, finding in each man the paternal figure that he barely remembered. Duty and fear weighed heavily on his young shoulders, but his godfather had faith that David would be restored to the Scottish throne. But no one was naïve enough to believe it would be without more battles against Balliol and the English.

David dispatched missives to King Philip informing him of the English involvement and the plot against his and Joan's lives. He detailed what he witnessed and what he'd learned. His was a complicated relationship with the French monarch. It was a rarely discussed, but impossible-to-ignore fact, that Queen Joan was King Edward III of England's youngest sister. Her own brother supported the man who fought to wrestle the throne from her husband—the man their father arranged for her to marry. Her grandfather was the infamous Hammer of the Scots, King Edward I Longshanks, while her mother, dubbed the "She-Wolf of France," was King Philip's cousin. This made David and Philip cousins-by-marriage once removed.

By the time the Sinclairs rode away from King David, Queen Joan, and Château Gaillard, the royal couple were safe from the most recent threat. Liam used connections with surrounding nobles to arrange more protection for the king and queen. While other nobles would send no warriors to join the king's sentries, they would deter and defend the king if needed.

"How are ye faring, *leannan?*" Blake glanced down at Cerys, who rode in his lap. She'd begun the day riding Kitten, but she'd grown weary after several hours. He'd questioned whether she was ready for the long journey north, but she'd insisted she was recovered enough.

"I'm well." Cerys glanced around and lowered her voice. "I'm tired, but I really just wanted to ride with you."

"And that's what I really wanted, too. Dinna think that we're fooling anyone, but everyone also kens ye arenae used to the long hours on horseback like we are. Do ye wish to sleep?"

"A little." As if to prove her need, she couldn't stifle her yawn. She nestled against her husband as her eyes drifted closed. He tightened his hold around her after he drew her Sinclair plaid arisaid tighter around her shoulders. Immense pride swelled within him when he watched his bride wear his clan's pattern. She was a constant source of admiration, and Blake was in awe of her. A flippant comment had both drawn her and pushed her away, but a chance second encounter showed them their destiny.

"Ye remind me of yer mama and me when we rode home to Dunbeath for the first time. Ye ken her family didna approve of us, nae when we handfasted nor when we had a kirking seven years later. Ye've already faced challenges that could have pulled ye apart, nae just by distance but in yer hearts. But I think ye love yer wife as fiercely as I love mine. Ye're both coming home. Dinna ever doubt that Cerys is welcome with our family and our people."

"But ye and Mama fell in love over several years, sending missives and seeing each other at Highland

Gatherings. Willna people question that we believe we're already in love?"

Magnus stared at his son before roaring with laughter. Blake scowled as Cerys shifted, huffing in annoyance even though he was certain she remained asleep.

"Lad, I kenned I wanted to marry yer mama the moment I met her. By the time we left that first gathering, I was besotted. I didna ken if I would ever see her again, so I lived ma life that first year much as I had before. But I never stopped thinking aboot yer mama. I kenned when I saw her again that there would never be anyone else. I was already in love with her. Yer grandda was in love with ma mama by the time she sat down for her first evening meal at Dunbeath. Tavish was in love with Ceit even though he denied it to himself. They didna always mix well, and they still bicker, but there was nay doubt they were destined for each other. I watched them. Callum and Alex kenned their hearts even though they doubted whether they could convince their women to love them. Yer cousin Liam kenned with Elene, even though they were cautious because of their circumstances. Yer aunt and Tristan were drawn to each other the moment they met and feared they couldnae be together until they were. That's the way of our family. We may love soon, but we love hard, and we never stop."

Blake nodded. He knew his family's love stories; they were ones of legend. But he'd wondered if he and Cerys could have such a strong union based on so little time. As he glanced down yet again, he chided himself for having a moment of doubt. He loved Cerys with a consuming passion and a steadfast loyalty. Time had nothing to do with it. It was their destiny.

The day progressed and one moved into two, then a week passed while they traveled to the French coast. By the time they reached Calais, Cerys's strength was nearly fully restored after napping every afternoon. With little privacy each night, they slipped away on the pretense of Cerys bathing, which happened, but there was inevitably a distraction. However, Cerys was soon asleep when they returned to camp, sleeping until the very last moment before they left camp each morning.

The Sinclairs boarded ships that sailed them across the channel, avoiding the English coast and giving the country's eastern coast a wide berth. They docked at Dunrobin, the Sutherland men disembarking from their boats. Cerys met Hamish and his wife, Amelia. She also met her mother's cousin, Arabella, who was the most beautiful woman she'd ever encountered. Her appearance was breathtaking. The clan's tánaiste, Hamish's son Lachlan, spent much of his time with his cousins, but he was cordial to Cerys. Amelia encouraged Cerys to spend the three-day respite eating and sleeping. There was something about the way Amelia looked at Cerys that she couldn't interpret at first.

Cerys's drowsiness seemed at odds with how well she felt when they reached Calais. She hadn't any aversion to being on the boat. But she felt an overwhelming fatigue while at Dunrobin. She assumed it was merely all of the events of the past month catching up with her, the strain finally demanding she rest. But the smell of porridge their last morning at Dunrobin had Cerys bolting for a chamber pot. Blake was already in the lists with the other men, but Amelia and Arabella rushed after her.

"Do ye wish to see the midwife?" Amelia asked softly.

"Do you really think I'm already with child?"

Arabella giggled. "The Sinclair men are just as randy and virile as the Sutherland men. I would guess ye got with child within a sennight of marrying. I'm certain all the practice has paid off."

Cerys's cheeks flushed, but she'd seen the affection between Hamish and Amelia, and Lachlan and Arabella. She heard Lachlan's sisters, Maude and Blair, were the same with their own husbands. Blake had already forewarned her that what she witnessed at Dunrobin would only be amplified by double once they reached Dunbeath. He assured her they would fit in perfectly.

She was less peaky by the time Blake returned to bathe before the evening meal, but she wasn't able to eat much. He noticed and worried, but she assured him she'd eaten a large midday meal, which wasn't untrue. She'd been ravenous by then. The Sinclairs retired early that night and were on the road to Dunbeath before dawn. She rode Kitten most of the day, but she could barely keep her eyes open as dusk approached. When she dozed off and nearly fell from her mount, Blake insisted they stop right where they were. The Sinclairs were too wise to argue with the newlywed who hovered over his bride. It was Cerys who'd had to shoo him away. However, the next morning revealed a surly, then panicked, groom.

Cerys woke to the smell of bannocks cooking. She covered her mouth and darted for the tree line, ordering Blake to leave her alone. She batted at him to leave her in peace. "I'm all right, Blake. Cease your whittling and give me room to breathe."

"Ye canna dash into the trees without a guard with ye. Ye ken that. I am giving ye space." Blake huffed as he crossed his arms. It wasn't that Cerys needing privacy bothered him. It was her refusal to tell him what was amiss. He sensed it, but she was evasive when he asked. However, the sound of Cerys retching, then heaving, pushed him out of his orneriness and into fear. She sounded utterly miserable with each moan between heaves. "Ye canna tell me naught is wrong. Ye're ill."

"I'm not ill, Blake."

"Ye are."

"I'm not."

"Healthy people dinna vomit before they've even eaten. They dinna sleep most of the day. Ye are ill."

"I'm not ill, Blake." Cerys repeated herself, unable to say more as another wave of nausea had her doubled over.

"Ye are."

"I'm not! I'm expecting a bairn." Cerys hadn't intended to blurt that admission. She'd planned to tell him that night when they were alone. She wished to share the news as a celebration of their first night together in their home and their bed. She'd seen the midwife at Amelia's suggestion, and the woman confirmed that it was early days, but Cerys was pregnant.

"What?" Blake barked as he kneeled beside Cerys. She reared back at his tone. He plucked her from her knees and settled her in his lap as he leaned back against a tree trunk. "I didna mean to yell."

"You roared. I told you, you are a Highland bear. You sound like one. God help our sons when they land on the wrong side of your temper."

"I dinna have a temper."

Cerys cocked an eyebrow, but she couldn't keep from smiling now that her nausea had passed. She leaned against him as she laughed. Blake didn't have a bad temper. He was more lighthearted than most men she'd met, and he took most things in stride. He'd proved that already.

"You don't. But you do roar."

"*Mo ghaol*, how do ye ken?" Blake blushed when he realized how naïve the question sounded. He understood how she would realize it, but it just seemed too soon.

"Amelia must have guessed the moment she saw me.

326

I haven't a clue how. Mayhap she's just been around a lot of expecting women in her life. But the porridge the morning before we left had me over a chamber pot. She suggested I see the midwife, who confirmed it."

"Ye scared me when ye wouldnae tell me what's wrong. I dinna want ye to think I willna give ye room to breathe, but I willna pretend I dinna worry aboot ye."

"I'm sorry. I wanted to wait until tonight when we were alone in our chamber."

"And I ruined that for ye by being so demanding. I'm sorry."

"You didn't ruin aught. We can still celebrate." Cerys glanced down between them and licked her lips, an exaggerated hint at what she planned. She felt Blake's cock pulse against her hip.

"I love ye, Cerys. And I love our bairn."

"So do I. I love you and the family we're making." Cerys sighed but then pulled away. "I would also love a drink of water and a mint sprig."

The travel-stained, weary Sinclair entourage rode into Dunbeath's bailey at noon the day after they set off from the Sutherlands'. An elegant woman with spiral-curled, honey-colored hair dashed forward, enveloping Blake as his feet hit the ground.

"Mama." Blake lifted Deirdre in the air and squeezed. He inhaled her floral scent, one that reminded him of all the times he'd crawled onto her lap as a child, of every time she'd tended to him when he was sick or injured, of whenever she'd chased him and his siblings with threats of the dungeon for one infraction or another. He kissed her cheek before taking her hand and leading her to Kitten. He reached up and lifted Cerys from the saddle. "Mama, this is ma wife, Cerys. *Mo leannan*, this is ma mama, Deirdre."

Cerys dipped a curtsy and bowed her head. "Lady Deir—"

"Ye can stop there, lass. I'm just Deirdre to ye. Mayhap one day, something more familiar. We dinna stand on titles here. Yer aunts willna have it either." Deirdre offered a motherly smile, and Cerys could tell she would offer an embrace if Cerys wished to accept it. She stepped toward the older woman and wrapped her arms around her lightly. But the moment Deirdre reciprocated, Cerys burst into tears. "Lass?"

"I'm so sorry." Cerys couldn't get her arms to let go. "I don't know what's wrong with me."

Deirdre looked at her son. She knew he tried to keep his expression impassive, but she saw the pride in his eyes. It was the same look Magnus had each time Deirdre was expecting.

"Ye're having a bairn. Ye're likely to be a watering pot and a thunderstorm for the next few moons. It's nae aught we arenae used to here. Ma felicitations, lass." Deirdre stroked Cerys's back, soothing her. But the younger woman still didn't release her.

"*Leannan?*"

"Your mother smells like a mama. She feels like one, too." Cerys knew that was likely the most asinine thing she'd ever said, but her mother's-by-marriage soft clucking and tightening embrace caused another wave of tears.

"I ken ye didna have a mother growing up, lass. Did ye have nay one?"

"My aunt Matilda, but it was never like this. This feels—right."

"Ah, ma sweet lassie. Ye warm ma heart. Ye're ma daughter now, just like Maisie."

Cerys accepted the affection she'd been starved of

her entire life. She knew her aunt did her best, but she simply hadn't been as naturally maternal as Deirdre was. Cerys couldn't help but stare when she finally let go, and Deirdre turned to find Magnus practically on top of them. The kiss they shared was virtually indecent. As Cerys looked around, trying not to stare, she spotted Callum, Alex, and Tavish greeting their wives the same way. Tavish's and Ceit's kiss was indecent, his hand on her backside, clearly squeezing.

"I told ye we will fit in," Blake whispered before he lifted Cerys off her feet, just like the other husbands did with their wives. And just like the other wives, Cerys's legs dangled as she readily accepted Blake's kisses.

"Och, aye, we ken ye love each other. We dinna have to see it every single day." Cerys turned her head and spotted a young woman who was the mirror of Deirdre. Her acerbic tongue didn't match the grin that lit her face as she approached Blake and Cerys. "Finally, a sister. Just what I always wanted."

"Maisie," Blake warned, but his sister merely smirked and pointed to the ground. When Blake put Cerys back on her feet, Maisie practically tore her from Blake's arms. Cerys was unprepared for the whirlwind that was Maisie Sinclair, but the embrace of her sister-by-marriage felt as natural as Deirdre's. She giggled at Blake's resigned grumble. "Bluidy hell."

"Aye, brother." Torquil slapped Blake on the shoulder before they embraced. "Now it's two against two. We barely survived Maisie. I dinna ken if we can last with the pair."

Cerys looked among the siblings, unsure what Torquil foreshadowed. But Maisie's giggles filled the air.

"Ye dinna ken the half of it, brothers." Maisie turned to Cerys. "Can ye shoot an arrow? Can ye throw a knife?" When Cerys nodded her head, Maisie's grin bordered on maniacal. "Och, we shall have such fun, sister. They dinna ken the half of it."

Cerys couldn't help but smile since Maisie's good nature was too infectious to ignore. Cerys looked up at Blake, her eyes twinkling with mischief, plots already hatching in her mind. There was mirth in his dubious expression. He was the most handsome man she'd ever seen, and she called him husband. She was finally home. She finally had a family.

"Let's introduce ye to everyone else. Then I'll show ye yer home." Blake leaned forward. "I think we shall start with our chamber. Mayhap ye'll see the rest in a sennight."

Blake held true to his promise, continuing the Sinclair tradition. Torquil wisely found somewhere else to lay his head at night. The newlyweds locked themselves away in their chamber, only opening the door to food and baths. The one exception was Blake's insistence that the midwife examine Cerys since she still felt ill throughout the days. After all they endured in the first two months of their marriage, the peace and privacy were much needed.

"I love ye, *mo leannan*." Blake said as they sat before the fire, Cerys's hair drying from their bath. "Now and forever."

"I love you, *m'eudail*. Now and forever."

Their bodies joined as their hearts and souls rejoiced that they were finally where they belonged. Home.

EPILOGUE

"**C**an you believe the last of the cousins is marrying today?" Cerys looked up at her husband of more than three decades. Fine lines etched into his skin around his eyes and mouth from years of laughter. Some of the exuberance of youth had faded from his eyes, and wisdom replaced it. Gray showed around his temples and in his beard. But those were the only signs that Blake was any different from when they married. He was still a mountainous man, made of chiseled and hewn muscle. He trained in the lists daily, now beside their sons as well as his father, uncles, and cousins.

"I canna. How have they all grown so auld so fast?" Blake stroked back hair from Cerys's temple and tucked it behind her ear as he considered his younger cousins. Threads of gray were interwoven with the nearly black locks he'd twirled around his fingers countless times. Her skin was darker than when they'd met; life in the Highlands had found her outdoors more than her life in the Lowlands ever had. The bridge of her nose and cheekbones were smattered with freckles that he knew even with his eyes closed, freckles that reminded him of stars in the night sky. Blake still counted his blessings daily that Cerys gave him a second look after their less-than-auspicious first encounter. She was just as beautiful to him now as she had been then.

"If they're auld, what does that make ye?" Cerys grinned as she wrapped her arms around Blake's waist as they stood surrounded by their family, awaiting the bride and her father. The air was filled with a love as potent as the strongest scent from spring flowers. They'd lived and loved together for more years than they'd been apart. There'd been good tidings and tribulations, happiness and grief. But they'd faced it all as one.

"Me? What aboot—"

"Dinna ye say it." Cerys winked, lapsing into the burr that sometimes flavored her speech after so many years in the Highlands. "I'm as much a spring chicken as when we met."

"Och, aye. And ye proved it this morning. But since I'm so auld, ma memory needs ye to prove it again tonight."

"Mayhap you aren't so auld, since you still chase me through the keep and into our chamber."

"And ye still let me catch ye."

"Always." Cerys rose on her toes to kiss Blake as the crowd turned toward the keep. Cerys followed suit, but Blake took a moment to look at the people he loved most. His grandfather was in his ninth decade, so Liam spent most of his time inside now. Callum had long ago taken over as laird, and there was even talk that Thormud might inherit the title soon. Callum stood beside Siùsan, his arm where it usually was—wrapped around her waist. It was the second-most common pose for the Sinclair men. If they weren't standing with feet hip-width apart, and their arms crossed, then they were just as likely to have one, if not both, arms wrapped around their wives.

Beside them stood Alex and Brighde. Cerys and her aunt had been immediate kindred spirits, and they were as close as mother and daughter, just as Cerys was with Deirdre. His parents stood beside Cerys. On the other side of Callum and Siùsan were Tavish and Ceit. Blake couldn't help but chuckle when his aunt poked his uncle in the ribs, scolding him about something. Everyone knew their bickering was merely a prelude, part of the dance they'd shared since they met.

Mairghread and Tristan stood across from the other Sinclairs, their Mackay family attending the wedding as well. Near them stood the Sutherlands, with Hamish in a chair beside Liam, and Amelia to his left. Maude, Blair, and Lachlan were there with their spouses and adult children. All of Blake's cousins and their spouses and children crowded around the kirk steps as the last of the second generation waited to exchange their vows. There'd been twenty-four other marriages before that day, the cousins ranging in age over two decades. The Sinclair legacy was as strong as the very Clan Sinclair itself. Their love and loyalty were immortalized in the Highlands, and the ceremony beginning at the steps of Dunbeath's kirk was a reminder that the Sinclairs, Sutherlands, and Mackays loved just as hard as they fought to defend their families.

"Do ye remember our wedding day, *mo leannan?*"

"Like it was yesterday, *m'eudail.* I didn't know how much I loved you then, but I know it now. You've given me a life that surpasses aught I ever imagined as a lass. Standing here with our weans and our family, I couldn't imagine a richer or fuller life. I love you, Blake."

"I grew up in a keep filled with love. But until I met ye, I couldnae appreciate, couldnae fully understand, the power of love between a mon and a woman and what they share for their weans. Ye've filled ma life to the fullest, and ma heart still brims over with ma feelings for ye. I love ye, Cerys."

They stood together as the young couple exchanged their vows on the steps before they moved into the kirk for the Mass. But as had become a tradition among the Sinclairs and Sutherlands, the newly married couple stopped on the steps once more as the sun set. They recited their own pledges, using the handfast vows Blake once proclaimed to Cerys. As the newlyweds spoke, Blake and Cerys looked only at one another as they mouthed those promises once more.

"Ye are Blood of ma Blood, and Bone of ma Bone. I give ye ma Body, that we Two might be One. I give ye ma Spirit, 'til our Life shall be Done."

THANK YOU FOR READING
HIGHLAND BEAR

Celeste Barclay, a nom de plume, lives near the Southern California coast with her husband and sons. Growing up in the Midwest, Celeste enjoyed spending as much time in and on the water as she could. Now she lives near the beach. She's an avid swimmer, a hopeful future surfer, and a former rower. When she's not writing, she's working or being a mom.

Subscribe to Celeste's bimonthly newsletter to receive exclusive insider perks.
Subscribe Now

www.celestebarclay.com

Join the fun and get exclusive insider giveaways, sneak peeks, and new release announcements in
Celeste Barclay's Facebook Ladies of Yore Group

THE HIGHLAND LADIES

A Spinster at the Highland Court

BOOK 1 SNEAK PEEK

Elizabeth Fraser looked around the royal chapel within Stirling Castle. The ornate candlestick holders on the altar glistened and reflected the light from the ones in the wall sconces as the priest intoned the holy prayers of the Advent season. Elizabeth kept her head bowed as though in prayer, but her green eyes swept the congregation. She watched the other ladies-in-waiting, many of whom were doing the same thing. She caught the eye of Allyson Elliott. Elizabeth raised one eyebrow as Allyson's lips twitched. Both women had been there enough times to accept they'd be kneeling for at least the next hour as the Latin service carried on. Elizabeth understood the Mass thanks to her cousin Deirdre Fraser, or rather now Deirdre Sinclair. Elizabeth's mind flashed to the recent struggle her cousin faced as she reunited with her husband Magnus after a seven-year separation. Her aunt and uncle's choice to keep Deirdre hidden from her husband simply because they didn't think the Sinclairs were an advantageous enough match, and the resulting scandal, still humiliated the other Fraser clan members at court. She admired Deirdre's husband Magnus's pledge to remain faithful despite not knowing if he'd ever see Deirdre again.

Elizabeth suddenly snapped her attention; while everyone else intoned the twelfth—or was it thirteenth—amen of the Mass, the hairs on the back of her neck stood up. She had the strongest feeling that someone was watching her. Her eyes scanned to her right, where her parents sat further down the pew. Her mother and father had their heads bowed and eyes closed. While she was convinced her mother was in devout prayer, she wondered if her father had fallen asleep during the Mass. Again. With nothing seeming out of the ordinary and no one visibly paying attention to her, her eyes swung to the left. She took in the king and queen as they kneeled together at their prie-dieu. The queen's lips moved as she recited the liturgy in silence. The king was as still as a statue. Years of leading warriors showed, both in his stature and his ability to control his body into absolute stillness. Elizabeth peered past the royal couple and found herself looking into the astute hazel eyes of Edward Bruce, Lord of Badenoch and Lochaber. His gaze gave her the sense that he peered into her thoughts, as though he were assessing her. She tried to keep her face neutral as heat surged up her neck. She prayed her face didn't redden as much as her neck must have, but at a twenty-one, she still hadn't mastered how to control her blushing. Her nape burned like it was on fire. She canted her head slightly before looking up at the crucifix hanging over the altar. She closed her eyes and tried to invoke the image of the Lord that usually centered her when her mind wandered during Mass.

Elizabeth sensed Edward's gaze remained on her. She didn't understand how she was so sure that he was looking at her. She didn't have any special gifts of perception or sight, but her intuition screamed that he was still looking.

THE CLAN SINCLAIR

His Highland Lass **BOOK 1 SNEAK PEEK**

She entered the great hall like a strong spring storm in the northern most Highlands. Tristan Mackay felt like he had been blown hither and yon. As the storm settled, she left him with the sweet scents of heather and lavender wafting towards him as she approached. She was not a classic beauty, tall and willowy like the women at court. Her face and form were not what legends were made of. But she held a unique appeal unlike any he had seen before. He could not take his eyes off of her long chestnut hair that had strands of fire and burnt copper running through them. Unlike the waves or curls he was used to, her hair was unusually straight and fine. It looked like a waterfall cascading down her back. While she was not tall, neither was she short. She had a figure that was meant for a man to grasp and hold onto, whether from the front or from behind. She had an aura of confidence and charm, but not arrogance or conceit like many good looking women he had met. She did not seem to know her own appeal. He could tell that she was many things, but one thing she was not was his.

His Bonnie Highland Temptation **BOOK 2**

His Highland Prize **BOOK 3**

His Highland Pledge **BOOK 4**

His Highland Surprise **BOOK 5**

Their Highland Beginning **BOOK 6**

PIRATES OF THE ISLES

The Blond Devil of the Sea **BOOK 1 SNEAK PEEK**

Caragh lifted her torch into the air as she made her way down the precarious Cornish cliffside. She made out the hulking shape of a ship, but the dead of night made it impossible to see who was there. She and the fishermen of Bedruthan Steps weren't expecting any shipments that night. But her younger brother Eddie, who stood watch at the entrance to their hiding place, had spotted the ship and signaled up to the village watchman, who alerted Caragh.

As her boot slid along the dirt and sand, she cursed having to carry the torch and wished she could have sunlight to guide her. She knew these cliffs well, and it was for that reason it was better that she moved slowly than stop moving once and for all. Caragh feared the light from her torch would carry out to the boat. Despite her efforts to keep the flame small, the solitary light would be a beacon.

When Caragh came to the final twist in the path before the sand, she snuffed out her torch and started to run to the cave where the main source of the village's income lay in hiding. She heard movement along the trail above her head and knew the local fishermen would soon join her on the beach. These men, both young and old, were strong from days spent pulling in the full trawling nets and hoisting the larger catches onto their boats. However, these men weren't well-trained swordsmen, and the fear of pirate raids was ever-present. Caragh feared that was who the villagers would face that night.

The Dark Heart of the Sea **BOOK 2**
The Red Drifter of the Sea **BOOK3**
The Scarlet Blade of the Sea **BOOK 4**

VIKING GLORY

Leif **BOOK 1 SNEAK PEEK**

Leif looked around his chambers within his father's longhouse and breathed a sigh of relief. He noticed the large fur rugs spread throughout the chamber. His two favorites placed strategically before the fire and the bedside he preferred. He looked at his shield that hung on the wall near the door in a symbolic position but waiting at the ready. The chests that held his clothes and some of his finer acquisitions from voyages near and far sat beside his bed and along the far wall. And in the center was his most favorite possession. His oversized bed was one of the few that could accommodate his long and broad frame. He shook his head at his longing to climb under the pile of furs and on the stuffed mattress that beckoned him. He took in the chair placed before the fire where he longed to sit now with a cup of warm mead. It had been two months since he slept in his own bed, and he looked forward to nothing more than pulling the furs over his head and sleeping until he could no longer ignore his hunger. Alas, he would not be crawling into his bed again for several more hours. A feast awaited him to celebrate his and his crew's return from their latest expedition to explore the isle of Britannia. He bathed and wore fresh clothes, so he had no excuse for lingering other than a bone weariness that set in during the last storm at sea. He was eager to spend time at home no matter how much he loved sailing. Their last expedition had been profitable with several raids of monasteries that yielded jewels and both silver and gold, but he was ready for respite.

Leif left his chambers and knocked on the door next to his. He heard movement on the other side, but it was only moments before his sister, Freya, opened her door. She, too, looked tired but clean. A few pieces of jewelry she confiscated from the holy houses that allegedly swore to a life of poverty and deprivation adorned her trim frame.

"That armband suits you well. It compliments your muscles," Leif smirked and dodged a strike from one of those muscular arms.

Only a year younger than he, his sister was a well-known and feared shield maiden. Her lithe form was strong and agile making her a ferocious and competent opponent to any man. Freya's beauty was stunning, but Leif had taken every opportunity since they were children to tease her about her unusual strength even among the female warriors.

"At least one of us inherited our father's prowess. Such a shame it wasn't you."

www.ingramcontent.com/pod-product-compliance
Lightning Source LLC
Chambersburg PA
CBHW011146100726
47899CB00010B/3185